Death at the Emerald

ALSO BY R. J. KORETO:

Lady Frances Ffolkes Mysteries

Death Among Rubies

Death on the Sapphire

Alice Roosevelt Mysteries

Alice and the Assassin

DEATH AT THE EMERALD

A LADY FRANCES FFOLKES MYSTERY

R. J. Koreto

NEW YORK

Published in the United States by Crooked Lane Books, an imprint of The Quick Brown Fox & Company LLC.

Crooked Lane Books and its logo are trademarks of The Quick Brown Fox & Company LLC.

Library of Congress Catalog-in-Publication data available upon request.

ISBN (hardcover): 978-1-68331-337-3
ISBN (ePub): 978-1-68331-338-0
ISBN (ePDF): 978-1-68331-340-3

Cover design by Andy Ruggirello
Book design by Jennifer Canzone

Printed in the United States.

www.crookedlanebooks.com

Crooked Lane Books
34 West 27th St., 10th Floor
New York, NY 10001

First Edition: November 2017

10 9 8 7 6 5 4 3 2 1

This book, about mothers and daughters, is dedicated to that most wonderful mother-and-daughter pair, my sister Abby and her daughter, Haley.

Chapter 1

Lady Beatrice Torrence, widow of Sir Arnold Torrence, reflected wryly that she knew all the names of everyone at the party but none of the faces. She had been abroad with her husband, from one posting to another, for so long and had come back to find that London was populated by the children and even grandchildren of those she had known a lifetime ago.

Consider that girl with the copper hair, Lady Frances Ffolkes. She had known her father, Lord Seaforth, who had served with Lady Torrence's husband in the Foreign Office, and Lady Seaforth had made her debut with Lady Torrence's cousin Edith. But the old Seaforths had gone to their final reward, along with cousin Edith. And now she exchanged a few pleasantries with this young, pretty girl, a brief discussion about her late parents. So full of energy, so full of confidence. It exhausted Lady Torrence just to talk with her.

When Frances departed, Lady Torrence thought that that was an end of it, but there was a lot more to discuss about her. Clara Astley, Lady Torrence's goddaughter, was practically quivering with excitement. She had a kind heart, was very solicitous of her godmother—and was also one of the worst gossips in London. Mrs. Astley knew everything about everyone, and at a party like this—one of Lord and Lady Moore's well-attended events—that was no small advantage.

"Dear Aunt Bea, do you have any idea who that was?" Her eyes glittered. This was going to be good. "Lady Frances is practically notorious. One of those suffrage girls pushing to get women the vote. Well, what could you expect—the family let her go to a college for ladies in America of all places, and it put all kinds of ideas into her head."

"Kicked over the traces, did she?" said Lady Torrence with a smile.

"Oh, and there's more. She involves herself with"—she lowered her voice—"the police. That fuss over the Colcombe manuscript that ended half a dozen War Office careers? She was in the thick of that. And then that unpleasantness at Kestrel's Eyrie? She was a guest there when it happened, hand in hand with Scotland Yard."

"With the police? You mean—more than just a witness?" Lady Torrence raised an eyebrow.

"So they say. Practically set herself up as a private detective, like Sherlock Holmes." Mrs. Astley was a mix of indignation that such a thing at happened and delight that she was in a position to tell about it.

"Really?" Lady Torrence was more amused than upset. "Her brother tolerates that? I assume she lives with him."

"Oh, dear, if only! She and her maid live in Miss Plimsoll's hotel."

"That's respectable enough, I'd have thought."

"Well, yes," Mrs. Astley conceded. "But it's really for elderly widows who don't want the bother and expense of continuing to manage the family home, not young ladies still seeking a husband and in need of a chaperone. It's unheard of."

Who'd have thought it—the Seaforth girl. She started thinking about it, and then Mrs. Astley was introducing her to more people, and Lady Frances went out of her head for the moment.

But she recalled the conversation later that night. Her maid was brushing out her hair before she went to bed, and Lady

Frances came back to her. *Louisa.* She had thought about her less and less in recent years but never really stopped, and with the return to London, she once again intruded frequently on her memory. Lady Torrence had made one futile try to follow up, but she was too old, too tired.

But that Lady Frances—a suffragist and, apparently, a detective. Could it be? Was God giving her one last chance? Lady Frances might laugh at her, a silly old lady. If she did, what did it matter? Write now, before she lost her nerve.

"I have a letter to write tonight," she told her maid. "Please hand me my paper and pen."

"Now, my lady?"

"Yes, now. Before I forget. Tomorrow morning, take it right after you serve me breakfast and have William deliver it by hand."

"Very good, my lady." She got the pen and paper for her mistress and then said good night.

Lady Torrence thought about the wording. She didn't want to spell it out—that would be too much. She didn't want to plead either. Or command. Just excite a little curiosity. She could find the right words—she hadn't been an ambassador's wife for all those years for nothing. Just a few lines. Then she sealed it and went to bed.

Could it be possible to find Louisa after all that time?

Lady Torrence saw herself to bed and turned out the light. For the first time in many years, she allowed herself to cry before falling asleep.

The next morning, as William was delivering the letter, Frances was not thinking of Lady Torrence. She was completely focused on the woman attacking her. Her opponent had her by her shoulder, but Frances seized her arm and let the woman's own weight send her off balance. But the woman was not fooled and, recovering more quickly than Frances had anticipated, swept her down until she was flat on her back.

Undeterred, Frances grabbed the other woman's ankle and gave a sharp tug. The woman fell down, and Frances scrambled back up again, ready for more . . . but then stopped at the sound of two hard claps.

Her opponent stopped as well, and they turned to the Japanese gentleman who was watching them closely.

"Improving," he said. "You still move like oxen, but you are improving."

"Improving as fast as your male students, sensei?" asked Frances. The other woman stifled a giggle. The man didn't laugh but considered her question carefully.

"Women follow directions more carefully than men. They learn faster that it is about *thought*, not *strength*. Now think on what I have said. I will see you at your next lesson."

The women bowed to him. "Thank you, sensei," they said and departed. In the changing room, a female attendant helped them change back into their street clothes.

"My goodness, Marie," said Frances. "Who'd have thought that London's best songstress could manhandle someone like a docker?"

"And who'd have thought the daughter of a marquess could kick like a mule?" said Marie. They both laughed. "I'm so glad you've been joining me. It's wonderful exercise, and I had almost despaired of finding a woman to practice with."

"Thank you for inviting me. We shall persevere and open our own dojo—for women only."

They said good-bye, and Frances caught a hansom back to Miss Plimsoll's. She realized that she looked a little worse for wear and was stiff in her legs. What would Mrs. Beasley, the manageress, say?

Miss Plimsoll's had been an elegant private house for generations until the elderly Miss Plimsoll found herself rattling around inside with too many rooms, too many servants, and a rapidly dwindling bank account. She had turned it into an elegant residential hotel for ladies, and despite the change in status, it still boasted beautifully maintained trimmings. But even though it wasn't a private residence anymore, Mrs. Beasley still kept up standards. Frances fancied the manageress turned a baleful eye on her. What was her ladyship up to now?

Wincing, Frances walked upstairs to her little suite. Mallow was waiting for her, and Frances watched her maid's eyes take in her hair and her dress, which were not as well-arranged as when Frances had left.

"Did you have a good physical education class, my lady?" That was what Frances had called it.

"Yes, very good, thank you. But I'm a little stiff, so maybe a hot bath." Mallow helped her undress.

"My lady, you have bruises!"

"Those happened during the class. We have advanced to the next level."

"I see, my lady." And Frances almost winced again at Mallow's subtle tone. *Imagine that, a lady going to a class of her own free will just to get hurt.*

Frances knew that she owed her an explanation.

"It's called jujutsu, Mallow. It's a method they developed in Japan to defend yourself against being attacked if you don't have a weapon, and a Japanese gentleman has come to England to give lessons. My actress friend, Marie Studholme, heard about it and asked me to join her since she needed a woman to practice with. I think it's an excellent idea for women to learn how to defend themselves."

"Very good, my lady." Mallow frowned. "So you and Miss Studholme take turns . . . hitting each other?"

"Well, not so much hitting as throwing each other."

"Very good, my lady," Mallow said, expertly hiding any thoughts she had about her mistress grappling with another woman. "I'll prepare a bath. Meanwhile, I picked up the mail for you earlier. There's a letter delivered by hand."

Frances looked at it. The handwriting and stationery were not familiar. She opened it.

DEAR LADY FRANCES,

WE SPOKE BRIEFLY LAST NIGHT AT THE RECEPTION, AND I WAS HOPING THAT WE COULD CONTINUE OUR CONVERSATION AT YOUR CONVENIENCE. I WILL BE AT HOME TO YOU FOR THE REST OF THE WEEK.

CORDIALLY,
LADY BEATRICE TORRENCE

"That's odd. Her late husband served in the Foreign Office years ago with my father. We had a few pleasantries, nothing more. Why should she want to speak with me again?"

"Perhaps she wants to join your suffrage club, my lady."

Frances laughed. "That would be a surprise. I've heard that Sir Arnold was strict and rigid even by the standards of his generation. Although . . . you may have hit on something, Mallow. She was with her goddaughter, Mrs. Astley, who is very gossipy. She no doubt gave Lady Torrence an earful about my suffrage work and other events. Maybe Lady Torrence just wants to lecture me."

Although an elderly aunt might do that, it would be insane for a woman who was practically a stranger to summon Frances to her home for that purpose. And Lady Torrence seemed of sound mind.

"Maybe she's just lonely and wants the company of someone young. I'm curious, at any rate, but I think I'll visit my sister-in-law first and see what she knows. But first . . . a bath."

"Very good, my lady. And I'll choose a dress appropriate for calling."

Once she was suitably relaxed and refreshed after her bath, Frances let Mallow dress her again and headed out to visit her dear friend Mary, her brother's wife.

Cumberland, the Seaforth butler, greeted her at the door. "A pleasure to see you again, my lady. Her ladyship is in the morning room."

"Thank you, Cumberland," she said, then turned a mischievous eye on the butler who had been serving the family since before she was born. "Don't think I didn't catch you making sure Mallow wasn't letting me out of the house without my dress and hair in proper form," she said. Mallow had been a Seaforth housemaid before Frances had promoted her to lady's maid when going out on her own. Cumberland bowed and gave Frances a small smile.

"I will only say, my lady, that Miss Mallow is a credit to the training she received in this house."

Which is more than you could say for me, thought Frances.

Frances found Mary writing letters when Cumberland announced her. "I'm so glad you called. We hardly got to speak last night, with Charles and I having to spend so much time making the rounds, speaking to everyone." Charles was Undersecretary for European Affairs in the Foreign Office. "The joys of being a political wife."

"And you like it. Even Charles's political opponents say that you're his best asset." The two women laughed. "I don't normally go to those events myself, but Lady Moore asked me specially, and as she was such a good friend of my mother's, I couldn't say no. But remember when you introduced me to Lady Torrence?"

"Yes. I hope she didn't ramble on too much about some house party she attended decades ago with some great aunt of yours. I was afraid she was getting a little dotty."

"No, she was clear enough, although we didn't talk long. But this morning she sent me a brief note asking me to call on her. It seemed such an odd request. They were hardly intimate friends with us, so I wondered why. You know everyone. What can you tell me about the Torrences?"

"That is strange. Let's see. I know Sir Arnold died some years back. He served mostly overseas in one country or another, in the continent and even the Orient. They have a daughter—oh, what's her name?—Sarah, yes. Raised a few eyebrows some years back when she married a fellow from the City, someone deep in finance rather than from the old aristocracy. Apparently, he did very well for himself, became extremely wealthy, and was even raised to the peerage, although I can't recall his name right now."

"Doesn't sound anything unusual," said Frances, but then Mary frowned.

"However, there was something about another child, I believe, something someone mentioned to me. An older daughter who died, but there was something more—a bad marriage, maybe. Louisa, I think the name was. You know how it is, a half-remembered story someone repeats over dinner, and then conversation stops because it's too painful or embarrassing. Sorry, I can't remember any more."

"Oh, but that's very helpful. If the late Louisa did something scandalous . . ."

"Then perhaps Lady Torrence wants to speak to a modern-day scandalous woman," finished Mary.

"Well done, dear sister," said Frances. "Perhaps my growing reputation precedes me. I'll call on her this afternoon and let you know what she says."

"Please do. And how are you faring otherwise? Or more specifically, how goes it with dear Mr. Wheaton?"

Mary smiled briefly at how the mention of Henry "Hal" Wheaton could still bring a blush to Frances's cheeks.

"Very well, thank you. As I told him, we'll have a long engagement. I see it as a way to make sure we are indeed fully suited to each other, to create an important stage between courtship and marriage."

"Dear Franny, does Hal share your noble goals?"

"Why, Mary, of course he does. He's more broad-minded and forward-thinking than people realize."

Mary arched an eyebrow. "As broad-minded and forward-thinking as you?"

At that, Frances gave Mary a look of mock horror. "I couldn't expect a mere man to go that far!"

Frances headed next to a Mayfair address where, over tea and sandwiches in a drawing room, she worked on speeches and pamphlets with friends from the suffrage group. And then it was time to call on Lady Torrence.

Frances continued to think about the message. Was it about the mysterious Louisa? But she was theorizing without the full facts. Her professors at Vassar would upbraid her severely for that. There were other possibilities. For example, Lady Torrence had been out of London for many years and might not know that Frances had become quietly engaged. Maybe she had a grandnephew she wanted to introduce to Frances, a chance for a connection to the large and influential Seaforth family. *I wouldn't have thought I was satisfactory to someone in Society anymore, between my suffrage work and police activities,* she thought. *But then again, maybe this mythical grandnephew isn't very satisfactory either.*

The house was typical for its fashionable neighborhood, well-kept on the outside, so Lady Torrence had the money to hire good servants and the ability to see they were well-supervised.

A proper butler answered the door and took her card. "Her ladyship is in the drawing room," he said, and Frances followed him. Although the outside of the house was nondescript, the interior was a delightful jumble, something she hadn't expected. She saw small jade statues from the Orient, oil paintings showing the Alps and the Hindu Kush, brass from India, and ivory from Africa. Souvenirs from a well-traveled life.

The drawing room was no different, with an attention-grabbing porcelain Buddha dominating a corner and a lacquered Japanese screen, decorated with fanciful pictures of mountains, stretched along the opposite wall.

"Lady Frances Ffolkes," announced the butler, which brought Frances's eyes to her hostess. Lady Torrence sat in a deep leather chair that was more comfortable than fashionable. Her dress was good, but a little old-fashioned, and she held the same elegant cane that she had had at the reception. They had only spoken a few minutes the other evening, and the lights had been dim, but now Frances saw that, although she was quite elderly, Lady Torrence possessed a clear eye and amused smile.

"Lady Torrence, a pleasure to see you again. And my apologies for my vulgar curiosity about your lovely artwork. My mother would've been appalled."

Lady Torrence just laughed. "Yes, my dear. I knew your mother, as I said, and she would've been appalled indeed. But I am flattered that you like the lovely objects we collected in Sir Arnold's postings over the years. They are reminders of other places . . ." Frances thought she could see a shadow pass across her face for just a moment. And then a maid came in with tea and cakes, and conversation stopped as she set up the tray.

"Will that be all, my lady?" asked the butler.

"Yes. And I am not at home to anyone else," said Lady Torrence. Frances raised an eyebrow at that.

"Very good, my lady," he said, and a moment later they were alone in the drawing room as Lady Torrence poured for them.

"A girl as curious as you is no doubt wondering furiously why I asked her to call on me," she said with the same amused smile. Her movements were slow but steady, and Frances could see her mind working, trying to find the words. "I seemed so sure the other night about what I would say. And here we are, having an ordinary tea. I fear that when you hear what I am going to say, you are going to laugh at me." She looked a little uncertainly at Frances.

"No. Nothing you could say would make me laugh at you," Frances said with great solemnity, staring intently at her hostess with her large gray eyes.

"Very well then. I don't know what you have heard, but I had two daughters. The older one was named Louisa. When she was twenty . . ." She shook her head. "I'm starting badly. I rehearsed this, but it's harder than I thought. A little background, I think, will better explain it. My husband was a very traditional man, very much a man of his time. But his one . . . frivolity, I should say, was theatre. He enjoyed plays very much, and we frequently attended. His people, and mine too, in fact, are from near Shrewsbury. His cousin inherited a title, a great manor, and land up there, and several times Arnold even arranged for plays on the estate when we visited. When our daughters became old enough, we brought them along too. Louisa loved theatre as much as her father did. She even entertained the family. She was a lively girl with a gift for mimicry, and she loved the attention she got at family events . . ." Lady Torrence had to pause for a few moments to gather herself. Frances drank more tea and ate a little cake to give her a little privacy.

"It became an obsession, I'm afraid, as she got older. There was no performance that she didn't want to see. I know I'm her mother, but she was very beautiful." She gave Frances a wry smile. "Young men who wanted her attention would arrange theatre parties—properly chaperoned, of course—to gain her company."

"Did any of those men ask for her hand?" asked Frances.

Lady Torrence shook her head. "No. I don't think any man really engaged her heart, despite all the attention she received. Oh, she did the season—dutifully went to the right parties to meet the right people. Maybe I'm imagining things now, looking back. But she seemed dissatisfied, somehow, eager for something else. My husband said that she just needed to get married and settled down. I thought maybe all those plays had turned her somehow, put her into a fantasy world."

Frances watched Lady Torrence's eyes lose their focus. She was back in time now, remembering Louisa as she was, and Frances knew from her tone that this story was heading toward a tragedy.

"My husband decided that she needed a change of scene. He had an older friend in India, a retired general, who died and left his widow out there. He thought to send Louisa as a sort of companion, with an idea of finding a husband among the officers there. She had talked about wanting to travel, but she had no wish to be tied to an irritable old woman, as she put it, until she was auctioned off to some major. She and my husband had a terrible row, and I . . . you will lose all respect for me, Lady Frances, but I did little to intervene. Arnold felt very strongly, and he was not an easy man to refuse. But nothing you could say would be worse than what I've said to myself."

Frances felt her heart ache for this woman. She knew more than her share of tyrants, men for whom their word was law, who commanded their families like they commanded their regiments, their government departments, their tenant farmers. This would have to change . . . but for now, she just listened to this woman reach into old memories.

"I understand and sympathize. Your position was impossible."

"Thank you," Lady Torrence said softly. "Where was I? Oh, yes. Arnold called a maid and told her to start packing for the trip to India. Louisa burst into tears and ran into her room, locking the door. She wouldn't speak to anyone . . . and that night . . ." There was no pretending anymore. Lady Torrence produced a handkerchief and wiped away the tears that flowed down her face.

"That night, she left the house. We found a note on her bed saying that she was going to become an actress. Arnold went into a rage, and I nearly fell apart with the horror of it all." Frances understood. Sir Arnold may have enjoyed the theatre, but for a man like him, an actress wasn't much higher on the social scale than a prostitute.

"And I never saw her again." All self-control disappeared now, and Lady Torrence sobbed uncontrollably into her hands. *My God*, thought Frances, *she probably hasn't been able to talk to anyone about this in years—in decades—keeping in the hurt because of the shame of it all.* She found herself full of pity and angry at how powerless Lady Torrence had been to prevent this. All the poor woman wanted was a sympathetic ear. Perhaps she was too embarrassed even to discuss this with her younger daughter.

Frances saw a sideboard with decanters. She got up and poured some sherry for Lady Torrence, then sat down on the couch next to her.

"This will steady you," she said, pressing the glass into her shaking hands. Lady Torrence drank slowly.

"You're very kind."

"Whatever I can do," Frances said, "even if it's just to listen."

"Oh, but there is," said Lady Torrence. She wiped her tears and mastered herself like ladies of quality were taught. She smiled through the final tears. "I've recounted this all very badly, I'm afraid. It isn't that I don't want your sympathy or value your kindness, but that is not why I asked you here." She finished her drink, then took Frances's hands in hers and looked her in the eye.

"My daughter, Louisa, disappeared more than thirty years ago, in 1875. I called you here to ask such a huge favor that I don't know how I can even say it." She took a deep breath. "Lady Frances, I want you to find my daughter. Or"—her voice broke—"proof of her death."

Chapter 2

Frances sat back down in her chair and thought before saying anything.

"I know—it's ridiculous," said Lady Torrence, perhaps thinking that she had overwhelmed her guest. "I'm so sorry for putting you in such an awkward position. Please forgive me." She looked diminished, Frances saw, as if she had experienced a final blow.

But Frances shook her head. "No, Lady Torrence; I'm not saying no. I'm simply surprised. I would have thought that you would engage someone who does this as a profession, a retired detective police officer, for example."

"Can you imagine, Lady Frances?" She smiled wryly. "A silly old lady calling on a private detective?"

"Of course. You might find yourself being bundled off to a rest home by the sea to soothe your nerves." Few would take her seriously, looking for a daughter who ran off after all these years.

"Exactly. My daughter and son-in-law are protective of me."

"I understand. But why me?" asked Frances. But she knew the answer the moment she spoke.

"You are not unknown, Lady Frances. There has been talk about you—how can I say it?—your involvement with the constabulary."

Frances grinned at that. She should be embarrassed, she knew, but she was rather proud of her growing notoriety. Her brother, Charles, would be horrified, as would most of her family, but

Frances said, "My reputation precedes me. Very well, Lady Torrence; let me see what I can do. But before I make any promises, tell me what you know. It's a big country, and it has been a long time. Are you sure that she ran away to the theatre?"

Lady Torrence nodded. "Yes. Her note not only said that—it said she ran away to the Green Players, who make their home, as you might imagine, in the Emerald Theatre. As if she dared us to follow her. I wanted to, Lady Frances, I truly did, but Arnold said that she'd come back with her tail between her legs and that that would be better than dragging her back. I thought . . . I hoped that he was right. But the days went by, and finally Arnold approached them, but it was too late. They swore at the theatre that they knew no one by her name, and they had meanwhile sent touring companies out of town, so there was no telling where she was. She had obviously taken a new name."

The whole awful story came out. By the time they realized that Louisa was not coming back of her own accord, Sir Arnold had become concerned that his daughter might have been "compromised." They spread it around that Louisa had become ill and had been sent to the south of France to recuperate. Then to a clinic in America. Months went by, and they heard nothing.

"Did you visit the Emerald Theatre in the hopes of seeing her there after the touring company returned?" asked Frances.

"My husband said no—if that's what had happened, he wasn't going to see his daughter on the stage. I kept my ears open for gossip, to hear if any of my friends said something like, 'Remarkable coincidence—saw an actress on the stage that could've been your Louisa.' But it never happened. And I know with costumes and makeup, even if she became an actress, she might not be easily recognizable. Anyway, neither of us felt we could stay in London, so Arnold took a foreign posting. We were mostly abroad for thirty years. We let it be known quietly that Louisa had died abroad after a long illness. Then we finally retired back here, and Arnold passed away. I did do one thing, though . . ." She sounded proud of that. "I know it was too little, too late, but about half a year ago, I approached the company manager of the Green Players, a man named Gilbert Rusk. I told him that I was a great lover of theatre and was thinking of writing a book in my retirement, a sort of guide to the theatre for ladies, and I asked if I could look through his company records."

Lady Frances perked up at that. "My word, Lady Torrence! You're on your way to becoming a detective yourself. That was very clever. Shall we start our own women-run detective agency?"

Lady Torrence turned pink. "Lady Frances, you flatter me. But I was a diplomat's wife for many years. A certain amount of . . . prevarication was part of the job. However, it was all for naught. I had only spent a week poring over their rather careless personnel records when Mr. Rusk said that the company had a new owner and there were new rules. He was afraid he could no longer open his records to me. He was very apologetic about it but firm."

Frances frowned. "That's odd. How would someone know? And why would they care?"

Lady Torrence shrugged. "I didn't make a secret of it. The actors in the company, the clerk who kept their books—all saw me there. Other than that, I mentioned it to my younger daughter, Sarah, but still kept up the fiction that I was writing a book."

Frances nodded, deep in thought. "Sarah . . . Were the sisters close?"

"Sarah adored Louisa, who doted on her baby sister. They were nearly six years apart. Sarah was brokenhearted when Louisa left. She was only fourteen."

"Did you ever tell her the true story?"

"When she married, we told her and her fiancé. We felt it was important that they knew."

"I heard your son-in-law was something in the City?" asked Frances.

Now Lady Torrence turned a sharp eye on Frances. For a few moments, Frances saw not a tired old woman but a sharp-witted political wife who had navigated through countless dinners, luncheons, and receptions with great aplomb.

"So you asked about me after you got my note. I was wise to choose you."

Frances gave a mock bow. "A consulting detective must be sure of all her facts beforehand," said Frances.

"Indeed. And yes, my son-in-law is 'something' in the City. What, exactly, I don't know. It's all a mystery to me. He was a rising young man when he asked for Sarah's hand. My husband was a little dubious, but the man was already making a name for himself. He made himself very wealthy and became Lord Freemantle some years back. He and Sarah move in more . . . commercial circles now, which is why they were not with me last night."

Of course. Lord Freemantle may have a title and vast wealth, but he was not of the old nobility. Perhaps Sarah, in choosing such a man, was also a little rebellious. That would bear looking into. And that was when Frances realized that she planned to take the challenge.

"I think you now know everything I can tell you. Please tell me—am I being ridiculous?" Lady Torrence looked both fearful and hopeful. She was not young and clearly realized that this was going to be her last chance to find out what had happened to her daughter.

"You are not being ridiculous at all. The real question is whether I am ridiculous to even try—but try I will, Lady Torrence. I can't promise results, but I will do my very best."

Lady Torrence closed her eyes for a moment, and when she opened them, she looked serene. "I have hope, and that is something. Now tell me, what do you need?"

"Do you have a photograph of her?"

"Not a very good one, just a few of her with other people, not easy to recognize. But we have a magnificent portrait of her, done just a year before she left. It's in a spare room upstairs. I never go in there." *And see the reminder*, was the implication.

"Excellent. I can arrange for a photographer to take a picture of the portrait and use that."

"I will bear that cost, of course. Which leads me to one more issue—your fee, Lady Frances?"

Frances blinked. A fee? It hadn't occurred to her. What did consulting detectives charge? Or was she just doing this to make a point about women entering the detective profession?

"I haven't really thought about that," she admitted.

Again, she saw a sharp gleam in Lady Torrence's eye. "Correct me if I'm wrong, Lady Frances, but don't you suffragist girls want to be treated like men? A man would charge a fee."

Frances laughed. "Splendid! You're absolutely right. Very well. I am treasurer of the Ladies' Christian Relief Guild. Perhaps a substantial donation if I give satisfactory service?"

"That I will, in addition to covering your expenses. And if you are successful, I will give a matching donation to your suffrage group—and deliver it personally at your next meeting."

"Wonderful! Now if you could show me this portrait."

"Of course. I'll have my maid direct you. She's the only servant I have from those days—everyone else in the house has only been in my employ since we returned to London. But Simpkins was a housemaid here before . . . before all that. She became my lady's maid, coming with us in all our overseas postings."

Frances smiled. "I haven't been to the East, but I've heard that English servants often have trouble adapting."

Lady Torrence laughed at that. "Simpkins thought it would be easier to make the entire subcontinent adapt to her ways, rather than for her to adapt to theirs. It's a testament to her that she came close to succeeding."

She rang for the butler, who came a moment later.

"A photographer will be coming in the next few days to take a picture of the portrait in the blue bedroom. He is to be admitted immediately and given all assistance."

The butler was too well-trained to show any surprise. "Very good, my lady."

"Now send Simpkins to me."

The butler bowed out, and a few minutes later, Simpkins entered. She instantly reminded Frances of Pritchard, her mother's maid—a formidable, even frightening woman, whom the junior maids had secretly dubbed "the tigress." Simpkins no doubt inspired a similar sobriquet downstairs. She was around sixty, Frances guessed, with hard black eyes that matched her dress. Her mouth was pursed as if she had been sucking on a lemon, thought Frances with some amusement.

"Simpkins. Lady Frances Ffolkes is assisting me with some personal affairs. I wish her to see the portrait of Miss Louisa. Please escort her."

Simpkins did what the butler hadn't—gave Frances a very quick review with those deep-set eyes, and Frances could practically see the gears turning in the maid's mind as she tried to sort this out. "Very good, my lady," she said in the end, just like the butler. She turned to Frances. "If you would follow me, my lady."

Frances followed Simpkins up the stairs, past walls lined with more artwork from far-off places. She made a note to request a visit at another time to take it all in. Hal, with his interest in art, would be fascinated. Perhaps they would have a celebratory dinner if she were successful . . . but she was getting too far ahead of herself, she realized. One step at a time.

For now, she turned her attention to following Simpkins, who had a ramrod back that would do credit to a sergeant major. Frances's brother had wanted her to engage such a maid to watch over her when she went out on her own, but instead she chose June Mallow, only nineteen at the time. She had never regretted it.

The guest bedroom, decorated in shades of blue, contained no eye-catching foreign artwork or knickknacks, probably because it wasn't used much. But the additional ornamentation wasn't necessary. The portrait was enough, and even Frances, used to fine portraits, practically gasped aloud when she saw it.

Lady Torrence hadn't exaggerated. If the portrait was true, Louisa was one of the most beautiful women she had ever seen. Midnight-black hair against a milky cheek and eyes like blue tourmaline gemstones. And that mouth—Frances had once overheard a cousin, after his third glass of port, refer to his favorite barmaid as having the "most kissable mouth in Christendom."

Was it a trick of the painter or really the way she had looked? There was something very inviting about her.

Frances let her eyes dart to Simpkins. The maid was clearly proud of her mistress's daughter and amused at Frances's reaction.

"You knew Miss Louisa, didn't you?" asked Frances.

"Yes, I did, my lady." And she no doubt knew the whole story, although she wouldn't admit it to Frances.

"In your opinion, is this an accurate portrait?"

Simpkins paused. She wasn't used to having her opinion sought after, beyond a question about a hat or dress.

"Yes, my lady. But if I may say, she was a wonderfully lively girl, and no artist could capture that."

"Many men must've courted her," said Frances.

But Simpkins quickly shut down at that. "I'm sure I couldn't say, my lady."

However, her eyes gave her away.

"Thank you, Simpkins. We can go back down now."

Simpkins showed Lady Frances back to the drawing room, and then Lady Torrence dismissed her.

"Simpkins tells me that the portrait is accurate. Louisa must've been the loveliest woman in London."

"Thank you. As I've said, I'm prejudiced. But she really was, wasn't she?"

"And I will do everything I can to find her. First, I would like to call on your other daughter, Sarah, as I need all the information I can get. And of course, I will keep our mission confidential."

"That will all be fine. Lady Frances, in addition to hope, you are giving me peace of mind."

Frances shook her head. "No, my lady. If I am good and lucky, I will get you the truth. Only you can give yourself peace of mind."

Lady Torrence raised an eyebrow. "Has anyone ever told you that you're wise beyond your years?"

Frances gave her hostess a cheeky smile. "My mother and a score of governesses. But they didn't phrase it quite as complimentary as you just did."

Chapter 3

Frances's mind was in a whirl as she returned to her rooms at Miss Plimsoll's. What a change this was! How should she get started? Should she have business cards printed up? That might be a little premature. And what would Mallow think?

"A pleasant visit, my lady?" Mallow asked as she helped Frances take off her hat.

"Very interesting, Mallow. And a bit of a surprise."

"Does Lady Torrence want to join your suffrage club after all, my lady?"

"Do you know, Mallow, she might in the end. But for now, she had a rather unusual request." The two women retreated to their little sitting room. "It seems Lady Torrence wants us to find a daughter she hasn't seen in thirty years." She summarized the commission she had been given. Mallow took it all in stride.

"So what do you think, Mallow?"

"I think you will bring the matter to a successful conclusion, my lady."

"Thank you for your optimism. I will need your help with this."

"I will be of assistance in any way I can, my lady."

Frances was going to warn Mallow that this was all highly confidential, but she realized it wasn't necessary. Frances's brother, Marquess of Seaforth, a minister in the Foreign Office, had more than once tried to trick Mallow into revealing details about Frances's private life. He had been unsuccessful every time.

"I know you will prove invaluable. I don't know if I ever told you, but Inspector Eastley once said that if they started opening the police service to women, you'd be his first choice as a recruit."

"I'm sure that's very flattering, my lady," Mallow said, clearly unsure if this was, in fact, flattering, "but I would prefer to remain in your service."

"And so you shall. For now, let's make sure that I have plenty of ink and paper. I'm not certain what Sherlock Holmes does, but I think it would be best to start my investigations with a written plan."

Frances woke up the next morning full of purpose. "I have a busy day ahead of me, Mallow, visiting with theatre folk."

Her maid produced one of the shirtwaist outfits Frances liked for daytime wear, especially when she had a lot of traveling.

"It's such a nice day, Mallow. I do like the beginning of spring, and it's finally getting warm. A perfect day for the bicycle."

The bicycle. That had made quite a change in their little household. Mallow had firm ideas on the correct forms of transportation. The best was a carriage drawn by matched horses. Hansom cabs were also acceptable. Trains were delightful, as long as you stayed away from that overwhelming locomotive. Motorcars were a bit frightening, with their engines right in front like that and all the noise.

And then Lady Frances had come home with the bicycle. "I can get around London more quickly than in a hansom when it's crowded, and it will save money. It's much faster than walking. And it's healthy exercise. I think it'll take a bit of practice to get going. In fact"—she had given Mallow a look—"it might be best if we learned together."

So it had been off to the park for some tumbles and spills, but soon they had been set, riding up and down the pathways.

"It is exciting, isn't it?" she had asked her maid.

"It feels like flying, my lady," Mallow had replied. Her face was normally placid, but just then her eyes had been bright and cheeks flushed. The bicycle was a welcome addition to Miss Plimsoll's.

Mallow took it to run errands for her ladyship, and Frances bicycled around town, as long as the occasion wasn't too formal. The theatre was certainly "not formal."

They kept the bicycle in a tool shed at the back of the house. Mrs. Beasley was a little dubious about a bicycle, but there was no denying the popularity of the vehicles among the young ladies of London. Horses could not be reengineered, so women had to ride them sidesaddle. But a minor design change allowed women to ride bicycles in skirts.

In a few moments, Frances was riding along the streets, her modest hat expertly pinned to her hair by Mallow so it didn't come off even as she rolled along. First, it was to a photography studio, where she was informed that they'd be pleased to make a photographic record of a portrait and would deliver the results to Lady Frances at Miss Plimsoll's.

Next, she travelled to the St. James Theatre, handed her bicycle to a startled porter, and walked in. She slipped quietly into the back and took a seat. Her friend from jujutsu class, Marie Studholme, was on the stage, singing a song to the accompaniment of a piano. The tune was catchy, and Frances knew well that Marie's sweet voice and lovely face would ensure cries of "encore" from the audience.

After hearing it a few times, the director announced that he'd rehearse the chorus, and Marie could rest for a few minutes. Frances waved to her friend, and Marie joined her in the back.

"Dear Franny. Hoping for another match? Not really fair; you're younger than I am."

Frances laughed. "And you're taller. That makes up for it. Anyway, I'm happy just to listen to your lovely voice and will see the whole show when it opens with great pleasure. But I'm really here for your specialized knowledge. As a favor for a friend, I'm trying to find an actress who worked for the Green Players some thirty years ago. I wondered if you knew anything about them."

Her face lit up with a knowing smile. "Ah, you're involving yourself in another mystery. Why don't you write a play about this one? We'll get it produced, and I'll play you onstage."

"Splendid idea! We'll add songs too."

"I'll look forward to it. But you wanted to know about the Green Players. They've been around forever. Good productions, very traditional. A bit of Shakespeare, some comedies, period pieces—anything to draw a large crowd. I never did anything with them myself, but they enjoy a good reputation. Oh, and they're getting into those new motion pictures."

"My maid will be delighted to hear that. She loves motion pictures."

"Yes, well, some of us are a bit worried about that. Will it take away from theatre crowds?"

"Whether singing or speaking, nothing will take the place of your lovely voice," said Frances.

"Thank you. But Frances, if you're going to insert yourself into the theatre world, know this: it's a very closed community, and as friendly as they are, they don't easily welcome outsiders."

"But you did."

"Yes, I am pleased to be your friend, Franny. You are unusual among the nobility to make friends with an actress. But I am unusual among actresses to make friends with a lady of quality. Think of what would happen if I paid a call to almost any other titled lady in this city. I'd never make it past the butler. For better or worse, it would be no different for a titled lady to visit the backstage of any theatre. Think on that, my friend. They'll want me back onstage in a few minutes, but if you have anything to ask, come by again." She gave her arm a squeeze and left.

Frances mulled that over for a few moments and then quietly departed for the Emerald Theatre. It was just a few minutes away by bicycle. The Emerald was one of the oldest theatres in London, going back to the eighteenth century, and the ornate facade spoke of a wilder city: glittering Georgian evenings with men in powdered wigs and fantastic dresses for the ladies, followed by an era of Regency rakes and demimondaines. It needed a good cleaning and some restoration work now, but Frances saw workmen setting up scaffolding. Improvements from the new owners? She found a porter that she could leave her bicycle with and asked him where she could find the manager, Mr. Rusk. He paused for a moment.

Frances watched the man think: *This woman was not an actress. There was no telling what a woman with an elegant accent like that wanted with Mr. Rusk. In any case, it wasn't his concern.*

"You'll find him right along that hallway, miss. He should be in."

"Thank you." She walked past the box office and down the hall. The door was labeled "G. Rusk, Manager." She knocked and heard, "Come in!"

As with Lady Torrence's drawing room, the decorations grabbed her attention first. It wasn't a big room, and it was made even smaller by the delightful jumble of objects. Posters for shows covered every inch of the walls. Some advertised recent productions that Frances had seen, and others—perhaps those with special meaning for Mr. Rusk—contained popular titles and actresses from before Frances had been born.

His desk was heaped with gaudy flyers for upcoming productions, swatches of cloth no doubt left by a costume designer for his approval, a couple of obviously fake daggers with paste jewels—*were they doing* Macbeth *this year?*—and a box of cigars, one of which Mr. Rusk was puffing away on. He seemed to be in his sixties, bald, with a face that looked hard. Here was a man used to giving orders. He was working in his shirtsleeves, and his cuffs were ink-stained.

He frowned at her. "Who let you back here? We're not holding auditions yet. Come back in two weeks."

Frances laughed. "I suppose I should be flattered that you think I'm pretty enough to be an actress. But no, Mr. Rusk. I'm Lady Frances Ffolkes. And I'm hoping you can help me."

"Oh! Well, I'm sorry then." His smile seemed genuinely warm and softened his face. "Take a seat, my lady. And no offense. I see now you're a lady of quality. How may I be of service?"

"I see you're busy, so I will get to the point." She had already worked out a story. "My mother had the most delightful cook for many years. She's retired, but she had a niece, the last of her family, who she believes became one of the Green Players some thirty years ago. I don't know how long she was a member of the company, though. As a favor, being here in London, I thought I'd see what I could do about finding her. I know it's going to be difficult, if not impossible. But I thought I'd try."

"Well, I'd like to oblige, my lady. In fact, I was working here thirty years ago. Do you have a name?"

"I wish I did. But the niece changed her name, and Cook couldn't remember what it was, if she ever knew. No offense, Mr. Rusk, but the family didn't want their name connected to the theatre."

Rusk chuckled. "No need to explain, my lady. A career in theatre has never been seen as entirely respectable, and it was even worse back then. Now any number of young, beautiful women join our company, or try to, each year. Any description at all?"

"I think you would remember this girl. She got work as an artist's model before deciding to become an actress, and I saw a portrait. She was exquisite. Only about twenty with midnight-black hair, eyes like blue gemstones, and a mouth that no man could resist kissing."

A dreamy look came over him—only for a few seconds, but Frances knew what she saw. "Oh, my, Lady Frances. I may have thought at first you were an actress, but it seems you're a playwright. Well, that's certainly a start, but I can't recall anyone like that offhand. I'm a manager, so don't have daily contact with the actors."

"Are there any actors, perhaps, from those times still working here?"

He thought about that for a moment. "Perhaps . . . could you wait here a moment, my lady? It's just that it's a bit of tumult backstage right now."

"Of course."

He stood up and headed out the door.

That was interesting, she thought. There was definitely something in his face when she gave that description. Well, if she didn't get any luck, she could come back with the photograph. She'd have to give up her story, but it would force the truth.

Frances amused herself studying the posters. Was Louisa in one of the older ones? But it was impossible to tell from the stylized designs.

Mr. Rusk returned with two men.

"Lady Frances, here are two men who might be able to help. This is Quentin Prescott, who has been an actor with our company for many years." He looked about the same age as Rusk but cut a more elegant figure. He was slim, and his hair was mostly dark with a refined touch of white at the temples. Prescott's face was mostly smooth, and only his wrinkled throat, visible through the open neck of his shirt, gave away his age. The shirt was probably part of a costume, thought Frances. Actors were vain, and an actor of his age and experience would no doubt be too careful to let himself be seen at anything less than his full advantage.

Prescott gave an exaggerated bow. "A pleasure, my lady."

"And this is Anthony Mattins, our chief stage manager. He has authority for everything that happens backstage. He's been with us his entire adult life." Mattins was Prescott's opposite in every way. He was a good decade older, concluded Frances, with a face like a walnut, dark and heavily lined, and his sour look seemed permanent. Frances had seen beggars who had given their clothes more attention.

"M'lady," he said as if it were an effort.

"I'd like to oblige her ladyship," said Rusk. "Some thirty years ago, we had a young actress here, the fairest in the land, with a kissable mouth and beautiful blue eyes. Either of you remember her? Lady Frances is trying to find her—the niece of her old cook."

Prescott made a great show of considering that. "Gertie Leister? Or did she have green eyes? Could be. Was your cook's niece from Yorkshire? It took Gertie months to learn how to speak the king's English. Ended up as a sort of nurse/companion to some old lady in the end. Or maybe Ophelia Darlington. Pretty enough, if I remember, though I wouldn't have thought her especially kissable. Heard she married a chandler in Liverpool, had a brood of children, and became quite stout. Those are the only two who come to mind."

Oh, here's a man who's deeply in love with the sound of his own voice, concluded Frances, who scarcely paid attention to what he was saying. It was all nonsense. What was truly interesting was Mattins's expression. He was looking at the actor with a mix of astonishment and irritation at his speech.

"Thank you for reflecting on that anyway," said Frances. "Mr. Mattins? Any memories?"

He gave Frances a deep look. She saw he had a certain shrewdness. It sounded like a complicated and difficult job, supervising the backstage of a large theatre, and if he had been a fool, he wouldn't have lasted.

"Your cook's niece, you say?" He sounded like he didn't believe her. *Lie like an actor*—wasn't that the phrase? Mattins probably had more experience with liars than any Scotland Yard detective. "Why does she want to find her?" It was a challenge.

"The last of her family," said Frances. "She's old and getting very sentimental. She would like to see her again."

"I'll have to think on it," he muttered. "Can't think of anyone immediately. Sorry, m'lady." But then he gave her a deeper look.

Frances would swear they were lying—all three of them. The glint of recognition in Rusk's eye. The silly little speech Prescott gave, working so hard to prove he was trying to remember. And then Mattins. Was it her imagination, or did he look like he was thinking it over, perhaps letting her know he might have a name? She thought about what Marie Studholme had said about theatre folk not trusting outsiders, but why should anyone care about an actress who had joined the company decades ago?

She could come back, though, when she had more information. But for now, this was it. "Ah, well. I appreciate your help." She produced three calling cards. "If you think of anything else, please call on me. I would appreciate it. Thank you again, and good day to all of you."

Mattins shuffled off quickly without saying anything else. Prescott said good-bye with another flourish. And Rusk—he seemed a little embarrassed.

"I'm sorry your trip was for nothing, my lady. Let me show you out."

"That would be kind." He walked her along the hallway. "I see you are making improvements to the theatre."

"New owners, my lady. Thought a fancier look would bring in a fancier crowd. Trying to upgrade our repertoire too—more modern plays mixed in with the old standards. Also expanding into those moving pictures."

"Really? That sounds enterprising of them. Who are they?" She lowered her voice to a conspiratorial whisper. "My family has a great many commercial interests," she said.

"I don't know," he said. Then maybe he felt, at Frances's dubious look, that he had told enough half-truths and outright lies for one day. He thought for a moment. "This is a very old company. We were founded right after the Restoration in the seventeenth century, when Charles II came to the throne."

"That's when theatre companies started letting women on the stage," said Frances.

"You know your history, my lady. Yes, until then, boys and young men played women's roles. Well, with Cromwell gone and a Stuart king back on the throne, new companies flourished, and Lord Beverly Greene, who had been a companion of the king in exile, was granted the right to form one of the first theatre companies. We were known as Lord Greene's Players then, but over time, things changed. The Stuart kings were thrown out for good, and we simply became the Green Players, just like the color, and eventually built the Emerald Theatre to continue the theme."

They were in the theatre lobby now, and Rusk looked around. "I owned a piece of this. A handful of us owned all this, this piece of history. Then all of a sudden, this fancy solicitor shows up, saying he represented the interests of someone in the City who wanted to buy us up—the company, the theatre, everything. We named a price, and the man didn't even negotiate. Agreed to it, right off, and said they'd keep me on as manager on salary, and we signed it all over two days later at the bank. Well, I'm a widower, my lady, my children are grown and settled, and I have a nice bit in the bank thanks to the purchase, so I'm all right. Who really owns it? I don't know—a group of City gents. The solicitor handles it all. I want you to know, my lady—I'm not hiding anything. I really don't know. And I'm sorry we can't help you more."

He did seem genuinely regretful. But there was something else there too—he was telling Lady Frances that she may be from an old and distinguished family, but his "theatre family" was, in its way, also old and distinguished.

"I understand, Mr. Rusk, and I thank you and your associates for your help. May I ask what show you're performing next?"

He cheered at the change of subject. "*Romeo and Juliet*, my lady. Very popular. We do it almost every season. Let me know a convenient date, my lady, and I'll have a complimentary pair of tickets for you."

"Thank you; I certainly will," she said. And Rusk handed her his business card.

"May I see you into a hansom?"

"Thank you, but I left my bicycle with your porter." Rusk seemed startled that a lady of quality had a bicycle, which amused Frances, and she headed off.

Her visit had not been successful—well, not directly successful. There was more going on there. They were lying to her, she would swear it, but it seemed like they hadn't wanted to. Rusk seemed sad, and Mattins—he might still come around. Prescott was an actor, and there was no telling what he thought.

CHAPTER 4

Frances rode home in deep thought. She'd let the theatre men stew for a while. For now, she thought it might be helpful to find out who bought the Green Players and the Emerald Theatre so quickly, for so much money. Was someone really willing to buy it just to block Lady Torrence from her researches? Were the men hiding something too?

She came back to Miss Plimsoll's, had lunch, and organized herself for some afternoon calls. Back in time for dinner, she came to the table with paper and pen. In her early days at Miss Plimsoll's, Frances's habit of working while eating raised a lot of eyebrows and caused gossip, but now it was just another little quirk her fellow residents accepted.

Who did she know in the City—the financial quarter of London? She assumed the lords of finances gossiped no less than the diplomats and generals in her family's social circle—or the fish mongers, butchers, and bakers, for that matter. Hal would know some of those men. Her mind wandered briefly. For Frances, engagement wasn't just a time to plan a wedding and gather a trousseau. It was time for real work . . .

But later. And it wasn't fair to Hal to use him to wheedle out some contacts. They would have their own separate careers, and she wouldn't live through him any more than he would through her. Meanwhile she made a list of relations who might know someone. There were no prohibitions in her own mind against using an uncle or cousin.

She was well along on her list when Mrs. Beasley entered the room, looking annoyed. Frances felt her heart sink as she approached her table. From greeting actresses in the guest lounge to entertaining visitors from the Metropolitan Police, it was usually Frances who tarnished the image of Miss Plimsoll's. What did the manageress want to speak with her about now?

"Lady Frances. There is a . . . messenger of sorts at the front desk. He says it is most urgent." Disapproval was etched deeply in her face, even though Mrs. Beasley usually approved of messengers. This probably wasn't a footman from a great house.

Frances gathered her papers and followed Mrs. Beasley to the foyer. The messenger certainly wasn't a footman, not in clothing like that. He was only about sixteen, wearing as lively an outfit of red and gold as had ever graced the hotel lobby. He was looking around with great curiosity at the room's expensive and lovingly cared for fittings.

"Excuse me?" said Frances.

"Ah, Lady Frances. Johnny Bridger, at your service." He bowed with a flourish. *Oh, dear, another actor.* "I'm in the chorus with Miss Studholme, and she put me in a hansom to fetch you most quickly. She said that you were interested in the Emerald Theatre and you'd want to know that, a little while ago, Tony Mattins was found dead in an alley behind the theatre."

Yes, she did want to know. *Thank you, Marie!* "This was very recent?"

"Within the hour, my lady. News flew fast. Never met the man myself, but he was well-known in the West End. Must've been some chance thief, poor bloke."

A dozen thoughts raced through her mind. But no, she could think later. Now was time for action.

"Did you keep the hansom?"

"Yes, my lady. Miss Studholme said to."

Frances suspected that she might need Mallow. "Bless you. Run back out, and tell the driver that I'll be out in a few seconds to head straight to the Emerald. I must fetch my maid." She practically ran upstairs. The maids usually had an earlier dinner, along with the hotel staff, who had to be free to serve at the resident meal, so Mallow would be sewing in their room.

"Mallow—there's been a development. A person of interest, as they say, has been killed, and we need to follow up."

"Very good, my lady." No fuss, no astonishment. She put down her sewing and said, "I will bring a wrap, my lady. It's often cool in the evenings this time of year."

Johnny was chatting with the cabbie but turned when the women came down the stairs. His eyes landed on Mallow.

"I'm sure we can all squeeze in," said Frances. "Johnny Bridger, my maid, Miss Mallow. Now let's go." But Johnny took time to doff his hat to Mallow and then help Frances and Mallow into the cab, ensuring that he'd be sitting next to Mallow. He had a winning smile, and his handsome features, reflected Frances, should be of great help in his career.

The door closed, and the driver pulled into the street.

"So, Miss Mallow. I'm an actor and singer in the chorus of the new show at the St. James. You like theatre?" Johnny asked. Mallow did like music hall entertainment and the new motion pictures, but that didn't mean she approved of actors. Or of men she had just met trying to chat her up.

"I go to respectable entertainments with my friends," she said, a little stiffly.

"We are most respectable too, Miss Mallow," he said. "I can leave tickets for you and a friend, and me and one of my mates could buy you a pint afterward."

Imagine that! Trying to arrange an assignation—in front of her mistress, no less.

"I am very busy serving her ladyship," said Mallow. Undaunted, Johnny turned to Lady Frances. "I'm sure you wouldn't mind if

Miss Mallow took an evening off? Very high-quality entertainment, my lady. The best people attend."

"My maid's social life is her affair," said Frances. Like most actors, he was shameless.

"There you go, Miss Mallow. Anyway, I can always be reached at the St. James Theatre if you change your mind."

They dropped him off at the St. James, and Frances told him to thank Miss Studholme. He tipped his hat again, and they continued on to the Emerald.

"I was being polite, my lady. I don't want you to think I would associate with actors."

"It's quite all right, Mallow. *I* associate with actors."

"Well, yes, my lady, but not a man and a woman together."

"Mallow, your behavior has always been above reproach. Now there's the Emerald and quite a crowd. Let's see what's happening."

It was dark, but even with just the streetlights, they could see a semicircle of the curious around the alley and the shields on the helmets of the bobbies holding them back.

Frances paid the hansom driver, and then she gave some thought to how to get into the theatre. She didn't think for a moment it was a coincidence that Mattins had been killed right after talking to her. There might be something among his effects that would help her.

Most of the officers were keeping the crowd back, but one was standing by the theatre doors. Up close, Frances saw that they seemed to be just curiosity seekers; they were not dressed like actors. They must all be inside the theatre. She stepped over to the constable.

"Excuse me, but I just heard about the tragedy. I am Lady Frances Ffolkes, and my family—my brother is the Marquess of Seaforth—are patrons of this theatre. It is necessary for me to speak with the company manager. May we—my maid and I—enter?"

"Sorry, m'lady, the whole theatre company is waiting inside for the inspector to speak with them, and none may leave without his permission."

"But I don't want to *leave*, Constable; I want to *enter*. Surely the inspector didn't say no one could enter."

"Well . . . not in so many words, m'lady, but it doesn't really matter. There was no performance today anyway. The theatre was closed to all except members of the company."

"And I'm practically a member of the company." She reached into her bag and produced Mr. Rusk's business card. "See? I even have the manager's card. I was here earlier today. If I had stayed a little later, I'd be in there with them anyway. I just need a moment to consult with Mr. Rusk."

"I'll have to check with the inspector—"

"—who won't thank you for interrupting him as he begins his investigations. I'll be in and out shortly."

The constable sighed. She was obviously someone of quality and it didn't do to thwart them, and it seemed silly to bother the inspector over something so trivial. And she was right—the important thing was that no one would leave, not that anyone would enter.

"Very well, m'lady," he said grudgingly, letting Frances and Mallow in. Frances quickly turned back to the bobby. "Can you tell me how Mr. Mattins was killed?"

"Oh, it'll be in the papers anyway. He was stabbed. That's often the way of it here, I'm afraid."

There was no porter on duty. *They must all be in the theatre itself.* With Mallow right behind her, she opened one of the heavy doors and entered the theatre proper. All the lights were on, so Frances could clearly view the interior. She had been there before but had never bothered to look closely at the decor. It was all gilt and velvet in rococo style, but in the brightness of the full house lights, she could see that it was looking a little faded. The Emerald was firmly rooted in the past, in a repertoire of another generation. Along with the facade, would the new owners refurbish the interior? And bring in new playwrights, as Rusk had thought?

The company was assembled in knots of people, some on the stage, done up to look like they were from medieval Verona.

Or rather, what Englishmen might imagine medieval Verona should look like. Others in the company gathered in the seats. A few looked up at them curiously, but no one called out, perhaps assuming that she and Mallow were just extras hired to fill in a crowd scene.

She looked around for Mr. Rusk and found him sitting a little apart from the rest of the others, talking to a couple of other men. One, judging from his dress, seemed to be some sort of clerk or accountant, and the other was dressed like Mattins—perhaps an assistant stage manager. Her eyes darted around, and she saw Prescott in conversation with some other actors in another corner.

Rusk looked up at Frances with surprise. "Lady Frances? What are you doing here? How did you even get in?"

"I just heard about Mr. Mattins and wanted to offer my condolences."

He blinked. That was an insufficient explanation, and they both knew it. Rusk turned to the other men. "We'll talk more later, but for now, the schedule stands as is." They glanced at Frances and shuffled off.

"Lady Frances, I didn't think you someone guilty of a gruesome level of curiosity. What are you really doing here? And who's this?"

"This is Miss Mallow, my personal maid."

"You travel with your maid, but—"

"Never mind that," said Frances, a little impatiently. "I am truly sorry about Mr. Mattins, but there will be time for mourning later. I am here because I am afraid that our conversation led to his murder."

Rusk started to speak, but nothing came out for a few moments. "My lady, that's ridiculous. I'm sure it was just a chance robber—what else could it be? If anyone in a theatre company died after gossiping about the old days, this place would look like the end of *Hamlet*."

"Perhaps. But who besides you and Mr. Prescott knew I was seeking this information?"

"Well, almost everyone here." He waved his arm to encompass the theatre. "When you asked about the company thirty years ago, I thought of Mattins and Prescott right away, but I also made a general announcement to see if anyone else had been there back then. I mean, you don't immediately remember if someone has been here for twenty or twenty-five or thirty years, but they were the only ones. At the least the only ones around now that I can remember. And I daresay both men discussed it later." He sighed. "It's not every day that a titled lady comes in asking about actresses of another generation."

"I see. But where did Mr. Mattins live? If he was killed for something he knew or had, there may be something in his rooms." Frances knew she wouldn't have any chance of convincing the local inspector of this, but she might get something out of Mr. Rusk.

"Lived? He had a room here. There's a gallery upstairs we use for some short-term storage, and there was a room carved out for Mattins, since he spent so much time here—a perk of the job. Lady Frances, I know you're upset, but I'm sure the police can handle this." He turned to Mallow. "Can you see your mistress safely home and give her something soothing?"

Mallow bristled. She took orders only from her lady—certainly not from theatre folk. Lady Frances matched her indignation. She didn't need "soothing."

"Mr. Rusk, I know you have lost an old friend and must continue to manage the company during this difficult time. I'll leave you now, and thank you. Come, Mallow."

Not waiting for any reply, she headed back to the entrance. She turned, though, before she exited. Most people seemed to be part of the company, such as actors in costume or stagehands in working clothes. However, her eyes lit on an exceptionally beautiful young woman who seemed a little apart from the others, sitting near a group of plainly dressed women who may have been dressers or seamstresses but not participating in their whispered conversations. She was just looking around. She could have been an actress, but she wasn't dressed as one.

Oh, well. Frances could think on that later, including the possibility of wheedling a list of interviewees out of one of her Scotland Yard contacts. For now, she and Mallow had work to do.

"Just follow me," she told her maid. "The man may have been killed, but let's make sure it wasn't for nothing." They went through the theatre doors, but instead of heading into the street, Frances took a quick turn down the hallway to where Mr. Rusk's office was. She kept going past it until they were by the backstage dressing rooms. Frances knocked lightly on one and, hearing nothing, entered.

It was a room for an actress. Clothes and cosmetics were strewn around. Frances heard Mallow give a little click of disapproval.

"Not very shipshape, is it, Mallow?" asked Frances with a smile.

"I'm sure actresses, being busy, do the best they can," said Mallow. The implication was that their best wasn't very good at all.

"We're just here to borrow a nail file," Frances said, and it took her only a moment to find one under the clutter. "And now to Mr. Mattins's room." She didn't know how to get to the upper gallery but saw a winding staircase at the end of the hall, along the back wall of the theatre. They walked up quickly and found themselves along another corridor. Most of the doors were open, revealing racks of clothes among baskets of props.

"My brother, our cousins, and I used to dress up for parties in the country when we were children. Imagine all the fun we could've had here. I dressed up as Boudica, the English warrior queen who defeated Roman legions."

"I'm sure you were very convincing, my lady," said Mallow.

One door was closed and, as Frances had suspected, locked as well. That was why she had brought the nail file.

"Mallow, we need to get in here before the police do. I think we may find a clue why he was killed inside. Stand by the head of the stairs, and let me know if someone is coming."

"Very good, my lady."

It only took Frances five minutes to get into the room. The more she practiced, the better she got at this. The door clicked open, and Frances motioned for Mallow to join her. They closed the door behind them.

The room was fairly large. There was a nook with a bed, a desk, a dresser, and even a closet. Unlike the dressing room, this one was neat. Mattins was in charge of the backstage, Frances knew, so being orderly was probably essential. A few posters adorned the walls, and there was a good supply of paper and ink, as well as a pile of scripts.

"What are we looking for, my lady?" asked Mallow.

"I'm not sure. But it will be old—papers, notes, a book, a photograph. These items all look recent." She opened the desk drawers one by one. She found some notebooks on various productions—how various plays were organized, scene by scene. She wished she had more time to review them, but there was no telling when someone else would come.

Mallow was going through the closet. Mattins didn't have much clothing—one Sunday best suit and good footwear appropriate for a man who probably spent a lot of time on his feet. Frances meanwhile went to the dresser, but there was nothing there either. How disappointing. She was so sure Mattins knew what she was asking about and had so hoped he'd have a tangible clue relating to Louisa Torrence. Her eyes darted around—the bed. Frances practically threw herself onto the floor. Yes—she could see a box there. Taking no notice of the dust on the floor, she wriggled until she could grasp the tin box and pull it out.

"My lady," said Mallow in a harsh whisper, "I hear footsteps."

Oh, dear. Frances heard them too now. No chance to leave unseen. She grabbed the box with one hand and Mallow with the other, and they slipped into the closet. Frances closed the doors as best she could from the inside but could still see through a crack between the doors. Mallow was right up against her, and Frances heard her shallow breathing. She found her hand and gave it a reassuring squeeze.

The door to the room opened, and a cloaked figure soon came into view. *Well, why not?* thought Frances. There was likely no lack of cloaks in the costume rooms, and whoever it was clearly didn't want to be seen going into Mattins's room. The figure followed their path, first checking the desk drawers, then the dresser. *Oh, God, will it be the closet next?*

But then the cloaked figure suddenly stopped and cocked his hooded head. Had he heard something that Frances and Mallow could not, in the closet?

He swiftly left, shutting the door behind him.

"We'll wait a few more moments to be sure," whispered Frances. She was right to do so, because then they heard heavy boots, and the door opened again. Frances could see it was a bobby, and Mallow tensed up. But the constable just stuck his head in to look around, then closed the door. His arrival must've chased away the cloaked figure. Frances cautiously opened the door.

"Mallow—I think it's time we left."

"I am in complete agreement, my lady," she said with such fervor that Frances had to smile. She tucked the box under her arm, and they headed back down, hoping they wouldn't meet anyone else. Perhaps the inspector was now in the theatre, talking to potential witnesses. It was clear to the front door, and after returning the nail file, they quickly slipped out.

The same constable was still out front. "See, Constable, in and out. Thank you for understanding."

"Very good . . . ah, my lady . . . that box? Did you take that from the theatre?"

She hadn't thought of that. "Of course not. I had it when I came here. Business I had to discuss with Mr. Rusk."

He frowned. "My lady, I think I would've noticed—"

Mallow jumped in, her young face as full of righteous indignation as if she had been a dowager duchess. "Constable, her ladyship is not accustomed to having her word questioned. Now it is late, and I need to get my lady to her bed."

The constable was a little astounded. So was Frances.

"I, um, see. Well then, have a good evening, my lady, and, ah, you too, miss."

There was no problem finding a hansom in the busy West End, and once they were seated, Frances said, "That was quite a little speech there, Mallow."

"I hope I am not guilty of taking a liberty, my lady, but listening to him question you like that, the word of the daughter of a marquess."

"Not at all, Mallow. A job well done, getting us out of there like that. Very quick thinking. But you do realize the constable was right. We did technically steal this box."

"Well yes, my lady. But I understood it was for a higher purpose, as they say."

"Nicely phrased. You should be appointed to a chair of applied ethics at Oxford University."

"Very good, my lady."

Soon they were back in their rooms, and Frances was excited about opening the box—but not before Mallow spread some newspaper on the table. "It's a bit dirty, my lady."

The latch was stiff but not locked, and Frances quickly had it open. One by one, she removed the items. First was a program from *Romeo and Juliet*, the play the Green Players were about to open. But it wasn't for the current production. "Look, Mallow, it's from 1875. It must have meant something to him. And that was about the time Louisa Torrence left." She looked over the cast. One name jumped out—Quentin Prescott played Mercutio, Romeo's colorful friend, who died in a duel halfway through the play. She didn't recognize any other names but saw Juliet was played by an actress simply named "Helen."

Next was what looked like another program but turned out to be a flyer from "The Halliday Mission, Maidstone, Kent."

"I've heard of them, Mallow. They work to provide spiritual comfort and charitable assistance to actors."

"A very worthy cause, my lady." In her opinion, actors needed all the spiritual assistance they could get.

"Yes. But it says here they were in Maidstone. I know this group, and they're located in London, not Maidstone. But again, this may be some years old. It will bear looking into."

The third item was handwritten on fine paper, like what Frances used for her personal stationery. A male hand had written in strong, elegant script:

> The Oath of Tyndareus: All men reading this shall know that the undersigned have signed the oath to support Helen in all things, according to the custom of the Greeks.

There were half a dozen signatures at the bottom: Gilbert Rusk, Quentin Prescott, Mattins himself, and three more men. One of them, Frances noted with a glance at the program, played Romeo in that thirty-year-old production.

"What is the Oath of Tyndareus, my lady?"

"It means, Mallow, that our quest for Louisa Torrence has become a lot more complicated than we may have thought. There's an ancient legend about a Greek queen named Helen, the most beautiful woman in the world," Frances explained. "She was kidnapped by a prince from a city called Troy, and the Greeks waged a long war before they got her back. There's a long poem about it called the *Iliad*. But before this all happened, many great men wanted to marry her. Her stepfather, Tyndareus, was afraid that war would break out among the rejected suitors. So he made them swear a sacred oath to defend his choice and always be allies. It was called the Oath of Tyndareus. They all swore, and then he gave her hand to King Menelaus of Sparta."

"I see, my lady. So maybe these men signed this paper because they all liked this actress named Helen, just like the lady in the legend?"

"It would seem so, Mallow. And I'm wondering if this Helen is Louisa Torrence. The time is right, and she was exceptionally beautiful. Anyway, I'm not going to get anything more out of the Green Players for now. Mr. Rusk already thinks I'm a madwoman. But there are other avenues to explore, like the Halliday connection. Why was this so important that Mattins saved it for so long in a special box? I'll visit their office tomorrow afternoon. Right after my luncheon tomorrow at Simpson's with Mr. Wheaton."

Mallow's ears pricked up at that. "Luncheon with Mr. Wheaton, my lady? I shall consider a dress most carefully. And you will need to give me time to do your hair up proper."

Frances sighed. "Yes, Mallow," she said, forestalling Mallow's usual comment that "gentlemen like to see ladies done up nicely. I heard this many times from your late mother the marchioness, God rest her soul."

Chapter 5

Frances met Hal in front of Simpson's. It was sweet the way he always seemed to light up at her arrival.

"Mr. Wheaton, are you sure you can take away time from your busy practice to romance a woman? What would the Law Society say?"

"But I'm not romancing a woman—not merely, I should say. I'm meeting with a deeply valued client of my law practice. But you, my lady—allowing yourself to be romanced when you should be working to get women the vote? How do you explain that?" He grinned.

"But I am working, my love. Today's lunch is all part of my master plan to convert men to our cause." And with that, she let Hal take her arm and escort her into the restaurant. The maître d' nodded to Hal and led them to a quiet table in an alcove.

"How did we get such a good table?" asked Frances. Hal shrugged. "I bet I know. This restaurant is owned by the D'Oyle Carte company. I can imagine such a distinguished company turns its business over to your equally distinguished firm. They are only too willing to show you to the best table."

"I am not allowed to confirm that, but . . . I can say that the Lady Sherlock is thinking along the correct lines."

"I am glad you brought that up," said Frances with more than a hint of pride. "Because I am about to become London's first female consulting detective. But first we order—I am absolutely ravenous for roast beef and sharp mustard."

She insisted on nothing but small talk until the food came. "Now listen to my story, dear Hal. I too have a client. A widow, whose late husband was a Foreign Office associate of my father's, asked me to find her lost daughter. It seems my reputation, good and bad, has caught up with me." She gave Hal a concise summary of the job she had been given and the results she had so far. But she decided to leave out the death of Mattins for now. The connection wasn't proven, and there was no need to worry him.

When she was done, Hal didn't say anything right away. He always thought before speaking. It must be something you learned while training to become a solicitor, Frances assumed.

"She must be a remarkable woman, this client of yours. She could've engaged any number of people in London. But she chose probably the only one in town who is both able and willing to truly help her." She flushed at that. "You must keep your client private, as I do mine, but if you need any legal help, I am at your disposal."

"I will call on you as necessary. But Hal . . ." Now Frances struggled for words. "I'm running all over town, associating with actors, smuggling boxes out of theatres. How could you introduce a wife like that to dinners at the Law Society?" She was half joking. Only half.

"Do you jest with me?" asked Hal with mock severity. "You'd be the most popular guest there. Come, Franny, you've met several of my friends from the legal profession. They're not a bad lot, are they?"

"Of course not, they are a delightful group—"

"Don't forget that I had to get you released from a police jail over that little mess at Kestrel's Eyrie, and still I'm more than willing to marry you." He smiled, and she returned it.

"But Hal, how can I do all this . . . while being mistress of a house, seeing the house is provisioned, meeting with the cook."

"You know my housekeeper. She'd put Otto von Bismarck to shame with her organizational skills and heavy hand running the house. She'll do it all happily."

"But as lady of the house, people will expect me to run things. As they did my mother."

"And since when did you ever care what other people think? You're worried about what I would think, right?"

Now it was Frances's turn to pause, and they ate in silence for a few moments. "Sometimes I wish I hadn't fallen in love with such a perceptive man," she finally said. "Oh, very well, I can't shake the fact that once we're set up as husband and wife, it just won't—I mean, I can't imagine myself protesting in the park, tracking down missing persons, and then returning to our townhouse." It was hard to admit this to herself, and she felt the frustration building up inside her, her love for Hal and her commitment to everything else. "So, Hal, isn't this where you tell me that if I really loved you, you and I would find a way of making it work?" She made the tone light.

"My dearest, I know you love me. I'm not going to ask you to prove it. I suppose it's for me to prove it to you. Now, Franny"—he held up his hand to stop any further protests—"you wanted to use our engagement period as a test, to see if we could really merge our lives as husband and wife. I think we can. As a solicitor, problem solving is what I do. Now can I tempt you with some treacle tart?"

"What are you up to? You sound of subterfuge."

"A solicitor? Dealing with subterfuge? You amaze me. But Franny, I don't run one of the finest firms in London for nothing. Trust me. I have some ideas. You'll see. We'll have it all." He reached over and squeezed her hand. "For now, I wish you success on your investigations." The promised treacle tart arrived. It reminded Frances of nursery years; she absolutely adored it. She would let him be mysterious—for now.

"Ah, Franny, speaking of fellow solicitors, I assume you're still joining me with my Law Society friends for dinner at my house? Or are you now too busy?" The man of affairs disappeared, and he looked shy and boyish now. It was important to him that she knew and liked those in his circle.

"I'm searching for a woman who disappeared thirty years ago. I don't see how a dinner would matter. I might even get a fresh perspective." He looked relieved, and she understood. Oddly, she had more freedom than he had. She was just "Mad Lady Frances." Any kind of disgraceful behavior was expected of her, but no one had to be more correct than a solicitor. And yet he wanted her to be part of his life.

Which brought Frances back to her original problem. How could she live with him? How could she contemplate life without him? When this was over, she knew, that problem would have to take top priority.

After their treacle tart, he dared risk giving her a kiss good-bye.

The Halliday Mission operated out of a genteel yet shabby two-room office filled with a couple of battered desks and a cabinet overflowing with papers. But there was nothing worn out about the mission's secretary, Mr. Jellicoe. He was in his fifties, a bit portly, and bursting with energy and most welcoming.

"Lady Frances, do take a seat. May I get you some tea? Are you sure? You know, your name is familiar to me. Are you active in charitable circles?"

"Yes, I am, Mr. Jellicoe. I work extensively with the Ladies' Christian Relief Guild."

"Of course, that's where I've heard of you. That's a very fine group, one that I greatly admire. I applaud your good works, my lady. Your guild makes a great deal of difference." He seemed genuine. She was used to many men who treated charitable work with an amused condescension, saying that it kept the ladies busy and gave them something useful to do.

"Thank you. I've heard of the Halliday Mission and your outreach work with actors. I am pleased to see someone with interest rather than contempt for them."

"Thank you so much. Do you know, I'm glad to see someone understand. We are not here to condemn actors or glorify them, merely to help save their souls."

You have set quite a task for yourself, thought Frances.

"But please tell me how I can help you."

"I am actually hoping you can solve a little mystery for me. I recently came across an old handbill regarding the mission, but the address was in Maidstone, Kent. Were you once there?"

"Oh, that is a long time ago, my lady. That's when Mr. and Mrs. Halliday themselves first ran the mission. They ran it out of their home in Maidstone at first, but eventually it was transferred to London, some twenty years ago at least."

"Are the Hallidays themselves still alive?"

"No, they were called to God about five years ago, I'm sorry to say. It was shortly after I started here—first Mr. Halliday, and then his wife not long after. I knew them somewhat. Very fine people, deeply religious but free from judgment, always ready to help their fellow man. But your mystery, my lady—is it about the history of the Hallidays? Maybe you would like to call on their son, the Reverend Samuel Halliday."

"So their son went into the ministry? Such pious people, who founded a mission, must have been very pleased with that." Frances wondered if the boy had been given any choice. But that was not fair, she realized. Her brother had been delighted to follow their father into Foreign Office service.

"I know that they were very proud, my lady. Especially Mrs. Halliday. She didn't live much longer after he was ordained—it was as if she had met her life's goal and was ready to meet her maker. Anyway, I've met Reverend Halliday a few times as well. He is very busy in his own parish and did mission work himself in Africa. He's vicar of Trinity Church in Wimbledon."

"I will seek him out, then. I'm merely investigating a possible connection with my own family, some years back. Thank you, and good luck with your mission, Mr. Jellicoe."

It seemed a thin enough clue—nothing really to connect the Halliday family with Helen or Louisa. (*Were they the same?*) But the flyer was in Mattins's box, so it probably had some importance. And it was old because it had the Maidstone address.

So she found herself a hansom and soon was on her way to Wimbledon, a pleasant neighborhood now best known for its tennis. The driver dropped her off at the Trinity Church vicarage, a substantial mid-Victorian brick building, and she knocked on the door. It was opened by the vicar himself.

She was startled at first. Frances had never thought of vicars as handsome, but then again, why shouldn't they be? He possessed well-formed features, welcoming eyes, and a shock of black hair over his brow. He also had a warm and cheerful smile.

"Reverend Halliday?"

"You have found him. Please come in, and let me know how I may serve you."

"Thank you." She stepped inside. "I'm Lady Frances Ffolkes. You will think I'm very forward, but in searching for an old family friend, I came across a connection to your late parents. I hope you may be able to help me."

He chuckled. "Most intriguing, my lady. Do come through, and we'll discuss it."

He led her through the hallway into a study. She was reminded of Lady Torrence's house because his home displayed examples of African art—no doubt mementoes of his time in the missions. The place was well-kept and the furniture modern and fine. Also, from the state of the house, he clearly could afford a good housekeeper and perhaps a housemaid as well. Mr. Jellicoe had said his parents had been well-off, so no doubt they had left their son a nice legacy, along with the mission endowment.

But she noted that he was not above answering his own door.

His study was also nicely appointed, with his papers well-organized and shelves of handsome leather-bound books. He showed Lady Frances to a seat and offered to ring for tea, but she politely declined and got to the point.

"I was doing some researches on behalf of a friend, and we came across a reference to your parents. The woman I was looking for was an actress, and I know your parents founded a mission to the theatre community. Did you know of a woman named Helen?"

She saw at once he did. The Reverend Halliday had a look of recognition and sadness.

"Yes, Lady Frances. My goodness, that was a long time ago. You were right; my parents did found a mission, and Helen was a woman that they helped. I'm afraid that many in the theatre community were not as receptive as my parents might've wished, but Helen was. I don't know the details, but I do know she married." He stumbled for a moment. "He died suddenly. And in her grief and confusion, she came to my parents for refuge. My mother was with child—me, as a matter of fact. So it was fortuitous, as my mother wasn't in good health at the best of times, and apparently this Helen was a kind and useful companion. The plan was for Helen to stay on after I was born and help until she made some long-term plans. But it wasn't to be. A week before I was born, she was hit quickly with a fever and died in two days. My mother was grief-stricken at the loss of her new friend, but as I was told, she recovered mostly with my birth—a healthy boy."

"Thank you for telling me that story. I grieve for the loss of your mother's friend, but I'm pleased that your mother came through. I was wondering—do you have a likeness of Helen?"

The vicar shook his head. "No, but my mother once mentioned that she was uncommonly beautiful, with the bluest eyes and blackest hair. She was a practical woman, my mother, and she once mentioned that had Helen lived, she would've had no trouble finding a new husband, as lovely as she was, and still so very young."

There could've been more than one actress named Helen, but Frances knew the men at the Emerald Theatre had recognized her description of Louisa. The vicar had just described Helen as Louisa. Helen had played Juliet in the program that Mattins had so carefully saved alongside the Halliday flyer that had led Frances here. So it seemed that Louisa was dead, without ever having seen her mother again. Frances had known that this was a possibility, but still she felt the sadness hit her hard. She had so wanted to effect a family reunion. She couldn't be completely sure yet, but it seemed like her search had led her to an unhappy end.

"Thank you, reverend. It's a sad story, but I appreciate the truth. I am acting as an agent for an elderly friend and will break the news. But tell me, I don't suppose you know Helen's surname, either her maiden or married name?"

He shook his head. "I don't ever remember my parents telling me. She went by her theatre name, just Helen."

"But surely there were some papers—a death certificate for Helen or her marriage license?"

"Yes, there should've been. When my mother explained this all to me when I came of age, she told me that any papers relating to Helen had been deposited with their local church, St. Mark's in Maidstone. But not long after, there was a fire due to a bit of clumsiness from the priest, who was elderly. About a year's worth of records were destroyed, I'm afraid."

"Do you have any siblings who might remember that time?" asked Frances.

"No, I was my parents' first and only child." He smiled sadly. "There was a tragic irony about it all. My parents had so hoped for a child and had not been blessed. My mother was thirty-seven and had long been in poor health, as I noted. And yet she survived the birth and delivered a healthy child. But the young and robust Helen died. An example of 'In the midst of life, we are in death.'

"Anyway, there's not much more I can tell you. My parents saw Helen buried at St. Mark's. I'm sure the vicar or sexton there can help you, if you or your friend would like to visit."

"You've been so kind. I was wondering, though—did your parents have any servants or nearby relations who might have a memory of Helen?"

"No one still with us, I'm sorry to say . . . but I know someone who might be able to help. As I said, my mother had been planning to keep Helen with them. But when she died, after my birth, she and my father sent for another woman to be a sort of companion. Aunt Em, I called her, although she was not a relation. She lived in Shrewsbury, I believe. I think her family had known my mother's family many years before, although I can't recall the details, if I ever knew them. She was with my mother for a while, and they were very close. Aunt Em never met Helen, of course, but my mother may have shared memories with her. Later, my father introduced Aunt Em to a carpenter friend of his, and they married and had a daughter. She was widowed a few years ago, as her husband was a bit older. We assumed she'd sell the business, but she was determined to run it. She promoted her late husband's most senior assistant as head carpenter and designer, but Aunt Em is very much in charge. A sharp lady, she is. I visit them about once a week. She has a shop on Bond Street. Be sure you mention I suggested you speak with her."

Frances raised an eyebrow. "A carpenter on Bond Street among all the fine shops?"

"Oh, they're not a typical carpentry firm. Emma's late husband had a sideline making fine jewelry boxes, cigar boxes, and so forth. Aunt Em saw the possibilities there and encouraged him to work on those full time. The shop has continued to prosper under Aunt Em's management and has become very fashionable, I hear. It is called Lockton's. She was born Emma Bradley but after her marriage became Emma Lockton, thus the name of the shop. I daresay you've passed it."

"I'm sure I have and look forward to visiting her." She stood. "I cannot thank you enough for your kindness and assistance."

"My pleasure. I just wish I had better news about Helen. Just one thing, my lady, if I may. My mother asked me, before she died, not to discuss this story widely. As you seemed to know about it already and appear to be the type of person to keep a secret, I didn't mind filling in the details, so to speak. But I would be grateful if you would help me keep my mother's wishes."

"Of course. My only goal is to help reconnect friends and relations with Helen, not to reopen old wounds."

"Thank you for understanding," he said. He walked her to the door, and Frances turned before making her final good-byes.

She had seen Reverend Halliday stumble over the death of Helen's husband. He hadn't wanted to discuss it. "One more piece of information—Helen's husband. Was it an illness that took him?"

He grimaced. "I'm afraid nothing so common. He was killed by a robber, it seems, although again, I don't know the details, just a chance mention from my father once. He was stabbed, my parents told me. No one was ever arrested."

Chapter 6

Frances and Mallow took their seats on the morning train to Maidstone, which was only about a one-hour ride. Her ladyship was in one of her thoughtful moods, observed Mallow, and not inclined to talk, but she would when she was ready. Meanwhile, Mallow produced some knitting to keep herself busy while the train headed into Kent.

"There's too much that's odd, Mallow," Frances finally said. "Helen's husband killed by a knife in an apparent robbery, and now Mr. Mattins killed the same way—and someone wanted to search his room. I called the local police station yesterday—no one has been arrested yet. And any trace of Helen disappeared in a fire. Then, the moment Lady Torrence quietly does a little research, the entire company is purchased without any negotiation, and her permission is revoked. And I'm lied to about Helen at the theatre. Finally, I hear that Mrs. Halliday's companion, Emma Lockton, is from Shrewsbury, where the Torrence family is from. Any one of these things happening is coincidence. But all of them happening together are very improbable."

Mallow nodded. "So we are going to look at Helen's grave, my lady?"

"Yes. But I don't know why. I just need to see if anything else is wrong, if anything else is just too coincidental."

They soon arrived at Maidstone station, and Frances saw Mallow look around approvingly. Her maid thought any town in England—or in the world—had to be second best to London. If you sought food, transportation, or accommodation outside of the capital, you did so at your own risk. But Maidstone was prosperous as a center for beer brewing and papermaking, and if it was nowhere near as grand as London, it was far from the sleepy country towns and villages that they had visited in the past.

"Shall I see about getting a hansom—or something similar, my lady?"

"Thank you, but when I looked on a map, St. Mark's was only a quarter mile from this station, so I think we'll walk."

Many of the commercial buildings they passed were new and in good repair, but when they headed around a corner to the appropriately named Church Street, they saw an older part of Maidstone.

"That is a beautiful structure," said Frances on seeing St. Mark's, and Mallow agreed. "I'm guessing fourteenth century. I don't wonder that the Hallidays were moved to religious devotion with such a building to inspire them," she continued. "The churchyard doesn't look very large, however, so I imagine we'll be able to find Helen's grave. And if not, we'll look for the sexton."

The iron gate to the churchyard opened easily, and Frances and Mallow wandered among the rows of tombstones, some so faded they were hardly legible anymore. The graves were for local aldermen, businessmen, veterans of wars that were mostly forgotten, and their wives and children. Many stones were touched with moss, and Mallow stopped to brush a stray twig from one. A maid's desire for order and cleanliness twinned with Mallow's reverence for holy ground. But overall, the place was well-tended, with the grass and bushes neatly trimmed.

Frances thought Helen's tombstone would be modest. It had been kind of the Hallidays to see to the burial of a woman whom they hardly knew, so she studied the small ones, keeping in mind it would still probably be in good condition, as she had died only about thirty years ago. But when they turned the corner around the back of the church, they both instantly noticed one of the most imposing stones in the graveyard:

In Memory of Helen, 1855–1876.
God Has Heard

Frances wondered at the epitaph. The wording seemed odd. What had God heard? Was this a peaceful end to a difficult life? However you considered it, there was more here than met the eye.

"If I may say, my lady, that was a very Christian act from Mr. and Mrs. Halliday, seeing Helen buried like this."

"Yes, it is, Mallow, but I wonder. Look at the other large stones. The only ones we've seen that are this impressive belong to a member of Parliament and a general who was knighted for service under the Duke of Marlborough. Monuments like this are very expensive. Would the Hallidays have spent that much when all that was needed was a simple stone?"

Frances frowned. It was too odd. But she admitted that there was a little thrill inside her too. Supposing this was Louisa Torrence—the years were right. Yet there was more mystery here. She peered at the grass growing over the plot, as if she could look underground. Did Louisa/Helen literally take something to her grave?

Her next plan was to seek out the sexton to see if he knew something, but he had already found her. A man in his sixties, dressed in work clothes, was approaching them. He had an outdoor complexion and the wiry build common to those who did physical labor.

The man gave them a welcoming smile. "Find what you were looking for, miss? I saw you from inside the church and came to see if I could help. Jethro Brent, sexton, at your service."

"Thank you, Mr. Brent. Lady Frances Ffolkes and my maid, Miss Mallow. I think we have found what we were looking for, the last resting place for Helen. But perhaps you can answer some questions about her. Were you sexton here back in 1876 when Helen was buried?"

She watched him closely. Brent had been openness and smiles, but now he frowned and looked a little cautious.

"Well, yes, m'lady. Been here since 1860. But I didn't know this Helen."

"I would have imagined that she'd been someone important, though, to merit such an impressive memorial. I spoke recently with the Reverend Halliday, and he told me that his parents paid for it. You must've known them. I understand they were prominent members of this church."

Frances watched him think. *Oh, he knows what I'm talking about, but there's some secret here, something he doesn't want to discuss.*

"Well, yes, of course, m'lady. Knew them well—very fine people. This Helen was a friend or relation, I think. I can't be sure. They saw her buried here and ordered this stone. Took some months, of course." It would, a marker that impressive. "That's why the vicar comes every month to visit. He said he promised his mother that he would."

"Was Helen's funeral well-attended? A woman so deserving of such an impressive remembrance must've had many attend her funeral service."

The frown deepened. Brent was unhappy with where these questions were going, and Frances watched him struggle.

"May I ask if you're a relation of Helen's, m'lady?"

Frances felt Mallow stiffen next to her. Frances knew her maid was dying to upbraid the sexton. *How dare you question the motives of the daughter of the Marquess of Seaforth?* She was keeping quiet because she knew Frances was questioning a witness, which was very important.

"No, but I am acting as an agent for someone who is, an elderly friend who cannot travel. The Reverend Halliday gave me some background but of course was too young to remember her himself. He suggested I come to you for details."

Now that stumped him, Frances saw. Brent didn't know what Halliday himself knew or what he had told Frances. If he lied, he could be caught out. But if there was a secret, he didn't want to reveal it. Loyalty to the senior Hallidays, perhaps augmented by some extra coins, was keeping him closed-mouthed.

He sighed. "It was a long time ago, m'lady. If I remember right, and I can't say I do because it's been thirty years, Helen got very sick, and Mr. Halliday was worried about illness spreading, with his own wife expecting a child. When Helen died, Mr. Halliday woke me up in the night and had me dig a grave at first light. I had a couple of local boys help carry the coffin, the vicar said his piece, and that was that. That's all I know." He was positively truculent at the end, as if daring Frances to push him further.

"The vicar. I don't suppose he's still with us, is he?" The Reverend Halliday mentioned that he was elderly thirty years ago.

"That would be the Reverend Uplands, m'lady. He passed away the following winter, and we've had two vicars since then. No one who remembers." He was gathering himself to leave, but Frances wasn't quite done.

"I'd like to see some parish records, but I heard there was an accident—the Reverend Uplands accidentally set fire to some of them?"

"I remember the accident, m'lady, but I have no responsibilities for the church records. And now, if you'll excuse me, I have to see about my duties." And not waiting for a response, he left.

"Well," said Mallow. "I must say that he could've been more polite."

"I'm sure, Mallow, but I had put him in a hard place. There are secrets and more secrets here. The gravestone is odd enough—but last-minute burials at dawn? It's ridiculous. And the Reverend Halliday didn't mention he visited regularly. Why omit that? Oh, there is something here, Mallow. Something deep. And we cannot forget that this isn't just about Helen. Mr. Mattins is dead, and he's part of our investigation too." She stared at the grave for a few more moments, then suddenly roused herself.

"Come, Mallow. There's a London train in thirty minutes, and I have much to do." They walked briskly back to the station, and Frances didn't speak until they were seated on the train.

"I am going to need to speak with Mr. Rusk at the Emerald Theatre again, but I want to know more before I do. Who bought the theatre and the Green Players? We need to talk to someone in the City—the financial center. I bet my brother can help us."

"Very good, my lady," said Mallow. But Frances heard something in her maid's tone.

"You don't think that a good idea?"

"I'm sure it's not my place to comment on your ideas, my lady, but if I may be so bold—his lordship has not been inclined to help your ladyship in such matters."

"You're right there," said Frances ruefully. "Perhaps I need to work on my delivery. Regardless, he should be home for tea this afternoon, so we'll see."

Soon they were back in London, and Frances was pleased to see that the photographer had delivered a print of the Louisa Torrence portrait.

"Even without color, it's clear how beautiful she was," said Frances, showing it to Mallow.

"Very lovely, my lady."

Frances watched her maid's eyes focus on Louisa's dress. "I am sure this was the height of fashion when the portrait was painted, although it seems so dated to us. It's all about change, Mallow. A Greek philosopher named Heraclitus said that the only constant is change. That is, we can never step in the same river twice. As we look back thirty years, we should remember that."

"Very good, my lady. Now do you wish to change before visiting his lordship and her ladyship?"

Frances declined, and when tea time came, said that she would take the bicycle.

"Has Mr. Cumberland adapted to your arrival on bicycle, my lady?"

Frances laughed. "Slowly, Mallow. Slowly."

"Perhaps, my lady, you should tell him what that Mr. Heraclitus said about everything changing."

Frances thought that was an excellent idea.

Chapter 7

Mary was pleased to see Frances again. "Charles will be joining us in a moment. He's been making arrangements with the French ambassador and his wife. We're having them for dinner next week. They speak English, but if you'd care to come, you could impress them with your excellent French."

"Yes. I can say to the ambassador's wife, 'Madame, would you like to come to the next meeting of our suffrage club?'"

Mary laughed. "Diplomacy via suffrage—you may open a whole new branch of international relations. But tell me, how did your meeting go with Lady Torrence?"

"Rather a surprise. I know I can trust you—she has asked me to find Louisa, her long-missing elder daughter, gone these thirty years. It just gets more and more complex, but I'm onto something. It's very exciting, becoming England's first female consulting detective."

"How extraordinary—people actually seeking you out! Your reputation is growing." Frances gave a mock bow. "Best of luck, my dear. You really are becoming the Lady Sherlock."

"Yes, and that's partly why I'm here. I need an introduction to a City gentleman, someone who knows what's going on in finance. It's for my investigations. I want to wheedle out of Charles an introduction to Sir Harold Spenser. He's the financial advisor to the Liberal Party, as you know, and I'd like to pick up some gossip from him. But Charles won't help me if he knows why."

"Aha! Well, you can count on me. But why not just ask Hal? He probably knows even more City figures than Charles."

Mary saw an evasive look on Frances's face, not something she saw often from her frank—no, overly frank—sister-in-law. She raised an eyebrow.

"It sounds silly, Mary, but that's not how I want to go into our marriage. I'm given something important to accomplish, and what do I need to do? Get help from my soon-to-be husband."

"But marriage is—or should be—a partnership, with each of you helping the other," said Mary gently. "Charles is undersecretary. And I see that his household and dinners support his career."

"Oh, I know that, Mary," said Frances, and she struggled for words. "You're the best political hostess in London. Everyone knows that. But about Hal . . . what can I give him? I'm not a hostess. I wouldn't be good at that even if I wanted to, and I don't think he wants that from a wife anyway. I can't ask from him and not give in return. That's not how to start a marriage on equal terms."

Mary just looked at her friend calmly with her gentle eyes and a demeanor that had soothed tempers at many a diplomatic soiree. "Dear Franny, you're so good at solving mysteries. I know you do more for Hal than you realize, and I'm sure if you talk with him, you will see that."

Frances frowned, but before she could say any more, Charles entered.

"I see I am a blessed man, taking tea with the two loveliest ladies in London."

Mary rang for the maid, and soon they were nicely set up with tea and plates of the Seaforth cook's best efforts.

"Dear Charles, I admit that although family feelings are enough to bring me here, I do have an ulterior motive."

Charles smiled wryly and shook his head. "Very well, Franny. What's this all about? Getting me to introduce a resolution supporting women's suffrage in the House of Lords?"

"How amusing! No, something much easier than that. I'm interested in learning more about City affairs—finances and so forth. And I'm hoping you could give me an introduction to Sir Harold Spenser. I'd like to spend a couple of hours with him learning about finances."

Charles sipped some tea, took a cucumber sandwich, and looked his sister in the eye. "Franny. What is this about? Hal could explain whatever you wanted to know. Why must it be Sir Harold?"

"It doesn't have to be Sir Harold. It's simply that I am aware how well you know him. And I'm not asking Hal because I want to surprise him over dinner with my newfound knowledge of City affairs."

Charles nodded, but he wasn't completely convinced, Frances could tell. "Really? That sounds very—how should I say—domestic of you, dear sister. Why not a reference to the Chancellor of the Exchequer, while we're at it?"

Frances just smiled. "With Mr. Asquith, the head of His Majesty's Treasury? I'd be delighted if you could work that out. I know how busy he must be. But Sir Harold would be more than satisfactory."

"Franny—" His tone rose, but Mary jumped in.

"Really, Charles. Sometimes I think there is no pleasing you. You upbraid Frances for involving herself in activities that you feel are none of her concern, yet when she works hard to involve herself in her fiancé's sphere in order to become a good wife, you react like this." She tsked and shook her head. Frances fought hard not to laugh.

Charles frowned. "My sister has been twisting the truth since she was old enough to talk, and you, my beloved wife, have been learning too much from the great diplomats of Europe." He sighed. "Oh, very well. I suppose I'll find out later, but if you want to convert Sir Harold to your suffrage cause, I don't think you'll find him a promising candidate. But that's your affair. I'll leave a message with him this afternoon."

Frances got up and gave her brother a kiss on his cheek. He forced a smile and sighed once more.

"So you found his lordship helpful, my lady?" asked Mallow the next morning as she helped Frances dress.

"Yes, Mallow. With the help of my sister-in-law. He let me have my way out of brotherly affection, but I don't think I can fool him anymore."

"I'm sorry to hear that, my lady," said Mallow, but she appeared not the least bit surprised.

"But the important thing is that Sir Harold Spenser will give me a lesson on how things work in the City. With any luck, he'll even tell me who bought the Green Players and Emerald Theatre." She sighed. "Those clubs we've passed so many times, Mallow, with their fine facades and servants in perfect livery. Five minutes of gossip there, and I'd know everything I want. But I think we'll see women in Parliament before we see them members of those clubs."

She thought of the fictional Diogenes Club, cofounded by Sherlock Holmes's still more brilliant brother, Mycroft. Would it have accepted women? Thinking about Sherlock and Mycroft, she had to conclude, probably not. *My goodness, I can't even get accepted into a fictional club.*

Initially, Frances had planned to take the bicycle, as it was another pleasant day, but she was already eccentric as a woman seeking advice on financial matters. No need to make herself look odder by leaving a bicycle with Sir Harold's chief clerk. It would be a hansom today.

The offices of Spenser, Ltd. were decorated in the faux Renaissance style favored by bankers, complete with columns, as if they were back in the days of the Medicis. It was just as smart inside, displaying gleaming wood and marble. An immaculately dressed clerk behind a desk rose to greet her.

"May I help you, Miss . . . ?" he said.

"Lady Frances Ffolkes, to see Mr. Spenser," she said. The clerk quickly consulted a leather-bound book.

"Very good, Lady Frances." He snapped his fingers for a uniformed page, who escorted Frances up the stairs and across a thickly carpeted hallway. Frances smiled to herself. If this place was designed to impress customers, it certainly succeeded.

Sir Harold held court in an office on par with the rest of the building. He sat behind a desk so large that Frances's immediate thought was that it was too big to fit through the door and had probably been built right in the office itself. The page announced her, and she walked across a magnificent Turkish rug to greet Sir Harold. The man himself was not as remarkable as his surroundings, being shorter than average and well-fed, which a talented tailor had done his best to work around. But Sir Harold had a welcoming smile and immediately came from behind his desk to meet Frances halfway.

"Lady Frances, it is a pleasure to meet the sister of so fine as man as Lord Seaforth. Please, take a seat." As the financial advisor to the Liberal Party, he was no doubt pleased to do a favor for a prominent party figure like Frances's brother.

Sir Harold showed her to a seat at a small table, and a moment later another page came with a tea service and then bowed out. He seemed pleased to see Frances, and she wondered what her brother had told him about the reason for her visit.

He answered her unspoken question in a moment. "Your brother tells me you are the volunteer treasurer of the Ladies' Christian Relief Guild. Very noble of you, Lady Frances. He says you wanted to know more about finance for your role, and to that end, I have put together a brief lesson for you—an introductory course, if you will, on the basics of investing . . ."

It was not the most entertaining half hour Frances had ever spent, but she had to admit that Sir Harold did not patronize her and explained matters clearly. He went over different classes in investments, how shares and bonds worked, and the organization of joint stock companies, and Frances filed much of it away for later. She realized that she had been long interested in political equality for women—but for economic equality, women would have to master the intricacies of the City.

However, Frances didn't lose sight of why she came here in the first place—to find out who bought the Green Players and Emerald Theatre.

"I hope I didn't go too quickly, Lady Frances. I do let my enthusiasm get away from me sometimes," he said, with a self-deprecating chuckle.

"Not at all, Sir Harold. You have given me much to think about and discuss with the other board members regarding our finances. But I wonder . . . what about investing in individual companies, such as purchasing an income-producing business?"

Sir Harold nodded sagely. "Very possible. But it requires a lot of investigation to make sure the business has a solid foundation. Large investors often have staffs to do it for them."

"That makes sense," said Frances, and she smiled. "In that case, if I had a sum, I might invest in, say, a theatre. I do see a great many plays and know London's theatre world so well, I daresay I am qualified to investigate their businesses." She had some more tea—but kept an eye on Sir Harold, who was looking at her with a great deal of curiosity. Had she been too direct?

"What an odd thing to say," he said. She looked back at him, full of innocence.

"Is that a foolish idea? I know I'm still very much a beginner here."

"No, not exactly. It can be a profitable, if rather risky investment, but—well, I really shouldn't say . . ." And he helped himself to a little cake.

Frances wanted to scream. Sir Harold had clearly heard something, and if they had been men together in a club with glasses of a vintage port, she'd have the information already. But perhaps she could still wheedle it out of him.

She put her hand to her mouth. "Sir Harold—don't tell me someone else has already decided to buy a theatre company as an investment! I feel rather proud to have thought of it as well."

"Ah, yes. Excellent idea, that, if you have enough capital to weather the occasional downturn. But it's more than that. I really shouldn't say, but it has been talked about in financial circles for some weeks."

"You can trust me to be discreet, Sir Harold. I sit on the board with the Duchess of St. Ives and the Countess of Edgewater, who was a lady-in-waiting to Queen Victoria. And our royal patron is the king's sister, Princess Helena. She frequently attends our board meetings."

That was too much for Sir Harold, Frances realized with some satisfaction. Her brother may be a gatekeeper to the leaders of the Liberal Party, but she had more than a few distinguished names to dangle in front of the man, as well as the hint that she had access to royalty. Businessmen made deals for information—why shouldn't she?

Sir Harold thought about it for a moment. "Of course, Lady Frances, as you come from a political family long used to discretion, I am able to trust you. Recently, a major investor, an important figure in the City, put together a syndicate to purchase the Emerald Theatre, home to the Green Players. There were a number of investors, but he was the principal. Everyone thought it a rather bold move, but he has since been pouring money into updates and expanding into these new motion pictures. His name is Lord Freemantle . . . I say, do you know him?"

It must've been plain all over her face, she realized. Lord Freemantle, the wealthy son-in-law of her client, Lady Torrence, was the secret purchaser of the Emerald Theatre. Now Frances knew that her belief that the purchase was engineered to keep Lady Torrence away from the theatre's records was correct. It was too much of a coincidence. But why? Why was Lord Freemantle so desperate to stop his mother-in-law that he would spend thousands of pounds?

She gathered herself. There would be time for reflection later. "I know his name, although we have never met. His late father-in-law, Sir Arnold Torrence, was a colleague of my father's in the Foreign Office."

"Ah, yes. Small world, of course." And it was. Nothing odd about a connection like that.

"But of course, Sir Harold, I will keep your confidence, since Lord Freemantle wanted to keep his business dealings private." She stood. "You've been most helpful, but I don't want to take up any more of your valuable time. I know the Guild's board would also appreciate your insights, if you would ever want to attend a meeting—the last Thursday of every month at the Duchess's house. I hope to see you there."

Sir Harold seemed happy with that, said he hoped to see her again soon, and rang for the page to show her out.

Back on the street, Frances felt proud of herself. Perhaps membership in one of the distinguished clubs was not always necessary for a successful negotiation, and if Sir Harold was good enough to advise the Liberal Party, he might very well have some ideas for her charity.

For now, though, it was time to focus on Lord Freemantle. Even for a man of his reputed wealth, the purchase of the Emerald Theatre was a major undertaking. *If he will do something drastic like that, what would he do to me if I interfered?* thought Frances.

Should she tell her client, Lady Torrence, that the reason she was banished from the theatre records room was that her own son-in-law had stopped her? No, that could start a major family feud that would be counterproductive to finding Louisa—never mind how Lord Freemantle would react! She would have to confront him herself. Just show up at his place of business? He might not even admit her, and he would certainly be on his guard if a lady suddenly showed up at his offices with no introduction.

But there were other ways to reach him.

CHAPTER 8

After lunch, it was off to call on Lady Freemantle. Once again, Franny thought about the bicycle, but this was another occasion not to look unusual, and anyway, the Freemantle townhouse was close enough to Miss Plimsoll's to walk.

She had never met Lady Freemantle, but that didn't matter. Ladies in society could call on each other with even the most tenuous connections. And as the daughter of the previous Marquess of Seaforth and sister of the current one, she'd be admitted anywhere.

Unless, she thought ruefully, her suffragist connections had preceded her.

Nevertheless, she was promptly admitted to the Freemantle house, and it was clear from the moment she stepped over the threshold that Lord Freemantle had done well for himself indeed. Frances had been in enough fine homes to recognize good furnishings when she saw them, but here everything was new. In homes where family fortunes went back generations, you saw old portraits on the walls and other faded mementoes from great-grandparents. Any items that Sarah Torrence, now Lady Freemantle, had brought to her marriage home were perhaps confined to her boudoir and not in evidence in the perfectly quiet entranceway.

The butler led Frances to the drawing room, where Lady Freemantle was seated with a look of curiosity on her face. Frances compared her to the portrait of her older sister, Louisa. Even accounting for the many years that had passed, she doubted Sarah had ever been as beautiful as her sister. But she was a handsome woman with a welcoming smile, and Frances saw friendliness in her eyes. No, more than that—some merriment.

"Lady Frances—how kind of you to call. Do have some tea." A maid expertly served the tea and silently departed as Frances sat. "Your brother is the Marquess of Seaforth, isn't he? The name is familiar. I believe our fathers served together in the Foreign Office."

"Yes, and I was pleased to meet your mother at a recent dinner at Lord and Lady Moore's. I do try to keep up with the family's old friends, and so I thought I'd call on you to reacquaint our families." She'd have to go slowly and draw upon the diplomatic skills the Seaforths were known for.

Despite that plausible introduction, Lady Freemantle frowned. "Fair enough, Lady Frances, but I confess to being disappointed. I was so hoping you were coming here to recruit me for your suffrage club."

So her reputation had preceded her. Frances looked at her closely. Yes, there was merriment in those eyes, and then she laughed, and Frances laughed with her.

"You'd be more than welcome, Lady Freemantle. You and your mother can share a hansom cab to the meeting."

Lady Freemantle laughed again. "I don't know what my husband would say," she said, but her tone indicated she didn't much care, and Frances wondered again if Louisa had been the only rebel in the family.

"I do confess to wanting to meet you for friendship's sake, but seriously, do think on our club. For now, I just wanted to tell you how much I enjoyed meeting your mother. So lively and intelligent. She must've been a great asset to your father's career as a diplomat."

Lady Freemantle was pleased at the compliment. She responded with a couple of anecdotes, and Frances matched her with stories of her own while planning to lead the discussion to the theatre.

"Although I see the advantages living abroad, I think I would miss much about London, especially the plays."

"I agree entirely," said Lady Freemantle. "I am fortunate in that my husband likes the theatre as well, and we go often—and to the opera as well. We used to make family parties, when my boys were younger. They're grown now, one an officer in the Royal Engineers and the other still at Oxford."

"You must be very proud of them. And it is so pleasant when a wholesome interest like theatre can unite a whole family." Then she spoke the next sentence very clearly, watching Lady Freemantle closely. "How fortunate, then, that your husband has seen fit to purchase the Emerald Theatre and its resident company, the Green Players. I assume that ensures you always get the best seats."

That got a reaction out of Lady Freemantle. The amused look disappeared, and Frances felt herself appraised, as if Lady Freemantle was seeing her for the first time.

"Yes," she finally said, a little tonelessly, "that's certainly an advantage."

Frances knew it was time to leave. A call on a woman she barely knew shouldn't last any longer than this, and she had done what she had come to do—let her know that the secret was out. She would tell her husband, and Frances hoped she would hear from him soon.

A maid came in to see if they needed more tea.

"Is his lordship in?" Lady Freemantle inquired.

"Yes, my lady, just a few minutes ago. He is in his study."

"Tell him to please join us here."

"Yes, my lady."

The maid left, and Lady Freemantle turned back to Frances. "My husband often comes back at this hour but finishes work in his study. I think you would like to meet him." And she smiled again, briefly, before both women lapsed into silence. *This was going to be interesting,* thought Frances. *But no one said the life of a consulting detective was always easy.*

Lord Freemantle entered the room. He was a striking figure, tall and lean, with a sharp-featured face and shrewd eyes that Frances thought would not be out of place on a police detective. He was about a decade older than his wife, Frances judged, an age difference exaggerated by a beautifully tailored but old-fashioned suit.

"Dear, this is Lady Frances Ffolkes. Her late father, the Marquess of Seaforth, worked in the Foreign Office with my father. Lady Frances was at a dinner with my mother and thought she'd call on us."

"A pleasure to meet you, Lady Frances. I have never met your brother, but he enjoys the same fine reputation that your late father did." His manners were impeccable, but Frances saw he was unclear about why his routine was interrupted to meet her.

"We were discussing the theatre," said Lady Freemantle. "Lady Frances likes the theatre very much. And she just remarked how wonderful it is that we can get the best seats because you purchased the Emerald Theatre."

Lord Freemantle's eyes got bigger, and he looked at Frances, but she looked right back at him. He didn't say anything but sat next to his wife, poured a cup of tea, and took a sip.

"May I ask how you heard about the purchase of the Emerald Theatre?" he asked. "It was kept deliberately quiet." His wife looked on curiously, wanting to see Frances's answer.

"You know, my lord, women are often accused of being gossips, but in my brief foray into financial affairs, I've found that City gentlemen are worse gossips than scullery maids." In the following long moment of silence, Frances helped herself to another cucumber sandwich from the plate.

Lady Freemantle burst out laughing. "Oh, you are so right, Lady Frances. Isn't she right, dear? Good lord, all the secrets spilled over good claret and roast meats in this house."

Frances had expected Lord Freemantle to be angry, or at least annoyed, and she was surprised at how coolly he reacted to the surprise. Indeed, he accepted the revelation in good grace, and Frances liked him for that. He gave Frances a small smile.

"I offer you my congratulations then. Yes, your information is correct. I lead the syndicate that now owns the Emerald Theatre and its resident company. I am being honest with you. Will you return the favor and tell me why this information is important to you?"

A fair question. "I have become friendly with your mother-in-law, Lady Torrence. She told me she was looking for clues to her older daughter's disappearance but that she was shut out after you purchased it. I confess that I'm astounded you would spend thousands of pounds just to prevent her from what would likely be a wild goose chase."

Lady Freemantle chuckled. "My wonderful mother. I told you, dear, that if we cut off that avenue, she'd find another one, and now she's set suffrage leader Lady Frances onto us."

"So it seems," said his lordship dryly. "Yes, your conclusions are right, Lady Frances. Although stopping my mother-in-law was a goal in fact, it also makes sense as an investment. As you can see, we're improving the theatre and moving into motion pictures."

"My maid will be so glad to hear that. She absolutely adores motion pictures. But why did you want to stop her so badly?"

Lord Freemantle looked at his wife. She shrugged. "You might as well," she said. "I daresay she's heard worse, and I'm sure she'll be discreet. Lady Frances, I don't see anything gained by telling my mother we thwarted her. It would just start a family argument. In exchange for your agreement not to tell her, we'll tell you why."

Frances nodded, and Lady Freemantle turned to her husband. He sighed. "If I really thought there was a chance of finding Louisa, I wouldn't have stopped her." He looked at his wife. "Unfortunately, I can't imagine that she's still alive. I'm sure she would've revealed herself again at some point. And not everything in the past needs to be dragged up. All I can say, Lady

Frances, is that Sir Arnold Torrence was a man of sterling reputation in his public life and was devoted to his duty, but there were aspects of his private life that don't bear close scrutiny." He looked very reluctant to admit it. Frances glanced at Lady Freemantle, and she was nodding sadly, agreeing with the analysis of her father.

"Can you give me more detail? Again, I will be discreet. I'm merely assisting Lady Torrence in finding out what happened to Louisa."

But Lord Freemantle shook his head. "I don't want to say more. It has no bearing on Louisa's disappearance and can only besmirch a dead man and embarrass his family. And I can also tell you that I personally looked through the old records, and there's nothing there that could help you. They were as careless and incomplete as you might expect from actors. As long as you avoid embarrassing the family, I wish you success in your task. My only concern is getting Lady Torrence's hopes up."

Before Frances could respond, Lady Freemantle jumped in. "I think, dear husband, that my mother is stronger and more clear-eyed on this than you give her credit for. If she wants to make a final search for Louisa, that's her decision." There was a hint of steel there, and his lordship smiled and nodded to his wife.

"Of course. I stand corrected. Lady Frances, again, best of luck. I share my wife's view that it's Lady Torrence's right to look for Louisa. And finding her would be wonderful. I am not optimistic you will find out anything after all these years, but"—he gave a wry smile—"as you have my wife's and mother-in-law's blessing, you have mine too."

After a few more pleasantries, Frances excused herself, and Lord Freemantle said, "I will show you out, Lady Frances." It was an unnecessary courtesy at a house that had plenty of servants, and Frances suspected it was an excuse for Lord Freemantle to have a quick private word with her. She was proved right at the front door.

"Lady Frances, I meant what I said about wishing you success. My wife deeply misses her sister. I know the Seaforths are a great family and an old one, long involved in diplomacy, so I hope I can trust you to be discreet about anything you find to my father-in-law's discredit."

His tone and look were pleading, not threatening. Frances knew he had the family name and business interests to protect.

"My only interest is Louisa Torrence, I assure you." He seemed relieved at that. As Frances left, though, she wondered, just what had Sir Arnold Torrence done?

Chapter 9

Back in her rooms, Frances thought over the exchange while she and Mallow sat over cups of tea. Whatever the late Sir Arnold had done, it must've been something pretty scandalous if it inspired Lord Freemantle to buy the theatre. He wouldn't tell Frances what it was, but she had a clue: It was something to do with the theatre, since that was where his mother-in-law had been looking. That was where she might find something. No—Frances corrected herself—Lady Torrence probably had an idea of what her husband was like, but did some horrible piece of proof exist among the records of the Green Players? Lord Freemantle had looked through them himself.

"Mallow, I think it's time we visited the Emerald Theatre again," said Frances.

"Very good, my lady."

"I'd like you to come too. There are a lot of people who work in the theatre, and I thought you might like to talk with some of them, collect gossip and so forth. Mention Sir Arnold Torrence, Lady Torrence's late husband. I want to know if his name is familiar to any of the older theatre folks. I'll tell them that, as a talented seamstress, you'd like to see where they create the costumes."

"I am glad to help in any way I can, my lady. It is my understanding that theatre people tend to be a little free with their gossip."

Mallow's voice was full of disapproval. But then she thought of the upside of this assignment. "I suppose, my lady, I'll be seeing the suits and dresses the actors and actresses wear. I wonder, though . . ." She paused while she was trying to decide what to say. "It's just that actors aren't really lords. They just pretend onstage. I wonder if their clothes aren't really a lord's clothes either."

"A wise observation, Mallow. I don't think anything in the theatre is real. We must remember that. And we should also remember that a man was killed and we are not the only ones seeking what he hid in his room."

They went downstairs, and Frances nodded to Mrs. Beasley at the front desk.

"Lady Frances—"

Inwardly, Frances groaned. What had she done now?

"Yes, Mrs. Beasley?"

"One of the maids noticed a man loitering outside, looking a little unsavory and dressed in remnants of an old army uniform. He keeps looking at our front door. I was wondering if he was one of your . . . acquaintances? If so, may I suggest you meet him somewhere appropriate? I was about to send one of the waiters to fetch a constable."

Frances met with a wide variety of people, so the accusation wasn't entirely unfair.

"I am not expecting any such visitors, but I will see for myself. And Mallow and I will take care of seeing him on his way, if necessary, with a reference to the Soldier and Sailor's Club."

She headed toward the front entrance, then stopped and turned.

"Mallow, we're going to outflank our spy, if that's what he is." She turned and headed instead toward the back stairs that led to the servants' hall. She imagined, rather than saw, Mrs. Beasley shaking her head.

The few hotel servants shot quick looks at Frances and Mallow as they strode out the service entrance in the side alley. The general consensus downstairs was that her ladyship was more than a little odd and that she was very fortunate that the excellent Mallow remained in her employ.

From the alley, Frances and Mallow walked around to the front of the building. A shabby-looking soldier was in fact loitering in front of Miss Plimsoll's. His collar was up, and between that and a slouch hat, it was hard to see his face. He kept glancing at the front door, though, as if waiting for someone to come out.

"Excuse me," said Frances. "Are you looking for me? I'm Lady Frances Ffolkes, and I may be able to help."

The soldier didn't expect the approach from the side and turned sharply, still hiding his face under the wide brim of the hat. Then he rapidly spun and practically ran along the street, disappearing around a corner.

"My goodness," said Mallow. "That was hardly gracious of him."

"Gracious is the least of it," said Frances. "Waiting for me because he didn't dare enter Miss Plimsoll's is one thing, but he likely wanted to follow us. That's why he bolted so quickly."

"Do you think he was the man who searched Mr. Mattins's room while we were in the closet, my lady?"

"Quite possibly. We will be on our guard. We've upset someone. And we're going to do it again."

They took a hansom to the Emerald Theatre, and the same porter was on duty.

"Good day, my lady. Can I help you . . . ?"

"We're just here to see Mr. Rusk. Don't bother; we know the way," said Frances, and without waiting for any response, they breezed right by him, down the hall to Mr. Rusk's office. Frances rapped sharply.

"Come in!"

When they entered, Mr. Rusk didn't seem pleased to see them. "Lady Frances . . . why are you here?"

"I'm still following up on my research, and I believe that you will find my task is connected with the tragic death of Mr. Mattins." Rusk started to speak, but Frances rolled right over him. "But I'm getting ahead of myself. For now, I think you full well know who I was talking about when I visited you last." She pulled the folder out of her bag and slapped the photograph down in front of him. "This is the woman who called herself Helen, isn't it? She's the woman I am looking for. Oh, don't bother answering, the look on your face is proof enough."

Rusk was staring at the photograph as if he was looking at a ghost. No one said anything for a few moments, and then he looked up with a face full of exquisite melancholy. Frances knew that her last talk with Rusk and his colleagues was just a show, a pretense at helping her so she would leave and not come again.

"Where did you get this?" he asked when he trusted himself to speak again. "Who had this portrait?"

"I'm not at liberty to say. But I am looking for Helen. And I think it's time you shared the truth with me."

He nodded automatically. He clearly was back in the past, some thirty years ago.

There was a knock on the door, but Rusk didn't seem to hear, and Quentin Prescott entered. He was dressed in rich robes of red and gold, clothes from another time period. Of course, they were presenting *Romeo and Juliet*, and from his clothes and age, Frances guessed this former Mercutio was now playing Lord Capulet, Juliet's father.

"Ah, the porter was saying how some lady came marching in, and I assumed it was you, Lady Frances," said Prescott. "Still researching . . . I'm afraid I haven't thought of who it might be—Gil, are you quite all right?" He finally noticed Rusk's stricken look.

"She knows," he said. "Helen. Look, she has a photograph." He held it up, and Prescott looked like he had been hit by a bolt of lightning. He snatched the photograph and just stared at it.

"This is not a photograph of Helen. I mean—it is her, definitely, but it's a portrait. Who painted this, and when?" Frances noted that they didn't know or suspect that Helen came from a background where expensive portraits were traditional.

"I cannot tell you that yet," Frances replied, "but I can tell you that, although I am annoyed you were not completely honest with me when I first visited, I forgive you, because I am assuming the Oath of Tyndareus prevented you from revealing it to me."

She felt another shiver of delight as she further astonished the men. Mallow barely hid a smile, Frances noticed. Her maid always enjoyed it when Frances left men speechless.

Rusk spoke first, his voice a mix of anger and surprise. "How do you know about that? No one outside the Green Players knew, and only the signatories knew the full details. Who told you? This happened before you were even born, my lady."

Frances just arched an eyebrow and let them stew for a moment before answering. "I won't tell you that either. I have no wish to reveal your secret; I just want to know about Helen. If you're honest with me, I see no reason to embarrass you by making this information public."

"And if we don't want to tell you?" asked Prescott with a thin smile.

Frances turned on him. "I have influential friends, Mr. Prescott. Powerful and wealthy people want to find Helen, and they also have influential friends. A suspicious death on your door just makes it all the easier. I have the ear of Sir Edward Henry, the commissioner of Scotland Yard, and I can have this place and every record here in the hands of a score of police detectives. And I know who your owners are—they wouldn't thank you for that."

But Rusk was already motioning with his hands for everyone to calm down. He was a manager, and he knew how to pour oil on the water. "There is no need for this. Lady Frances; we will assume you are a woman of honor and that your mission is not one of vulgar curiosity. I don't know how you found out about the oath, but"—he looked at Prescott, who seemed resigned—"we will tell you what we know."

"That sounds acceptable and reasonable. But there's no reason for my maid, Mallow, to be part of this. She is an excellent seamstress and perhaps can assist your costume mistress and her staff while we speak. The recent tragedy must have set you back, and she can help."

"Oh . . . yes, thank you. Miss Mallow, continue down the hall and ask for Mrs. Mancini. Tell her Mr. Rusk sent you."

"Very good, sir. My lady . . ." She gave her mistress a meaningful look and departed. Frances and Prescott took seats, and by a silent understanding, Rusk began to talk.

"This is going to seem very silly and romantic to a modern young lady like you. Helen just appeared here one day. She didn't say where she had come from and never spoke about her past, and we never asked." He smiled. "She begged to join the company. She had a way with a nice upper-class accent but could also sound like a Cockney wife. I remember so well what she said—'I'm a good hard worker, Mr. Rusk; I'll remember my lines, follow all direction, and never give you a moment to regret engaging me.' So earnest. I bet she had written down and rehearsed those lines."

He lost himself in the memory. "That was all well and good, but in fact, none of us had ever seen such a beauty. It was more than that . . . she had a presence." He smiled shyly. "I was bewitched by her—we all were—but we weren't idiots. She was only an adequate actress, no more, but with her beauty and unapologetic boldness, she commanded the stage, and for many roles, that was enough. It was more than enough."

"And you all wanted her? That's where the oath came in?"

Rusk looked a little embarrassed. "Yes. I know we look like fools, but we were young, my lady, and those were different times. There were six of us. Myself, Prescott here, Mattins, and three actors no longer with the company: Nicholas Garfeld, Dennis Oppington, and Alexander Braceley. We swore we would support whoever she chose to marry with no hard feelings and that her happiness would always be foremost with us."

Braceley's name was familiar—he had played Romeo opposite Helen's Juliet according to the program Frances had uncovered. "Which one did she choose?" she asked.

Prescott laughed at her question. "That's the thing, my lady. It never occurred to us she would take anyone but a man of the theatre, but full of surprises was Helen. We had a man of business here who kept our books, working while he studied for his accountancy exams. His name was Douglas MacKenzie, a pleasant enough fellow for a Scot, who seemed likely to make his way in the world, but you never would've thought he'd capture the heart of a woman like Helen."

"Women are romantic but also practical," said Frances. "You men thought of her beauty, but for a life partner, she thought about more than a handsome face and glamorous figure."

Prescott burst out laughing at that, and Rusk forgot his melancholy long enough to smile. "Oh, Lady Frances, you are too right," said Prescott. "I bow to you." And he did just that, like a Stuart-era cavalier. "He wasn't even one of the signatories."

"So she married him?" asked Frances.

"Yes," said Rusk. "He passed his exams and landed a government position in Jamaica. They were going to take a brief visit to his people in Edinburgh before sailing. She had only been with us for about year. We kissed her good-bye, shook MacKenzie's hand, and we never saw them again." He buried his face in his hands.

"No letters? You never heard from her?" asked Frances. Rusk looked up and shook his head.

"There was no point. She was starting another life, halfway around the world. Our part was done. Helen left us with memories, and for us, that was enough. We continued with our lives."

Frances nodded. Unless they were lying beautifully, they had no idea that there was a grave with Helen's name on it in Maidstone, MacKenzie was apparently murdered, and a vicar in Wimbledon knew at least some of the story.

"Thank you for being frank. I know about the two of you and Mr. Mattins. What happened to the other three signatories?"

"Oh, that was a long time ago," said Rusk. "Let's see, Nick Garfeld was tall and gangly and completely tongue-tied around Helen. Did well in comic roles. He left a few years later, didn't he?"

"Yes, met an innkeeper's daughter while on tour in Rye and took over the business. He had a couple of sons, but the last time we were there, three or four years ago, we heard he had died."

"And Dennis Oppington—" continued Rusk.

"Big man. Always bought flowers for Helen," said Prescott. "Might've made a good Falstaff someday if he could've lost that accent of his. His family were gamekeepers or something in Yorkshire, and eventually he went home to do whatever gamekeepers do. He sent a letter every year at Christmas until he went to his final reward."

"And then there's Braceley, Alexander Braceley," said Rusk, grinning at the memory. "My God, there was never a more ardent suitor."

"Pressed his attentions hard?" asked Frances.

"The poor girl was flattered at first. He was handsome and could be amusing, but he became tiresome very quickly. She once doused him with a pitcher of wine."

"I don't blame her," said Frances. "What happened to Mr. Braceley?"

Rusk grimaced and Prescott shook his head. "That was a tragedy, my lady," said Rusk. "He always thought Helen would come around. He was already making a name for himself, receiving good reviews. He was going to be celebrated. I thought he might actually win her. But he was always a little high-strung, and when she announced her marriage, he broke down. He hoped she would change her mind, but sometime after she married, he left the company and joined the army."

"He was the best actor this company ever had, and you can imagine, I don't like to admit anyone was better than I, so you can believe it," said Prescott.

"Better than you—he must truly have been great," said Frances with a wry smile.

"He was young, scarcely older than Helen, but we knew he'd be a great leading man. It broke my heart to see him give up like that. Just the kind of grand gesture he'd make. He thought he'd come back with a row of medals, covered in glory, and win her back in some manner. She'd leave her husband. What a waste," said Rusk.

Prescott even relaxed his mocking features long enough to look sad. "I, and a few of the other lads, saw him off on the train.

So cheerful he was, still pledging undying love for Helen. And that was that."

"He died?" asked Frances.

Rusk shrugged. "He was sent to the Sudan with the Suffolk Rifles. I don't think I need to tell you, my lady, what happened there."

No, he didn't. No one had come home from the Sudan campaign.

"That leaves just me and Prescott here," said Rusk. "I married a few years later, raised children, eventually became manager, and am now a widower. Prescott here remains a confirmed bachelor and an adaptable mainstay of the company." Prescott gave another bow. "And so now you know all, my lady. I wish we could help you with your task, but if Helen and Douglas remained in Jamaica, or came back to England, or went to another colony—we have no idea."

"We still have to account for Mr. Mattins's murder," said Frances, drumming a finger on Rusk's desk for emphasis. But he just rolled his eyes, and Prescott chuckled.

"You are thinking like a playwright, my lady. In a play, the death of Mr. Mattins would dovetail with the disappearance of the divine Helen. But this is real life, and in real life, scenes don't work themselves out so neatly," said Prescott.

"Perhaps," said Frances, not wanting to give up her idea. She looked to both men and smiled slyly. "Mr. Prescott, I've heard of the others. But how did the rest of you love Helen?"

"Oh, my dear, what a question!" said Prescott. "I'm in danger of forgetting that you are of the aristocracy. I loved Helen most poetically. The late Mr. Mattins was older. He loved her protectively. And you, Gil." He looked at the manager. "There was no dissembling there. You were the only one of us, I think, who wasn't just entranced by her. You really loved her, completely."

Frances looked closely at Rusk's face and realized that Prescott might well be right.

Chapter 10

Mallow found the backstage as busy as a kitchen in a great house before a dinner party. Men were hammering away at some sets and painting others. Dressers were holding costumes for fittings, and actors shouted lines on the stage. A pair of women were sorting through props—scrolls, fans, bottles, and swords.

Mallow found the costume mistress with pins in her mouth as she held up a dress, giving it a critical look. She was pleasantly round in body and face, and her brown hair, shot with silver, was pulled back neatly and simply.

"Excuse me," said Mallow. "Are you Mrs. Mancini? I'm Miss Mallow, personal maid to Lady Frances Ffolkes, who has business with Mr. Rusk. My lady thought I could assist you in the meantime."

Mrs. Mancini put down the dress and removed the pins from her mouth. Mallow pulled herself up and tried to look haughty, as befitted a lady's maid in the House of Seaforth, while Mrs. Mancini looked at her with a shrewd eye.

"You can sew?"

"I am an excellent seamstress," she said.

"Very well then." She picked up a dress and a sleeve and handed Mallow needle and thread. "Take a seat and sew this on, thank you."

Mallow began sewing and was well aware of how closely Mrs. Mancini was watching her. Very well then. Mallow had repaired costly dresses from the finest dressmakers in London, even dresses brought all the way from Paris.

"You do fine small stitches, I'll give you that. But if that's how you're planning to do it, on opening night, half the cast will be naked."

"I was taught to make it perfect," said Mallow. Indeed, Frances's late mother, the old marchioness, had more than once praised Mallow's work.

Mrs. Mancini laughed, though not unkindly. "Fair enough, my dear, but this isn't a Belgravia ball. Look at the other sleeve. It doesn't have to look good for the other actors, just for the audience. We do it fast, just good enough for the front row, and after we're done with the show, we tear the sleeves off again and use it for something else. It's all make-believe, Miss Mallow."

Mallow thought on that. It made sense, when you thought about it. A lady on the stage was not a lady in a fine house. She felt the cloth carefully while Mrs. Mancini watched her.

"It's not very good material," said Mallow, with a little hesitation.

"Of course not. We're not going to buy the finest silks and satins for the stage." She sighed. "Everyone is always surprised the first time. But never mind. Just have a go, and try to be fast rather than perfect. The other seamstresses are busy with fittings, and I could use the help and the company."

And soon they were sewing away together. "So, Miss Mallow," said Mrs. Mancini. "I can tell that you're a fellow Cockney."

"Yes, Mrs. Mancini, born within the sound of Bow Bells, though I have been in service in good houses since I was thirteen."

"Good for you, my dear, being a maid to a fine lady. You're set up proper, you are, but we've had some fun here, I can say. Though my father was an Italian, I've lived my whole life in London. Been at the Emerald since I was your age."

Oh, good, thought Mallow. Since Mrs. Mancini had been here more than thirty years, she could help with their investigations. But when sharing gossip, it didn't pay to be too direct.

"It must be exciting, being around all the actors and actresses," said Mallow.

"Oh, that wore off long ago. I'll tell you the truth; they can be rather exhausting."

"We don't see many actors where we live," said Mallow. "Lords and ladies and so forth."

"I can imagine," said Mrs. Mancini. She gave Mallow a sharp look. "What is your lady doing here, anyway?"

"She's a patron of the arts," said Mallow grandly, and Mrs. Mancini nodded. "Lady Frances's brother is a marquess and in government. She knows all the best people. The king even came to dinner once."

"Ooh, he did, did he? The king has also been to this very theatre."

"Did Queen Alexandra come too?"

Mrs. Mancini smirked. "No. He brought a 'friend.'"

Mallow blushed a little. *Well, kings did that kind of thing . . .*

"Just last week, Viscount Hallifax came to dinner at the house of her ladyship's brother and sister-in-law. Eldest son of the Duke of Uxbridge, he is, and grandson, on his mother's side, of the Bishop of Borham."

Mrs. Mancini laughed. "Dear Andy! He practically lives here. Sweet on one of the actresses, takes her out to dine two or three nights a week and keeps half the florists in London in business."

Well, thought Mallow. *My goodness.* She knew that not all of the nobility showed perfect behavior, but for the heir to a dukedom to take actresses out to dine . . . It was one thing for Lady Frances to make friends with an actress, but when it came to romance . . .

From there they went back and forth, with Mallow mentioning the leading members of Society who the Seaforths knew and Mrs. Mancini responding with names of gentlemen who (with various degrees of discretion) called on actresses after performances. There was a lot more overlap between the two groups than Mallow had suspected.

"As I said, her ladyship is a patron of the arts," said Mallow, "and she knows others in the best society who also support respectable theatre. Indeed, a friend of her late father's, the Marquess of Seaforth, was such a patron as well, Sir Arnold Torrence."

"Sir Arnold? Oh, dear lord, Miss Mallow, really!" And Mrs. Mancini laughed and laughed. "A patron of the arts, was he? Is that what they called it?"

"Did I say something funny?" said Mallow, a little stiffly.

"Sorry, Miss Mallow, no wish to give offense. Sir Arnold—haven't heard his name in . . . well, it must be thirty years. He must've gone to his final reward by now. But back in the day, he spent more time here than with his wife and children, I'll tell you that."

"Are you saying," said Mallow with some hesitation, "that he had an affair with an actress?"

"Oh, my dear, not with *an* actress. With *all* of them."

"But . . . he was such a distinguished man, I heard."

"Ha—they're the worst. Being proper all day and then in the evening . . . I could tell you stories, Miss Mallow. Anyway, Sir Arnold certainly loved actresses, wooing half a dozen at a time. You should've heard the talk. Anyway, he moved overseas, I heard, and we never saw him again. Don't know if he ever came back to London. He'd be very old if he was still around."

Were any of his actress lady friends still around? Mallow knew her ladyship would want to know, but it was hard to ask something like that directly without making Mrs. Mancini suspicious. Mallow was rather horrified at Sir Arnold's behavior but thought it best not to appear too unsophisticated.

Mallow sighed. "It's an unfair world for women. The men can have their bit of fun no matter how old they get, but think of those actresses—they'd be in their fifties and sixties now. I don't suppose anyone wants a bit of fun with them anymore."

Mrs. Mancini gave her a curious look. "Funny thing to say, especially from one as young as you, but I daresay you're right. Still, the men would give their women gifts, and the smart ones saved them for a rainy day. They got by." She paused in her sewing. "You made me think of Genevieve. Do you like motion pictures, Miss Mallow?"

"Oh, very much!" Mallow said with much enthusiasm. Mrs. Mancini smiled.

"Yes, you young people do love them. Genevieve D'Arcy was in this company once, and she aged into character parts. Then her voice started to go, but she was able to keep working at Emerald Film Studios, where they make motion pictures. They're not far from here. Tell her Mrs. Mancini says hello, and maybe you can see a motion picture being made. But I wouldn't bring up Sir Arnold. That was a long time ago, and I'm not sure she wants to think about it."

"It ended badly?" asked Mallow.

Mrs. Mancini shrugged. "I couldn't say. The thing of it is, there aren't many roles for older women. People want to see young beautiful women on the stage, and gentlemen want young beautiful women in their beds." Mallow flamed at that, and Mrs. Mancini chuckled. "As you say, Miss Mallow, it's an unfair world."

Shortly after that, Frances came to fetch her maid.

"Thank you for the loan of Miss Mallow, my lady. She's a fine seamstress and helped me get a lot done."

Mallow enjoyed the compliment.

"I am glad to hear it. I hope to see these costumes onstage during a performance. By the way, I was speaking with Mr. Rusk about the history of this company, and the name of an actress who worked here briefly, many years ago, came up. Helen. Did you know her?"

Mrs. Mancini looked amused. "Can't say she was a close friend of mine, my lady. I was just a simple seamstress back then, so I really didn't know the actors and actresses well. I remember her because she was so beautiful, and if I may say, the men all made themselves fools over her."

"But which one did she like?"

"I don't recall her caring much for any of them, my lady. Married someone respectable, if I remember right, an accountant who did some work here, and headed off to the colonies.

Mr. Rusk, who was just an assistant stage manager then, didn't come to work for two days, he was so broken up, and Mr. Rusk never missed work, before or since."

"Because he was losing a valuable actress or the love of his life?" Frances smiled, and Mrs. Mancini matched her.

"After all this time, my lady, I really couldn't say."

Frances and Mallow said their good-byes and left. They were heading out of the door just as another man was coming in. He was tall and narrow with a full beard. His eyes lit up as he saw Frances.

"Major Frances, what a pleasant surprise," he said in an Irish accent. "It's been a while. When did we last meet?"

"Mr. Shaw, a happy meeting. It's been nearly a year since we saw each other at a house party, where you tried to get me to become a Fabian."

They both laughed, as Mallow looked on with more than a little confusion. "So I did. Anyway, I have some business here with Mr. Rusk. What about you? Are you producing plays? Writing them?"

Frances laughed lightly. "Very amusing. I am here for some . . . personal business."

Mr. Shaw raised an eyebrow. "Not another mystery, my lady?"

She looked Mr. Shaw in the eye. "Perhaps."

He chuckled. "I've heard stories about your recent exploits. Trying to work with theatre folk? I won't press you on details, but I will offer some advice: you will find them a clannish group."

"So I've noticed," said Frances, a little ruefully.

"But if anyone can break in, it will be the determined Major Frances. I will leave you with one more piece of advice then. This is a world of illusion. Everyone is creating an illusion. The director has one line of illusions, the actors another. The audience brings their own illusions when they show up. Navigating through them to find reality is not easy. Perhaps not even possible."

"And the playwrights, Mr. Shaw? What about them?"

"Oh, we're the worst of all. Trust nothing, not even your own eyes. I will wish you success and send you two tickets to my next play." They said their good-byes, and Frances and Mallow left the theatre.

"That was George Bernard Shaw, Mallow. One of our very best playwrights and one of our wisest. I will take his advice to heart."

"Very good, my lady." Then after a pause, she asked, "May I ask why he called you 'Major' Frances, my lady? I know his lordship, your brother, was a major in the army."

"That's Mr. Shaw's little joke. It's after *Major Barbara*, a play Mr. Shaw wrote about a woman who's a major in the Salvation Army—you know, the Christian group that does so many good works."

"Yes, I know of them, my lady. But you aren't a member of that group."

"No, but the character of Major Barbara is dedicated to improving the world and goes about it in a very energetic and forthright manner, sometimes to the point of being annoying. Mr. Shaw likes to tease me that I resemble her, even that he based her on me." Mallow studied her mistress. Her expression was half irritation and half pride. "I don't really see the resemblance myself."

"I'm sure I don't either, my lady."

They quickly found a hansom cab, and Frances summarized her meeting with Mr. Rusk and Mr. Prescott.

"It seems certain now that Louisa Torrence and Helen the actress are definitely the same, but other than that, we have still more questions. Why did the men who professed to love her not know that she had died so soon after leaving the theatre—and still in England? You'd think word would've spread. No one seems to know much about her husband, a man not glamorous or wealthy. Ah, well, we make progress. Did you get any useful information from Mrs. Mancini?"

"Oh, yes, my lady. Quite a talk we had. I am sorry to say that Sir Arnold was not—well, according to Mrs. Mancini, who seemed to be a truthful person, Sir Arnold's behavior . . ." She sighed, while Frances waited for her maid to find the words. "As the vicar would say, my lady, he fell short of the ideal. He had mistresses, my lady, and a fair number of them were actresses in the company. One of them is now an actress in motion pictures." She summarized the rest of her talk.

"Mallow—well done! That is fascinating. Louisa Torrence—now renamed Helen—joins the same company as her father's mistress. She may have heard rumors, especially as she spent a lot of time in the theatre, and her father misbehaved so extensively. Was it anger? Just plain curiosity?" *And was Lady Torrence too embarrassed to tell Frances about that? She must've known. Wives always knew.*

"Will you want to question the actress, my lady? Mrs. Mancini said her name is Miss Genevieve D'Arcy."

"Absolutely, Mallow, for several reasons. Sir Arnold may have shared something about his family with her, and there seem to be some aspects of family life that Lady Torrence doesn't want to discuss, even though she engaged me. Helen almost certainly knew—maybe even made friends with—her father's mistress. That may give us more information. I'll think on that—and you'll get your visit to a motion picture studio," she said, smiling at Mallow.

"I do admit, my lady, I am curious to see where motion pictures are made."

"I am as well. But we can't forget what we're really trying to find out—and that's where Helen ended up. I keep getting back to that strange grave. I am going to report to Lady Torrence, and then I'm going to see about getting an exhumation order for Helen."

"Beg your pardon, my lady? Exhumation?"

"Dug up. We're going to have Helen's grave opened up and see what's in there."

Mallow was silent for a few moments. She had done a lot with her ladyship, but grave robbing was a new one. Frances noted how stricken her maid looked and quickly reassured her.

"We'll be perfectly legal about this. I have friends at Scotland Yard. We'll just have to be a little . . . diplomatic about it. I am going to leave you at Miss Plimsoll's before going on to Lady Torrence."

"Very good, my lady." She paused. "I will go through your closet and see what we have that might be appropriate for an exhumation."

Lady Torrence received Frances right away and again told her maid that they were not to be disturbed. Frances could see how the woman was almost quivering with excitement. Only Lady Torrence's ingrained good manners prevented her from bursting forth with questions before tea was served.

"I have some news for you, Lady Torrence. Nothing definite yet, but we have made some progress. To cut to the heart of the manner, it seems your daughter Louisa changed her name to Helen and joined the Green Players. I think she toured briefly before returning to the London stage, where no one apparently identified her as your daughter." Soon after, the Torrences had put it out that Louisa was abroad under treatment, and then they had left for foreign shores anyway.

"As far as I can tell, she married, but there's no telling under what man. Her husband was a man of business, a Scot, and I think she was widowed soon after. And I am sorry to tell you—but she might have died shortly thereafter herself of a fever."

"I see." Lady Torrence sipped her tea, and they were both quiet for about a minute. "You promised me the truth, no more and no less, and you have kept your word. But you said, 'might.' Is there some hope she might be alive? Or that you have more details?"

"There is a grave in Maidstone that claims to be the last resting place of Helen. I promised other people I would keep their secrets, so I can't say any more. But within that grave may be your daughter. Or more questions. What I need from you now is your permission to have the grave exhumed. From there, I could work out the details of her last weeks and months, if that's what you want. I don't want to hold out false hopes, but there is reason to think Louisa's remains might be . . . elsewhere."

Lady Torrence didn't answer for a while. Frances wondered for a few moments if she had overwhelmed the elderly woman. But no. She was made of sterner stuff.

"I am unfamiliar with the procedures of exhumations," Lady Torrence finally said. "Will it be sufficient if I write you a letter giving my permission for a reburial among my husband's people near Shrewsbury?"

"I assume so. There will be some paper work, as the grave says 'Helen' and not 'Louisa.' But I am confident we can overcome any difficulties. I also believe that it is traditional for a member of the family or an appointed agent to attend the exhumation. I will serve in that capacity, if you don't want to attend."

"I would appreciate that. I will add that to the letter myself and have it sent to your rooms this evening. Please let me know when arrangements have been made."

She clearly was trying so hard to be brave, to be poised, talking about the daughter she had hoped for so long that she might see again. Frances knew that she couldn't discuss with this woman her husband's apparent infidelities, adding more to her heartache. *Would Sherlock Holmes be as kind? Am I too soft to be a consulting detective?* wondered Frances.

"I will leave you now, Lady Torrence, and let you know as soon as the matter at hand proceeds."

"Very good. And I should say—you have already done more than I could have hoped for. Thank you."

Chapter 11

"What shall I lay out for you this morning, my lady?"

"Brisk and businesslike, Mallow."

"One of the shirtwaists, my lady?"

"Perfect. I am calling on Inspector Eastley at Scotland Yard."

"Very good, my lady."

Frances detected the subtlest of tones, indicating that Mallow was not in complete agreement with her ladyship's course of action.

"You don't approve, Mallow?" Frances asked with a smile.

"I'm sure it's not my place to approve or disapprove of your ladyship's visits."

"But you're concerned that the inspector will not welcome a visit from me? He seemed pleased enough with the results of our work at Kestrel's Eyrie."

"Yes, my lady. I believe he also strongly suggested that you and I travel to America for an extended stay so you could share your detecting skills with the New York City police department."

"I interpreted that remark as a compliment, Mallow."

That was not Mallow's interpretation, but she dropped the subject.

"Anyway, I'm just asking for a little advice, not involving him in a case. Not yet, anyway. And I'll be taking the bicycle. I'm sure the constables will be pleased to watch it while I meet with the inspector."

So after breakfast, Frances hopped on the bicycle and pedaled her way to Scotland Yard. Another advantage of bicycling: not having to face the confusion of every cab driver who couldn't believe a lady wanted to go to police headquarters.

The constables now recognized Lady Frances, but the bicycle was new. "Could you please see if Inspector Benjamin Eastley is in?" she asked the constable at the front desk. "And I assume it won't be inconvenient if I leave my bicycle in this corner? Very good then."

By leaning over the desk, she heard half of the constable's telephone call to the inspector's office, even though he turned away as far as possible. "Lady Frances Ffolkes, sir . . . she didn't say . . . I would say more cheerful than upset, sir . . . very good, sir . . ." He hung up the phone and offered to accompany Frances.

"Thank you, but I know the way." She walked briskly to the Special Branch suite and saw Eastley's huge assistant filing papers.

"Hello, Constable Smith," she said.

"M'lady," he said, betraying no emotions. *He must be an excellent card player,* Frances thought.

Frances knocked on Eastley's door, heard a weary, "Come in," and entered.

"Inspector. It is good to see you again. You are well, I trust?" Sitting behind his desk, he was wearing his usual poorly ironed suit. He didn't bother getting up but waved Frances to one of the two visitor's chairs.

"Well enough, Lady Frances. And I hope you are doing well too?"

"Very well, thank you. But you're probably wondering why I'm here today."

"Consumed with curiosity, my lady. Perhaps you want to help me with one of my current cases?" He waved his arm over the folders on his desk.

"Actually, that's not why I came . . . although I'd be happy to offer my assistance in any way I can." She got a thin smile in response. "Oh, very well then. I'm actually just here for advice. A friend of mine has a relative who died some years ago while estranged from the family, and now my friend wants her exhumed to be buried in the family plot. I assumed that no one would have more insights into the people with whom we ought to speak than you." She gave him a hopeful smile.

Eastley looked back and studied her. She had known in advance that he wouldn't just give her a name and say good-bye. He'd be as difficult to trick as her brother.

"My lady. You have family solicitors to consult. Why come to a Special Branch inspector for a question like that?"

"Well, there's a slight wrinkle in the situation. The deceased was buried under an assumed name, so there is no immediate connection to her actual family. However, I have a photograph of a portrait of the woman, which those who knew her under her assumed name will swear is her. So perhaps that will allow us to overcome any difficulties. I also have a letter authorizing me to act as my friend's agent in this matter."

Eastley listened and nodded when Frances was done. Then he leaned back in his chair. "In all honesty, I am sure there is a long and fascinating story there, my lady, and had I more leisure, I would like to hear the full tale."

"It's rather simple, actually."

"No, it's not. If it were simple, a solicitor would be in the office of some Home Office undersecretary. Instead, the daughter of a marquess is sitting in the office of a Special Branch inspector. Convince me, Lady Frances, why I should help. Give me a little more." His smile became broader.

Oh, very well, thought Frances. He was giving her a chance. And Inspector Eastley would give very few women—or men, for that matter—such an opportunity.

"Some thirty years ago, the daughter of a well-born family ran away to join a theatrical company, acting under the name 'Helen.' I showed a photograph of the missing girl to her former theatrical colleagues, and they confirmed Helen and the missing girl were one and the same. After she left her brief theatrical career, she moved in with another friend and died in

Maidstone. There is a tombstone that says 'Helen,' and the dates are right." It wasn't the entire story, she knew, but enough to get the inspector to help her while avoiding awkward questions. Frances hadn't forgotten that she had stolen her main clues from Mattins's room.

Eastley nodded. "Do you have this photograph?"

She produced it and handed it to him.

"She's a beautiful girl," he said. "Girls like that often have a story about them."

"Why, Inspector, that sounds almost poetical," said Frances.

"Not at all. I don't know this Helen. But I know men and what they would do for a face like that. Anyway, this friend of yours—does she have any family?"

Frances was surprised at that question. "Yes . . . a younger daughter and two grandsons."

"Then have her say her good-byes at Helen's grave. Leave some flowers. And spend the rest of her life and energies with the family she has left."

"That's not what she wants, Inspector. She wants her daughter buried with her own people, under her true name, not forgotten in Kent."

"I don't know what you did to find a woman who disappeared thirty years ago, but I am impressed that you brought your investigation to a successful conclusion. And yet, that isn't enough. You want—how should I say—a more complete solution. I don't know of any detective inspector who would need that."

"Is that a compliment or an insult, Inspector?" He seemed a little amused, and Frances didn't know if that was a good sign.

"Part of me wonders about the many details you no doubt left out, my lady. Do you have another reason for requesting this, other than your friend's sentimentality?" She didn't respond, and it was very quiet in the office for a long moment as they just looked at each other. "Did you not understand my question?"

"I assumed your question was just a rhetorical device," she shot back.

He laughed dryly. "Oh, very well, my lady. What exactly do you want?"

"The connection between my client and Helen is clear to me and any thinking person, but the situation is not legally perfect. If I handed this over to solicitors, my request would be bounced from one department to another for weeks and months, because no petty bureaucrat would want to take responsibility for signing an exhumation order when the case is not entirely solid. I need to reach the right person. And who would know more about the inner workings here than a Special Branch inspector?"

"Thank you," he said. "So you assume that I could cut through these functionaries? That I would know the one correct department?"

"No. Not the department. You know the one right person, and I'd like you to introduce me to him. We're a political family, and I've learned that, for all the talk of Parliamentary groups and Ministerial committees, decisions like this tend to come down to one person."

"That, if I may say, is a surprisingly shrewd comment."

"Oh, and you are surprised because a woman made it?"

"No, I'm surprised that anyone who doesn't hold a position in government realizes that. Oh, very well, my lady. You want my trust. But will you give me yours? And that question is by no means rhetorical."

He was serious. And she matched him with a grave look. "Yes, Inspector. I will."

"Then let me see your letter of permission." She would have to trust the inspector with Lady Torrence's secret—to a certain extent. There was no other way. She handed it over, the inspector read it, and then he handed it back to Frances. He stood.

"Wait here, my lady. I'll be back in a few minutes."

"Where are you going? Can't I come?"

"None of your concern, and no."

The inspector left quickly, leaving the door open. Frances was momentarily nonplussed, pleased that she seemed to be getting what she wanted but irritated that she was being left in the dark. There was another advantage to this, though—the inspector had left what were no doubt fascinating case files on his desk.

But a moment later, Frances realized that the inspector was no fool. He had left his door wide open in full sight of Constable Smith and other officers. There was no way to quietly shut the door or secretly consult the files. Oh, well. She sat back on his chair and waited for him to return, musing about the case in the meantime. She might need continued help from Eastley and other Scotland Yard inspectors. It wasn't just Helen's fate she had to investigate—who was still so concerned about her queries that he had killed Mattins?

Eventually Frances became impatient, and she was considering striking up a conversation with the constables in the outer room when Eastley returned. His face was unreadable, but he had a sheaf of papers.

"Good news, Lady Frances. Despite the somewhat thin evidence you gave, I was able to convince a senior clerk to sign off on the necessary documentation on my authority. Lady Torrence will receive a notice and will be responsible for the costs. She can attend the exhumation herself or name a solicitor as her agent. I assume you will fill that role, of course."

"Of course," said Frances. "I do want to thank you for your help and trust. I am grateful. I would be even more grateful if you could tell me how you got these papers signed when it would take weeks or months through conventional channels."

Eastley chuckled. "How so like you, my lady. Your joy at getting what you want is trumped by your irritation at not knowing how. There are people here you don't know about with powers you aren't aware of. And we'll have to leave it at that."

But Frances knew in broad strokes what had happened. In any group, there were always insiders—friends and associates who could get things done by working around the rules. Whether it was Charles and the other aristocrats in their Pall Mall clubs or secretive Special Branch men among deceptively obscure

Whitehall suites, it was all the same. Social classes may differ—but women were always excluded. That would have to change. But then she saw the paper in Eastley's hands and was reminded that it was already beginning to change. Someday, women too would have not only the vote but the even more important access to the halls of power, where the real work of London, the real work of the Empire, was done.

"I have some arrangements to make, Lady Frances, but we should be able to proceed shortly. This will be done at night in order to not excite curiosity. A Home Office representative needs to attend, and I will fill that role myself."

"Really? I wouldn't have thought that a mere exhumation required a Special Branch inspector."

"With you, my lady, there is no 'mere' anything." Again, Frances didn't know if that was compliment or an insult. "So I will be there with Smith. A pair of diggers. A Home Office physician to review the remains, as required by law. Oh, and it's holy ground, so we have to have a vicar."

"Wouldn't the St. Mark's vicar be the obvious choice?"

Eastley smiled. "Ah, but we are trying to keep this quiet. I don't want the local vicar slipping and discussing this with his flock."

Frances nodded. That made sense. "I suggest you see about the sexton too. I sensed a slyness about him."

"Thank you. A word in the bishop's ear will mean the vicar will be invited to a dinner party at the diocesan residence. This means the sexton will get a couple of days off, and he won't be hanging around. We've done this before, my lady."

"Of course. My apologies. So you need a cleric you can trust. I suggest my cousin, Michael Ffolkes. He's Archdeacon of Westminster and, like all in our family, can be trusted to be discreet. He would do his duty and show up no matter how late."

He thought that over. "What would he think about his cousin involving herself in something like this?"

Frances laughed. "He'll be horrified. Almost as upset as when I joined the suffragist club."

"That sounds delightful. Very well then; I'll arrange for the archdeacon to join us. Quite a jolly party."

"And Mallow. She'll be with me."

Eastley rolled his eyes. "Your maid? You're dragging that long-suffering maid of yours to a midnight exhumation?"

Frances looked astonished. "Inspector! Have you learned nothing about Society during your career? Do you know how inappropriate it is for a lady in my position, daughter of a marquess, to attend an exhumation without her personal maid? What would people say?"

Eastley just looked at her with amazement. And then laughed and wagged a finger at her as Frances grinned. "Very good, my lady. I deserved that. Fine, Mallow too. Yes, it will indeed be a jolly party."

CHAPTER 12

Frances said her good-byes and retrieved her bicycle from the front desk. It had been a most odd process, but it had been worth it. She had gotten what she had come for—an exhumation order, something even a solicitor might've taken weeks to get. Would Hal have been able to get it more quickly? She was proud of herself.

Then she felt ashamed. Why was she making a contest out of this? Was she so determined not to be seen just as Hal's wife? Hal had always told her that he fully expected her to live her own life after they were married. This struggle was in her own mind, but she'd have to come back to it later.

Frances mounted her bicycle, and thoughts of Hal and marriage left her. Checking to make sure the road was clear, she saw the soldier again, half hidden behind the corner of a building across the road. Seeing he was caught, he started walking rapidly away.

But I'm on the bicycle now, thought Frances and took off after him. It was a wonder. Although she was short, even a fit man at a brisk place was no match for her. She pedaled harder—oh, Mallow was right, it was like flying! The soldier practically started running, but he clearly didn't want to: a running man in shabby clothes would be sure to catch the attention of a constable.

Frances was coming up to him and was dimly aware of people watching her. Ladies on bicycles had become a familiar sight, but they were supposed to ride at a sedate pace, not race along like they were in the Tour de France.

The soldier's collar was up and his hat pulled down, and he glanced back at Frances as she rode. Now pedestrians were looking at him too as he bumped into them. He could've ducked into a building, but then he'd be trapped. A hansom or motorcar would be easy to outrun on the busy streets, but not a bicycle, and even turning down a narrow alley wouldn't stop her.

"You there! Stop!" she called out as best she could while pedaling. She was almost ahead of him and thinking about how she could stop him when she came to halt so suddenly she thought she'd go over the handlebar. Unfortunately, while she was looking at the soldier on her right, a burly young constable had grabbed her from the left.

"Whoa, miss. You're going to kill someone, and possibly yourself."

"Constable, I was chasing someone. Now let me go." The soldier glanced back and disappeared quickly around the corner.

"Chasing someone? That's for sure." The constable laughed. Frances wanted to hit him.

"A soldier has been following me, and I needed to confront him."

"Ah, well, soldiers and pretty young ladies—it's a common enough situation, but not illegal, if you don't mind me saying."

"I do mind you saying," said Frances. "I do not have to put up with a man stalking me." A crowd started to gather, men and women. Frances appealed to them. Why not an impromptu suffrage speech? "Do any of you women here appreciate a man pressing his attentions on you uninvited? How many of you really find yourselves flattered by that?" The women smiled and nodded. Frances wrenched her bicycle from the increasingly bewildered constable.

"Next time, Constable, I suggest you worry more about criminals and less about women on bicycles. Good day."

She pedaled at a more sedate pace home. She had lost her stalker, but he wouldn't take her by surprise again.

Frances got up early the next morning, excited about the impending exhumation and eagerly awaiting notification from Inspector Eastley. Everything was riding now on what she might find in Helen's mysterious grave.

Mallow had proved a little anxious at first when Frances had explained that this was all approved.

"Begging your pardon, my lady, but is it . . . that is, I assume the church fully approves of this?" It had been Mallow's understanding until recently that once you were buried, you stayed buried.

"Oh, quite, Mallow. A vicar attends to make sure that the deceased is treated with respect. In fact, my cousin, Michael Ffolkes, Archdeacon of Westminster, will be there. You no doubt saw him when he dined at my brother's house."

All doubt cleared from Mallow's face. Not a mere vicar, but an archdeacon, and a member of her mistress's family.

"Very good, my lady. Now, as you said it would be a nighttime event, I have chosen a warm dress, and I will take wraps for both of us." She continued in a tone that indicated an important conclusion had been reached after a lot of thought. "I will make us tea and pour it into the vacuum flask." To Mallow, the vacuum flask was even more of a marvel than a train. You poured hot tea into it, and it stayed hot for a long time. Frances's patient explanation of how it worked, accompanied by a diagram out of a magazine, did nothing to dim Mallow's amazement.

"An excellent suggestion. Make it good and strong to keep us awake. Now my brother's assistance with the City, plus recruiting my cousin, the Venerable Michael Ffolkes, to attend the exhumation made me think of other relations who might help. So this morning, after breakfast, I'll be calling on my great-uncle, Lord Hoxley."

"Very good, my lady."

Frances grinned. "Meaning, not very good at all."

"I'm sure it's not my place to comment on your ladyship's family."

"Ah, but it was my mother's place. She always referred to him as 'Uncle Scapegrace.' The word 'scapegrace' means just that, someone who has somehow managed to escape God's grace."

"I'm sure none of us can, my lady," said Mallow solemnly.

"A theologically sound statement, but Lord Hoxley certainly gives the Almighty a run for his money. Anyway, the timing of a visit to his lordship is tricky. It must be after he has breakfasted but before he has retreated into one of his clubs, far from the reaches of reforming nieces. And dinner is out—the Lord only knows whom he'll be dining with or where. But my uncle knows something of the theatre and may know about Helen, or at least know someone who does. I believe he's had dinner with every pretty actress in London for the last half century. It occurred to me I'm not getting a very clear picture of Helen, just from her mother and men who fancied themselves in love with her. Maybe my uncle can be more objective—or as objective as man can be about Helen. Now about our stalker . . ."

She told Mallow about her adventure on the bicycle, and her maid was indignant that the soldier was still following her. "And it should have been obvious to that constable, my lady, that you had the matter well in hand." Mallow knew well that her ladyship *always* had the matter well in hand.

"Absolutely. And I have no doubt our stalker will try again. This may be darker than we think. I could tell it was an army uniform, but it wasn't what we're used to seeing on soldiers today, is it? It was worn by soldiers in the Sudan campaign years ago. And we learned from Mr. Rusk and Mr. Prescott that one of Helen's suitors was in that campaign, and it was assumed he died, but no one knows for sure."

Mallow's eyes got wide. "Do you think he came home and is still looking for Helen, my lady?"

"I don't know, Mallow, or why he's following us. He does make me think of a Sherlock Holmes story, 'The Crooked Man,' about a soldier everyone thinks is dead but who shows up again many years later. It bears consideration—I'm not the only one who read that story. As Oscar Wilde said, 'Life imitates art.' But whoever he is, he won't catch us again. We're going to catch him."

After breakfast, Frances got her bicycle out of the shed, and once on the street, she looked around for the soldier, but he wasn't present. Perhaps he couldn't get away all the time, or maybe she had scared him yesterday. If the latter, she assumed it would only be temporary. He wanted something from her—to know what she was doing or perhaps eventually to attack her. If he had seen her outside Scotland Yard, he knew that she was involved with the police.

Frances pedaled off to Lord Hoxley's house, which wasn't far. She parked her bicycle around the back and then rang the front doorbell. She was admitted by Lord Hoxley's butler, Llewelyn, who smiled at her.

"It is good to see you, my lady, and I know his lordship also appreciates your visits," he said with his musical Welsh accent.

"Thank you, Llewelyn." Over his shoulder, she could see a maid carrying a tray. "Excuse me," Frances said. "Is that tray for his lordship?"

"Yes, my lady," said the startled maid. Frances marched over to her.

"Is his lordship unwell?"

"He confessed to being in perfect health," said Llewelyn, "although I believe he was out late last night, my lady."

"A gentleman should be able to make it down to his breakfast unless he is ill or infirm. And it's too late for breakfast anyway." She reviewed the tray. "Also, this is too much food for a man as inactive as his lordship." Frances scraped what she felt was unnecessary food onto the toast plate and then took the tray from the maid. The girl looked up at the butler for instructions, but he just shrugged. "You take this plate back to the kitchen and may have it yourself if you want. I will carry the tray up to his lordship. Lead the way, Llewelyn." The maid took the plate with the extra food and headed back to the kitchen, where she was looking forward to sharing gossip about another visit from his lordship's niece.

Frances followed Llewelyn up the stairs, where he knocked on Lord Hoxley's bedroom door and entered.

Lord Hoxley was sitting up in bed, wearing an elegant dressing robe. His white hair had been neatly combed, and a smile played around his pudgy face at the anticipation of breakfast. But he lit up even further at the sight of Frances.

"Franny! What a delightful surprise. As you are serving as a maid this morning, I take it you'll be moving into my house and taking care of me from now on?"

"Don't be ridiculous, Uncle. I am far too busy to be your nurse or nanny or whatever you require, although it is a pleasure to see you." She set the tray in front of him, while Llewelyn pulled up a chair for Frances and began opening the curtains.

"Llewelyn, this breakfast is . . . incomplete."

"It was prepared as you ordered, my lord, but her ladyship believed it was more food than good health dictated."

"Llewelyn, I pay your wages and the cook's. Why are you listening to Lady Frances?" The butler didn't respond. Lord Hoxley sighed and began eating. "I suppose Lady Frances is a force of nature," Lord Hoxley added, answering his own question.

"If I may say, my lord, your metaphor provides an accurate description of her ladyship's activities," said Llewelyn. He bowed to Frances. "No offense intended, my lady."

"None taken," she said.

The butler turned back to his master. "Will that be all, my lord? . . . Very good."

Alone with her uncle, Frances made herself comfortable in the chair.

"Ah, well, a visit from my favorite niece is compensation for the loss of some of my breakfast. The two black sheep of the family."

"Oh, dear Uncle, it's true that we have both upset many in our family, but I do it because I want to make the world a better place, and you do it because of your selfish pleasures." He laughed at that. "But never mind. I'm here this morning to give you a chance to redeem yourself, in part."

"By giving you money for one of your charities? I give all my nieces and nephews a very nice check on their birthdays, and that's all. And at my death, I'm leaving everything to a home for fallen women."

"Why shouldn't you? You're the reason half of them are there." That provoked more laughter. "But no, this has nothing to do with money. I need your memory. You love the theatre as much as I do—and have done so for much longer. In the 1870s, there was an actress named Helen. Do you remember her?"

He didn't have to say anything for Frances to see that he did. He was in midsip of tea when he put down his cup and stared into the distance. It was rather like when Gilbert Rusk thought back on her. *This Helen must have been something,* thought Frances wryly.

"My goodness. Helen. Beautiful Helen. That takes me back. She disappeared before you were born, my dear. Why are you interested in her?"

"I'm helping a friend who wants to find out what happened to her."

"Is this more policing on your part? I've heard bits and pieces about your continual involvement with Scotland Yard—but never mind." He held up a hand to forestall her response. "You want to know about Helen. She was an exquisitely beautiful actress. I saw her in several productions, and one night I sent her a bouquet of flowers and a dinner invitation." Frances felt a thrill. Someone who knew Helen, outside of the Torrences and Helen's theatre family! And she suspected her uncle, a lifelong bachelor, was too shrewd to actually have fallen in love with Helen or the scores of women he had dinner with.

"You dined with her?"

"Oh, yes. Flowers and a card with the family crest. As a viscount with a substantial income, I could get an actress to join me for dinner at least."

"I'm not going to comment on what you meant by 'at least' and ask you to tell me about her. I assume you can distinguish her from all the others?"

"You think such horrible things about me. And yes, I do remember her well. And not just because she was exquisite. Not just. She knew her own mind. First, although I asked her to dinner, she responded that she was particular about where she dined and suggested an out-of-the-way place." *Of course,* thought Frances. *Nowhere she'd be in danger of being recognized as Louisa Torrence.*

"Was she bright? Sharp?"

"Yes, and yes. Quite sharp. Refused to discuss her background. She was intensely focused on her future—odd for someone so young."

"But wise. Actresses' careers don't last forever, and her face was her fortune. I heard that she had a good stage presence but was not necessarily talented."

Lord Hoxley nodded. "A fair assessment, looking back. We spoke about the stage, and she was very emphatic about her life. I remember another actress—oh, what was her name—married a lord with a good income. His mother was incensed, never spoke with her daughter-in-law. But Helen said she'd starve before becoming the wife of a rich man—or worse, his mistress. She was not giving up control like that. That's what she kept saying. She said she'd never let a man control her, never let a man dictate her life. I remember being fascinated."

Frances leaned closer to her uncle. "What else? What did she want?"

"My goodness . . . what is this about? But you won't tell me, and I'm not sure I want to know. We had dinner once more, and then she said that was all. She said I was amusing but nothing more. I saw her onstage again, some months later, and then, one day, she was gone." He looked sad.

"Gone?"

Lord Hoxley shrugged. "She just left the stage. I asked other actresses what had happened to her, and all they said was that she'd gotten married to an accountant of all things and moved to parts unknown. It seemed odd. A bright girl. Marriage wasn't for me . . . and I'm more progressive than you realize, dear niece. I accept that some women don't want to get married either. So why not be mistress to a duke? She'd have been very well taken care of, for minimal work."

"It is astonishing, Uncle. Just imagine, wanting to be an honest man's wife rather than spending years as a nobleman's whore."

Lord Hoxley turned red. "For goodness' sake, Franny. Language like that. I'm still eating. And don't look at me like that. The actress Nell Gwynn was mistress to Charles II. Their son was made Duke of St. Albans. Everyone went home happy."

"I'm very happy for Nell Gwynn and her son the duke. But what of this accountant? What do you know about him? What kind of person was he, and where did they live?"

"Good gracious, Franny. I wasn't invited to their wedding. Another actress mentioned that some man who had helped keep the theatre's books had proposed, Helen had accepted, and they were moving out of London. That's all I know, I'm afraid."

Frances suddenly thought of another woman who had made sure that she'd never be the prized wife of a great lord—herself. She loved Hal, surely, but she had never considered that part of her attraction to him was equality. As successful as he was, he was middle class—someone, perhaps, that she could be a helpmeet to instead of just a decorative lady of the manor. Was that what Helen had thought? Times were even harder for women back then, and a marriage alliance with a rising professional was the perfect balance between independence and security. Louisa may have had jewelry to pawn for her own money, and if her uncle was right, she was smart—someone who could be of true help to her husband, not just an entrancing doll. A man who didn't just love her but needed her. *And what do I want?*

Lord Hoxley broke into her thoughts. "Woolgathering?" he asked with a smile.

"You gave me something to think about. A lot to think about. Self-determination. That's what she wanted?"

He nodded. "That's what she wanted."

"So not mere comfort, but some measure of independence too."

"You're the philosopher, my dear. I will accept your conclusion as fitting the facts. But indulge me. There's a box of chocolates on the little table there—"

"Uncle, you're not going to finish your breakfast with candy!"

"Of course not, my dear. It's unopened. A present for a . . . friend. Just fetch it, and look at the cover." Frances did. Like many chocolate boxes, it displayed a picture of a lovely young woman with cherry lips and raven hair falling over her shoulders.

"Chocolate-box prettiness—that's the phrase," said Lord Hoxley. "Beautiful, idealized, yet doesn't always age well."

Frances thought about that. "Was that Helen—just chocolate-box prettiness?"

Lord Hoxley just answered with another question. "Have you spoken to any women who knew Helen? I am well aware of the limits of my sex. Call on a woman who knew her. You'll get another point of view, certainly more accurate."

"I agree. I'll do that." She thought of the gossip Mallow had picked up about Sir Arnold's mistress. Perhaps she had known Helen without realizing that Helen was her paramour's daughter.

"But speaking of marriages, how are wedding plans with your young man, the solicitor? And this is something on which we can agree: I haven't met him, but from all accounts, he'll be a fine partner for you and a fine addition to the family."

"Well said, Uncle. I'll keep you apprised of our plans. And maybe you can give us dinner some evening."

"Excellent idea. And here's a thought—Marie Studholme is a friend of yours, isn't she? Bring her along, and perhaps we'll make a foursome of it?"

Frances just rolled her eyes. "I won't even bring it up. You're old enough to be her father. And she's independent too." She leaned over and gave her uncle a kiss on his cheek. "Be good. Take care of yourself, and I'll visit again soon. And maybe, just maybe, I won't tell Llewelyn to give me all your port, which I can auction off for charity."

She headed downstairs, and Llewelyn showed her out after thanking her for visiting and raising his lordship's spirits. Her mind, meanwhile, was a jumble of thoughts. What had driven Helen? It seemed to be less a love of theatre than a love of independence. Frances had upbraided her uncle, but he had a point: a mistress to a wealthy man—especially back then—would have been given great comfort and a large degree of independence, but Helen hadn't wanted to be at some lord's beck and call. Frances felt full of admiration for the woman.

The clatter of a hansom cab brought her out of her reverie. A man clambered inside. It was a soldier, *her* soldier, entering the hansom. How had he found her there? She hadn't seen him when she left Miss Plimsoll's. The cab drove off quickly, and Frances knew she'd never catch it on her bicycle. But she smiled. She knew something now. This man was a little afraid of her. He no doubt had the cab ready, knowing she could—and would—follow.

But that wasn't the most important thing. She had been sure that the soldier hadn't been waiting at Miss Plimsoll's. Did he have a confederate spying and reporting back? Or perhaps he had multiple disguises; it had been a busy street—he might've been dressed as a dustman or laborer or clerk. And yet, here he was, back as a soldier outside her uncle's instead of trying another disguise. Whatever else he wanted, he needed Frances to see him *as a soldier.* That was interesting. Very interesting.

Chapter 13

Lady Torrence had sent Frances a note, delivered by a footman, saying that she had responded to the Home Office form, officially appointing Frances as her representative for the exhumation. Inspector Eastley followed with a message saying that he had made the arrangements for the following night. He told Frances to arrive inconspicuously with a trusted driver. The church would be open, and any coachmen and chauffeurs could wait comfortably inside.

Frances was excited about the evening, but nevertheless, she and Mallow both took naps after lunch so they'd be fresh for the night.

After a quick dinner, Mallow laid out a simple outfit for her mistress. Frances had initially suggested the outfit that she saved for her volunteer work at the soup kitchen, but Mallow felt even an exhumation deserved something better. She also produced jackets for both of them and made tea for the vacuum flask.

"Sorry we have to do this so late, Mallow, but apparently exhumations are typically done at night when no other activities are going on and people aren't around to ask questions and gossip."

"Of course, my lady. I understand we will be traveling in his lordship's motorcar?"

"Yes, Mallow. I told my brother that an elderly friend was having a relative exhumed and moved to a family vault and that she felt more comfortable with a woman friend representing her than a solicitor. I even told him my cousin Michael would be attending in his official capacity. His lordship thought it a little odd but didn't seem upset."

"Very good, my lady." No doubt, reasoned Mallow, Lord Seaforth thought her ladyship could not get into trouble surrounded by the officials, including a doctor and an archdeacon.

"However, we do have something else to concern ourselves with. Our soldier-spy is still following us. I don't think he means us harm, not directly, but he wants to know where we go. He wants us to see him. I don't know why yet, but he won't do it tonight, that I can promise you. I have a plan. Do we have everything? Time to be off for our very first exhumation."

Ridgeway, her brother's chauffeur, was waiting for them downstairs, and he helped them into the elegant and comfortable sedan.

"I understand we are driving to St. Mark's church in Maidstone, my lady. I already consulted the map and will head there straightaway."

"Excellent," said Frances. "But first, please head around the hotel once before driving to Kent. I have a friend on the next street over, and I want to see if her light is on. We may stop there briefly."

"Very good, my lady." He no doubt thought the request strange, but he was too well trained to show surprise. And Seaforth servants expected the unusual from Lady Frances.

As they drove off, Frances leaned over to Mallow. "Our stalker won't be able to easily figure out where we're going if we don't directly head to Maidstone." Once they reached the next street, Frances told the chauffeur that it seemed her friend's house was dark, so they could head on. It was still cool at night, and they were glad of their jackets. Frances enjoyed watching the passing scenery, the dark houses and countryside, and listening to the powerful hum of the engine. Mallow simply wished they were on a train.

It was only about an hour to St. Mark's. Frances saw a police wagon already there and lanterns in the churchyard by Helen's grave. Even as they were pulling up, a local constable walking outside the gate approached them.

"Lady Frances? The inspector said you may join him by the gravesite. I have to stay here, but it's just along the path."

"I will walk you there, my lady," said Ridgeway.

"That's quite all right. You may head directly into the church."

"I beg your pardon, my lady, but his lordship instructed me most particularly to escort you and Miss Mallow to the official in charge."

"Oh, very well," said Frances with a sigh. Mallow seemed pleased with the escort, however. Cemeteries weren't cheerful in bright sunlight, and in the night they were sinister. With shadows falling across shadows and the dimly lit church hovering over them, it was easy to imagine some nameless monster behind every stone. A scrabbling noise seemed louder than it really was—just a rabbit out for a midnight feeding.

Ridgeway walked them to the gravesite, where Inspector Eastley, Constable Smith, and two diggers were waiting for them. Eastley took in Frances, with her maid and her uniformed chauffeur, and greeted her with a brief nod, just visible in the light of the lanterns.

"As you can see, I am now safe. You may wait in the church," Frances instructed her chauffeur.

"Very good, my lady." Ridgeway bowed and left.

"Good evening, Lady Frances, Miss Mallow. I am glad to see you looking so eager. The Home Office physician and your cousin the archdeacon should be here shortly," Eastley said. "Can you tell me what you expect to find tonight?" His tone was teasing.

"Inspector, merely the remains of Louisa Torrence, known as Helen," Frances replied, full of innocence.

"If you say so, my lady," he said with a thin smile. He turned his gaze on her maid. "Tell me, Miss Mallow. I don't know a great deal about London society. Do other ladies' maids also attend their mistresses in churchyards at night?"

"A proper lady's maid would not gossip about such an activity, so I couldn't say, sir," said Mallow.

Eastley chuckled. "Well spoken." More footsteps, and the Archdeacon Michael Ffolkes appeared. His height was emphasized by the beautifully tailored cassock he wore. His expression was serious, as befitted a high-ranking clergyman, but even in the dark Frances could just make out a slightly sardonic smile.

"Thank you for joining us, Archdeacon," said the inspector. "I am sure it's tedious for you to come so far, so late."

"Members of the clergy are used to traveling far, and late," said Archdeacon Ffolkes. He looked down at Frances. "Plus, I am also assuming the additional duty of chaperoning my young cousin."

"Very kind of you," said Frances. "But Inspector Eastley is more than capable of guarding my virtue. You are well? The rest of your family?"

"Yes, in perfect health, thank you. Can you explain why you are here representing the family of the deceased and not a solicitor? The inspector wasn't entirely clear on that point."

Frances glanced to Eastley, who raised an eyebrow. "The mother of the deceased felt more comfortable with a woman representing her for such a delicate situation. Perhaps if there were women solicitors, it wouldn't be necessary—"

"Oh, I see. This is to make a point for your suffrage group. That you have come to Maidstone from London in the middle of the night is proof of your dedication, I'll give you that."

"Suffragists are used to traveling far, and late," said Frances, quoting his own words back to him. He relaxed enough to laugh. A sense of humor was common among all Ffolkes, even archdeacons.

"Touché, Frances." And then he became serious again. "But this has brought you to church at least. You will join me in prayer afterward?" he asked. Frances agreed.

They heard rushed footsteps and a stumble followed by a muffled curse, and a young gentleman stepped into their midst.

"Am I the last? So sorry. I've never been to Maidstone before. Dr. Edward Grayson from the Home Office." He straightened his tie and smoothed his jacket.

Frances concluded that Dr. Grayson was new to his profession. A tedious job like this, outside of London, would be assigned to the most junior man available.

"Quite all right," said Eastley. "Thank you for joining us. This is the Venerable Michael Ffolkes, Archdeacon of Westminster, representing the Church of England. And Lady Frances Ffolkes, representing the mother of the deceased." He turned to the diggers. "You may begin now." The men picked up their shovels, and the silent night was broken with the rhythmic crunch of metal on soil.

Dr. Grayson greeted the archdeacon and then Frances. "I say, I've been to a few of these, but it's always some chap from a solicitor's office." And Frances had to explain again she was a friend. "Very nice of you. So, both of you named Ffolkes? Just a coincidence?"

"The archdeacon is my cousin," said Frances with an amused look. "He can watch over me this way."

"Very nice," said Dr. Grayson, a little confused. And then he turned to Frances, saying in a reassuring voice, "I wouldn't worry, Lady Frances. I don't think the results will be disturbing, and although by regulation I must review the remains, there is no need for you to look."

Mallow felt a stab of pity for the doctor. Her ladyship hated to be patronized like that, as she would no doubt make clear in a moment.

"There is no need for concern, Doctor," said Frances. "I'm not inclined to faint at the first unpleasantness. I took science courses while obtaining my degree, so I am not expecting any great surprise." In the dark, she thought she could sense the inspector stifling a chuckle and her cousin rolling his eyes. "Indeed, I am proud to call Dr. Elizabeth Garrett Anderson my friend and a colleague in the suffrage movement. I am a great admirer of hers. Have you met her?" Dr. Anderson had gained fame for her successful fight to become the first woman physician in England.

"Ah, no," said Dr. Grayson, a little overwhelmed, and then hastened to assure Frances that he understood that Dr. Anderson "was an admirable member of the medical profession."

"But speaking of remains," said Frances, "what will they be like? The body was buried about thirty years ago, probably in a plain box without any embalming process." There would've been no time for elaborate preparation or a well-sealed casket, if she was buried as quickly as the sexton said she had been.

"Good question," said Dr. Grayson, who clearly decided not to "protect" Frances any further. "This is southern England, so we have damp soil and mild weather for the most part. I'd say the body has been reduced to bones after all this time."

"I don't suppose there is much you can tell from just bones?" she asked. It was a pity. She knew much could be told about death from bodies, but not when only bones were left. Dr. Grayson looked at her a little oddly.

"Not much," he admitted. "You can look for signs of breakage. You can estimate age at death, if necessary."

"Can you tell the sex, just from the skeleton?" she asked.

At that, she heard the inspector shifting. The doctor fell further into confusion.

"Is that a question here?" When Frances didn't answer the doctor, he cleared his throat. "Yes, you can. The shape of bones, with women's bodies, of course . . ."

Frances heard the embarrassment in his voice.

"That is very helpful, Doctor. Thank you."

"Yes, fascinating. Thank you indeed, Doctor," said Eastley dryly. *The inspector wants to know why I'm asking this,* thought Frances.

They fell into silence while the men worked. The inspector produced a flask and offered a drink to the doctor, who accepted a quick sip, and to the archdeacon, who politely declined. With a smile he offered the flask to Frances and Mallow, but they had their vacuum flask of hot tea.

The pile of dirt by the side of the grave got higher, and then they heard the thud of the shovel on wood. Frances felt her heart beat faster. There had to be a clue here somewhere—the secret burial, destroyed records, elaborate tombstone. But what?

"Careful," said the inspector. The diggers eased out the box and placed it on the ground. The Inspector said they would go into the vestry to open it up.

It was warmer inside, and brighter. The inspector already had a plain table set up, and the diggers placed the box onto it. After they left, the inspector nodded at Smith, who produced a jimmy. Frances was looking expectantly at the coffin, and Mallow stood a half step behind her. A moment later, the top was off.

No one breathed for a moment. There was a body in the coffin—but it certainly wasn't Louisa/Helen. It was quite obviously the skeleton of an infant, wrapped in a blanket that probably had been new and fresh thirty years ago but was now falling apart. The skeleton was on its side, curled up, as if for a nap. Mallow noticed a tight smile on her mistress's face: her ladyship had hoped for a surprise, and she certainly had got one.

Alongside the skeleton were three bags of coarse hessian cloth. Eastley lifted one up and reached into it. He pulled out a handful of what looked like soil and then put it back. "Dirt. Common dirt. No doubt placed inside to add weight, to make it seem as if the coffin contained an adult. Doctor, what can you tell us about the child?"

Dr. Grayson carefully unwrapped the infant and began his brief examination. The inspector focused intently, and the archdeacon paused from his prayer book to also listen.

"Nothing to indicate a violent death," said the doctor, carefully examining the bones.

"So he died a natural death," said the inspector.

"I think the doctor means that the skeleton's condition is not inconsistent with a natural death," said Frances.

The inspector sighed, and the doctor cleared his throat. "Yes, actually. That is correct, Lady Frances."

"From the time she was eight, my cousin never missed a chance to show how clever she was. How reassuring it is to see she hasn't changed," said the archdeacon. Frances gave him a dirty look.

The doctor continued. "You asked about the condition of the skeleton, Lady Frances. I don't know what you learned about anatomy, but bones in our infancy fuse as we age. And the skull doesn't completely close until later in infancy." Frances looked closely at the skull as the doctor continued. "So aside from the size of this skeleton, it's clear from the skull this was a very young infant. As you quite rightly put it, it's consistent with a child who died shortly after birth." He looked at the inspector. "I think that's all I can tell you."

"Can you tell the child's sex?" asked Frances.

"Unfortunately, no, Lady Frances. The changes that, ah, differentiate the sexes don't appear until close to adulthood."

"Thank you, Doctor," said the inspector. Frances realized she was still smiling, understandable in her hope for something unusual but inappropriate under the circumstances, and she quickly modified her expression. She looked up. Her cousin had raised an eyebrow in surprise, and Mallow seemed quietly pleased that there was something unusual, as her ladyship had hoped for.

And Inspector Eastley? *He seems . . . angry. He's angry at me. He thinks I knew something. He's going to want to have a talk with me,* thought Frances.

"So, Lady Frances, can you enlighten us?" asked the inspector.

"What makes you think I know anything?" asked Frances.

"Call it a hunch. We have a history, my lady, and I saw the expression on your face when you looked into the open coffin. We will talk about this."

If I'm going to be a consulting detective, I must learn to better mask my feelings, Frances realized.

The archdeacon spoke before Frances could respond to Eastley. "Inspector, this is a mystery for you to solve, as a representative of the lords temporal. But as a representative of the lords spiritual, I must make a report of this to Lambeth Palace," he said, referring to the London seat of the Archbishop of Canterbury, the head of the Church of England.

"Of course, Archdeacon," said the inspector, his mind somewhere else.

"And naturally you are blessed to have my cousin assisting you," the archdeacon continued. The inspector looked up sharply, but the archdeacon appeared absolutely serious, as befitted the occasion and his senior position in the church. Again, only Frances could detect a hint of a smile.

Eastley snapped out of his brief fog and began issuing orders. "We have no idea who this infant is or the reasons for hiding him—or her—in Helen's grave. But I don't see any reason to assume he is a relation to the lady who requested this exhumation. Lady Frances, as representative of the next of kin, and Archdeacon, on behalf of the church, shall we place the deceased into the ground again? That is my recommendation."

France thought on this. "I agree, Inspector. I see no other useful course at this time." The archdeacon concurred.

Eastley told Smith to supervise the reburial and told Dr. Grayson he could go home.

"I'll write up a report on the infant and send it off to you in a few days. If there are any questions meanwhile, you can reach me at the Home Office laboratories at University College," said the doctor. After saying his good-byes, he left.

"It's up to you, Archdeacon, but you can go home too, I believe," said the inspector.

"Thank you, but I think I'll say a quick prayer in the church. You may join me."

Frances looked at Mallow. "I think my maid would like that," said Frances.

"You are most welcome, my child. And your mistress may attend as soon as she's available."

"Thank you, cousin. But first, to the lords temporal." A few moments later, Eastley and Lady Frances were alone in the vestry.

Chapter 14

"You knew, my lady. I read you from the moment you came into my office, again when you came this evening, and finally from your face when we opened Helen's coffin. This is now a police matter, so we need to have a more complete conversation," said Eastley.

"I don't see how this is a police matter," said Frances.

"Think on it, my lady. It's sacred ground. The archdeacon was right—Lambeth Palace will be calling my superiors tomorrow. They are going to wonder how this happened under the supervision of the vicar here thirty years ago. Was this graveyard profaned? What happened to the body that was supposed to be here? Helen was supposed to be destined for Christian burial. Instead some unknown baby was put into her coffin, an adult coffin. They are going to want me to find answers, starting tonight with you, my lady. I want the truth this time."

"I gave you the truth," said Frances. "But perhaps, out of concern for your busy schedule, I omitted some details." She could see that she wasn't making him happy. He'd want everything now, and she quickly went through all the details in her head. She couldn't give everything away. He'd want to know how she found out about the Oath of Tyndareus, which involved theft, and she didn't want him to warn her off if he knew she was being stalked. True, he might eventually connect Helen with the recent murder at the Emerald, but London was a violent city, and it might take him a while to make the connection.

"Oh, very well. There are a few more details. Helen's life and death were a little more complicated than I first indicated. Helen had many suitors and appealed to the Hallidays as a widow. That's the story she told the Hallidays. She was trying to hide from her family. Maybe someone else was after her as well. I don't need to tell you that a beautiful actress had many suitors, and some of them may have been aggressive, so maybe she wanted to disappear. Or if she was killed, it was elsewhere."

"That is very possible," he said, "but what I don't understand is how you knew Helen wouldn't be in that grave and why you didn't tell me beforehand."

Frances sighed. "Inspector, I'm a consulting detective, not a wizard. I had no idea she wasn't there, and that some unknown child would be, but I knew something was wrong and, I admit, I hoped that the exhumation would reveal further clues. There were too many coincidences. I found that the records for this period were destroyed by accident. I spoke with the sexton and learned that the burial was handled with unusual haste. And yet, the Hallidays spent a princely sum to give Helen one of the finest headstones in this churchyard. There was something wrong here, but I couldn't be sure anyone with the police would agree with me. But now I see I was right." She felt very proud of herself, and even the inspector nodded in agreement. "I don't know if Helen is alive or dead. But I will keep working until I find out."

"I compliment you on your reasoning. For now, we are working toward the same ends, Lady Frances. I will also have to put in my report a finding, or at least a reasonable supposition, of what happened to Louisa Torrence, who was presumably also the actress named Helen."

"Will you share with me what you find?" she asked.

"If I can," he said with a wry smile.

"Likewise," said Frances. "I think I will join Mallow and my cousin now. And perhaps you'd like to pray for guidance?"

"Perhaps you'd like to pray that your cousin doesn't tell your brother what you're up to."

Frances said good-bye to the inspector and joined Mallow and Archdeacon Ffolkes in the church. When they were done with their prayers, Frances spoke with her cousin.

"Thank you for attending this evening," she said.

"Never a dull moment with you, cousin. What are you going to tell your friend?"

Frances realized she would have to give a report to Lady Torrence. After just accepting that her daughter was dead, she would now learn that Louisa might be alive—and that the police were involved. "I suppose I'll tell her about the virtue of hope. Good evening, dear cousin. Come, Mallow. Let's collect his lordship's chauffeur and go home. It is past our bedtime."

Frances and Mallow were too excited to rest as they drove through silent streets in the small hours. Fortunately, in the back seat of the large motorcar, they could talk quietly without the driver overhearing.

"Mallow, we have to proceed in the belief that Louisa Torrence may be alive. I don't see how, or why, something like this could've been done without her cooperation. A very cool hand planned this, Mallow, destroying records and arranging for the burial of this unknown child. But there are so many unanswered questions here. No matter who that child is, why wasn't he given his own burial? What has this to do with the soldier who has been following us? Why did her theatre friends think she was safely in the colonies when the Reverend Halliday told us she was buried in Maidstone?"

"You don't think that the Reverend Halliday was telling an untruth, my lady?" Mallow could barely utter the words.

"No, Mallow," Frances reassured. "He may not know the whole story, but I think he told us the story as he knew it. There's a lot we don't know here, but there are two things we are going to do. We are going to find out more about Louisa Torrence, after she became the actress Helen. If she helped engineer her own disappearance, as I believe, she's a woman of great intelligence. But what happened to her later? Second, we are going to have to watch out for the soldier and continue to find ways to thwart him."

"Do you know yet why he is following us, my lady?"

"No, although I'm once again thinking of that Sherlock Holmes story, 'The Crooked Man.' If this stalker is Alexander Braceley, formerly of the Green Players, he's an experienced actor, well-versed in disguises. We will take the offensive at some point. For now, however, we need to visit Genevieve D'Arcy, the mistress of the late Sir Arnold Torrence."

"Very good, my lady," said Mallow without much enthusiasm. Visiting actresses was bad enough, but an actress who was a mistress . . . it was for her ladyship's work, but still.

Frances's amused look was hidden in the dark. "But Mallow, remember we will be seeing her at the motion picture studio. We will see how the motion pictures are made. I should think that would be very exciting."

"Oh, yes, my lady," said Mallow, this time with great enthusiasm, seeing the bright side after all.

CHAPTER 15

Frances and Mallow did indeed sleep late the next morning, right past breakfast.

"We'll have some tea and rolls in a tearoom on our way. And after, I'll need to visit Lady Torrence to give her a report," said Lady Frances.

Quickly fortified, they found a hansom cab and made their way to the Emerald Studios. It might've been an old warehouse, but onto it the builders had added what looked like a large greenhouse.

"I believe, Mallow, that it requires lots of light to make a motion picture, and it's simplest to use natural light. I suppose we'll learn more inside." And they walked up the steps and entered the building.

Frances expected a reception desk or at least a porter, like at the Emerald. There was a desk up front, heaped with papers, but lacking an attendant. Some sort of caretaker was sweeping up.

"Do you know where we can find someone in charge?" asked Frances.

He looked them over. He apparently decided Frances and Mallow looked respectable and said, "Couldn't say, miss, but you can look around." Mallow was about to give him a dressing down for his casual attitude, but she saw that her ladyship was eager to find whoever managed this place and so followed her past the desk.

All seemed to be chaos inside. Actors and stagehands roamed over the large space, which ran from the "inside" portion to the glasshouse area. They saw motion picture cameras on tripods, and as no one seemed to care, they stepped up to one. It looked similar to a typical camera with a lens and a viewfinder and also contained what Frances understood was a reel of film.

"Do you know how it works, my lady?" asked Mallow. She loved motion pictures but hadn't given a lot of thought to how they were created.

"I know the basics. You've seen regular cameras, Mallow. Well, this one takes many photos, one after the other, and when they're run through a projector, it gives the illusion of movement."

"Very interesting, my lady," said Mallow, who was looking at the camera with what approached reverence.

"I know you said they need sunlight, my lady," said Mallow, looking at the glass portion of the studio, "but you don't get a lot of sunlight in London."

"No, and that's why they have those lights." Frances recognized arc lamps, which she had read about but had never seen. They created strong illumination that could be focused on a particular area, especially when there was no sunlight.

The lights seemed to be powered by heavy electric cables that snaked along the floor. Mallow looked at them with some skepticism and gave them a wide berth as they walked around the studio.

Everyone seemed to be giving directions or just shouting instructions, and actors began to place themselves on one of the sets, little boxes set up as various kinds of rooms: a bedroom, a parlor, and a kitchen.

Mallow looked at it all with wonderment. "I always thought that they made the movies in a house, but instead they make the house inside here, my lady," she said.

"It would seem so. I guess it wouldn't be practical for them to bring all this into a real house to film. They may have to bring the camera back to show the whole room, and they need to add the lights. There wouldn't be enough space for that in a normal room. Again, Mallow, another illusion. Now I wonder who's in charge? I think, as in the theatre, there is a director."

There didn't seem to be anyone to ask without interrupting the organization, as men in work clothes moved sets and the cameras, and as young women with sheaves of papers marched briskly from set to set consulting with actors.

But then a man in his shirtsleeves, his clothes a little better than what the others wore, shouted above the fray. He seemed to be in his forties and had an air of command about him, as if he was used to managing a regiment.

"Everyone! We'll be filming scene two in fifteen minutes. We can do the rest later today, but that one must be done first. Costumes and lights need to be ready. No excuses!" He shook his head, but the chaos gradually resolved itself around one of the little rooms.

One of the young women with the papers strode over to him, and the moment she left, Frances was on him, with Mallow right behind her.

"Are you the director? I have some business to discuss," Frances said.

The man gave her a shrewd look. He was sharp, and Frances watched him take in her clothes, voice, and bearing.

"Abel Pyecroft, miss, chief cook and bottle washer, at your service."

"Lady Frances Ffolkes and my maid and assistant, Miss Mallow."

Pyecroft's look deepened. "Ffolkes . . . I know that name. The Marquess of Seaforth, right?"

"Very good, Mr. Pyecroft. I wouldn't have thought that you'd keep up with the aristocracy." She was genuinely surprised.

"Motion pictures are a new business—a funny business, I have to say—and it pays for me to know a wide variety of people. Or at least know about them. Perhaps the Seaforths would like to rent a theatre out for a private showing? It would be easy to arrange."

"So your new owners are encouraging you to expand your opportunities?"

That seemed to take him aback, as Frances knew it would. It was his turn to be surprised.

"You know about that, do you? You're not interested in seeing a motion picture then. You want to invest in one."

Frances laughed at that. "I know very little about motion pictures. Miss Mallow adores them."

"You do?" said Pyecroft, who seemed pleased.

"My friends and I attend frequently, sir," said Mallow.

"Very good." But he wants the quality to come, Frances realized. People with more money to spend would allow them to make more elaborate pictures. Oh, she was learning all about business.

"I'll speak with my brother about a showing," Frances said. "We've always liked theatre, but motion pictures are new to us. For now, I'm looking for one of your actresses, Miss Genevieve D'Arcy." She smiled. "We have some mutual friends."

That surprised him again. It seemed impossible that a picture actress and a daughter of the House of Seaforth had anything in common.

He started to say something, thought again, then snapped his finger for the young woman he was just speaking with.

"Is Jenny in the next scene?" he asked her.

"No, sir." She thumbed through the pages. "She's not until the parlor scene. She's probably in the dressing room."

"Please show Lady Frances and Miss Mallow there."

She gave them a quick look with her cool blue eyes. "My lady, Miss Mallow—follow me, please." They headed toward the back of the building.

"What is your job here?" asked Frances as they worked.

"Script management," she said, a little surprised that anyone would ask. Then seeing the look of interest on Frances's face, she continued, "We've started making longer motion pictures with more elaborate stories and multiple scenes—more like a play, my lady. Such motion pictures are not filmed in linear order, my lady. We film all the scenes in one set at once, then film all the scenes for the next set together. It's all sorted out during editing."

"That is fascinating," said Frances. "One doesn't think of these things. What did you do before this?"

"I worked in an office, my lady." *She's wondering who I am and why I'm so interested*, thought Frances. *Any job a woman has is always of interest.*

"Just between us," said Frances, giving their guide a conspiratorial look. "Is this more interesting than working in an office?"

The woman laughed. "Oh, my lady, have you ever worked with motion picture actors?"

They had passed through a warren of small rooms and storage spaces in the back of the building. One door was marked, "Dressing." The woman knocked and opened it without waiting for a reply. The room looked much like the dressing rooms at the Emerald, with pots of cosmetics and clothes thrown around rather slapdash.

There was one occupant, a woman of middle years, in a faded dressing robe. Yellow hair fell across her shoulders. Her skin wasn't as youthful as it no doubt had once been, which accounted for the little jars of cream all about, but she had a good figure. She looked at them curiously with her soft brown eyes.

"A couple of friends, Miss D'Arcy," said the guide. "I'll see someone is back in about half an hour to help you dress." With that she left, closing the door behind her.

"Friends?" asked Miss D'Arcy, sounding a little amused. "I'm afraid I don't remember you." Her voice was whispery. As Mrs. Mancini had said, her voice had faded.

"We have friends in common, I should say. We were visiting Mrs. Mancini at the Emerald Theatre, and she mentioned your name," said Frances.

"Dear Daisy. I do miss working with her. She knows a thing or two about dressing women." Miss D'Arcy looked over Frances and Mallow. "I daresay the two of you do as well. But make yourselves at home, if you can."

Frances knew Mallow was itching to clean up the room, and her maid indeed quickly removed dresses from the chairs, hung them up neatly, and took a seat along with her mistress.

"I'm Lady Frances Ffolkes, and this is my maid and assistant, June Mallow. Genevieve D'Arcy—are you of French background?"

"Good lord, no, my lady," she said, smiling. "A lot of actresses do that, take a fancy name so people remember us. Jenny Derby I was born, and Jenny is what they call me."

"Very well then. We're helping an old friend of ours, tracing some family history. Your name came up as someone who was a friend of the late Sir Arnold Torrence."

"Oh, dear God!" She threw her head back and laughed. "A 'friend'—that's a good one. Yes, I was his 'friend,' if that's the way you want to put it. Dear Arnie. That was a long, long time ago, but we had some fun, I can tell you." Then suddenly she glared at Mallow.

"You there, Miss Mallow, you can stop looking so surprised. I wasn't always on the far side of fifty. I had skin as smooth and soft as yours once upon a time, and I had a line of men waiting outside my door after every performance. Let's you and me meet again thirty years from now and we'll see what you look like then."

"I am sure I don't know what you mean, miss," said Mallow coolly. It took more than that to cow Mallow.

"Mallow wasn't judging you," said Frances. "She and I come from a different world than yours, and behavior is different. Neither better nor worse, but different. But we three have something in common. You, Mallow, and I are women in a world of men. Mallow spent years answering to a butler. You answer to a director. And for all I am the daughter of a marquess, my late father tied up my principal until I marry or pass the age when no man will have me. I come not as a lady to an actress but as one woman to another, for your help. To help a friend, I need to know what happened many years ago."

I've heard other ladies say her ladyship is the best speaker in the suffrage club, and I'm seeing why, thought Mallow.

Miss D'Arcy seemed a little stunned by this, as if she didn't know how to respond. It took her a while to find her voice.

"I don't know what I can tell you. Arnie—Sir Arnold—was a 'friend' of mine, as you say. Oh, he had a lot of 'friends.'"

"And his wife? Do you think she knew?"

"Oh, my goodness. I heard that Sir Arnold had died, although I hadn't seen him in many years. Don't tell me his widow has sent you to make trouble for me after all this time. What will she get from me? Vengeance?"

Frances shook her head. "No. She doesn't even know about you, not personally. She is old, and I believe has made peace with any shortcomings in her marriage. Indeed, I ask you: Did she know about her husband's many friendships?"

"Very well then, my lady. I don't see how she couldn't have known. Some men have a certain—what you might call discretion. Sir Arnold did not. Sometimes he'd spend days with me. Where did she think he was?"

"He had daughters. Do you think they knew?" asked Frances.

Miss D'Arcy shrugged. "I didn't know anything about his children until I read about him dying. I have no idea if they knew. My lady, what's the point in any of them knowing?"

Frances nodded. "Back then, when you were one of the Green Players and working at the Emerald, another actress joined the company. She was just a little younger than you, I think. Her name was Helen."

Frances watched Jenny's face fall. Was she sad? Upset?

"What can I say about Helen, my lady? She was a funny one. Not a bad girl, but not especially popular here. Didn't fit in, I should say."

"Was she unpleasant? Unfriendly?" asked Frances.

"No. Nice enough, I guess, but thought very well of herself. She lost no time setting herself up at the Emerald. Every man in the company panted after her, and she toyed with them, with her teasing and smirks. Could've had half a dozen men taking care of her, but she wouldn't do more than have a dinner or two with any of them, and I always got a sense she looked down on any woman here who . . . well, who did more, if you get my meaning."

Frances thought about her next question carefully. She didn't want to give the game away, but she had to know. "Did Helen have it in for you particularly? Was she jealous of you for having a wealthy friend like Sir Arnold?"

"Well, I wouldn't say exactly jealous, my lady. But she would ask me, like butter wouldn't melt in her mouth, what I saw in him, was it really worth it having to be with a man like that to get some nice meals and a few trinkets? So pure she was. I told her to stay away from him, and from me. She'd just say, 'Don't worry. I have no intention of meeting him. I can do better than that.'" Miss D'Arcy seemed to forget Frances and Mallow were there, lost in old memories of Helen. It made sense, thought Frances. Louisa may have thrown in her lot with the theatre crowd, but her sense of superiority would've been ingrained. And considering what she knew about her father, her contempt for actresses who took second jobs as mistresses was only to be expected.

"What happened to Helen?" asked Frances.

"She was as stupid as she was beautiful. She didn't do better after all. Married an accountant and moved away. Africa? India? I don't remember after all this time. She said they were moving to the colonies, where her husband had a government job. She could've been set up with a wealthy man. Every man in the company practically went into mourning when she married."

"It doesn't sound like Helen had ever met Sir Arnold. And yet she had formed an opinion about him."

Miss D'Arcy looked curiously at her. "Very interesting you should ask that, my lady, because I wondered about that myself at the time. I even asked Helen how she had formed such a low opinion. She'd just smile and say, 'Oh, we've met.' I asked Sir Arnold about her. He just shrugged and said he never knew an actress named Helen, and if he was lying, he did it very well. But wait—" Light came into her eyes. "You're not interested in Sir Arnold. It's Helen you want to know about."

Frances saw no reason to lie, especially as Miss D'Arcy would never guess that Helen was her lover's daughter. "Yes. As you said, she got married and moved away, but that's when she disappeared. She came from a family that would like to find her, and I've been asked to help them."

"Well, I can't help you there," said Miss D'Arcy. She gave Lady Frances another shrewd look. "It must be someone with money if a lady like you is asking. I suppose there's a reward? But not for a thousand pounds could I tell you. I can say this though—there were plenty of actresses who were happy to see her leave. As I said, she wasn't really one of us."

Frances stood. "Thank you for being so frank. I appreciate your assistance." She produced a card. "If on reflection you think of anything more, you can find me here, and you will be paid for your time and trouble. Good day." With that, she left with Mallow right behind her.

The women paused in the hallway as another woman passed by them, probably to help Miss D'Arcy get dressed for her scene.

"My uncle was right, Mallow. We got a very different view of Helen—Miss Torrence—from a woman. She wasn't much liked, it would seem."

"I have observed, my lady, if I may say, that beautiful women are often subject to the jealousy of other women."

"That's a wise observation, Mallow. That may be part of it. So the men worshipped her, and the women wanted her gone. Was she killed? Did a woman do it? And for all she ran away, Miss Torrence was gently bred and would not have been a good enough actress to hide that. If she even wanted to. I was thinking too far ahead. I had wondered if a jealous lover killed her, but it may have been a jealous woman. If in fact she was killed! We don't even know if she's alive or not. If she is dead, we don't know whether she died a natural death or not . . . Anyway, it's time to give a report to Lady Torrence."

They were seeing themselves out the door when Mr. Pyecroft intercepted them. "Lady Frances . . . Miss Mallow. Did you find Jenny D'Arcy all right? Listen, if you aren't busy, how would the two of you like to be in a motion picture?"

"We are not actresses, sir," said Mallow, and Frances felt the frost from her maid. Mr. Pyecroft hastened to reassure them.

"No, of course not, Miss Mallow. As ladies who appreciate the performing arts, this would be a chance to see it from the inside, so to speak. We have a need for a brief scene of a lady being served. You would wear your current clothing."

"Oh, let's do it," said Frances. "We'll learn something."

"Well, if you put it like that, my lady," said Mallow, a little reluctantly. And so they were quickly ushered into one of the fake rooms. A woman came up to them with some powder. "Your faces can't be shiny, or they will look wrong on the film," she said, liberally applying a powder puff to their faces.

Mr. Pyecroft came up to them. "It's very simple, ladies. I will be standing there by the camera. You sit here, Lady Frances. When I say 'Action,' you, Miss Mallow, will pick up the food on the plate over there and serve it to your mistress. You can see the camera over there." He pointed to where stagehands were setting up the camera they had examined earlier, some twenty feet back, far enough to get in the whole room.

"Do we look at it?" asked Frances.

"No. In fact, pretend it isn't there. Even trained actresses have a hard time remembering that when they look at the camera, they look at the audience. Unless you're addressing the audience, you never look at the camera."

Mallow was meanwhile reviewing the setting. "Excuse me, sir. But your place setting is backward," said Mallow.

"What?" Mr. Pyecroft didn't seem to understand.

"This is not the way a table is properly set. I served meals at the household of the Marquess and Marchioness of Seaforth, sir, and this is how the table setting should be arranged." And Mallow proceeded to fix it. Standards must be maintained, even in motion pictures. As she was doing it, she could hear in her head the solemn approval of Cumberland, the Seaforth butler.

"She's right," said Frances with a little amusement. "If you want to expand your audience, you do need to get the details right."

"Oh . . . very well. Fix it as you see best, Miss Mallow." Mallow laid out the table as carefully as if it were a formal dinner party, not a shabby motion picture set.

"Very good. Are you ladies ready now? This will be about thirty seconds. You should talk to each other, but it doesn't matter what you say, of course. Again, in a moment, I'll say, 'Action.' The cameraman will start moving the film through the camera, recording your movements. You should keep going until I shout 'Cut.' Also, it's a little overcast today, so we'll need some extra light." Frances saw more stagehands carrying one of the heavy arc lamps near the camera. They connected it to a cable and turned it on. Both women jumped; it was like having a streetlight right next to them. The scene was washed in harsh, white light.

"Sorry, ladies. I forget how startling that is, but we need plenty of light to film." The men then adjusted its direction a little and spoke with Mr. Pyecroft before settling on a direction and adjusting the movable shades for the light.

"Very good, ladies. Take your places. Now, *action*!" Mallow did as instructed, serving her mistress as she would during her days as a housemaid.

"It's a little bit of history, Mallow. We will learn about this new form of entertainment. It's just starting, so there's a chance for women to grow with it—not just as actors, but as directors and managers."

"Very good, my lady." Mallow poured a glass of water for Frances. "I'm not sure what your late mother would say, God rest her soul, my lady." Frances laughed, and then Mr. Pyecroft called, "Cut," and the scene was over.

"Very nice, ladies, very nice indeed. The film will be developed, and I will send you a note inviting you to come and see it at your convenience."

"Thank you very much, Mr. Pyecroft. I look forward to hearing from you," said Frances. They headed outside. "I know it was a little unusual, but it was a little fun, wasn't it?"

Mallow smiled. "I will admit it, my lady. After seeing so many films, to actually be in the place where they make motion pictures and to actually be a part of one is very exciting, my lady." Then she became serious again. "Of course, it was mostly to help you for your work. I normally would not be doing this."

"Of course not, Mallow."

Frances looked for a hansom—and frowned. "There's a workman in a street worker's uniform across the street—he's been poking at that sewer cover since we got here. Why is he working alone? And why is that hansom waiting there on the far side? There's no reason for him to be there. I am willing to bet that the moment we step into a cab ourselves, that so-called workman will follow us in that cab, which is waiting for him. He's our soldier, I'm sure. We will have to thwart him." She thought a moment. "Mallow, how would you like to be an actress again, just one more time . . . ?"

A few moments later, Mallow headed along the street. The stalker would be looking at Frances, not at her. It didn't take her long before she was out of sight, behind a delivery van, and she swiftly crossed the street and headed toward the waiting hansom. She approached it from behind and quickly jumped in. Her heart was pounding, but her ladyship was counting on her.

"See here, miss, I'm already taken," the driver yelled down.

"I don't see anyone here. Now I'm going to Miss Plimsoll's hotel. I assume you know the way."

"But Miss—"

"Are you going to take me, or am I going to have to call a constable? I have my fare." She held up the bills Frances had given her. "Now please be on your way." Meanwhile she saw that there was a cloak on the seat next to her—the stalker was no doubt holding it in reserve to hide himself.

Frances gave Mallow a few minutes to take charge of the hansom and then headed straight for the "workman." He didn't even pretend that he wasn't watching Frances and, pulling his hat down, started walking quickly for the hansom. He was just a few feet away when he saw that Mallow was now occupying it, despite the driver's complaints to the contrary, and Frances was bearing down on him.

"You, sir! You won't get away this time!" Frances took out her silver police whistle and started blowing it. The man pulled his hat down and began running. Frances kept blowing, and people started to stare. *Oh, please, may there be a constable around now, when I really need one,* thought Frances. To her delight, she saw a constable running toward them. It seemed inevitable that the constable would catch the man, but the stalker surprised both of them by turning into a large building nearby. Frances followed closely after him with Mallow—who had abandoned the hansom to join Frances—and the constable behind her. The building seemed to be some sort of hardware wholesaler, realized Frances, with workmen of all kinds bringing goods in and out through large doors she could see at the back. It was a busy place, and some of the men looked at the trio curiously as they strode in and out of the aisles between the tall metal shelves that reached to the dimly lit ceiling fifteen feet above them.

"Did he rob you, miss?" asked the constable.

"No. He's been following me. But we should be able to find him. He's wearing a street worker's uniform, so he should stand out." The constable nodded, looking around. "You two ladies stay here for safety. Let me see if I can flush him out. If you see him meanwhile, blow that whistle of yours." He turned to a couple of hefty workmen who were loitering by the door. "You two—there's a man in a street worker's uniform. If you see him, grab him and call for help." They nodded, and the constable disappeared down the nearest aisle.

"We're not going to safely wait here, Mallow."

"No, indeed, my lady." And together they headed down another aisle, between rows of metal pipes. They heard muffled clanks as workmen moved items in adjoining aisles, but they seemed to have this aisle to themselves.

"You look on the right, and I'll look on the left," said Frances.

"Yes, my lady," said Mallow. They walked slowly, seeing if their stalker was hiding in the shadows, behind a pipe. They'd have him yet. He couldn't hide forever, and in his uniform he'd be challenged and stopped if he tried to leave. Slowly, they walked. Between them and the constable they had the first two aisles, and she didn't think their assailant had time to go farther.

"My lady," said Mallow. Frances turned and saw her maid had noticed a discarded street worker's uniform.

"Good catch, Mallow. He anticipated us, unfortunately, and probably had another outfit under this uniform so he could easily escape. But why leave the uniform right here?"

A second later, Frances realized why. She looked up and saw a man sitting right above them on the upper shelf. He now wore a workingman's rough clothes that would let him fit in anywhere. A wide-brimmed hat obscured his face.

"You, get down, now." And she blew her whistle. But the stalker jumped off suddenly, which the women didn't expect. Frances tried to block him, but he pushed by both of them, sending them stumbling. Frances blew the whistle again, and she heard the constable come running, but it was too late. By the time they made it to the front, the newly disguised assailant had slipped out with some other workmen.

Frances stamped her foot in frustration. "He was prepared and had another set of clothes under his first disguise. We would've had him otherwise."

"I'm sorry, miss," said the constable. They looked around the warehouse. In fresh clothes, there would be no finding him. "Would you like to come to the station and file a report?"

"Thank you. Maybe later. But I appreciate your diligence," she said. She looked at Mallow. "My maid is with me now, Constable, so I will be all right. Thank you again; you may go back to your post."

"Very good, miss," he said and left them. Frances and Mallow stepped outside.

"What do you have wrapped around your waist?" Frances asked.

"His cloak, my lady. He probably meant to use it as an additional disguise. I tied it around my waist to keep my hands free while we were searching. But—well, there's something wrong with it."

Frances frowned. "What? It seems normal."

"But feel it, my lady. It's very poor-quality cloth. What good could it do? It's like what Mrs. Mancini showed me at the Emerald Theatre. It's all poor quality. It doesn't have to work; it just has to look right for the audience."

Frances smiled. "Very good observation, Mallow. That's a real clue. We'll save this, and now we must be off to Lady Torrence."

Running up to them was the cab driver, who had followed Mallow. "Miss, you chased away my passenger, then left yourself—and you took that cloak. It should be given back to him."

"I am sorry we cost you a fare," said Lady Frances. "But you can take me to my next stop so you won't lose a fare."

"But what if he comes back?" said the increasingly confused driver.

"He won't be coming back. Did you get a look at him?"

"What? No, not really. He just gave me some coins and told me to wait. Quiet voice, and he hid his face under his hat. Now what is going on?"

"This is Lady Frances Ffolkes, sister of the Marquess of Seaforth," said Mallow. "She is not accustomed to answering questions, only asking them. Her ladyship has some urgent appointments, so please show us into your hansom cab without further delay."

He started to talk but then stopped and led the women to his cab.

Chapter 16

"Empty?" asked Lady Torrence. "My daughter's grave was empty—but a child was buried there?"

Lady Torrence and Frances sat having tea in the Torrence drawing room.

"Yes. We don't know why no adult was buried in that casket or who that mysterious child was. We don't know if Louisa is alive. All we know for certain is that there was a clever plot here, and judging from the complexity, I don't think your daughter was a victim. I think she was a willing participant. Perhaps even the orchestrator. To what end still remains to be seen, but with your agreement, I will keep looking. I am confident of answering these questions."

Frances had been afraid of upsetting her elderly client and was prepared to quickly call for her maid. But she underestimated her. Instead of fainting, Lady Torrence smiled wryly. "I feel like I've landed in one of Baroness Orczy's melodramatic works. It's like a scene out of the *Scarlet Pimpernel*."

"I agree," said Frances. "Although I find her writing a little overheated." Lady Torrence laughed in agreement.

"One more thing. As I once told you, I have to keep some secrets. But do the names Halliday, Lockton, or Bradley mean anything to you?" She wanted to see if there was a connection between the Torrences and the Hallidays or Emma Lockton née Bradley, the Halliday's former companion.

"No, I'm afraid not. As a diplomat's wife, I've always been good with names, but those are not familiar. I'm sorry."

"No need to apologize. It actually would've been a surprise if you had heard of them."

"So what next?" asked Lady Torrence.

"I have more people to speak with. There is clearly a strong connection to some incidents happening recently at the Emerald, and I believe that there are still clues waiting to be uncovered. I will report when I know more." She paused. "I am assuming you want me to continue." Frances couldn't bear the thought of quitting now, but she had to remind herself that she was serving a client. How could she continue if Lady Torrence didn't want her to?

"Of course. You never promised me peace of mind, only the truth. But I could no more ask you to stop than I believe you'd be able to. God go with you, Lady Frances."

Frances went home and had lunch, scratching comments into a notebook in Miss Plimsoll's dining room. It was time to tackle Emma Lockton. It was true that she was not part of the Halliday household until after Helen had supposedly died, but if she was close to the family, she might know something. She'd bring Mallow too, who was doing a fine job as her "Watson."

She'd have to approach Emma Lockton carefully. A well-regarded shopkeeper couldn't afford even a breath of scandal or the hint that she gossiped about her distinguished clientele. Very well then; she'd approach Mrs. Lockton as a possible customer. If she owned a Bond Street shop, there was no doubt she knew the names of London's leading families—including the Seaforths.

Finally, knowing that she had to appear more "ladylike," Frances allowed Mallow to dress her up a bit, which delighted the maid. Mallow fussed with her hair and discussed dress choices until Frances was driven to distraction. But she did realize that being a consulting detective required some sacrifices.

"I thought we'd try putting your hair up and back like this, my lady," said Mallow as Frances sat in front of her mirror.

"That will be fine," said Frances.

"Unless, my lady, you would rather that we do it like this . . . of course, the first way, it would go perfectly with the neckline of your blue dress."

"Whatever you think best, Mallow," said Frances with impatience.

"Very good, my lady," said Mallow with just a trace of censure. She knew that Frances's late mother, the old marchioness, happily had held lengthy discussions with her maid over every detail of hair and fashion. Ah, well, being the maid to a consulting detective required some sacrifices.

Dressing done, they made their way to Lockton's store. A boy was cleaning the glass window and brass fittings out front. Mrs. Lockton clearly knew how important it was to make a good impression before a customer even entered the store.

A cheerful bell rang as Frances and Mallow entered. Two shopgirls were seeing to customers, one attending a middle-aged woman while the other was bent over the counter, showing an elegantly crafted jewelry box to an older gentleman.

"Lovely, just lovely. I'm sure my goddaughter will enjoy it. Here is my card. Have it properly wrapped and sent to my house," said the gentleman.

"Very good, sir," said the shopgirl. The man thanked her again and tipped his hat to Frances as he left. The shopgirl carefully put away the box and then looked up. Frances recognized her immediately—the beautiful girl who had been sitting with the seamstresses in the Emerald Theatre right after Anthony Mattins had been killed. Frances thought she saw a flicker of recognition from the girl, but it was gone in a moment.

"Good afternoon. How may I help you today?" the shopgirl asked.

"Do you have gifts for men? I thought my brother might like something here," said Frances, affecting the somewhat languid tone used by ladies who devoted much of their time in shops like this. "Perhaps a cigar box? I'm Lady Frances Ffolkes. My brother is the Marquess of Seaforth, an undersecretary in the Foreign Office. Smokes entirely too many cigars, but he might as well do so from an elegant box."

"Oh, yes, my lady. We have some very handsome boxes that would nicely complement any Whitehall office. Let me show you." She produced several boxes, and Frances cast an appreciative eye over them. They were indeed beautifully crafted.

"Are these made in your workshops?"

"Yes, my lady. Everything we sell is made in our workshops from our own exclusive designs."

"Very nice. Mallow, which do you think his lordship would like? You have such a good eye."

Mallow looked over the boxes. "They are all fine, my lady, but I think he'd especially like this coloring."

"I agree, Mallow. You can send the account to me at Miss Plimsoll's Hotel," she said to the shopgirl.

"Very good, my lady." The girl looked pleased with herself.

Frances jumped in. "Have we met before? You look very familiar. I've seen you somewhere else, I believe."

"I'm sure not, my lady," said the girl, but she looked nervous and cast an eye on the other shopgirl, who was still seeing to the woman customer.

"Yes, I'm sure we have." The girl bit her lip as Frances continued, "The Emerald Theatre, right after the tragic death of the stage manager, Anthony Mattins. You were there; I'm sure of it."

"Yes, my lady," she stammered. She glanced now to a door behind the counter. Then she said in a low voice, "I sometimes assist with the costume work there, when I am not scheduled here, but the proprietress doesn't like me working there."

"I don't see how it's any of her business," said Frances. "She's your employer, not your owner. You have a right to any other respectable occupation during your own time."

"Yes, my lady. Except that the proprietress is also my mother. It is my ambition to become a fine dressmaker, and I would like some practical work experience. My mother supports me in this, but she doesn't like me mixing with theatre folk."

Frances smiled and nodded. "I see. Mothers are a different group altogether. Discretion is the better part of valor. I will keep your secret, of course. So you must be Miss Lockton?"

"Yes, my lady, Susan Lockton. My mother is Emma Lockton and has run the shop on her own since my father's death some years ago."

"May I meet your mother? It's unusual to see a woman running such a fine shop, and I am curious to meet her. I am a member of the League for Women's Political Equality, and I encourage other women to patronize women-owned businesses."

She watched a variety of emotions chase themselves across Susan Lockton's face: surprise, confusion, and pleasure that this well-born lady was willing to recommend her shop. Never mind that she was a suffragist!

"Of course, my lady. Please follow me around the counter."

"Thank you. This is my personal maid, June Mallow. I make no important purchases without her advice."

They went through the door and down a hallway. Frances could hear a loud woman's voice as they approached a closed door. The words became clearer as they approached.

"I'll tell you again: those designs are not today's fashion. We went over this already . . ." Susan knocked and entered without waiting for a reply.

"Mother? An important new customer would like to meet you." Frances stepped into the office. A middle-aged woman sat at a desk piled with neatly ordered business papers. Her hair, black with some silver creeping in, was arranged simply but fashionably.

Her face was strong and cheeks a little flushed from conversation with a man standing over her. He appeared just a little older than Susan and was dressed in working clothes. He was a tall man, fair-haired with a heavy build and calloused hands.

He didn't seem too upset at the woman's loud words, more resigned with a hint of amusement.

"Lady Frances, this is my mother and the proprietress, Emma Lockton, and Hiram Alton, head carpenter at our workshops. This is Lady Frances Ffolkes. She has just purchased a cigar box for her brother, the Marquess of Seaforth."

Mrs. Lockton pulled herself together quickly, stood, and pasted a smile on her face. "Lady Frances. I am so glad you are pleased with our goods. May I ask which model you picked?"

"The new line of mahogany," said Susan. Mrs. Lockton smiled with a little triumph and glanced at Alton. "I told you it would be popular with those who know quality, like Lady Frances," she said.

Hiram smiled good-naturedly at Mrs. Lockton. "So you did, ma'am. Anyway, I should be getting back to the workshop. I will work on the designs as you suggest, ma'am. Lady Frances, I hope your brother enjoys his cigar box." He bowed out and left the women to themselves.

"You have a very fine business here, Mrs. Lockton. I am active in the women's suffrage movement and so take a great interest in women who run businesses on their own."

Mrs. Lockton's face wasn't immediately readable. There was some amusement there. *What are you thinking? That humoring ladies of quality with their fads is part of good business?* thought Frances.

"I am glad for your interest, my lady. Managing both this store and the workshop takes all the hours of the day. I don't have any time for politics." Then perhaps Mrs. Lockton felt she had been too sharp, based on what she said next: "Of course, I do believe in the importance of a woman being prepared to make her own way in the world. She should not be dependent on a husband." She glanced at her daughter, whose look said, "We've had this conversation before."

"I completely agree," said Frances.

"I am proud of my daughter's skill as a seamstress and am looking to apprentice her to a fine dressmaker when she's a little older. I think it's best for a young woman to be of a certain age before going out on her own. Meanwhile I have saved money to eventually buy her a partnership."

"How fortuitous we are here, then," said Frances. "My maid Mallow is a very fine seamstress. Miss Lockton, if you have samples of your work here, Mallow would be happy to review them, and I can make an introduction to my own dressmaker, who also does work for my sister-in-law, the Marchioness of Seaforth."

"An excellent idea, Lady Frances," said Mrs. Lockton, who seemed excited, as did her daughter. "Susan, show Miss Mallow into the back room where you have some of your work. Bessie should be able to handle anyone up front."

Susan practically skipped out the door, and Mallow followed, but before leaving, she met Lady Frances's eyes.

Alone now with Mrs. Lockton, Frances turned to her and got a shrewd look back.

"I think you have more to ask me, my lady? I can imagine how busy you are. You didn't come just to compliment my firm's skill with mahogany."

"Very good," said Frances. "Actually, I am here at the suggestion of a mutual friend, the Reverend Samuel Halliday, from Wimbledon."

At that, Emma Lockton's face quickly softened and became full of warmth. "Yes, he is an old family friend." She blushed a little.

"I understand that you joined the Halliday household shortly after he was born."

"Yes. My family knew Mrs. Halliday's once. Her health was weak for a long time after the birth, and she and her husband thought a companion would be good. I was . . . well, I needed a job and was looking to move. They were the kindest, most Christian people I have ever met. Their son, Samuel, was as fine a legacy as parents could hope for. As he grew up, he called me Aunt Em, although there was no blood relationship. Now that he's grown . . . well, it sounds silly, but he still calls me that." She blushed again, then seemed to remember herself, and Frances saw the businesswoman come back. "Do you have some interest in the Halliday family or the mission they founded?"

"Actually, I have an interest in another friend of theirs. At the same time Samuel Halliday was born, they had given sanctuary to another woman, known only as Helen, who had been recently widowed. Helen died while living with them. I am trying to find out more about Helen on behalf of some old friends of hers. I know this was before you joined the Halliday household, but if you were close to the family, perhaps you were told something."

Mrs. Lockton was silent for a few moments. *She knows something, but she's trying to figure out what I already know and what she can safely tell me*, thought Frances.

"I know a little," Mrs. Lockton said slowly. "Mrs. Halliday mentioned that they had sheltered a young widow and that she died, as you said. Naturally, she didn't want to reflect on it, as it happened about the same time that her son was born. I know they buried her. Mrs. Halliday cared for the young woman and tended her grave for the rest of her own life."

"That's interesting. I've heard Helen was an actress, and friends and colleagues from the theatre told me that she had married and moved away. But it seems she was a widow."

Mrs. Lockton shrugged. "I can only tell you what Mrs. Halliday told me. I didn't come until some months after Helen's death."

"Yes, of course. Where did you say you came from?"

Mrs. Lockton hadn't said. She was clearly thinking about her options—telling Lady Frances, or simply refusing. Or lying.

"From near Shrewsbury, a village called Blackthorpe. Mrs. Halliday's mother had a cousin from those parts, so there was a connection."

Shrewsbury. The Torrences had originally come from there. Lady Torrence had said that her husband held private theatre parties at his cousin's estate, so they must've been people of note.

"You may have known some other friends of mine, the Torrences. I understand that they had a large manor there."

Now those shrewd eyes flickered. Frances felt her heart beat faster. She had hit a sensitive area for Mrs. Lockton. Frances would have bet anything at this point that Mrs. Lockton knew of the Torrences, even though Lady Torrence didn't know her.

"They were a prominent family in Shrewsbury. Lord Torrence was a large landowner."

"Did you know them well?"

"Hardly, my lady. My family was very modest. We didn't socialize with aristocracy. I'm sorry I couldn't be of more help." She started to stand to indicate the discussion was over.

Meanwhile, Mallow was in a room at the back of the shop, a small storage area. She was looking intently at some of Susan's stitchwork. The girl looked hopefully at this much-praised lady's maid, hoping for a good response.

"You have fine, even stitches. As good as the work done on her ladyship's dresses," Mallow finally concluded. She was impressed. Very little work reached her standards.

"Thank you, Miss Mallow. It's my dream to have my own dress shop someday. Perhaps . . ." She eyed the maid. "Perhaps Lady Frances would favor me with her custom then? And her sister-in-law the marchioness?"

Mallow knew Lady Frances wanted her to be encouraging and find out what she could. "Perhaps. Once you make a dress for one fine lady, your reputation will spread."

"That would be wonderful. I am so awfully tired of selling boxes all day."

"But it's such a fine shop," countered Mallow, who had noted the elegant fittings and the prestigious address. Shopgirls here would work only with the very best people.

"Well, yes. But day after day, selling boxes. I bet your life is more exciting, going with your mistress to fancy house parties and great estates all over England . . ." She let the sentiment hang, hoping for some gossip to enliven her day. And Mallow indulged her.

"Oh, yes, it can be interesting. The king himself came to dinner at her brother's house. And her ladyship knows other famous people. We've even been to police headquarters at Scotland Yard."

"Oh, I wish I did all those things. Of course"—and now she gave Mallow a sly look—"one can always get married."

"Marriage is a fine and noble goal," said Mallow, "but her ladyship believes that the choice of a husband is a very important decision reached only after a great deal of consideration."

Susan looked a little startled at the gravity of her words and expression.

"Ah, yes, well of course. But I'm taking it very seriously. And while I am ready to earn my own way in the world, I just turned twenty-one, which is not too young to get married if I get a suitable offer." And then she looked sly again. "There's a family friend, the Reverend Halliday. He should be getting a wife at his age. A very fine vicar he is, handsome, and he has a private income that lets him live nicely. I have a dowry, and I think it should be delightful to be a vicar's wife. Everyone looks up to you, presiding over tea with the most important people in the parish, dining regularly with the bishop."

Mallow nodded. There was a lot to be said for marrying a vicar, but she wasn't sure Susan was taking it as seriously as she said. A vicar's wife had to be very proper.

Susan frowned, coming out of her daydream for a moment. "But my mother isn't being very encouraging. She doesn't want me working at the theatre—you'd think she'd be glad I was earning good money. I could also do well at a dressmaker's, but she keeps telling me she wants me to stay here until I get a little older. I don't know why. And she gets very annoyed every time I talk about the Reverend Halliday. Surely she can't think I'd find someone better." She sighed rather dramatically. "I wish had a normal life like yours, Miss Mallow."

That was the first time anyone had called Mallow's life with Lady Frances "normal."

Susan said she should really be getting back to the front, and Mallow said she'd wait with her until her ladyship came out. It wasn't long before Mrs. Lockton and Frances joined them.

"How did you find Miss Lockton's sewing skills?" asked Frances.

"Very good, my lady. I think she would do well at your dressmaker's." Both Locktons beamed.

"Excellent. We'll be sure to pass on your name. Thank you for your help, and I look forward to giving my brother that lovely box."

They were about to leave when the door opened, and the Reverend Samuel Halliday entered.

Frances's eyes took in everyone's faces instantly. Mrs. Lockton resumed the warm and soft look from when she had spoken of the vicar earlier. The vicar himself seemed pleased—and startled—to see Lady Frances. And there was a smile, almost a smirk, from Susan.

"This is a pleasant surprise, Samuel," said Mrs. Lockton as he kissed her on the cheek.

"Yes, it is," said Susan. She took the initiative to kiss Halliday on his cheek. Mrs. Lockton frowned but only for a moment.

"I had a diocese meeting nearby, so I thought I'd drop in," said Reverend Halliday. "And I see you met Lady Frances Ffolkes. She's been trying to find more about Helen, the poor woman my parents took in. Were you able to help her, Aunt Em?"

"Perhaps a little," said Mrs. Lockton.

"Oh, she's being modest," said Frances. "She was very helpful indeed. I'm closer than ever to finding out what happened to Helen."

"Helen is dead and buried in Maidstone," said Mrs. Lockton with a heavy finality.

"So I understand. But the dead don't always rest easy, do they, Reverend Halliday?"

"Are you referring to Helen, my lady?" replied the vicar, looking a little puzzled. "I should think she lies peaceably."

He seemed genuinely confused. Mrs. Lockton didn't react to that at all. *So the good vicar doesn't know about the mystery of the grave*, thought Frances. *But I bet that you, Mrs. Lockton, could tell us something.* "Of course, Reverend Halliday. I am sure she is at ease. Good day to you all. Come, Mallow, we have other appointments." And with that, they left.

But before they were more than halfway down the street, the Reverend Halliday overtook them. He still looked a little confused—and upset.

"Excuse me, Lady Frances. I am sorry to waylay you like this."

"Not at all, Reverend. You want to talk to me away from the Locktons?"

He spent a moment gathering his thoughts before answering. "I've had occasion to think about your request for information, my lady. I was pleased to help you then and to send you to the Locktons, but nevertheless, it seems . . ." He paused, clearly trying to find a way not to offend her.

"I understand," she said. "You're worried my continued investigations will end up publicizing family secrets. I have been discreet, I assure you."

"Oh, I'm sure," he said, hastening to reassure her, "but it is worrisome. My mother was so concerned about it . . . I know it seems odd." He broke off lamely. A few people slipped by them on the street, but Frances wanted to press on while she had his attention.

"Your mother and Helen were very close?" she asked, making it half a statement and half a question.

"They were. My mother spoke of her often, but nothing about where she came from or anything else about her. She visited her grave every week."

"Yes. And since you bring it up, it's a very impressive monument. Seeing her properly buried was an act of great charity. But a stone of that size for someone who's not even a member of the family . . ."

The reverend sighed and looked around before turning his eyes on Frances again. "I've thought on that myself. Helen was a mystery. I can't help but wonder at what tied her to my parents. They were the finest people, my lady, and their mission among the actors was a living testament to their Christian faith. But none of us is perfect, and I am afraid that something, some long-ago misdeed, could come to light and tarnish their reputation when they are no longer around to explain it."

"I appreciate that. I can tell you this: I am acting for the family of Helen. I know nothing to her discredit. My goal is to explain her life . . . and death."

"And who was her family—can you tell me that?"

"I'm afraid the rules of my profession preclude me telling you, as it is confidential," said Frances.

"Your *profession*, my lady?" he asked, more confused than ever.

"I'm a consulting detective. I believe the first female one in all of London."

He appeared as though he was trying to decide if he should laugh but, looking at her face and the equally serious face of her maid, decided against it.

"I see. Well then. Can you tell me if you have learned anything to the discredit of my family?"

"I can share that much. No, I have come across nothing that shows your parents behaved in any immoral or illegal manner." The baby was a mystery, but not necessarily evidence of a crime.

"Thank you for that, my lady. Just one more question. My mother mentioned Helen acted at the Emerald Theatre. Have you spoken with anyone from there, and were they able to tell you anything about Helen? I am sorry, I know I sound like a gossipy old woman, but my mother's friendship with Helen . . . she made me promise to visit her grave regularly. It's a piece of my family history that's missing, and I never thought I'd find out anything—until you said you were acting on behalf of Helen's family."

He looked so hopeful that Frances hated disappointing him. "Yes, I spoke to some of the actors, but again, I can't reveal anything. I am sorry, but I can promise you this much: I have more to discover about Helen. I will recommend to my client that she allows me to share my findings with you."

He nodded. "That's very encouraging, my lady. Thank you for listening to me. God go with you on your quest."

A moment later, Frances and Mallow were alone on the street.

"Family," said Frances. "He's concerned about reputation. He thinks something was strange regarding Helen's death and her relationship with his family."

"Do you think there was something wrong, my lady?"

"Not necessarily. But he fears there was. Secrets lead to so many problems, Mallow. I have to think on this."

Chapter 17

Frances and Mallow proceeded to walk along Bond Street in silence. Mallow recognized her ladyship's mood and could practically see the gears turning in her head. She was lost in thought and would walk right out of London if she hadn't finished thinking.

However, her ponderings only took a few blocks. "Mallow, was Miss Lockton's sewing as good as you said?"

"Definitely, my lady. I think she'd do well at any fine dressmaker's." She summarized her talk with Susan Lockton.

"Very good," said Frances after Mallow was done. "I wonder why her mother objects so strongly to her theatre work. Of course, many people don't trust theatre folk, but considering how the Hallidays supported the actors, it seems a little hard of her."

"Yes, my lady. And one more thing. As you know, I don't like to gossip . . ."

"Of course not, Mallow. But we're not gossiping. We're investigating."

"Very good, my lady. It seems Miss Lockton is a little sweet on the Reverend Halliday."

"Is she now? Well he's nicely set up, charming, and handsome. I daresay he'll make some woman a good husband, and sooner rather than later might be best if he wants to avoid more fuss among the young women of his flock."

"It's very serious to be married to a vicar," said Mallow, "and, although it's not my place, my lady, since we're investigating, I must say I'm not sure if Miss Lockton realizes how much responsibility comes with being a vicar's wife."

"Perhaps, Mallow, half of her infatuation is just to tweak her mother. I think Mrs. Lockton, for all that the vicar calls her 'Aunt Em,' is a little sweet on him herself."

"My lady!" said Mallow, shock spreading across her face. "She's known him since he was a babe in arms."

Frances laughed. "It's a little unusual. She's probably twenty years older than he is and beyond childbearing years. But age sets no limits on the heart's desires, and she'd be a marvelous vicar's wife." She had no doubt Mrs. Lockton would approach parish business with enormous energy and efficiency. "Also, we should be fair. My uncle, Lord Hoxley, has been sweet on women twenty or more years younger than he is. And I believe Mrs. Lockton has matrimony in mind, which is more than you could say for my uncle. But this is all a side issue, Mallow. I think Mrs. Lockton knows what happened the night Helen supposedly died. She seemed very uncomfortable when we spoke about it, and she comes from the same town as the Torrences. There are secrets and more secrets there, Mallow. This is about perspective and illusion. I wonder if the answer lies in Zen Buddhism, a religion practiced in the East."

"You mean there are answers in a non-Christian religion, my lady?" said Mallow, a little nervously.

"Well, yes, Mallow. But it doesn't mean it's anti-Christian. For our purposes, it's more about how you look at a problem. For example, remember our last visit in the country, where my brother and his friends were practicing archery?"

"Yes, my lady. Sir Avery Rowley shot an arrow into the herb garden and frightened Cook so badly she had to lie down for an hour."

"Yes. That was unfortunate. But the point is, especially as far as Sir Avery is concerned, that in the West, we look at things separately. In the East, they look at things together. That is, the arrow and the target are not separate but part of the same reality. When you look at things like that, everything becomes more understandable."

"Very good, my lady. I know Cook would appreciate that."

"I'm sure. For now, I think I'll visit Inspector Eastley and see if he's come up with anything since last night. I recently had an idea, something I had forgotten, that will keep him and Constable Smith busy."

They went home, and Frances changed back into her business-like shirtwaist before bicycling off to Scotland Yard. She didn't see their stalker out front, but she suspected she wouldn't be free of him forever.

The sergeant at the front desk frowned at her approach. "My lady, are you planning to be a frequent visitor with your bicycle?"

"Yes, I am, Sergeant."

"Of course. It's only that we have limited room here, my lady . . ." He let his voice trail off under Frances's full gaze, his hope dashed that she would pick up his implications.

"I think over time you may expect more visits from women, and since bicycles are a healthful and economical form of transportation, you might consider creating a space to easily park them. In fact, thank you for bringing this up. I will write to the Commissioner myself."

"My lady—"

"It's quite all right. I'm just here to see Inspector Eastley. I know the way."

It was business as usual in the Special Branch suite, with Constable Smith and others working at their desks and the door marked, "B. Eastley, Inspector," shut.

Frances rapped on the door sharply and heard, "Come in."

"Ah, Lady Frances," said Eastley as she entered. "I have been expecting you. This is a little quicker than I thought, but please, take a seat. I suppose, full of energy, you've made a great deal of progress since our graveyard surprise and want to make sure that I have been just as busy."

"Inspector, although you and I may differ on approaches, I have never doubted your dedication or work ethic."

"I am relieved," said Eastley. "As expected, with the agreement of Lambeth Palace, I have been asked to look into any crimes arising from the supposed missing body of Helen. Indeed, my lady, if you had come earlier today, you would not have found me. Constable Smith and I were in Maidstone. The sexton was back in service, and we had a talk with him about Helen's grave."

"Did you tell him it was empty of Helen but containing an infant?" asked Frances.

"Good question. We didn't for now, but he isn't a stupid man, and when a Scotland Yard inspector started asking him questions right after a marquess's daughter did, he knew something was up. He was alternately frightened and truculent when we asked him about the grave, but although I think he knew something was odd about the burial, he didn't know what. You're looking very proud of yourself, my lady."

Frances did feel proud of herself. She had done better than she had expected. "Rather. It is pleasing to know a Special Branch inspector wasn't able to get any more information than I could."

Eastley rewarded her with a rare laugh. "Indeed. We didn't get any more out of him, which narrows the field down. Who was involved in the deception? Mr. and Mrs. Halliday, both deceased. If there were trusted servants, I'm sure they're gone too."

"And Helen. Don't forget Helen, née Louisa Torrence."

Eastley frowned and leaned back in his chair. "So you don't think she was a victim or even a bystander to this but an active conspirator? That's interesting."

"Yes, I do. She was an unconventional woman, a daring woman. I don't know why or how she did what she did, Inspector, but I think I know her. I can imagine her having the presence of mind to plan something like this. Faking her death. Also, I thought of one more thing that may be of interest to you. We were only concerned with the grave, but we didn't talk about how Helen came to be at the Hallidays. I don't suppose you've spoken with the Hallidays' son, the Reverend Samuel Halliday?"

"Not yet. And it is possible I may never. You need to understand, Lady Frances, my writ extends to the possible desecration of a grave under the authority of the Church of England. The sexton, I believe, has been cleared. I know nothing about the vicar, except Lambeth Palace told me he was dead, and while alive there was no blemish on his record. Burying a mislabeled coffin may be bizarre but is not a crime in itself. And there's no evidence the child was a murder victim."

"But aren't you concerned that Helen's body is . . . somewhere? Desecrated?"

"Ah, but you have convinced me, my lady, that Helen planned this and is out somewhere happily leading her life. Maybe the child was just the offspring of an impoverished family and Helen and Hallidays gave this child a well-appointed grave. At any rate, that's what my report will conclude." He smiled.

Frances shook her head. "So you're going to use my own words against me? Can you stop just like that? How can you just let a mystery like that go?"

"My lady, look at my desk. Look at these files. Real cases, real crimes. I am a public servant. We can't all be independently wealthy aristocrats spending time doing whatever we want."

Frances turned a little red at that. Why did he start having to bring class and money into their discussion? "That was needlessly insulting."

Eastley raised an eyebrow. "I don't see how. It's true. And for the record, my lady, I would've said the same thing to an independently wealthy *male* aristocrat sitting in that chair."

Yes, you would've, thought Frances. *Inspector Eastley may not like working with members of the nobility, but he will work with women. Give him his due.* "Point taken, Inspector. Very well, an agreement. I know you well enough to say in confidence that you don't want this investigation to end, even if you plan to issue a report saying that, whatever happened, there was no crime—"

"And I know you well enough to say that you're going to pursue this to a conclusion. Very well. As long as you don't wade into police matters, I wish you luck. So if that's all . . . ?"

"It is certainly not all, Inspector. I need something from you. Yes, I have time and money. But you have access and resources. We will share. I am going to tell you something that I forgot in the shock of our discovery last night. I spoke with Reverend Halliday, and he said that his parents told him Helen was a widow. Her husband had been murdered."

Eastley frowned, and Frances watched him think. "You want me to solve a thirty-year-old murder? Even if I wanted to, that's not my department."

"He was stabbed, Inspector. That's what the Reverend Halliday told me. And just days ago, another man who had courted Helen, a member of the Green Players, was stabbed to death outside the Emerald Theatre. What do you say to that?"

Eastley sighed and spread out his hands. "What do you want me to do, Lady Frances? Draw a line between stabbings thirty years apart?"

"I want you to go through records. There must be records. I need the details of the murder of Helen's husband. We can narrow down the dates. You and Constable Smith can surely find them. Then we can compare the two murders. It can't be that difficult, and I know you want to solve the mystery as much as I do."

Eastley thought some more as Frances watched him. She suddenly realized that she had half jumped out of her seat. Her mother would not have approved of her getting so excited—in a police inspector's office, no less.

"I could arrange for you and Miss Mallow to wander through the stacks of records. But records that old would be found in a dusty basement storeroom. Your maid would only be upset at how dirty your hands and dress got. Oh, very well. I make no promises, but I'll see what we can find."

"Thank you," said Frances, forcing herself to calm down. "I appreciate that."

"I'm glad that's settled," he said. "Just one more thing. As you swept passed the front desk, the duty sergeant called to inform—or should I say, warn me—that you were on your way. He also asked me to advise you not to leave your bicycle in the lobby."

Chapter 18

It had been a busy day, and Frances was looking forward to putting her feet up—but her hopes were dashed when she returned to Miss Plimsoll's. Mrs. Beasley, the manageress, intercepted her the moment she walked into the hotel. "There is a guest waiting for you in the lounge, my lady."

Frances had become an expert in judging the type of guest visiting her by Mrs. Beasley's voice. When it was one of Frances's own class, the tone was warm and sweet. An actress? The words were frozen. This time, her voice was neutral. So not a member of the nobility, but someone respectable—more acceptable than the police.

"Thank you," said Frances. When she entered the lounge, sitting straight-backed in a chair was Mrs. Lockton. She was looking around the room curiously. Frances saw she had changed out of the businesslike dress she had worn as proprietress of Lockton's into a more elaborate outfit. It might be her best dress, thought Frances, saved for special occasions. Like visiting the nobility.

"Mrs. Lockton? You wanted to see me? Is it about the box I purchased today?"

Mrs. Lockton stood. "No, my lady. That is being properly packed and will be delivered tomorrow. If I may, I wanted to speak with you again about the Halliday family. You may think it's none of my business, and I daresay you're right, but they were very close to me. They treated me like family when I had no family. I wanted to talk to you about them, if I may, my lady. There are some things I think you should understand before you proceed."

She was forthright, a mix of bravery and anxiety. She had a shop, a life, and a livelihood that depended on the goodwill of the best families in London. And yet she was showing up here to talk with, and possibly upbraid, the daughter of a marquess.

"Of course, Mrs. Lockton. But we can talk in more privacy in my rooms. Please come upstairs with me. My maid, Mallow, will make some tea for us."

"If you're sure it's not inconvenient, my lady . . ."

"Not at all. It's just upstairs." Frances watched Mrs. Lockton look around wide-eyed as they walked up the stairs at the elegant furnishings and the oil portraits of lords and ladies from the middle of the last century, going back to the days of the prince Regent.

Mallow was catching up on her sewing in their little sitting room.

"You remember Mrs. Lockton from earlier today, Mallow. Put on some tea for the three of us, will you?"

"Very good, my lady."

Frances told her guest to make herself comfortable while Mallow boiled the water.

"It must be difficult to run such a fine establishment as a woman alone," said Frances. "May I ask if you have trouble with male employees and suppliers taking you seriously?"

"They didn't take me seriously when I took over from my late husband, my lady. Sometimes they still don't. But I have money, and they take that seriously."

Frances nodded. "That is very telling. You are a philosopher, Mrs. Lockton."

She shrugged. "I don't know about that, my lady. I am a woman of business, and that is enough."

"So it is. And you have allies, such as the Reverend Halliday. I was very impressed when I met him at his vicarage and spoke to him about his family." She looked closely at Mrs. Lockton. Perhaps sensing that Frances was digging for more information, she now looked a little tense at the mention of the vicar's name.

"He's a good friend. As I said, almost family."

Frances continued. "And it seemed your daughter was especially delighted at his visit. As her father is deceased, I'm sure it's good for a girl to have an older male relation—you said the Hallidays were practically family—interested in her welfare."

Mrs. Lockton darkened at that and struggled for words. "He is the most charitable and kindest of men, but Susan, despite other fine qualities, is a little willful. Young girls often are." She smiled wryly. "I was at that age, my lady. Willful and foolish. I am sure the reverend looks upon her as a daughter or younger sister, as you say. But she may think . . . otherwise. I tell you this so that if you meet again, my lady, you don't inadvertently encourage her in those feelings. I don't think being a vicar's wife is the right path for Susan."

She was firm in her talk, and Frances realized she had gone as far as she could. There could be no probing of Mrs. Lockton's own feelings. Frances had told Mallow those feelings were a side issue to the case—but it was odd for a woman as sensible as Mrs. Lockton to apparently harbor romantic feelings for a man so much younger, to the point where she'd prevent what could be an excellent marriage for her daughter. And Frances had seen too many oddities in this case.

Mallow served tea and made to take hers to her room, but Frances stopped her. "Do stay, Mallow. You don't mind, do you, Mrs. Lockton? Mallow is as discreet as I am."

Her eyes flickered for a moment as Mallow quietly took a chair. "No, of course not, my lady. And our recent talk about the Reverend Halliday is the reason I came—or, actually, about his parents." She gathered her courage and continued. "I know you are busy, so I will cut to the heart of the matter. As you know, I never met Helen. She died before I joined the household. But I can tell again you that Mr. and Mrs. Halliday were the finest, most charitable, and most Christian people I ever met. When Helen came . . . it caused a problem. Not that the Hallidays did anything shameful, but there are secrets they took to their own graves, and if you continue your search for Helen, it could reveal them."

"Very well. But if the Hallidays are in their graves, how can the revelation of any secret hurt them? The religious foundation they started is surely so respected that even if something embarrassing came out, it wouldn't be harmed."

"Perhaps not, my lady, but it might reflect on their son, the Reverend Halliday. Things happened that might . . . impede him in his calling." Frances watched her blush. *Oh, my, her love for the Reverend Halliday goes deep.*

"I have no wish to cause any embarrassment to the Reverend Halliday. I am only trying to locate this actress, Helen. I have been approached by family members who haven't seen her in thirty years and want to know what became of her."

"You know what happened, my lady. Widowed, she sickened and died quickly. She's buried in Maidstone. What else does her family need to know?"

Frances watched Mrs. Lockton lick her lips. She's nervous, she thought. Because she's starting an argument with a daughter of the House of Seaforth? Or because, unlike the Reverend Halliday, she knew all was not right with that grave? Frances had a decision to make: the secret of the grave was powerful. Should she use it now to force Mrs. Lockton to reveal what had really happened? Frances suspected Mrs. Lockton would do anything to spare any hurt or humiliation for the Reverend Halliday.

"Mrs. Lockton," she said quietly. "I know, for a certainty, that Helen is not in that grave. And I think you do too. Is she still alive to your knowledge? Or if not, where is she buried?"

Mrs. Lockton just stared at Frances, and she wondered if the woman would get up and leave rather than continue the conversation.

"I won't ask how you know that, my lady." The words came out as a tortured whisper. "But I beg you not to tell anyone. Please. You have no idea what secrets had to be kept. What are still being kept."

"I have no interest in your secrets—I told you," said Frances, letting a little impatience creep into her voice, "I want to find Helen."

"Helen is dead. I can tell you that much," said Mrs. Lockton.

"Where may her mother go to mourn her?" asked Frances. "Helen had a mother. She is very old, and she wants to lay flowers on her daughter's grave."

"If I told you where she was, my lady, it would give away the secret. The reputation of the Reverend Halliday—if you could see what good work he does, the souls he cares for. And . . . I have a daughter . . ." She stood, a little uncertainly. "I beg you, my lady, to think on what you do. I assure you I give you no threat, but do understand that I'm not being melodramatic if I say that these are secrets some might kill or die for. A mother's love is . . . but I can say no more. Thank you, my lady. Please—I will see myself out." She left the room and closed the door firmly behind her.

Frances and Mallow sat quietly for a few moments before speaking.

"Why won't she tell us, Mallow? What kind of thing could be so terrible that she can't tell us? What would be so awful? I wanted to hold back on the secret of the child for now. We might want to use it later. But does it have to do with him or her?"

Mallow thought on that. "I can't explain the child, my lady. But perhaps this Helen had done something illegal and wanted it believed she had died." In the neighborhood Mallow had grown up in, criminals often found themselves better off if they were thought dead.

"Very possibly," said Frances. She also remembered that Mrs. Lockton and the Hallidays were middle class, and a rigid adherence to rules was common. In their milieu, an adulterous affair was alarming—what would the neighbors say! Among the aristocracy, many men had mistresses yet everyone just shrugged as long as the parties were reasonably discreet.

"Also, Mallow, perhaps the Hallidays were not quite as perfect as everyone says. For example, what if Helen had an affair with Mr. Halliday? Where does that take us?" Frances was just thinking out loud, but she had horrified her maid.

"My lady! Everyone says they were the finest people. They established a Christian mission."

"Perhaps, Mallow, they did so out of guilt."

"If you say so, my lady," said Mallow, ending the conversation as far as she was concerned. Frances smiled to herself and thought about the words. A mother's love? Was that Mrs. Halliday for her son? Or Mrs. Lockton for her daughter? But Susan had been born long after Helen had died—or rather, before Helen was presumed to have died.

Frances kept a small collection of books and references on a shelf in their sitting room, including a map of England. With Mallow's help, she spread it out on the table.

"Here, Mallow. Blackthorpe, just outside of Shrewsbury. I think it's time we opened a second front, so to speak. Emma Lockton, née Bradley, knows too much to be a casual witness here, and I am wondering about her, the Hallidays, and her background. Let's find out more about her."

Mallow knew her mistress well enough to know what was next and was fetching the train schedule before Frances had even asked for it.

"Well done, Mallow! Let's see, there's an early morning train out of Euston with a connection to Blackthorpe. We shouldn't even need to stay overnight. But this has to be secret. Our occasional stalker may be around, and I don't want him to see us going to Euston station. Mallow, see if one of the housemaids is around."

Mallow went into the hallway and brought in Ethel, a sweet-tempered young maid who was obliging, if not especially bright.

"Yes, my lady?" Ethel asked.

"For some reason, a soldier has been following me."

Ethel's eyes got wide. "That is very wicked, my lady."

"More annoying than wicked. But I need you to check to see if he's still outside. Could you stick your head outside and see if he's still there? I don't want him to know that either Mallow or I are aware if he's there."

"Of course, my lady. I'll be right back," said Ethel as she practically raced out of the room. She returned a few moments later. "Yes, my lady, I looked out the hall window. He's loitering outside. Shall I ask for Mrs. Beasley to send for a constable?" She seemed pleased at the thought of some excitement in her routine.

"Thank you, but no. Mallow, what time is the morning train tomorrow?"

"At seven twenty-five, my lady."

"Ethel, what time do you go on duty tomorrow? And Violet, the other maid for this hall?"

"We're on late shift this week, my lady, so not until nine."

"How would you like to make a little extra money tomorrow morning for almost no work at all?" Hotel rules allowed residents to pay maids for extra work in their off time. Different emotions chased themselves across Ethel's face. Some extra coins would be most welcome, but everyone knew she was called "Mad" Lady Frances for a reason. What might she ask?

"Thank you, my lady. I would be happy to assist before I go on duty, and I'm sure Violet would too. What, ah, would you like us to do?"

"It's very simple, really. I just want you to change your clothes."

Chapter 19

A little before seven the next morning, a hansom pulled up to Miss Plimsoll's. There was an early morning chill, and two well-bundled women stepped out of the hotel and into a cab. One was dressed plainly but neatly, as befitted the maid to a lady, and the other was dressed in a more expensive outfit, simple but well-tailored. The cab took off. A man in a soldier's uniform stepped out of the shadows and ran quickly to another waiting cab, which took off after them.

A minute later, Frances and Mallow left the hotel as another hansom pulled up. A crack of the whip, and they were on their way to Euston station.

"I knew it would work," said Frances, full of triumph. She and Mallow had watched it all from an upstairs window. That morning, Ethel and Violet had come into Frances's suite. Ethel, the same height as Frances, changed into one of Frances's outfits. Violet, a little taller, changed into one of Mallow's. Then the two maids walked out of the hotel. They were about the same age as Frances and Mallow and now were dressed like them. Wide-brimmed hats half hid their faces. It had not been hard to fool their stalker.

"I am very glad it did, my lady. I just hope Ethel and Violet are careful with their borrowed clothes."

Frances laughed. "I'm sure they will. They're good girls, and they won't be having dinner in them. I told them to go around the park and lead our stalker on a merry chase. Even if he eventually realized he's been fooled, we'll be on our way to Shrewsbury."

"It serves him right, my lady," said Mallow stoutly.

"Yes, it does. He's a shrewd one. His persistent and careful stalking of us has convinced me he's the missing Alexander Braceley, the actor-turned-soldier who was one of Helen's suitors. If he somchow survived the Sudan and came home, he's a formidable opponent. As an actor, he's used to disguising himself, and as a soldier, he can live by his wits and make quick decisions. But what does he want? Just to frighten us? To send us a message? We'll have to think on that. He won't attack Ethel and Violet, not in a cab or in front of the hotel. But we will need to watch out for him, and sooner or later we will have to catch him."

It was a three-hour trip to Shrewsbury, and the train served a very nice breakfast. Mallow watched the countryside go by as they ate. A London girl born and bred, Mallow always found the countryside exciting and a little scary. Although she felt at home in London's worst slums, it took a lot of reassurance from Frances before she accepted that there weren't wolves lurking behind every tree.

"I've never been to Shropshire, my lady."

"I've only been once or twice myself," said Frances. "It's a very rural county known for the River Severn, the longest river in England."

"Longer than the Thames, my lady?"

"Yes, even longer. Blackthorpe, where we're going, is built on a stream that flows into the Severn. I expect it will be rather picturesque. Anyway, we're going to look up the Bradleys, and we'll start with the church. In small towns like this, everyone knows everyone else. I want to find out about Mrs. Lockton's past."

Mallow poured more tea for Frances and herself. "So much wickedness in your investigation, my lady. Everyone seems to be lying."

"Yes. We have a great many lies, but they are not necessarily all due to wickedness. Remember what we know about Helen and all the men who loved her. She married a man who I suppose she loved. Some people do the most terrible things for love, Mallow."

Mallow gave that a lot of thought.

At Shrewsbury, they changed to a small local train that took them the few miles to Blackthorpe. It was indeed picturesque. The train station, even as small as it was, seemed to intrude on a town that didn't look like it had changed much since Henry IV had fought a major battle there in the fifteenth century. There were thatched cottages, muddy streets, and an ancient church with black stone stained in places with moss. One of the more substantial buildings on the main street was the Boar's Head Tavern, where farm workers, who had no doubt been hard at work for hours, were taking an ale break.

"It's a rare situation that I'm the best-dressed person in sight," said Frances wryly.

"I think, my lady, that you're the best-dressed woman in the entire history of this town," said Mallow.

"You may be right. I bet the Boar's Head does a very nice lunch with fresh country food, but we'll find that out later. For now, let's visit the church and see what we can find out about the Bradleys."

They got more than a few curious glances as they walked. There was probably a local squire who owned much of the farmland and served as the justice of the peace, and his wife would be the de facto social leader of the community. But even she wouldn't be able to compete in status—or in the expense of her clothing—with the London-born daughter of a marquess.

The church was dark inside, but there was enough light to see that it was clean and well-maintained. A figure in black was tidying the altar, making sure everything was perfect. He was elderly and moved surely but slowly. His silver hair was brushed straight back from a well-lined face.

He looked up, and Frances saw him squint. Perhaps his eyesight wasn't as good as it had been, and the church was not lit as brightly as it would be during a service. "Can I help you?" he asked. From the strength of his rural accent, Frances was willing to bet he had spent his entire life in Shropshire.

"Perhaps you can," she said and walked closer. "I see from your robe you are a verger here."

"Yes, I have that honor. Peter Doakley at your service. But perhaps you seek the vicar? He should be here shortly."

"Thank you, Mr. Doakley. I am Lady Frances Ffolkes, down from London, and this is my assistant, Miss June Mallow. I think you may be able to help us. We're involved in a little family research project, and I was hoping to view your baptism records."

"Happy to oblige, my lady." He was clearly tickled at having someone so well-born in his church. "We have some very old records here. May I ask how far back you would like to look?"

"Only about fifty or sixty years."

"That will be easy then. Please follow me, and I will set you up nicely." They followed him out of the nave and into a records room, adjacent to the vicar's office. It was lined with bound books, neatly labeled by hand, going back about a century.

"Here they are, my lady. Baptisms, weddings, and funerals. May I bring you some tea?"

"Thank you. That would be very nice." He left, and Frances and Mallow looked over the books. "We're going to assume Emma Bradley, as she was then, is between fifty and sixty years old, judging from her appearance and the age of her daughter. It's a pity we don't have a photograph of her to show anyone here, but we'll make do with what we have." She heaved one volume off the shelf for Mallow and one for herself. They pulled chairs up to the desk, opened the books, and got to work. Mr. Doakley came with the promised tea. He was clearly curious about their mission but was too polite to ask. He said he'd be in the church if they had any questions.

"Certainly a well-populated town, Mallow. A great many baptisms."

"And a vicar who wrote them all down with an elegant hand, as they used to do, my lady."

It took them about an hour until Mallow found a name. "My lady, this may be it. Emma Bradley, baptized in this church in 1855. Daughter of Edmund Bradley and Elizabeth Bradley, née Dean."

"Good show, Mallow. That seems right. How many Emma Bradleys could there be of that age here? Now comes the next part, finding out if anyone knows her or about her. I imagine Mr. Doakley could help us."

They replaced the books and found Mr. Doakley still pottering about the church, making sure all the hymnals were in place. *This must be the most well-ordered church in England*, concluded Frances.

"Did you find what you're looking for, my lady?" he asked.

"Yes, we did. We were looking for a name—and we found it. Emma Bradley, baptized in this church in 1855. You are a local man, I assume. Can you tell me if she is still in this village, or if you know where she moved? We know something to her advantage if we can find her."

Mr. Doakley looked at her curiously and frowned, as if he didn't know how to respond. Frances suppressed a shiver of delight. There was something odd here. As with Helen's grave, something wasn't as it should be.

"Come with me," he eventually said. They walked out of the church and through the yard. Were they visiting Emma? If so—then who was Mrs. Lockton? They continued across the main street and down a narrow lane past some houses until they came to a cemetery. Now despite her warm jacket, Frances felt a chill, and a glance at her maid told her that Mallow did too.

"We outgrew the churchyard some sixty years ago," said Mr. Doakley. "This land wasn't particularly suitable for farming, and the lord of the manor at the time donated it for church use." The verger seemed to know the way. He probably knew each section by decade.

"Here you are, my lady." He pointed to a small stone, nothing like Helen's elaborate one. It read, "Emma Bradley, 1855–1865, nestled in God's arms."

"It was a fever, my lady. Swept through the village that year and took many. Emma was one of six children in that family, and it was a small mercy that she was the only one who didn't have the strength to resist."

"I see," said Frances. "You seem to know them well."

"Everyone knows the Bradleys hereabout, my lady. A large family and a good one. It was a sad day when we buried young Emma here. I was there myself, along with most of the village, out of respect and affection for her parents." He paused. "I'm sorry you had to find out like this, my lady, but when you said 'something to her advantage,' I didn't know what you meant."

"Are there are no other women named Emma Bradley?"

He shook his head. "If there were, it was long before my time. This Emma here had two brothers who married local girls, but neither is named Emma. But come to think of it, I tell a lie, my lady. Her brother Luke has a daughter named Emma after his late sister, but I didn't think of her, as she's much younger than the Emma you were looking for, only about twenty-five. She married last year and now lives in Shrewsbury."

"You've been most helpful. I appreciate it." She stared down at the tombstone, her mind working furiously. Another lie. Another hidden person. "But tell me, Mr. Doakley. You mentioned the lord of the manor. Which lord is that?"

"Oh, the Torrences. They own all the land over here, my lady, from this field and behind toward Shrewsbury. The farms over there, nearer to the stream, mostly belong to Squire Henley, a very fine man, like his father before him."

"Torrence. I think I know about one of the family—not the lord but his cousin, Sir Arnold Torrence, who was a colleague of my father's many years ago." She would have to be careful here. The Torrences were an old family, wealthy and no doubt with a lot of influence. Someone like Mr. Doakley would not criticize the family, especially to a stranger.

"Aye, I knew him," said Mr. Doakley. And that was it. No "very fine man" comment for Sir Arnold. "His cousin, the old lord, died about ten years ago. Lord Reginald Torrence, he was, and Sir Arnold visited frequently with his wife and daughters. A good man, Lord Reginald Torrence." But not, apparently, Sir Arnold.

"I never met Sir Arnold myself," said Frances. "But I know his widow, Lady Beatrice Torrence. She had two daughters."

He nodded. "A gracious lady," said Mr. Doakley. He gave Frances a look. "May I ask if your inquiries are on her behalf?"

"We are trying to locate a member of the Bradley family, but my information may not have been accurate," she said, not quite answering him. "I also know the younger Torrence daughter, Sarah."

He perked up at that. "I remember her, my lady. A lovely little child, scrambling after her older sister, Louisa. A very spirited girl, was Louisa, but not unkind, and very sweet to her little sister." Everyone seemed to deserve a compliment—except Sir Arnold. "May I ask if the daughters are well?"

"Yes, Mr. Doakley. Sarah married well and lives in London with her husband. She is now Lady Freemantle. She has two grown sons. Louisa—I never met her. She is married too, and her husband holds a government position in the colonies."

He nodded. Frances saw he wanted to say something but was struggling.

She spoke gently. "Mr. Doakley, I am acting as an agent for Lady Torrence in London. What you tell me will only be shared with her, and I will not tell her the source. But for reasons I can't say, I am researching both the Bradleys and the Torrences. What can you tell me?"

He smiled sadly. "For all that, my lady, I don't know much. A silly thing, really. I can't see how it will help. It's just that the young Louisa and young Emma were the same age, more or less. When the London Torrences came for visits, they'd come to the village. There are some very pleasant walks and the ruin of an old abbey, which ladies like to sketch. They got on nicely, the two girls, with the younger one tagging along."

He sighed, as if girding himself for the rest of the story. "Unfortunately, on one of the last visits before Emma's untimely death, Sir Arnold put an end to the friendship. He said that his daughter should not be associating with . . . with a girl not of her class, my lady. It was a public scene, I'm sorry to say, leaving both girls in tears and Lady Torrence deeply upset. She saw no harm in the friendship. It was a very unhappy moment, my lady. Left a lot of bad feeling in the village. It might've been forgotten, but with Emma's death the following winter—well, it lent a tragic pall over it all."

They stood in silence for a while as the cool spring breeze passed over the field and ruffled the grass. Frances reflected that Lady Torrence hadn't told her that story, but it had been so long ago, perhaps forgotten among Sir Arnold's other cruelties.

Finally, Mr. Doakley cleared his throat.

"If that is all, my lady, I should be getting back to the church."

"Of course, Mr. Doakley. Thank you for being so frank. I will keep your confidence."

"Thank you, my lady." He turned and headed back toward the church.

They were alone for a few more minutes before Mallow broke the silence in a hesitant voice. "My lady. Are we going to arrange for another exhumation?"

"No, Mallow," she responded with a smile. "I have no doubt that a girl named Emma Bradley is in this grave. The real question is, who is the woman pretending to be Emma Lockton, running a fine shop on Bond Street? But it's getting late. Let's see what kind of lunch the Boar's Head offers."

"Very good, my lady. Do you think they serve proper London food there?"

"I shouldn't think so," said Frances with cheer. Mallow sighed.

The proprietor of the Boar's Head may have known nothing about London society, but he could tell Frances was a lady of quality and Mallow was a superior servant. He led them to a table in a semiprivate alcove, and Mallow brushed a hand across the chairs before declaring them suitable for sitting. It turned out that the pub actually served savory meat pies, and even Mallow, after some close examination, pronounced the food quite acceptable, especially when accompanied by half pints of the local ale. One didn't drink ale in London drawing rooms, but Frances had a "When in Rome" attitude.

"So let's think here," said Frances. "The mysterious woman known as Mrs. Lockton takes the name of a childhood friend of Louisa Torrence and then goes to work for the Hallidays—who had given shelter to that same Louisa Torrence, then called 'Helen.' But she arrives after Helen went missing. The Reverend Halliday seemed certain that Emma didn't show up until after Helen died. Of course, he also wasn't sure where his mother knew Emma from. The families had known each other, he said, and 'Mrs. Lockton' mentioned that it was a connection through a cousin. Perhaps Mrs. Halliday had never met the real Emma, so it was easy for the imposter to disguise herself."

Mallow frowned. "I see that, my lady. But why? She helped Mrs. Halliday and then got married and runs her shop."

"I don't know . . . yet. I'm seeing a triangle here: Emma Lockton. Emma Bradley. And Helen. But how . . . ?" She shook her head. "This may be much larger than a missing daughter. We may be looking at an act of exquisite revenge, Mallow. Someone wanted to punish the Torrences by killing their daughter. Even if she was Emma's friend, it could've been a grim 'eye for an eye' logic, brought to extremes. Even assuming the Reverend Halliday is honest—and I do—we can't be sure that Emma actually didn't show up earlier, when Helen was still alive. But that's still all supposition. And that soldier, Alexander Braceley, showing up after all these years? It's quite a mess so far. But step by step."

The proprietor came by to ask if he could get them anything else.

"He's a local man," said Frances when he left. "That accent marks him as being from Shropshire. Mr. Doakley is the same. It's the Welsh influence—a similar intonation to Llewelyn, my uncle's butler. Did you hear it from Mrs. Lockton?"

"She sounded like a London native to me, my lady."

"Yes, she's been living there for years and would want to sound as if she fit in. She's gotten rather good at it. Unless . . ."

"Unless she was never from Shropshire at all, my lady?" asked Mallow.

"Exactly. I was thinking that we should confront Mrs. Lockton, letting her know that we know she's a fraud, but I'm going to hold onto that for now. I may have made a mistake in telling her we knew the grave was empty of Helen, but at least we found out that she also knows something isn't as it should be. Is she fearful about that anonymous child? I'm going to hold back on telling her we know she's not Emma Lockton. I want her to think her disguise is safe, and I won't bring up the child. We don't know who is on whose side right now. For all we know, Mrs. Lockton may be in league with our stalker, and I don't want them to panic. Emma Lockton may know where Helen is or what happened to her."

"Very good, my lady. What will you be doing next?"

"We can't forget that there were two murders: Helen's husband, Douglas MacKenzie, and Mr. Mattins. Inspector Eastley is trying to find the details of MacKenzie's murder, and we'll see what clues his work brings up. For now, we're going to have to wait, I'm afraid." She wasn't happy about that but could think of no one else to talk to, no other avenues to explore for now.

"You're dining at Mr. Wheaton's house this evening," Mallow reminded her.

"Yes, Mallow, a proper dinner party." She smiled wryly. "Don't worry; there's a train back to Shrewsbury and then to London within the hour."

"I'm not worried, my lady, but we need time to do your hair up proper, get you into a dress, and choose jewelry. The green dress with your grandmother's necklace should work very well, my lady."

"I put myself in your capable hands," said Frances, and that made Mallow happy.

CHAPTER 20

Although her head was full of her investigation, Frances realized that it was good to have an evening off visiting with Hal. And of course, there was the pleasure of being in his company. There would be other couples at dinner, his solicitor friends from the best firms in London and their wives. And Frances. She was not a wife yet but would be, and these would be the people she'd socialize with when she moved into his house. Which would become their house. She had to sort out her feelings—as soon as she solved the mystery of Helen.

She had looked for the soldier when they left, but it had been too dark. And he'd be more careful now that Frances had almost caught him twice and had fooled him that morning. Still, all he'd find this evening was that she was visiting her fiancé.

Mallow was with her in the hansom. Ladies' maids did not normally accompany ladies to evening engagements, but Mallow would soon be part of this household too and usually joined Frances to get to know her fellow servants. She could also help collect the ladies' wraps as they arrived.

"How do you find Mr. Wheaton's staff, Mallow? Just between us?"

"Satisfactory, my lady. Of course, a rather small staff compared with his lordship's household." Frances's brother did a great deal of entertaining because of his position. Hal had a butler who doubled as a valet, a cook, and a couple of maids. For large dinners, like tonight, he hired an extra waiter. "Also, the food is not as . . . elaborate, my lady."

"No. Mr. Wheaton leads a somewhat simpler life," said Frances. Not because he couldn't afford to do better, but because that was the way he chose to live. Frances's mother had had long weekly conversations with her cook, and if there was an important dinner, they'd spent even more time. That wouldn't happen to Frances. She wasn't going to lead that kind of life.

They alighted from the hansom, and Mallow headed down to the servants' entrance. Hal greeted Frances at the door himself.

"Am I the first?" she asked.

"Yes, my dear." He kissed her on the cheek.

"My mother would be annoyed with me for arriving so early, but Mallow did an efficient job getting me ready."

"And a fine job it was. You look lovely. But then you always do."

"Flatterer."

"Come sit down, and I will pour you some sherry if you'd like. Tell me how your detective work is going."

Frances studied him. From most men, she could expect at best an amused condensation about her work. But not from Hal, and she felt ashamed of her suspicions. She should have known better. There was genuine interest and admiration there in those pale-green eyes.

"I've found out a lot, but it keeps getting more complex, and the lies keep growing. I am beginning to suspect that even my own client isn't being entirely honest with me—not deliberately, but out of embarrassment or a wish to forget the past."

"A client not being completely forthright with you? I am shocked, Franny. That has never happened to me or any other solicitor." He laughed.

"Perhaps I am naïve," she said.

"No, just inexperienced. Years ago, I was engaged to make financial arrangements for a client's distant cousin, a widow with a child, who had fallen on hard times. It was years before

I figured out that the 'widow' had been a poor farm girl he had gotten into trouble. It wasn't that he didn't trust me but that he was ashamed. Maybe your client is the same."

Yes, thought Frances. Lady Torrence was ashamed—for letting her husband hurt their children all their lives, finally driving one away. She had said she hadn't remembered the name "Bradley." Indeed, if Emma was her daughter's playmate, she might not have known the girl's surname. As a girl, Frances remembered romping with the fishmonger's daughter near their country estate. She doubted either of her parents had known the fishmonger's name.

Soon, the butler was announcing the next arrivals, and in short order, there were ten in the drawing room, greeting each other and talking. As always, Frances found herself the subject of curiosity as a member of the aristocracy and a well-known suffragist. Although they presided over highly formal offices during the day, in the evenings—especially after a glass of wine or two—Frances found Hal's solicitor friends and their wives a lively bunch. And who knew? Maybe one or more of the women could be enticed to attend a suffrage club meeting.

The butler called them all to dinner, and as they were eating their soup, Hal drew everyone's attention by standing.

"My dear friends and colleagues, gentle ladies, and beloved Frances"—the last item was met by approving laughter from the company and a blush from Frances—"although I invited you here out of friendship, I also want to use this occasion to announce a momentous change in my office. I have found myself busier than ever of late. To that end, I needed another senior clerk, to be promoted from among my pool of clerks. And dear Frances, I know you of all people will be thrilled to hear that I promoted one of my female clerks, Miss Wilmington, to the position."

More laughter followed with cries of, "Hear, hear!" from Frances.

"Well done, Hal!" said Frances. "As you know, I've met her several times and think no one, man or woman, is more deserving of such a promotion. I daresay she's the first woman with that title in any solicitor's office."

"Quite, Franny. But it's what happened after I told her of her promotion that makes the story so humorous. She was very pleased and thanked me most warmly, especially when I told her what her new wages were—the same as the male senior clerks. And she said, 'Thank you very much, sir, and please extend my thanks as well to Lady Frances Ffolkes.' Well, ladies and gentlemen, I asked her why I should thank my intended for a promotion in my firm—in *my* firm—and she stammered something about assuming Lady Frances had had a hand in the promotion. Which she did, if indirectly. But it seems I have to remind my staff that her ladyship is soon to be my partner in life but not in my business."

With loud cheers, everyone toasted Hal for his progressive step and Frances for being such a good influence on him.

"I am glad to have inspired you to take such a step, Hal. And I hope when next we all meet, I'll find out that other gentlemen here have also promoted women in their firms."

The ladies were particularly vocal in their support.

"Perhaps," said one woman, "someday we'll even have women solicitors. And then Frances can be his partner in life *and* his firm."

Frances and Hal met each other's eyes and shared an unspoken message: *Wouldn't that be nice.*

The dinner proceeded with good conversation and good humor. All went well until the roast was being cleared in preparation for afters, when Mrs. Dilmouth knocked over her wine glass, spilling some of the red liquid onto her dress.

"How terribly clumsy of me," she said.

"Come with me," said Frances. "My maid Mallow is downstairs, and she's a genius with stains."

The two women excused themselves and headed to the servants' hall, where Mallow was helping with the sewing.

"A stain, madam? I'm glad you came quickly. I can keep it from setting and have you all fixed in a moment. Just wait right here." Mallow went into the kitchen and came back with a damp cloth and a few other ingredients. The stain was handled quickly.

"Thank you so much, Mallow," said Mrs. Dilmouth. "It's a wonder."

"I am pleased to be of assistance, madam," said Mallow, full of pride.

"I'll follow in a moment," said Frances, and Mrs. Dilmouth headed back upstairs. She turned to her maid. "Thanks again. All is well here? The dinner is going beautifully, Mallow. Hal seems to have good staff."

"Oh, yes, my lady." She lowered her voice to avoid being overheard. "Mr. Wheaton's staff is fine, my lady, and the hired waiter knows his business. But the extra kitchen maid, Gladys—although I'm no cook, I know how a kitchen should be run, and I wouldn't think that she had ever been in a kitchen before."

"That's odd, Mallow. Mr. Wheaton never mentioned hiring an extra kitchen maid."

"She showed up with the waiter, my lady. She said the agency was lending her for the evening as a gift because Mr. Wheaton is a good customer of the agency. The waiter didn't know her, though, and Cook says she isn't much good, free or not."

"Mallow, where is this Gladys now?" She felt her heart pounding.

"Washing up, I believe, my lady. Do you think . . . ?"

Frances realized that, much like in a military campaign, planning was everything. There just wasn't time. If she alerted the butler, she'd risk losing her quarry. She had to think on her feet.

"Mallow, there's no easy way for you to leave through the kitchen exit without attracting attention. Go upstairs quickly, exit through the front door, and stand on the street. Alert a constable if you see one, but I doubt we'll be that lucky."

Mallow said a quick, "Yes, my lady," and headed upstairs at a rapid pace. Frances slipped into the kitchen. Cook was busy putting the finishing touches on the final dish, and one of the regular maids was helping her. By the time Frances's presence was recognized, she had already placed herself between "Gladys," who was working at the sink, and the only exit to the street. The maid's hair and sloppy oversized cap shadowed her, but Frances could see her face, masculine despite clever theatrical makeup.

No one ever looked closely at a mere kitchen maid, and the soldier—their stalker—had counted on that.

"Gladys. Although that is not your real name. You have been found out and are done stalking me. Sit down at the table right now and face the consequences of your actions." She put every ounce of her patrician upbringing into her tone.

The cook and her maid looked up from their tasks, stunned. The stalker didn't move right away. He was considering his options, Frances knew.

"I said, 'sit down,'" Frances commanded. Then, turning to the staring maid and cook, she ordered, "One of you—go get the master now. We have an intruder in the house." The maid ran, and then "Gladys" made his move, rushing Frances with his head down. She had half-expected that and stood her ground. Frances wasn't tall, but she would not be easily moved, and she knew no man, even an actor, would be used to moving in women's clothes. That was her advantage.

The stalker grabbed her and tried to throw her aside, but Frances pushed back. She was turned around and felt strong arms surround her. She couldn't move.

And then she remembered her jujutsu. She relaxed for a moment, fooling her attacker, who moved forward to escape—but Frances neatly stepped forward and tripped him with a well-placed foot. He stumbled, and while he was off-balance, Frances grabbed him again. When he turned to attack her, she nimbly stepped aside and threw him with the aid of his own weight into the table, where he slammed his hip.

Clearly panicked, the assailant rebounded and gave Frances another shove while trying to use his longer legs to race past her to the door. Frances saw him try to pick up a rough bag, like a workman would carry, that was lying unobtrusively at the exit. But Frances caught up with him and was ready with her foot, despite the restrictions of her clothes, and tripped him again as he tried once more to run past her toward the door. He pulled himself up again, scrambling for the bag, but Frances managed to step on it, and the worn strap tore as he pulled it hard.

Unfortunately, his sharp tug also sent Frances off balance, and she fell against the wall. Snatching the bag from the floor, he stumbled out the door. Frances heard noise upstairs; Hal and his company were coming. But would they be fast enough?

Frances followed the man out the door and onto the street. He was running along now, and Frances realized that she had no chance of catching him. But then, out of the night, she saw what seemed to be a brass cannonball coming from the direction of the front door. She vaguely realized it was a decorative doorstop from the main entranceway—a sphere flattened on one side—and it caught their culprit right between his shoulder blades. He went down yet again, and without its strap, the bag went sliding away into the darkness.

He had no time to retrieve the bag, so he abandoned it and disappeared down the street. A moment later, Hal and the other men appeared behind Frances, coming from the front entrance.

"I'm unhurt—follow him!" Frances shouted, and Hal and one of the men did. But in the dark, the man had no doubt shed his maid's outfit and vanished. They came back a few minutes later, shaking their heads.

"Franny, are you sure you're unhurt?" asked Hal.

"Yes. A little shaken, but fine—Mallow, was that you with that doorstop?" Mallow reappeared, having retrieved both the missile and the lost bag.

"Yes, my lady. I am sorry that I failed to stop him more permanently."

"But Mallow, you succeeded. I tore his bag, and you made him drop it. If he wanted it so badly, it must be important. We will examine it."

"But later," said Hal. "Come upstairs. Mallow will see to you, and you'll have some brandy." He looked at her in the eye and embraced her, and she let him comfort her. "I'll tell you later," she whispered.

She looked up at the assembled company gathered in front of the house, looking on with concern and more than a little curiosity. Frances owed them an explanation.

"It's my own silly fault. I was just checking in on my maid downstairs and noted that something about the hired kitchen maid looked wrong. When I challenged her, she attacked me and fled."

"I imagine that she was a petty thief using forged references to get a temporary job to steal spoons or whatever else she could quickly grab," added Hal. "Frances, with her sharp eyes, no doubt rattled her. No point in making a fuss with the police now. I'll have a word with some contacts of mine at Scotland Yard in the morning, but there's no reason not to go back upstairs and finish our dinner."

It was a good speech, Frances realized, but didn't entirely account for everything, especially Frances's fight, part of which may have been witnessed by some of the guests. And how had Mallow been in place unless Frances had sent her there? The shrewd solicitors and their clever wives would know there was more to this. There would be talk . . . and Society would be treated to another colorful story about "Mad" Lady Frances.

But for now, an efficient Mallow rearranged Frances very quickly downstairs and dinner concluded with afters, coffee, and brandy.

"I say, Wheaton," said one of the gentlemen. "You promised us a memorable evening, but we had no idea. Once more, a toast to your remarkable fiancée."

The evening concluded on a cheerful note, and as the other guests left, Frances saw more curiosity from the gentlemen—and admiration from the ladies. Perhaps, if nothing else, one or more of them would come to a suffrage meeting to see what else Frances was getting up to.

When Hal and Frances were alone, they retired to the library, sitting next to each other on a settee, finishing their brandies.

"I owe you an apology," said Frances. "What happened this evening was a result of my detective work. I dragged it into your house." She sighed. "Although I am taking it seriously, I confess I also saw it as amusing. But I have introduced danger into your home. That was . . . thoughtless of me." She looked at Hal for understanding and forgiveness.

"It is my house, Franny. But soon, it will be yours too. Ours. It's the point I keep making. We are joining our lives together."

His easy dismissal of the drama she had caused was endearing but vaguely irritating. He should be annoyed. Even angry.

"Mr. Wheaton, you're going to spoil me. You're too good to me." She was only half joking.

"Is it so hard to believe that what is important to you is also important to me? After all, my lady, we're all in agreement that you're the one who got me to promote Miss Wilmington to senior clerk."

"So you did it just to please me? You don't think she really deserved it?" she challenged him.

"No. Despite my great love for you, I wouldn't have done it if I didn't think Miss Wilmington deserved it. But the point, Franny, is that I wouldn't have even thought about it before I met you."

She nodded. "Thank you," was all she could say. Yes, there were some things to work out before they walked down the aisle, but she did love him and knew that he loved her. She'd work out the details later. She always did. Meanwhile she still had a mystery to solve.

"Thank you for not calling the police. I don't want any more complications in this case," said Frances.

"So I assumed. Now I saw Mallow retrieved the bag the culprit dropped. I won't ask you to violate your client's privacy, but I hope it has a clue for you."

"I expect it does," says Frances.

"Shall I ring for Mallow so you can examine it now? I'll give you the privacy of my office. Or I can have a cab summoned so both of you can go back to your rooms."

"I do want to examine it, but the clue will still be there later tonight. Or tomorrow. It will keep." She put down her brandy and leaned over to give her fiancé a long kiss.

CHAPTER 21

It was late when Hal saw Frances and Mallow into a hansom for the short drive home. He was a little nervous and wanted to come with them, but Frances dissuaded him.

"We're not going to be attacked together, and he's licking his wounds, not seeking to start trouble with a London cabbie who probably has a club under his seat. Thank you, dear Hal, and we will talk very soon." A final quick kiss, and then they were off into the night.

"I didn't get a chance to say, Mallow, but I was deeply grateful, and deeply impressed, at your aim with that doorstop. Thank you."

"You're most welcome, my lady." With a little hesitation, Mallow said, "I think, my lady, that I did that Zen Buddhist trick you spoke of earlier. That is, the arrow and the target are the same."

"Mallow, I truly believe you did. Meanwhile, one of Mr. Wheaton's friends told me I'd make a very good prop." Mallow saw the mix of pride and embarrassment on her ladyship's face, as when Mr. Shaw had called her "Major Frances."

"Is that a position in government, my lady?" It was her ladyship's dream to get women into government, although Mallow wasn't entirely sure what that entailed.

"I wish. A prop is a position in rugby. You've probably heard my brother mention it—a violent sport played by boys and by men who think they're still boys. A prop is apparently one of the strongest and toughest men on the team. It was a compliment. I suppose."

"I see, my lady. When I was giving the ladies their cloaks as they left, one of the gentlemen told me I'd make a very good fast bowler. Is that also a position in rugby?"

Frances smiled. "That truly is a compliment, Mallow. It's a reference to cricket."

"I've seen gentlemen play that at the country estate when we visited."

"It's a much more civilized sport. Anyway, a fast bowler is someone who can throw a ball with great speed and accuracy, as you did this evening."

"I am pleased to hear that, my lady, although should we take up sports, I hope that we'd be playing the same game on the same team." She spoke earnestly with no trace of a smile.

Frances took Mallow's hand. "Always, dear Mallow. You and I will always be playing the same game on the same team."

"That pleases me, my lady. Thank you."

"But as for Mr. Wheaton. Will he have such a storm petrel as his wife?" She looked at her maid with a half smile.

"If I may be so bold, my lady, my impression of Mr. Wheaton is that he is most steadfast and unlikely to change his mind, despite this evening's unpleasantness."

"I do believe you're right. But I have been careless and won't be again. We will not let our stalker sneak up on us again. Although I daresay that he's found attacking us is far more trouble than expected. I am getting a sense of what this is all about. I still have much to figure out, but I think a lot of what we've been through is window dressing. What we really have here is a woman, this Louisa-Helen, who had to run away. Everyone else is just trying to hide their parts in her disappearance—or their parts in her husband's death—and making sure we do not find out the truth."

"What do we do next, my lady?"

"That bag you have—I'll wager we have a clue, and as tired as we are tonight, we'll have a quick look. Soon, we'll see if Inspector

Eastley has found anything about Helen's murdered husband. And we will have to take another look at the Emerald Theatre. I think there are more secrets there. They have had a little time to gather themselves after Mr. Mattins's murder, and now that we know more about Helen and Sir Arnold's penchant for actresses, we are in a better position to ask questions. We are by no means stuck."

Despite Frances's assurance that they were under no more threat that night, Mallow looked around carefully before alighting from the hansom cab. The hotel's night porter let them in, and Frances checked the mail rack on the piecrust table in the foyer.

Oh, my—three interesting items, one stamped with the seal of the Metropolitan Police Service and the other two in a lavish green script of the Emerald Theatre. The police and actors both writing her in the same evening. Mrs. Beasley would have been very displeased.

"We advance, Mallow!" cried Frances, opening all three and scanning them quickly. "Inspector Eastley writes us that he has discovered something and invites me to call on him at my convenience. Very nice. And here are two tickets for the opening night of *Romeo and Juliet*, as Mr. Rusk promised, as well as the opening night party. Two nights from now. That is perfect. The actors will be there, and I can question them. Perhaps I can hear more from Mr. Rusk and Mr. Prescott, and maybe there are others. And this second letter is actually from the Emerald Theatre film studios. They have developed our film, Mallow, and are inviting us to see it. That should be fun. All this is excellent. Now, upstairs. We're going to see what our stalker has been hiding."

In their rooms, Mallow again laid out some newspaper to protect the table, and Frances carefully reached into the bag. First she came out with a long, tapered blade.

"It's like a small sword, my lady."

"It's a bayonet, Mallow. Infantry soldiers attach them to the ends of their rifles when attacking."

"My lady, you don't think—" Her eyes were wide.

"I don't know what to think, Mallow. But it's a horrible, lethal-looking weapon. What else do we have?" She pulled out a piece of cheap paper. Frances read the heavy block letters: "'You will stop meddling in the search for Helen. She belongs to me and me alone.' Now that is very odd, Mallow. Let's say our attacker is Mr. Braceley, Helen's suitor, the actor-turned-soldier. This is a weapon he might have. He was going to leave us this note. Perhaps dramatically pinned to Mr. Wheaton's wall with the bayonet. He wanted us to know how easily he could threaten me, even in my fiancé's house. How terribly theatrical. But why have we made him nervous now, just because we're trying to find Helen? Unless we're being elaborately played with?"

There was one more item—an old newspaper, folded open to a particular page. It was a small news item that related to the murder of Mr. Mattins. It was circled in bright-red ink.

"Our stalker has little faith in our intelligence, Mallow. Or our courage, for that matter. He was going to leave this with the note to indicate that we'd be courting death to continue with our investigations. As if we didn't know or care."

"Very wicked, my lady," said a deeply affronted Mallow, "and insulting."

"Agreed. But about this ink . . ." Who would have red ink? Accountants used it—was it a statement about the murdered Douglas MacKenzie, Helen's late husband? Frances looked more closely and then tested the ink with her finger.

"My lady—it isn't blood, is it?"

"No, Mallow. He's not quite that horrific, although maybe he hoped we'd associate it with blood. It's like what my friend Miss Studholme once showed me. This is theatrical makeup. Lipstick, it seems, which actresses use for full, red lips. It can be found in dressing rooms at the Emerald or any other theatre."

"So is this a soldier who wants us to think he's an actor, my lady?"

"Yes. Or maybe an actor who wants us to think he's a soldier. Perhaps Mr. Braceley, returned from the Sudan, or someone who wants us to think he is. But I can't think anymore. We're both exhausted. I think we'll be sleeping through breakfast again."

CHAPTER 22

They both fell asleep quickly and slept well, so they actually did make it to breakfast the next morning. After eggs, toast, and plenty of tea, they met again in their sitting room.

"A busy day ahead of us, Mallow. I'm first going to see Inspector Eastley and then make a quick visit to my sister-in-law, Mary. Also, all of the excitement at Mr. Wheaton's house shouldn't make us forget what we discovered in Shropshire. Lady Torrence didn't seem to remember the name Bradley, but I wonder if her daughter, Lady Freemantle, can help us more with the story. I'll call on her again. Finally, I have a meeting with some members of the suffragist club—the executive committee and our founder and president, Mrs. Elkhorn." As Mallow well knew, there was no one in London whose good opinion Frances wanted more than Mrs. Elkhorn's. "Then back here for lunch, after which you and I will go to the film studio."

"Very good, my lady. I assume you'll be taking the bicycle for this morning's travel?"

"It's a bright and clear day, Mallow, and the fresh air and exercise will be invigorating."

"I'm sure it will, my lady. Meanwhile, I will consider what you will wear to the Emerald Theatre tomorrow."

"Excellent. And bring out your best dress and hat. We shall look most impressive for the opening night of *Romeo and Juliet*."

"I beg your pardon, my lady. My best dress?"

"Yes, Mallow, for the theatre. We want to look our best."

Mallow's hand flew to her mouth. "My lady, I assumed you would be going with Mr. Wheaton or the marchioness."

"Dear Mallow, my turn to beg your pardon. As pleasurable as the theatre is, it's also part of our work, and you are my Watson. We will be going together."

Mallow's eyes shone. *Imagine that*, she thought, *going to a fancy theatre like the Emerald, and on opening night*. "I am pleased to attend you there, my lady."

"Excellent. And if you'd like, I have a copy of the play on my bookshelf, and it has a summary. Shakespeare's plots can be a little complicated, and it pays to know the story beforehand. And now, I must be off. I'm practically living at Scotland Yard these days. Maybe they can find a small office for me there."

Having retrieved her bicycle, Frances paused in front of Miss Plimsoll's, but there was no one suspicious in sight. She figured that the close call she and Mallow had given their stalker last night—and the seizure of his bag and threatening note—would ensure they wouldn't see him again for a while. *He wanted to terrify us. We ended up terrifying him*. But it paid to be cautious.

She happily pedaled off to Scotland Yard, where the sergeant on duty gave her a sour look.

"I had assumed, my lady, that you would be making other arrangements for your transportation."

"A thousand pardons, Sergeant. I have been so busy that I have not yet been able to contact the Commissioner about making arrangements for parking bicycles. But I will get to him shortly, I promise. Meanwhile, I see that you are hardly overwhelmed with them yet, so I'll just leave it here, for now."

"But, my lady—"

"Thank you so much. I see how busy you are, and I know the way." She took off down the hallway and heard the sergeant dressing down a couple of constables for snickering at the exchange.

Constable Smith gave Frances his usual taciturn, "M'lady," and then she knocked on the inspector's door and entered.

"Ah, Lady Frances. Perhaps I should've just met you at Miss Plimsoll's. You're continually upsetting our desk sergeant."

"I do apologize. I was saying to Mallow how much time and bother we'd save if you could see your way to finding me a small office here. I could keep my bicycle in the corner."

"As soon as our meeting is over, I'll ask the chief super about it," he said dryly. "Meanwhile, I have done as you requested. We found the records of that murder in 1886. An accountant by the name of Douglas MacKenzie was stabbed to death. The motive was assumed to be robbery. According to these records, there was no arrest. You are fortunate that the detective sergeant who investigated it took excellent notes, something that doesn't always happen in cases like that, especially back then." He slid a folder to Frances. "I doubt anyone will be looking for the file anytime soon, but please return it at the end of your . . . investigations," he said with a thin smile.

"I will guard it carefully and return it as soon as I reach some sort of conclusion. Do you have the file for the more recent murder of Mr. Mattins?"

"That, my lady, you will have to get elsewhere. It's not something I could do. Or to be more exact, I could do it, but it isn't worth the cost."

"But surely you could call the inspector in charge of that case? Why wouldn't he share his findings with you?"

"Oh, he would. But he'd want to know why a Special Branch inspector is interested in a common murder. There would be questions and talk. He'd speak with his superior, who would talk to mine."

"And you can't say it's to oblige London's first female consulting detective?" asked Frances.

"Not even that. But I am sure you will prove equal to getting the information through other channels."

"Thank you. I take that as a compliment. Very well, you've given me this, and it will get me started. Now, Inspector, I have been stubborn and difficult during our acquaintanceship.

I realize that." She paused and then sighed before saying, "This is when you're supposed to say, 'Oh, no, my lady, it has always been a pleasure working with you.'"

Eastley laughed. "Oh, no, my lady. I am not one of the Society gentlemen you are used to. You have been stubborn and difficult, and I won't insult you by pretending otherwise."

Frances laughed in return. "Well said. Where was I? Oh, yes. Despite it all, I am indescribably grateful to you for doing this. I give you my heartfelt thanks."

Eastley seemed almost embarrassed at her sincerity. "Yes. Well, you're welcome. But the favor is not entirely free. I have two requests for you. One, if someone is going to be arrested at the end, I would like to be one doing it."

"But of course. Doesn't Sherlock Holmes always let Scotland Yard take the credit?"

He smiled thinly. "Thank you. But that's not the issue. We've cut some corners here, what with the exhumation and this file. We don't need more people knowing about it."

"A very fair request, Inspector. I give you my word. And the second item?"

He sighed.

Oh, this is going to be a big one, thought Frances.

"Please be careful, Lady Frances."

"Why, Inspector, you care for me. I am flattered."

"Don't be too flattered. I'm imaging all the paper work required if harm comes to the sister of a marquess." He stood. "Best of luck. And don't forget your bicycle on the way out."

Frances headed back to the lobby. She had the file in her bag, and she still had the bayonet. She would've shared her finding with Inspector Eastley if she had needed more leverage but was glad it wasn't necessary. There would be too many questions from a man who was very good at asking them, and Frances didn't want the police pulling her off the case because of the danger. Meanwhile, she had heard about finding fingerprints on objects and matching them with culprits. But, she realized ruefully, she had no one to compare it to. Not yet.

But how to get the information on Mr. Mattins's murder? What she really wanted were the details of the killing, which would be in the police surgeon's report.

Medical—of course. Dr. Edward Grayson, the Home Office physician who had attended the exhumation. He said he had an office at University College. Perhaps other murder victims ended up there. Dr. Grayson may have handled Mr. Mattins himself or be in a better position to ask for information than Inspector Eastley was. Back onto the bicycle; it wasn't far. Once she arrived, a helpful student directed her to the medical hall. There was no problem with the bicycle here. A dozen of them were lined neatly by the porter's lodge, and no wonder—they were popular with students.

In the building, Frances saw a sign to the Home Office laboratories. A clerk was manning the front desk, and above him a sign noted, "Only Home Office Staff Beyond This Point."

The clerk looked up and smiled. "I'm sorry, miss, but this is a Home Office suite, not an area for students."

Ah. He thought she was a student. In fact, University College had been one of the first institutions in London to grant degrees to women.

"Thank you, but I'm not a student. I'm here to see Dr. Edward Grayson."

Now the smile turned to open merriment. "Ah, I see the problem. I think you've got the wrong Dr. Grayson, miss. This isn't Harley Street, and our Dr. Grayson isn't the kind of doctor who sees patients."

Frances matched him with a sweet smile of her own. "Oh, I'm aware of that. He's the kind of doctor who cuts people up to see how they died." She watched the color drain from the clerk's face. "I have business with him. Would you be so good as to tell him Lady Frances Ffolkes is here to see him at his earliest convenience?"

"Ah, yes, Miss . . . my lady." He cleared his throat. "May I ask what this is in reference to?"

Frances held up her bag. "I would so like to tell you," she said, lowering her voice to a whisper, "but it's secret government business."

That seemed to confuse him even more. As Frances expected, he picked up his telephone to call the doctor. So much easier than continuing to talk with this lady of quality in a conversation that was threatening to turn into something out of Lewis Carroll's works.

"Dr. Grayson, I'm calling from the front desk. You have a visitor . . . a lady, actually . . . she won't tell me . . . Lady Frances Ffolkes . . . very good, sir." He hung up the telephone. "The doctor will be out in a moment."

While she waited, Frances began reading the papers in the file. There wasn't much there—Douglas MacKenzie had been killed by a blade in the early evening. The street was near the Emerald Theatre; perhaps he had been going home. The alley was used as a shortcut, but no one had been around to hear anything. Had the killer known MacKenzie's habits and been aware of that alley?

There was also a detailed description of the wound, which Frances hoped would be helpful to Dr. Grayson.

The doctor came out a moment later, dressed in a suit and looking at Frances with a mix of pleasure and curiosity.

"My lady, what brings you here? Although I am glad to see you."

"Thank you, Doctor. I actually have some questions as a result of our . . . meeting the other day. Do you have a few minutes for me?"

The doctor now looked bewildered, and the clerk was looking a little stunned.

"Of course, my lady. Do follow me to my office," said Dr. Grayson. He led her back through several hallways. Some doors were open, revealing men working in offices. They passed by one room separated by large double doors marked, "Operating Theatre," but to Frances's disappointment, they were closed.

The doctor's office was small and rather messy. Mallow would've been very unhappy. There was nothing on the walls except for his framed medical degree and just one photo on his desk. Curiosity got the better of Frances, and she also needed to build a personal connection to the doctor to ensure his cooperation.

"Your wife, Dr. Grayson?"

He blushed a little. "My fiancée, Arabella. We're to be married as soon as I'm a little more established."

"She's very sweet looking."

"Thank you, my lady. I'm very fortunate to have found her. She's very quiet and shy. I didn't think girls like that existed in these modern times." His blush turned crimson. "I'm so sorry, my lady, I didn't mean to imply—"

But Frances just laughed. "No offense taken, Dr. Grayson. I am bolder than most ladies, I fully admit. Meanwhile, take my card. I'm an officer of the League for Women's Political Equality, dedicated to achieving the vote for women. Tell Arabella she's welcome to contact me about joining." That left the doctor speechless. Frances continued, "But I am sure you're busy, so I'll get to my reason for coming. I told you the other night that I was at the exhumation as a service for a friend. That is true, but it's a little more complex."

Dr. Grayson looked a little wary. "Complex" was clearly not something he wanted to hear about.

"And what can I do for you?" he asked.

"The woman who should've been in that grave was married. Her husband was killed in London not long before she died herself. Through friends of mine in the Home Office, I was able to get the police report for his murder." She produced it for him. "I want you to look at the description of the wound and tell me how he died."

He opened the folder and read the description. "Fairly detailed description. It seemed to be caused by a long, flat knife from the description. However . . ."

"Yes?" said Frances eagerly.

"It was a very deep wound. Too deep for a typical kitchen knife."

"But might a professional killer carry a blade like that?"

"I perform autopsies, Lady Frances, but I'm not an authority on criminal weaponry. Although, to be fair, I've seen my share of murdered bodies, and, well—" He looked up at Frances.

"Please, Doctor. I managed to get through an exhumation without fainting. I daresay I can handle whatever you are going to tell me."

The doctor grinned. "Fair enough, my lady. I was going to say that you can kill with a short knife as easily as a long one if you know what you're doing. And how would you conceal something this long?"

Frances nodded. That made sense.

"I'm not sure what else I can tell you, my lady."

"Oh, there's much more; we're just beginning," said Frances cheerfully, watching the doctor's face fall. "There was another murder just a few days ago of someone who I have reason to believe had a connection with the deceased Mr. MacKenzie. I want you to compare these wounds to those of a man named Anthony Mattins, killed outside the Emerald Theatre."

Dr. Grayson just stared at her for a few moments, blinking. "I can't imagine what we could possibly learn from a comparison."

"Oh, but we have a weapon we can compare it to: a long, flat blade, as you said." She reached into her bag and slapped the bayonet onto his desk. She took pleasure in watching him jump.

"Lady Frances . . . where did you get this?" Dr. Grayson looked at it for a while, and then his professional curiosity got the better of him. He picked the blade up, handled it, and then looked at the police report again. "I have to say that this, or something like it, could've been the murder weapon."

"Not inconsistent with the wound. Is that how you would put it?" she asked. She took great pleasure in his smile.

"You have it perfectly. But you mentioned Anthony Mattins—the theatre chap? He was one of mine."

"What a delightful coincidence," said Frances.

"Not really," he said, a little ruefully. "I'm junior man here. I get all the 'plum' assignments, like murder victims and midnight exhumations. It's a recent case, and I think I still have the file here." He reached into a desk drawer and pulled out a file that was similar to the one Frances had.

"Let's see what we have here," he said, and Frances was pleased to see that he was forgetting that he was discussing deadly wounds with the daughter of the marquess and was throwing himself into his professional curiosity. He reviewed the file, then from another drawer produced a ruler. He took careful measurements of the bayonet and made some notes. Then he smiled.

"So again, 'not inconsistent' with the weapon?" asked Frances.

"Oh, I can do better than that, my lady. I would say that the MacKenzie and Mattins wounds seem to have a great many similarities. And the bayonet would definitely account for Mattins's death. Look here. See the blade's edge? It's not completely smooth. That means there would have been tearing, and see my notes . . ." He handed her the file. "Read right here—the flesh wasn't neatly cut, but torn in places, as we'd expect from a nicked blade like this."

He was clearly excited by his discovery.

"So this was the murder weapon? This bayonet?"

"I would say very likely. One doesn't think of a bayonet killing someone—that is, outside of a battlefield. It's long and awkward to handle unless it's at the end of a rifle, and you don't see rifles on London streets. Either thirty years ago or today."

Frances leaned back. There was a lot to think about. She had made the mistake of underestimating her stalker, but he had also underestimated her. If the bayonet was going to be left as a warning, he clearly didn't expect her to realize it was a valuable clue.

"Dr. Grayson, you have been very helpful, and I am deeply in your debt." She took the MacKenzie folder and the bayonet and put them back in her bag.

"You're taking it back? Shouldn't the police be called to take charge of that weapon? It's an important clue."

"Of course. I have friends in the Home Office, as I said."

"But Lady Frances, you can't just walk around London with a bayonet—a possible murder weapon!" Once again, Dr. Grayson was a little overwhelmed.

"I didn't walk. I bicycled. And you can be sure that as an established consulting detective, I will take good care of it. Good day, and thank you again. I've used up a lot of your valuable time and know how busy you are, so I'll see myself out."

Feeling very pleased, she headed back to the lobby. She saw the operating theatre was still closed, and she briefly thought of slipping in and seeing what was there. But no, she had other appointments, and there would no doubt be an opportunity some other time.

For now, it was off for a visit with Mary. She retrieved her bicycle and, after checking again for stalkers, pedaled off to the Seaforth house.

Chapter 23

Cumberland greeted Frances at the door. "I am sorry for any delay in answering, my lady. I am used to hearing the sounds of horses or motorcars in front of the house, not bicycles."

"I have a bell on the handlebar. I'll try that next time," said Frances, grinning.

"I shall look forward to that, my lady. Meanwhile, her ladyship is in the morning room. If you would like some tea, I'll send some up straightaway."

It was early in the day for making calls, so Mary wasn't yet in the larger drawing room or out making calls herself. She was busy planning dinner parties that she would host and considering those she and Charles would attend, as befitted socially prominent people and Charles's senior position in government.

"Dear Franny, you are here just in time," said Mary as Frances entered the room. "Next month we're having a rather intellectual evening. The chancellor of the University of Bologna—I think that's his title—is coming, and among some government functionaries, we'll have an Oxford don or two. It should be interesting. Maybe my appetite will come back by then; this early seasonal warmth seems to have killed it. In any case, would you and Hal join us?"

"I'm sure I can say yes for both of us."

"Excellent. And since we will not need to engage any outside staff, you won't have any opportunity to get into a wrestling match with a kitchen maid." A moment later, she was laughing at the look of shock on Frances's face.

"How on earth did you know? Is it already all over London?"

"Too many witnesses, my dear. You know how gossip spreads. One brief mention to a maid, who chats with the predawn milkman, and so on. It made it to my kitchen even as breakfast was being cooked, and my maid, Garritty, with great flourish, told me the story with so much drama one would think you had been kidnapped by gypsies."

"Does Charles know?"

"He won't hear it from me. But I daresay some valet will hear it soon enough and pass it to his master, who will tease Charles about it in the hallway of some government building. I knew if you had been seriously hurt that Mallow or Hal would've called us, but I am consumed with curiosity. According to Garritty, you caught out a sneak thief in Hal's kitchen."

"Oh, if it was only that! My investigations have earned me a stalker, someone who is very unhappy even after all these years that I am trying to find Louisa Torrence. He disguised himself as a kitchen maid. But don't worry. Even though he escaped, Mallow and I gave him a thrashing he won't soon forget. And I am getting closer. I think I might know who the stalker is and perhaps why he's acting this way. Louisa remains a mystery, but bit by bit I am finding out more about her."

Mary smiled and shook her head. "I'm at loss for words. I won't tell you to stop, but I will tell you to be careful." She took a sip of tea, frowned, and put it down.

"What's wrong with it? You always have the best tea here."

"It tastes a little off somehow."

Frances looked more closely at her sister-in-law. She had always been pale and willowy, but now she seemed almost wan. And she had said something about having no appetite.

"Are you sick, Mary? Should I ring for Garritty?"

"No, please. It will pass."

Frances's eyes narrowed, then her face lit up. "Of course, you're not sick—you're with child!"

Mary laughed. "I should've known the Lady Sherlock would figure it out. I was going to tell you but didn't want to interrupt your investigations. Only Charles and I know. I haven't even told my mother yet. I imagine Garritty has guessed, but she isn't saying anything."

"This was well worth the interruption." She gave Mary a hug. "What could be more important? I am looking forward to my nephew or niece, whom I will spoil terribly."

"You'll take them to all kinds of unsuitable places and be their absolute favorite aunt." They both laughed. "But for now, I can't seem to eat anything, although I'm told in a few weeks I won't be able to stop eating."

"I'm so happy for you, my dearest friend. You can now be my source for all things maternal because my case seems to be full of maternal feelings."

"I'm not quite a mother yet," said Mary.

"Oh, but you are so very nearly, and more maternal than I will ever be. I am faced with a kind vicar, who was deeply loved and wanted by his parents. Although they have gone to their final reward, he is close to his mother's companion, a widow who seems to love him too—but perhaps too much like a woman, rather than a mother, if you take my meaning. But he's rather unworldly, and I don't think he realizes it."

"How deliciously scandalous!" said Mary.

"Exactly. The vicar's parents knew Louisa when she took refuge with them. And this widow has a child of her own and is very protective of her daughter, just a few years younger than we are. And finally, there's Lady Torrence herself, who so misses her older daughter. Mothers and motherhood keep cropping up."

"Well, I am not a detective like you, my dear, but if you want a perspective from an almost-mother, know this: mothers will do anything, things you cannot imagine, for their children."

Frances considered that. "The Greeks even had a special word for the kind of love a mother has for her children."

"And well they should. Could the passions that impel your stalker be a love you hadn't thought of?"

"You have sent me in a whole new direction, dear sister. I hadn't considered that. There is deep romantic love here, but perhaps I wasn't considering all kinds of love. This something to think about."

"Then think on your own mother."

"Really? Mine?" Frances had considered herself close to her mother, despite having been largely raised by a series of nannies, as all children in her class were. Of course, there had been battles. A lot of them.

"Yes, yours. I knew her well, you know. Do you realize how hard she fought to get your father to allow you to go to Vassar?"

"Well, I knew she was on my side, even if she didn't want to admit it," said Frances, a little uncertainly.

"She didn't want that life for you. She wanted you to stay home and marry well, not sit in a classroom on the other side of the world. It went against everything she wanted and meant that she had to stand up to your father. But she did, because it's what you wanted so much, and she loved you."

Feeling a little humbled, Frances nodded. "This has been very helpful. I need to come here more often—for your love and your common sense, which I often lack."

"Excellent. I'll be your Watson."

"I'm afraid Mallow is already Watson."

"Then I will be your landlady, Mrs. Hudson." They laughed once more.

"I must go now. I've one more call and then a suffrage meeting. Do take care of yourself."

"And you too. Your brother is so very excited. He says if it's a boy, he'll be prime minister."

Frances smirked. "I'll do my brother one better. I say, even if it's a girl, *she'll* be prime minister."

It wasn't far to Lady Freemantle's house, and the butler just said, "Very good, my lady," when Frances told him that she was leaving her bicycle just inside the front gate. Lady Freemantle received her, and Frances saw a mix of emotions play across the woman's face. The last time Frances had come, it was to reveal secrets and bring up a painful past. But it also had also given her and her husband a little hope. Now Frances was back. What was it this time?

"Please make yourself comfortable and have some tea." Lady Freemantle paused while searching for the right words, and Frances watched. It was interesting to see what Sarah's feelings were. There would be joy if Frances could find her sister. But what else would come out? "I know you work for my mother, not me, but do you have anything to tell me?" Then she smiled wryly. "Or are you here to ask me more questions?"

"I know it's terribly vulgar of me to show up again to question you about your family."

"Oh, it is—but that won't stop you, will it?" said Lady Freemantle, laughing with such good nature that Frances joined in.

"Oh, I'm afraid not, but it won't take long. I came across a name that wasn't familiar to your mother, but maybe it is to you. A name from your childhood: Bradley."

Lady Freemantle closed her eyes for a moment. "Dear lord, I haven't heard that name, or thought about it, for many years. I assume you mean Emma Bradley from Blackthorpe, in Shropshire. How did you come across that name? But don't answer. I'm sure you can't tell me, and I'm sure I don't want to know. What do you know?"

"That she was a childhood companion of your sister's. That your father discouraged the friendship. And that Emma Bradley died tragically young."

Lady Freemantle nodded. "That's the basics. I can tell you that Louisa was never happier than when we went to the country.

With our cousins and local children, a certain . . . informality was allowed, at least at first. Now I'm not a fool, and I know that it was never forgotten who lived in the manor and who lived in a thatched cottage, but when you're chasing butterflies in the field, positions in life tend to seem less important."

Frances nodded. That was true.

"So Louisa loved the country, and I was allowed to play with the local children too, although I was younger. And then . . ." She sighed. "And then my father had to intervene. He decided that Louisa was too old for such foolishness, that it was time to separate her from those in the working classes, and he banned her from playing with them. Mother pushed back, but when our father made up his mind, there was no discussion. I was too young to really understand what was going on, but Louisa discussed it with me for years afterward. She had a lot of bitterness. When we found out later that Emma had died and Louisa hadn't been allowed to go to the funeral or even been told, she was furious."

"I can understand. I don't wish to criticize your father in your own home, Lady Freemantle, but his behavior sounds unusually strict. My brother and I were allowed to socialize with the local children at our country estate."

"Don't hesitate to criticize on my account. It was terrible and unreasonable. Especially for Louisa, who was high-spirited to begin with. She spoke about it to me until the day she left. She swore she'd go back to Shropshire someday. It's odd, really, that you bring it up. It seems when she finally ran away, it was to join the stage. But I always thought her choice would have been to settle in Shropshire. I'm afraid I can't tell you any more. My mother may have forgotten the name—she may not have even known Emma's surname—but she couldn't have forgotten the event. Unless . . . unless she wanted to forget it."

Frances could see why she'd want to, the pain of seeing her daughter hurt and being unable to do anything about it.

She stood. "Thank you again for your frankness."

"Lady Frances—" Lady Freemantle hesitated, and her voice became almost a whisper. "Will I see Louisa again?"

"I cannot offer a guarantee right now. But I can tell you that I am optimistic. If Louisa lives, and I think she does, I will produce her. Thank you again, and good day." With that, she let the butler show her out.

So the friendship with Emma was a defining moment for Louisa, a disappointment she held onto for years. Why had the false Emma Lockton taken that name? It tied her somehow to Louisa, but the reasons were obscure. Was the imposter somehow an agent of Helen's, if Helen was the author of the conspiracy that let her disappear?

She thought of Mary's impending motherhood. Mothers were a theme here. Lady Torrence, losing her daughter as an adult, and Emma Bradley's mother, losing her daughter as a child. And some mother losing the baby they found in Helen's grave.

It would no doubt become clear later. Meanwhile, it was back on her bicycle to the suffrage meeting.

Chapter 24

Frances found the meeting very refreshing, giving her the chance to be among other strong and focused women. Feeling full of purpose, she pedaled back to Miss Plimsoll's. Her legs were getting weary. Bicycling was all well and good, but on a busy day, it was tiring. She had some lunch, allowed Mallow to clean her up a bit, and then they were off to the film studio in a hansom.

"Although I'm excited to see ourselves on film, I also want to talk to Genevieve D'Arcy again," said Frances. "I only thought of her as Sir Arnold's mistress, as someone who knew Helen, but now that we've grappled with our soldier, I realize I need to ask her about Alexander Braceley and Helen's other suitors. Miss D'Arcy was one of the Green Players and is the right age to have known them. The other men who signed the Oath of Tyndareus appear to be accounted for, but we don't know for a fact that Braceley died in the Sudan."

"So was that Mr. Braceley who attacked us last night, my lady?"

"Perhaps. But even if he wasn't, someone wants us to think it was him. And even if the stalker is only pretending to be Mr. Braceley, that doesn't mean that he's dead. I shouldn't have taken Mr. Rusk's and Mr. Prescott's accounts of themselves regarding Helen at face value. We need another point of view. Miss D'Arcy can provide that. She knew Helen, but she can also tell us about the rest. I'm also thinking about babies, Mallow. I know I can trust you with a secret—Lady Seaforth is expecting."

"That is wonderful news, my lady. I am most pleased to hear it."

"You and I and his lordship are the only ones who know."

"I will be most discreet, my lady."

"There is a baby in this case, Mallow. We can't forget about the infant child in Helen's grave. Who was the oversized monument for? We assumed it was for Helen, who wasn't even there. Was it for that child?"

"But why was the child so important, my lady?"

"I don't know, Mallow. Who were those child's parents?"

Mallow frowned. "And why bury him secretly, my lady?"

"That is something we must find out. Step by step, Mallow."

The hansom pulled up in front of the movie studio, and Frances and Mallow walked right in. As before, the room seemed a study in controlled chaos, with actors walking around, young women consulting their papers, and workmen dragging scenes, sets, and cameras into place. Mr. Pyecroft was giving directions, trying valiantly to maintain an authoritative air, but he smiled when he saw Frances and Mallow.

"Ladies, thank you for acting in our film, and now please join me. We have a small theatre here, and I have asked our projectionist to queue up the reel with your scene. We think it came out very well."

"We are looking forward to it," said Frances, glancing at Mallow. Her maid, as usual in a public situation, stood demurely behind her mistress, but Frances could see her eyes sparkling with excitement.

Mr. Pyecroft led them into a side room about the size of drawing room. A dozen chairs were arranged as in an auditorium, while a screen sat at the far end of the room. They looked at the projector, an intricate collection of knobs and levers, which had a spool of film already loaded. Mallow had never considered any job aside from being in service, but now she imagined being a projectionist, getting to see the pictures every day . . .

They took their seats as Mr. Pyecroft turned off the lights and started the projector. The screen flickered for a few moments—and there they were, Frances and Mallow flashing across the screen, with Mallow serving her mistress and the pair of them talking in silence. Frances heard Mallow gasp next to her, and Frances herself was a little stunned too.

The screen went dark, and the lights came back on.

"Did you like it, ladies? Very startling, isn't it, to see yourselves on a screen?"

"Yes, it is, sir," said Mallow firmly, blushing a little.

"I agree. Very exciting, Mr. Pyecroft. Thank you very much."

"And thank you both for appearing in my film." He coughed delicately. "And I do want to remind your ladyship that we are available for private showings."

Frances turned to Mallow. "Should we have my brother and sister-in-law rent out a theatre at the height of a season for a party?"

"I think that would be very popular, my lady."

She turned back to Mr. Pyecroft. "I'll talk to my brother, the marquess. For now, is your actress Miss D'Arcy around? We had a lovely conversation last time, and I would like to see her again."

"Jenny? She just finished filming for the day and probably is getting changed in her room. I'm sure she's still here."

"Thank you again," said Frances. "We know our way to the actors' rooms." They made their farewells and headed to the dressing rooms.

"So, Mallow, did you find it as exciting as I did to see yourself on the silver screen?"

"Oh, my lady, I couldn't believe it. It was like . . . magic. To watch yourself moving like that. It's like, well, being in two places at once, isn't it?"

Frances stopped. "That's a very insightful comment, Mallow." Another illusion. Helen in two places at once, in her grave and perhaps . . . wandering about somewhere? Was their attacker in two places, both stalking them in London and lying dead in the Sudan? And Mrs. Lockton, both a long-deceased child in Shropshire and the proprietress of a distinguished Bond Street shop. Frances thought about what George Bernard Shaw had told her about theatrical illusion—directors, actors, and playwrights.

"Thank you, my lady." And then, with a little hesitation, Mallow said, "Although I will not publicly discuss your investigations, my lady, would it be all right if I mentioned the filming to my friends?"

"I see no harm in that," said Frances, and Mallow lost herself for a few moments imagining telling other maids in great houses that she, June Mallow, had been in a motion picture.

When they reached the correct door, they knocked and heard someone say, "Come in."

Genevieve D'Arcy had just changed out of her costume and was adjusting her dress as they walked in.

"Oh!" she said. "The two of you again. If you have more questions, I'm afraid I told you all I know about Sir Arnold and Helen. I'm done filming for the day and will be heading home now."

"Actually, we're interested in some other members of the company, the men who loved Helen."

"They're gone, mostly, my lady. And those that are still with us are friends of long standing. I won't gossip about them now. But I do have a long trip home, so if you don't mind . . ."

Miss D'Arcy's dress was well out of fashion, and Frances had no doubt that it was kept together with careful stitching. It had been a long time since men lined up outside of her dressing room, and any gifts she had received over the years were probably being sold one by one to pay for rent and food.

"I see I've started very badly," said Frances. "I'm not here to interrogate you, but I am still trying to find Helen. I believe the men are hiding things from us, but you as a woman would know about them. So it's not sordid gossip I'm after but important memories. If it helps, I won't tell anyone what we discuss."

She saw Miss D'Arcy waver a little, and then Frances sweetened the deal. "But I'm being rude. You probably want to get home to your evening meal. If there's a place nearby you know of, I'll buy the three of us something to eat."

Miss D'Arcy's eyes lit up at that. "Seeing as you're doing this for the good of the family, my lady, it wouldn't be very nice of me to refuse you. The Nell Gwyn around the corner has a very nice steak and kidney pie with potatoes and a more than passable beer. Of course, it is quite respectable, my lady. You need not be ashamed to go there."

"I'm sure I won't," said Frances. "It sounds more than acceptable, and as it's a little early, we should be able to find a quiet table."

"Certainly, my lady," said Miss D'Arcy and, cheered at the prospect of a generous meal, grabbed her jacket and bag, and the three headed out.

"Nell Gwynn—I suppose that's a reference to the actress, as we're near so many theatres," said Frances as they walked. Her uncle, Lord Hoxley, had mentioned the name.

"Oh, yes, my lady. Something of a legend here, as you can imagine. Became mistress to the king, she did, and their son became a duke, so they say." She sighed. "Some women have all the luck."

The Nell Gwynn was better than Frances had feared. It was clean and reasonably well lit. The few midday patrons appeared to be actors, talking over drinks at the bar. A waiter seemed a little surprised to see someone of quality and quickly sat them at what was clearly the "best" table, toward the back. Mallow inspected the seats and grudgingly accepted them as suitable.

Frances and Mallow had already had lunch, so they requested some little cakes and tea, but Miss D'Arcy ordered a pint and her steak and kidney pie with a side of potatoes. Frances watched Mallow's hint of a bristle there. When women ordered beer, which shouldn't be too often, it should only be *half*-pints. But Miss D'Arcy was in too good a mood to notice.

"Miss Mallow, I owe you an apology from last we met for speaking to you so sharply. It isn't easy getting older, especially for a woman in the theatre, and so I was a little oversensitive, as they say. I want to tell you that you have a pleasing face and figure, and I have no doubt that if you had a mind to, you could do well for yourself on the stage."

Mallow wanted to say that no amount of money would ever tempt her to be actress (except for a brief film role, just to help her ladyship), but she realized this was meant to be a compliment, so she just smiled. "That is very kind of you to say, Miss D'Arcy," she said, and the actress was as pleased with the restoration of good humor as she was with the arrival of the beer.

"So, my lady, you'd be wanting to know about the men and how they made fools of themselves over Helen with some sort of oath they made—the Oath of Tyneside, I think they called it. I don't know why; we rarely traveled that far north. They thought it was secret, but there are no secrets inside a theatre."

"The name is actually . . . well, never mind," said Frances, not wanting to give Miss D'Arcy a mythology lesson. "There were half a dozen men involved. At least two are dead from natural causes in the past few years. Mr. Mattins, as you know, was killed recently."

"Yes, I was at his funeral just yesterday," Miss D'Arcy said solemnly. "He had no family, like many of us, but we all turned out from the Emerald and other theatres, so he had many to see him in the ground. We take care of our own in the theatre."

"I am pleased to hear that. He struck me as a good man, if a quiet one."

"Yes, that's the truth of it, my lady."

"But in his quiet way, he loved Helen?"

Miss D'Arcy nodded. "Yes, he did, my lady, but I would say, to be fair, he loved her almost as a father. He was somewhat older than the rest, you see. I think he felt protective of her."

"I can see that. But what about Mr. Rusk, the company manager?"

She smirked a little at that. "Oh, my lady, you see him now, a plump manager of middle years, but he was a fine man back then, still just an assistant manager. Afraid to say 'boo' to a woman as beautiful as Helen but devoted nonetheless. Indeed, most of them were like that." She snickered at the memory. "But I'd have to say, of all of them, his love was truest."

"That's interesting. What makes you say that?"

"After all this time, my lady, I can tell those who love a girl from those who just want to get her into bed. Pardon my frankness."

"On the contrary, I admire your honesty," said Frances. "And Mr. Prescott?"

"Oh, him? He couldn't shut his damn mouth."

Mallow had heard far worse words than that but not from those taking hospitality from her ladyship. Frances watched her maid's lips purse, and Miss D'Arcy looked a little embarrassed.

"Pardon me, both of you. But you should've known him. Poetry, compliments that were old back when Nell Gwynn herself was on the stage, flowers. Made quite a pest of himself with wandering hands, let me tell you. She slapped him more than once. But I don't know if he was truly serious." She shrugged.

So Prescott's description of his and Rusk's love for Helen had been accurate, thought Frances. Except that Prescott had been a little more aggressive than he had admitted. Prescott certainly sounded a lot more forward than the rest, but if Rusk really loved her . . . that could be a powerful emotion. More than mere lust.

And now for the one she really wanted to know about. "What about Alexander Braceley?"

"Ah, yes," Miss D'Arcy said. "Dear Alex. Just between the three of us here, he belonged in Bedlam."

The conversation was temporarily suspended by the arrival of the food. Frances and Mallow were left wondering why Braceley should be confined to London's infamous insane asylum while Miss D'Arcy savored her hot pie.

"He went mad?" Frances finally prompted.

"I don't think he went mad. I think he was born mad. He was always a little nervy—full of odd humors, my mother would've said. And it all came out for Helen. He worshiped the ground she walked on."

"So like Prescott?" asked Frances. But Miss D'Arcy shook her head.

"No, Prescott was irritating, but with him it was more the thrill of trying to seduce her. He took it hard when she turned him down, but I don't think he mourned over her."

"It hurt his pride, not his heart," said Frances.

"Well put, my lady. That's exactly it. But Braceley felt it deep down. He'd seat himself in front of her dressing room for hours, waiting for her to arrive. Spent all his wages on flowers for her."

"Did they act together? That is, in the same play?" Frances remembered from the program they had found that Helen and Braceley had been Romeo and Juliet—did Miss D'Arcy remember too?

"Oh, yes, my lady. They played Romeo and Juliet together. To have a Romeo who was really in love with Juliet!" She laughed.

"But Juliet didn't love Romeo."

"Well, sometimes things don't always work perfectly. Helen had to act." Then she paused. "As best she could, anyway."

Frances tried leading her to a deeper discussion of the clash of personalities. "My impression was that Prescott's pride might have been hurt that he didn't get to play Romeo."

"Oh, yes, my lady. Funny you should say that." She was enjoying her visit to the past. Everyone else she knew had already heard these stories. "Prescott thought he'd get to be Romeo, that maybe Braceley wasn't seasoned enough, as they say. But Helen said she wouldn't take the role opposite Prescott because of his behavior, so they gave him Mercutio, which I think he was better suited for anyway. But he was very upset. Took it personal, and Mr. Rusk had to calm him down."

"Helen wasn't afraid of Braceley's behavior?"

"Oh, no, my lady. He was crazy, it's true, and would even sing poems to her under her window. But he was well-behaved, and they acted well together. But I knew it was one-sided. When she married, he just went to pieces, and the next thing you knew, he had joined the army. Said he couldn't stay in the theatre anymore. Most people didn't think he was serious, but I did. And there he was off to the Sudan, and we never saw him again." She looked a little mournful and gestured to the waiter for another beer.

Frances nodded and caught Mallow's eye. Her maid wasn't impressed with anyone's behavior here.

"My understanding was that Braceley went off cheerfully when he joined the army," Frances said.

"Ha! Who told you that, my lady? Not the other men who signed that silly oath. He was furious with Helen. He felt he had been humiliated and had to run off. He said he couldn't show his face around the theatre. I remember him saying that if Helen had run off with a Duke or Earl for a soft life, he might have understood. But to turn down love like his for an accountant. He roundly cursed her and all women."

"That is a revelation," said Frances. "But tell me about this accountant. You mentioned him briefly when last we spoke, yet no one seems to know about him."

Miss D'Arcy took a healthy sip of her second pint. The alcohol would loosen her tongue, Frances realized. However, she also knew that she'd better get all her questions answered while the actress was still upright.

"Not much to say. Well-dressed, well-spoken when he spoke, which wasn't often. He took care of the money on payday. Hardly a man to stand out in a theatre full of actors. Now you, Miss Mallow. You're like me, women who work for their bread. You tell me why Helen married an accountant."

Frances watched Mallow pull herself up and order her thoughts. "An accountant is a respectable position. Steady work, as I understand it, and a good Christian life. Why take an actor if you can have an accountant? At least, that's my opinion."

"Well said!" cried Miss D'Arcy, who turned her attention to Frances. "Do you agree, my lady?"

Frances smiled. "You and Mallow have made your point clear."

Miss D'Arcy smiled sadly. "That's about it, my lady. Braceley, hurt and angry, running off to war to prove something. Rusk shrugging and marrying a hostler's daughter from down the street. Prescott licking his wounds, and the others eventually moving away, the oath forgotten." She sighed. "This has been very nice, my lady, but it's been a long day, and I should be getting home." She stood a little unsteadily.

Frances produced some money and gave it to Mallow. "You have been so helpful," she said to Miss D'Arcy. "I'd like to thank you by sending you home in a hansom. Mallow will see you into one."

"Well, you are a lady. A nice drink and meal and a hansom cab. Thank you so much." Mallow led Miss D'Arcy out of the restaurant and came back a few minutes later.

"I told the driver most particularly that he was to take Miss D'Arcy home and that she was a friend of Lady Frances Ffolkes, sister of the Marquess of Seaforth, so to treat her with full respect."

"Very nice, Mallow. Thank you. There's a bit more tea here, so let's finish and talk. We certainly got a lot of information. Miss D'Arcy didn't have such a good view of Mr. Prescott. And a decidedly less romantic view of Braceley. Love's young dream on the surface, but decidedly unbalanced."

"Romance is all well and good, my lady, but Mr. Braceley sounds more like a spoiled child."

"I agree. None of them look very good. Rusk and Prescott sticking together, putting a more romantic view of the world on display. They didn't want to make Braceley look bad, as he was one of those who signed the oath. Not going to betray him in front of each other. I expect we'd have heard something different if we had questioned them separately. That's something to remember. And one more thing—Helen humiliated both Prescott and Braceley, but it seems Rusk was able to work with her. We're going to need to speak to the actors after the show tomorrow, when they've had a drink or two and are likely to talk freely."

CHAPTER 25

The next day Frances had some calls to make on behalf of the suffrage club as well as other charities. Later, after a quick dinner, she put herself into Mallow's hands. They had earlier negotiated just how much time Mallow would need to "get her lady done proper" and how much time Frances would be willing to give her.

"I have my good dress and hat ready for myself, my lady. I confess to being excited about this."

"Oh, it will be exciting, Mallow. It's opening night, so we may see other distinguished members of society there. And of course, we have to keep our ears open at the theatre. I think there is more that we don't know. Perhaps that box we found in Mr. Mattins's room contains clues we haven't fully plumbed yet. We know the importance of the oath and the reference to the Hallidays. But what about that program? It may have been just a keepsake, but I think it was something more. Like the other two items, it was designed to say something."

"It was the same play we're seeing tonight, wasn't it, my lady? *Romeo and Juliet*."

"Yes, and that may also be significant. In fact, after our discussion with Miss D'Arcy, I'm wondering if there is more in the background we weren't told about. In fact, I'm sure of it. I think I'll drop some hints that we know more to frighten Prescott and

Rusk into making a mistake. There was a plot all those years ago, Mallow, and it's still going on."

"I will keep my ears open, my lady. Meanwhile, I read the summary of the play, as you suggested."

"What did you think?"

"Very sad, my lady. But they're not English, are they? Verona is in Italy, I believe?"

"Yes, Mallow."

"Well, that explains a lot, my lady. I'd expect the English to be better behaved."

Frances raised an eyebrow. "That's a fascinating piece of theatrical criticism. I am sure my mother would've agreed with you wholeheartedly."

"Thank you, my lady. Just one more hairpin, and you should be all ready."

They quickly found themselves a hansom cab and were off to the theatre.

"As you said, my lady, many fine people will be there tonight."

"Yes, Mallow, and we'll be among them."

"What I meant is that there won't be many personal servants in the audience."

"No," said Frances, giving her maid a grin, "and not that many suffragists either."

Mr. Rusk had left them very good seats in front of the center orchestra, amid ladies and gentlemen in fine clothes. Mallow felt a little out of place. This was a lot fancier than the music halls she attended with her friends, but no one seemed to notice or care about her appearance. The theatre was certainly a lot more casual than a drawing room.

They waited for the curtain to rise, and suddenly there was a rustle to one side. Everyone craned their necks to the see the small group entering one of the boxes—including His Majesty, King Edward VII.

"Oh, my lady. The king himself!"

"He does like theatre, and it is opening night. And that's Mrs. Keppel with him." Frances whispered to her maid that Mrs. Keppel was the king's long-term mistress. "Do you disapprove?"

"My lady," said Mallow, shocked, "I would never criticize His Majesty's choice of companion."

The lights dimmed, so there was no more time for discussion of the king's relations, as an actor walked onstage and began to recite: "Two households, both alike in dignity . . ."

The production was beautifully staged and acted. Frances enjoyed the music of the language, and Mallow paid close attention, watching each scene with great seriousness.

Prescott made an impressive Lord Capulet. He commanded all his scenes with a strong presence and a powerful, flexible voice. Frances felt a twinge during the scene where he bullied his daughter into marrying Paris. Fathers and daughters; an echo of Sir Arnold pressing his daughter to go to India to become an officer's wife. Had Sir Arnold sat in this theatre, watching this same play? Had he seen any irony in Lord Capulet's behavior—especially while trying to seduce the Juliet?

The play flew by under nimble direction, and before they knew it, the prince was saying, "For never was a story of more woe than this of Juliet and her Romeo."

Mallow applauded with great enthusiasm. "Oh, my lady. Very exciting . . . very affecting."

"I agree completely, Mallow. I look forward to telling the actors ourselves, as we've been invited to stay after for a reception."

"I should very like to meet the actress who played the nurse, my lady. She was very amusing."

The crowd dispersed, talking and gossiping. Frances and Mallow made their way to the lobby and then along the hallway to the back.

"The reception will be in the greenroom. It's where the actors gather during the play," Frances explained.

"Why is it painted green, my lady?"

"It isn't painted green."

"Then why do they call it the greenroom?"

"After we solve this mystery, Mallow, we'll devote our full attentions to that one."

Many of the actors had not yet arrived, busy taking a quick rest and cleaning off their makeup, but Rusk was in the greenroom along with a few other ladies and gentlemen—and the king and Mrs. Keppel.

"Oh!" gasped Mallow.

"You've seen the king before," said Frances.

"But as a servant, my lady. I am a guest here."

"And like me, his most loyal subject. Come."

The king's eyes roved and landed on Lady Frances.

"Dear Lady! So pleased to see you here. I hope you enjoyed it as much as Mrs. Keppel and I did."

Frances and Mallow curtsied. "Yes, we did, your Majesty," said Frances.

"I wonder how you find time for the theatre, being so busy working on suffrage for women."

"I find it very refreshing, sir, and will be able to address members of Parliament with renewed vigor the next day."

Mrs. Keppel laughed. "Well said, Lady Frances." She greeted Frances warmly. "I enjoy meeting you again. Wit binds together all members of your family."

"You are too kind, Mrs. Keppel. May I present my friend, Miss June Mallow." Mallow was standing in Frances's shadow, never expecting to be introduced, but she was equal to the task.

"Your Majesty. Mrs. Keppel," she said and curtsied again.

"Did you enjoy the play as well, Miss Mallow?" asked Mrs. Keppel.

"It was very full of emotion, Mrs. Keppel," said Mallow.

The working-class accent and simple clothes identified Mallow as a servant, but Mrs. Keppel pretended not to notice: If Lady Frances chose to bring her maid to opening night at the

Emerald, that was just another one of her eccentricities, and nowhere near the most egregious.

Frances started to take her leave, but first the king said, "Have your brother send me another invitation. The conversation was amusing, and his cook was unparalleled with game meats." Frances said she would. They stepped away, but not before Frances caught a look on Rusk's face. She had impressed him. Oh, he had known she was of the aristocracy, but being in a position where she could banter with the king . . .

Actors were beginning to show up. Junior cast members set up a table with drinks and food, and people spilled into the hallway and onto the backstage.

Mallow dabbed at her forehead. "Did I . . . was I correct, my lady?"

"I was the one who jested with the king about suffrage, and you ask if you were correct?" Frances laughed, and Mallow looked relieved. "But let's not forget we came here to work. We need to talk to the actors and see if we can pick up any gossip. I'd be surprised if we didn't, what with Mr. Mattins's recent death. And I have a feeling that Helen's spirit hovers over this play. I do want a private word with Mr. Rusk. And over there, unless I miss my guess, is the actress playing the nurse. Go over and introduce yourself."

"What shall I say, my lady?"

"Start with a compliment. Actors can never get enough compliments. I see Mr. Rusk has left the king and Mrs. Keppel to speak with some of the other actors. Time to get to work. I'm sure this has been a difficult period for the surviving signatories of the Oath of Tyndareus, and gossip and rumors may have spread after Mr. Mattins's death. Be sure to help yourself to a glass of wine. I'm sure it's little better than vinegar, but we want to look relaxed."

"Very good, my lady."

Even at a party where the king was in attendance, Mr. Rusk was busy. She found him upstage in a relatively quiet spot, talking to a couple of stagehands. As they departed, Frances approached him.

"Theatre work is never finished, is it, Mr. Rusk?"

He forced a smile. "A few things have to be fixed before tomorrow's curtain. I hope you enjoyed the show, my lady?"

"Very much. I came specifically to thank you for the tickets. Nimbly directed, handsomely staged, and every performance was gripping."

He laughed. "What a wonderful line. I wish you were a theatre critic."

"If I were, I would single out Mr. Prescott. It's not a large role, but he commanded the stage in all his scenes. He played very well with Juliet."

"Thank you. He's aged rather nicely into paterfamilias roles, although I believe he still wishes he could play romantic young leads as he used to. He did a very good Henry V once."

"I can imagine. Once upon a time, I believe he was a very commanding suitor to Helen. More than you led me to believe. Made quite a nuisance of himself, so I heard."

Mr. Rusk looked uncomfortable. "May I ask who told you that?"

"Actors are terrible gossips, as I'm sure you're aware. Still, the real surprise is what I've heard about Alexander Braceley. If Mr. Prescott was annoying, Mr. Braceley sounds mad by all accounts. A love that intense can lead to a bad end. But again, I'm stating the obvious—look at the play we just saw."

Rusk was now even more nervous and ran his finger under his collar. "My lady, this was all many years ago. I can't recall the details after all this time. But can I ask if you've made any progress in your search for Helen?"

"Oh, yes. That's why I was asking about Mr. Braceley. It's part of the lore that no one came home from the Sudan campaign, but we don't know that really, do we?"

"What could that possibly have to do with Helen?"

"Mr. Mattins is dead. I wonder who killed him?"

"That was a robbery, my lady. That's what the police said."

"Police? Who's talking about police?" It was Prescott, and on his arm was the actress who played his wife, Lady Capulet. Frances noted that her face was strong with sharp cheekbones, so she probably didn't get the ingénue roles. Frances thought she'd make a great Lady Macbeth.

Rusk seemed to welcome the interruption. "Nothing at all," he said, dismissing the police talk. "Lady Frances, this is Edith Lasalle, our Lady Capulet."

"I enjoyed both your performances. The deep and complex relationships among the Capulets made for some very poignant scenes," said Frances, and both actors were pleased with their compliments. Seeing their arms were linked, Frances thought to tweak them. "I am glad the two of you seem to have a greater friendship than Lord and Lady Capulet, however."

"How observant of you, my lady," said Prescott. "Because we do have such a deep appreciation for each other, it requires all our acting skills to pretend we have a coolness onstage."

"Oh, don't listen to him, my lady," said Miss Lasalle. "He's only being affectionate with me because the actress who plays Juliet won't have anything to do with him."

Prescott fought looking irritated at that.

"What a shame," said Frances. "You don't seem to have much luck with Juliets, do you?" She saw a flash of anger, but it was gone in a second. Her eyes quickly turned to Rusk, who was also unhappy. Miss Lasalle looked confused. Of course—she probably hadn't even been born when the oath was signed.

"Luck with Juliets?" Miss Lasalle asked.

"Only that he doesn't get along with either the actress or the character," said Frances. She realized that she had upset both Prescott and Rusk. Good. She wanted them off-balance. Someone had been hunting her, and the secrets were lost in the origins of the oath.

"But we should speak of Romeo too," said Frances. "He was exceedingly appealing. One could see why Juliet fell in love."

"I may be accused of being immodest," said Prescott. *Oh, really,* thought Frances. "But when we did the play some thirty years ago, I daresay I was a most ardent Romeo." He looked at Frances, as if daring her to disagree.

"You weren't Romeo then. You were Mercutio. Braceley was Romeo," said Rusk with a weary patience.

"I was Romeo," Prescott said insistently. "We decided Braceley wasn't quite ready to play Romeo."

"You were Mercutio. You twisted your ankle during your death scene rehearsal, and we were nervous you wouldn't be ready for opening night."

"I won't argue it. It's pointless. But I was Romeo. You don't think I remember each role?"

Rusk shook his head. "I ought to thank His Majesty again for coming," he said, looking to leave. Then he glanced at the stagehands toward the back, who were fixing some sets. "But someone needs to keep an eye on them until we can properly replace Mattins."

Frances's mind worked furiously. She saw Rusk and Prescott lock eyes. They wanted to get rid of Miss Lasalle and talk about Frances's comments, and Frances saw an advantage in keeping them there. As she well knew, it was easy to hide if you knew how.

Her eyes darted around.

"The king will no doubt exit through here," said Frances. "If you want to be sure not to miss him, just move a little downstage. You'll see the stagehands and can be sure not to miss the king."

"I suppose you're right," Rusk said. "I thought he might want to leave through the alley door to avoid the crowds, but they'd be dispersed by now."

"Meanwhile, please excuse me. I do want to find and compliment the rest of your cast. Thank you again." And she left them, the men looking just a little astonished.

Chapter 26

Mallow did compliment the actress who played the nurse, pleasing her with the praise. Seeing her up close, Mallow realized she was much younger than she had seemed onstage. Makeup had tricked the audience. London was full of maids working to make their aged mistresses look younger, but here the opposite happened. It was a different world.

Before she could engage the actress in further conversation, however, an actor came by and gave the nurse a kiss, and with laughter they ran off. Things didn't happen like this in the drawing rooms of good houses, that was certain.

But Mallow wasn't alone long. A few moments later, she saw Mrs. Mancini, the costume supervisor she had helped earlier.

"Miss Mallow, I'm so pleased you and your mistress could come. And fancy that, the king and Mrs. Keppel showing up again. It's always exciting when royalty attends. Did you enjoy the play?"

"Very much so," said Mallow, "and so did her ladyship."

"I'm so pleased. His Majesty seemed entertained as well." She sighed. "It was hard to pull it off, I don't mind saying, without Mr. Mattins. He was so good at organizing everything, and also there was a lot of sadness about his passing. But Mr. Rusk said the production would be a tribute to him so we'd all pull together. And everyone did. Even the actors, and let me tell you, getting actors to behave is something."

"Yes, that was very sad about Mr. Mattins. Have the police made any arrests?"

"No. We're all guessing it was just a chance robbery. But Mr. Rusk has been powerfully affected by it. He even hired extra porters to watch the doors—said he was afraid of criminals pushing into the theatre. I thought it was a little strange. No one is going to do anything when the place is packed with people. But men get cautious as they get older."

"It does sound strange," said Mallow. "Did Mr. Prescott also get nervous? I know he is also older, and he seemed to be a particular friend of Mr. Rusk's."

"Funny you should mention it, Miss Mallow. He wasn't worried about that, but he has been very nervy too, of late. The young man you saw play Romeo tonight? Well, I'm sure you noted that there's a fair amount of swordplay, and there was some frustration that young Romeo wasn't as convincing as he might've been. So quietly after rehearsal, just yesterday, he asked Mr. Prescott if he'd show him some pointers with the sword—apparently because he was good with weaponry. Well, Mr. Prescott screamed that he was insulted—who was spreading the word that he knew anything about blades?—and that he wasn't a damned fighting instructor, if you'll pardon my language. He said he didn't want to hear any more about blades. He was so loud, people came running. Poor Romeo slunk off, and Mr. Rusk had to take him aside to soothe him."

Mallow wrinkled her nose. "But why get so upset? It sounds like Romeo was complimenting Mr. Prescott by asking for his advice. The late marquess, her ladyship's father, took great pride in his shooting during hunts, they say, and was tickled when young men spoke with him about improving their skills."

Mrs. Mancini shrugged. "I agree. Maybe Mr. Prescott was feeling old and saw an insult where there wasn't one. He is no longer young enough to play the active roles as the young men do. Actors don't like getting old."

"Neither do gentlemen," said Mallow.

Mrs. Mancini shook her head. "It's different in the theatre, dearie. The gentlemen you know, running their estates and serving in Parliament—well, they can still do that when they get old. But there are things actors, no matter how good, can't do any more once they get old, and they feel that."

That made sense to Mallow, but she was thinking about weapons, Mr. Rusk suddenly posting guards in the theatre, and Mr. Prescott getting so upset because he was seen to be knowledgeable about swordsmanship. Her ladyship would find that very interesting, Mallow was sure.

"Ah, well," said Mrs. Mancini. "There's always a lot of fuss when you're working with actors. It's hard to tell when they're acting and when they're just behaving like children. Anyway, I only came to catch a look at the king. There are seams to fix before tomorrow's show—"

As she said that, Susan Lockton appeared. She seemed surprised and a little dismayed to see Mallow, but she didn't admit to knowing her in front of Mrs. Mancini.

"I was just looking for you, Mrs. Mancini. Did you want me to start on those hems?"

"Yes, please. And I'll probably have more." She turned back to Mallow. "A pleasure to see you again. Although I know you have a good position, if you ever want a job at the theatre, just come by."

"Thank you, Mrs. Mancini." But she would never consider it. Lady Frances may be unusual, but the theatre was a madhouse.

Mrs. Mancini left, but Susan hung back, saying she wanted to see if she could grab a peek at the king. When they were alone, she said to Mallow, "Please don't tell my mother I was working here again. She thinks I'm visiting some cousins, who support me in this."

Mallow didn't approve of lying, especially to mothers, but lord knew she had helped her ladyship evade her mother many times . . .

"I will be discreet, and so will her ladyship," said Mallow.

"Oh, thank you, Miss Mallow. Every shilling I earn will go to buying a dress shop."

Or provide a dowry to marry a vicar, thought Mallow. She watched Susan turn and stride back to the workroom. Meanwhile, Mallow headed toward the stage, where she had last seen Lady Frances, but her mistress was already rapidly approaching her.

"Mallow, come with me. We have had a bit of luck. If I played my cards right, we will be able to eavesdrop on Mr. Rusk and Mr. Prescott."

"Eavesdropping again, my lady?" She hadn't forgotten hiding in the closet in Mr. Mattins's room.

"It's the wonderful thing about theatres, Mallow. There are lots of places to hide."

"Very good, my lady. I found out some interesting things."

"Good. Tell me while we walk." Mallow quickly summarized her talk with Mrs. Mancini.

"Very good. So they're frightened and on edge. Mr. Rusk is worried about security, apparently for no reason. And Mr. Prescott is unaccountably nervous when blades come into conversation." She frowned. "Did Mrs. Mancini say exactly when Mr. Prescott got so upset about swordplay?"

"Just yesterday, my lady."

"Ah. So after we foiled the attack at Mr. Wheaton's house. That is very telling."

"Oh, and Susan Lockton is here, my lady, sneaking around her mother to work on the costumes. I told her we'd keep her secret."

"You told her you'd tell an untruth?" teased Frances.

"In Proverbs, my lady, the Bible talks about the virtuous woman, saying, 'She seeketh wool, and flax, and worketh willingly with her hands.' We're just helping Miss Lockton live a virtuous life."

"I don't think there's a theologian alive who could dispute your reasoning," said Frances.

She led them to a staircase, but not the one that led up to the storage rooms. This one went down to the basement.

"What's down here, my lady?"

"Every theatre has a space below the stage. It helps move scenery and allows actors to appear suddenly through hidden doors in the floor. Now it's going to be dim in here, and we risk being overheard, so let's walk carefully."

The room reminded Mallow of the basement at the Seaforth country manor, where she had occasionally had to go to fetch something when she had been a housemaid. It was low ceilinged and dusty, filled with boxes of what seemed to be carpentry tools and some old furniture no one knew what to do with. A stab of light at the far end provided the only illumination. It took Mallow a few moments to get her bearings. The light was coming from a hooded box she saw at the front of the stage. There were a few rickety stairs that led to it.

"It's called the prompter box," whispered Frances, following her gaze. "It's for the director to help the actors with their lines without the audience knowing. If I worked things out right, Mr. Rusk and Mr. Prescott are talking just above us, and we can overhear them. We'll sit on those steps. With two pairs of ears, we should be able to catch everything."

It was clear "Lady Capulet" was still talking with Mr. Rusk and Mr. Prescott, and Frances was hoping she'd leave so the two men could talk about what was no doubt on their minds. There were a few minutes of catty gossip about who had missed a line or stumbled over an entrance, and then they heard her laugh and say, "I'm going to find some of that awful wine you bought." Her footsteps faded away overhead.

It didn't take too long for the men to get to the heart of the matter.

"What the hell was that about you playing Romeo? You damn well know you played Mercutio," said Rusk. "Did that have to do with the tantrum you threw over the fencing lessons?"

"The boy was an idiot. I'm not his assistant."

"Don't play games with me of all people," said Rusk, and Frances heard real menace in his voice. "You and I were boys together in this theatre, but that doesn't give you carte blanche." She didn't hear anything immediate from Prescott. Perhaps he had shrugged.

"It's just nerves," he eventually said. "Mattins is dead, and Lady Frances keeps asking questions, poking around. I thought she was just bored, making excuses to visit a theatre, but she keeps coming back."

"I noticed," said Rusk dryly. "I gave her tickets and an invitation but never thought she'd stay after the performance. And she wasn't bluffing about her connections. Her brother is a powerful government minister, and she's close enough to the king and Mrs. Keppel to feel comfortable joking with them. Worse, she knows something. She was taunting us."

"Just showing off some gossip she picked up backstage. You know what those toffs are like."

Frances heard Mallow tense up. Insults, even overheard, were not to be borne.

There was a long pause, and Frances was afraid they were leaving, but then Rusk continued, "Do you think he came back?"

"Who?"

"Braceley, of course. We never had proof he died, and he was mad on his best day. Can you imagine what he'd be like after the Sudan campaign if he managed to find his way back to England?"

"Are you saying you think he killed Mattins? That's why you hired extra porters?" Frances heard doubt in Prescott's voice, but also fear. A mad ex-actor with a soldier's training was something to be frightened of.

Rusk didn't answer him. "Do you know who visited me yesterday? The Reverend Samuel Halliday."

"Halliday? You mean that group that keeps trying to drag us off to church? I knew they were still around, but I thought the Hallidays themselves were long gone."

"It's their son. He's not involved directly in the mission, but he asked if I knew anything about Helen. Apparently, she was close to his parents. Said he'd heard some new information and was trying to locate her."

That was interesting, thought Frances. She had inadvertently excited the Reverend Halliday's curiosity. Or perhaps he was worried about damage to his family's reputation just like Emma Lockton had been. Was the Helen connection the real reason she didn't want her daughter at the Emerald?

"So what?" asked Prescott.

"He was discreet, but vicars have trouble lying. Just like actors have trouble telling the truth." Rusk laughed without humor. "He kept talking about her in the past tense—like she was dead. Why would he think that if he didn't know? She'd only be in her fifties. And why is anyone showing up at all?"

Of course, thought Frances. *The actors still imagined Helen living abroad with her husband. Only the Reverend Halliday knew she was buried, or should have been buried, in Maidstone. And he wouldn't give that away to the actors, having promised his parents he would be discreet.*

The men shifted, and Frances heard a dramatic sigh from Prescott. "For a man who's not an actor, you certainly have a lively imagination," said Prescott.

"And even for an actor, you're not being very bright. Some of us have more to do than read a few lines and chase girls young enough to be our daughters. Did you know who our new masters are?"

"Some city gents. Who cares?"

"I had to ask around a lot and call in some favors. It's a syndicate led by a very wealthy peer, Lord Freemantle. And guess who he is? The son-in-law of the late Sir Arnold Torrence, who had half the actresses in the company."

Prescott laughed. "That's funny. I wonder if this Lord Torrence knows? For God's sake, Gil, you know how many gents have worked their way through the female company here. It would be odd if our owners did *not* have a connection. You know how close and tight Society is. Mattins spooked you. And me too, I admit it. But that's all."

There was another moment of silence before Rusk said, "I searched his room, afterward. It was locked. You know he kept it locked. But I didn't find anything."

"You didn't? I'd have thought he'd have saved something about Helen. He was very sentimental, despite his behavior. You can't think Braceley killed him for some reason after all these years and then stole something from his room."

"Killed him? Maybe he came back to avenge him."

"Gil, do you know something you're not telling me?"

"Me? I'm an honest man." Rusk's voice was heavy with sarcasm. "You're the actor. What are *you* hiding? Would either of us even know what Braceley might look like after all these years?"

There was the sound of another pair of shoes on the floor, a light tread, probably belonging to a woman.

"Excuse me, Mr. Rusk." It was Susan Lockton. "I do sewing for Mrs. Mancini, and she wanted me to tell you we're almost done with the hemming and she'll do those new sleeves tomorrow."

"What? Oh, yes. Fine. Tell her thanks. Tomorrow is soon enough for the sleeves."

"Very good, sir," she said, and they heard her walk away.

"Who was that?" asked Prescott.

"You heard her—one of Mrs. Mancini's seamstresses."

"I mean, what is her name?"

"Sally? Susan? There's always an army of them in and out. Why—? Oh, God, Quentin. It's bad enough what you do with the actresses, but leave the respectable girls alone. I mean it. I don't need any more problems, like Mrs. Mancini yelling at me that decent seamstresses won't work here anymore." The tone carried the full weight of the company manager.

"Don't be ridiculous—although she is a lovely thing. That's not what I meant. Didn't she remind you of someone? Perhaps she's some actress's sister or niece or something?"

"And if she is? So what? Look—there's the king's equerry. His Majesty will probably be following. Change and go home, Quentin. And be careful."

"You too, Gil." There was no word or movement for a few moments. Frances imagined both men looking at each other, wondering what the other one knew. After a few seconds, footsteps departed in different directions, and then there was nothing.

Frances hadn't realized how tense she was, concentrating so hard on the conversation. Mallow, now that they were alone, made herself busy brushing cobwebs off them both.

"We have a lot to think about," said Frances, "but let's do our thinking in our comfortable rooms instead of below the Emerald stage." She giggled. "If some stagehand finds us here, I don't think we'll get away with claiming we got lost on our way to the front door."

CHAPTER 27

With all the security due to the king's attendance, Frances didn't expect any attack when they left the theatre. There were plenty of hansoms, and soon they were back in their rooms. After their good dresses were hung up nicely, Frances got out the biscuits, Mallow made the tea, and then they put their feet up in their sitting room.

"A very entertaining evening, Mallow. And a very profitable one. Both Mr. Rusk and Mr. Prescott think Mr. Braceley has come back. Or they want the other one to think so. And we've upset the Reverend Halliday."

"He seems like such a good man, my lady," said Mallow, sorry that they had disturbed a vicar.

"I believe he is, Mallow, but we may have touched on some sensitive family history. Something can be embarrassing without being in any way sinful. We're making the surviving signatories of the oath increasingly nervous. They're *afraid* that Mr. Braceley has come back. Mallow, aside from those we've directly upset from our investigations, have you ever been afraid of someone trying to avenge themselves on you?"

"Certainly not, my lady."

"Because you have led a good and virtuous life. But what if Mr. Rusk and Mr. Prescott have not? Their agreement was based on an ancient Greek oath. The Greeks spoke of a sort of avenging angels, the Erinyes, or Furies, which were hideous creatures who attacked those who committed grave crimes, tormenting them to death."

Mallow suppressed a shudder. "They sound terrifying, my lady."

"Oh, they were. The Greeks believed in vengeance, Mallow, and they didn't forget. Not for years, not for generations, and one of the worst crimes was breaking an oath." Frances had seen pictures of the Furies, but there was no reason they couldn't wear the uniform of a soldier of the Suffolk Rifles and mete out punishment with a bayonet. Or avenge a death with one.

They drank their tea in silence. Frances's mind wandered to a remark Mallow had made the previous day about how a motion picture let one person be in two places at once. There had been a lot of that, and the same thoughts kept going through her mind: Helen buried in Maidstone but quite possibly alive elsewhere. Emma Lockton née Bradley, a dead child in Shropshire and running a fine shop on Bond Street. Mr. Braceley, who should have died with the rest of his battalion in the Sudan but was possibly running around with a bayonet in London.

Actors were like that, and not just film actors. They changed clothes and masks, moved from one side of the stage to the other without the audience seeing them, rising or disappearing from the stage. She thought not of Romeo and Juliet but of Rosalind from *As You Like It*, one of her favorite Shakespearian heroines. A strong, resourceful woman, she spent much of the play disguised as a boy. Of course, as Mr. Rusk had reminded her, before the Restoration, men had played women's roles. So Rosalind would've been a male actor, playing the role of a woman pretending to be a boy.

The kitchen maid. Frances and Mallow had been threatened by a man dressed as a woman.

Frances got up and fetched the program from the old staging of *Romeo and Juliet*, the one starring Helen. What an odd argument to have after all these years—whether Mr. Prescott had played Romeo or Mercutio. Was he that vain?

"Mallow, we thought that Mr. Mattins's secret was the oath. But what if that wasn't all? The items in this box were important because they were essential clues. They led us to the Hallidays and the rest of the signatories of the oath. But what about the program? It doesn't really tell us anything. I mean, everyone knew Helen played Juliet. We would've found that out. But what if there is something else? Something to do with Mr. Prescott playing Mercutio. We did find out that Helen prevented him from playing Romeo."

"Was he embarrassed, my lady?"

"Perhaps, even after all these years. But why try to make everyone forget? Was it aimed at me? What is special about Mercutio? He dies in the play, of course."

"It seemed that by the end, half the cast was dead, my lady," said Mallow, a little disapprovingly. "I kept count: Mercutio, Tybalt, Paris, Romeo, and Juliet."

"Oh, Mallow, you've hit on it! Yes, but Mercutio was first; he was first to die. Fairly early in act three." She grabbed some other papers in the case file she had assembled, and Mallow saw the unmistakable smile of triumph on her ladyship's face.

"Have you figured it out, my lady?"

"I've figured out a lot, Mallow. What a horrible situation this was. You were right when you noted that the inhabitants of Verona did not behave like Englishmen—there is something very un-English about all this. But there is one thing I still haven't figured out . . ."

She sat back down in her chair and smiled ruefully. "The reason we started all this. Where is Helen? I bet Emma Lockton knows, but she's sharp and tough—I'll never get anything out of her. She's the gatekeeper here, I sense. Her name connects her to Shropshire. Let's say that somehow Louisa ended up there—she told her sister that's where she'd be happy. So I can't force something out of Mrs. Lockton. Let's say Mrs. Lockton's 'stolen' name,

Emma Bradley, is a hint of some kind that this is really about Shropshire; then perhaps Louisa has been in Shropshire for all these years, and Mrs. Lockton is the only one who knows under what name Louisa is living. We can't frighten Mrs. Lockton or she'll get word to Louisa, and she'll disappear again—for good. It's maddening. Still, if I'm to be thwarted, Mallow, I take some perverse pride that it's by a woman. We need to attack from another angle."

"So who will you visit next, my lady?"

"We may need another visit to the Reverend Halliday. I think he knows something. He's more curious than I expected him to be."

"You mean he's hiding something, my lady?"

"Not intentionally, Mallow. Remember that fuss in Seaforth Manor when it was discovered that the gamekeeper's daughter was with child?"

"Very clearly, my lady," said Mallow, pursing her lips. "I can't say many of us were surprised belowstairs. Anyway, she wouldn't name the father, and the gamekeeper was most wrathful. Even the vicar was afraid to intervene." The gamekeeper was about six and a half feet tall with fists like battering rams, and it took all of Charles's diplomatic skills to soothe the man. Still, the girl protected her lover's identity.

"It was old Mrs. Weldon who knew, even though she didn't realize she knew. Half-dotty she was by then, talking about nice young Davey Pribble, who always waved hello to her at her cottage door on his way over the stream. The thing was, there was nothing on the other side of the stream except the gamekeeper's cottage. And she said he waved to her day after day. She knew, Mallow, but didn't put it together."

"I see, my lady. She couldn't draw a conclusion, as you say."

"Exactly. And I'm afraid that time I drew my conclusion a little too quickly and vocally." Indeed, it had taken Charles and two undergardeners to hold back the enraged gamekeeper. The incident had been a lesson to Frances in *how* information was to be revealed. A lesson that Charles later told Frances he hoped she had learned well.

"For all that, my lady, it was a most jolly country wedding, and the baby boy no less handsome for having been born just seven months after."

"Yes, it was. So tomorrow we will visit my cousin, Archdeacon Ffolkes."

"I beg your pardon, my lady; I thought you said we were going to visit the Reverend Halliday."

"Yes. But as an archdeacon, my cousin should know something about the Reverend Halliday. I think that we will try to find some background about him first. Who knows what we're missing here? Even the Reverend Halliday may not know what he knows. For example, he was a missionary in Africa—and that's where Mr. Braceley served. The archdeacon may have some connections we can draw on."

"Do you think, my lady, he will feel inclined to help us?" Her voice was full of hesitation.

"That will be the difficult part, Mallow. You'll come with me, of course. The Venerable Michael Ffolkes seemed impressed with your devotion to prayer. Everyone seems to have one piece of the puzzle. And I'm thinking there's just one left. We'll find it, even if the person who has it doesn't even realize it."

Chapter 28

Mallow felt that getting ready to visit an archdeacon in the diocesan offices was at least equal to a dinner in one of the great London houses.

"Modest is good enough, Mallow. I don't have to look . . . elaborate."

"I would think 'Sunday best' would apply here, my lady," she replied with just a hint of censure.

"But it's not Sunday, and we're going to an office, not a church."

"As you wish, my lady," said Mallow stiffly. Then came the counterattack: "But it wouldn't be respectful to not do your hair up proper, my lady."

"Yes, Mallow."

And then it was off to the archdeacon's office.

Archdeacon Ffolkes occupied a suite that was as sedate as Hal's law office if a little less elegant, as befitted a religious setting.

"Lady Frances Ffolkes, here to see my cousin, the archdeacon," Frances told the archdeacon's soberly dressed clerk, who guarded the inner sanctum, "if he has a few minutes."

"Of course, my lady. I will see."

It turned out that, yes, the archdeacon was available, and he came out himself. "Franny, a lovely surprise. You aren't here to drag me into another exhumation, are you?"

"Not at all—well, in a way. We do need your assistance with a related manner. Could Mallow and I see you in your office?"

He raised an eyebrow. "I am consumed with curiosity. And filled with dread. Come in; we'll have some tea and see what we can do."

Archdeacon Ffolkes had a large office, a little disorganized with a few piles of paper. But the pride of place was given to a large leather-bound Bible within easy reach. He invited Frances and Mallow to take seats as he settled behind his desk, and a few minutes later, the clerk from the front office served them tea.

"So are you going to tell me you solved the mystery of the grave?" the archdeacon asked with a smile.

"I quite honestly don't know. But if I ask for your help, you deserve the details. The grave was supposed to be the last resting place of an actress named Helen, which was an assumed name. The last place she had been known to reside was in the care of a couple named Halliday, who at that time lived in Maidstone. By all accounts, they were a good Christian couple. The last we know, or believe we knew, was that she died of a fever. The Hallidays are long gone, of course, but they left two legacies, so to speak."

"The first, their mission to the theatre community. I know of it. Good work." The Venerable Ffolkes chuckled. "A rather Sisyphean task, but in my profession, we are obliged to take a long view. The second is their son, the Reverend Samuel Halliday, in Wimbledon, I believe."

"I'm impressed. How do you know that?"

"Oh, yes, how do we poor men manage to stumble through life, how do we run the Church of England, without the brilliant Franny Ffolkes leading the way?"

"Very amusing," she said.

The Venerable Ffolkes looked at Mallow. "Tell me. Has your mistress ever been wrong?"

Would Mallow lie to a senior church official? wondered Frances.

"In my experience, sir, she has quickly corrected any errors she made."

"Nicely answered. Honest yet loyal. Very well. Yes, I know of the Reverend Halliday. Well-regarded for his mission work. He apparently delivers a good sermon and is assiduous in his duties but not ambitious. He seems content to be a parish priest and has a legacy from his parents that makes life comfortable for him. He isn't married but has dined frequently at the home of a prominent barrister who has an eligible daughter. Anything there to help you?"

Frances folded her arms across her chest and frowned. "No. There has to be something else, something hidden. I will need to speak with him directly, of course, but I need to know where to start. There must be something unusual there."

"Are you looking for gossip or scandal? There are details about the priests I oversee that I can't share, but I can tell you that there has never been a hint of any impropriety about him. Does that disappoint you?"

"No. It's not him. It's his family. It's something that may have come down to him. His birth was . . . dramatic," she said, thinking of him coming into the world as Helen was leaving it.

"Indeed? You're ahead of me. I generally don't enquire into the birth of our priests. That you know something about it, oddly enough, doesn't surprise me. Appalls me, but doesn't surprise me."

"He related it to me himself. He was the only child born late in life to an unwell mother who was unusually old to bear a first child. The night he was born, a family friend, Helen—the actress I mentioned—was dying. Do you know the Reverend Halliday visits her grave?"

"A vicar who visits the grave of a family friend with no one to mourn her. What an odd task for a man of God to perform," he said sarcastically.

"But, dear cousin, his mother had to have known Helen wasn't there."

He spread his hands out. "I'm an archdeacon, not a detective. That's your profession. His parents knew, and they're with God. We have no knowledge that the Reverend Halliday knows anything. How can we guess what secret shame or fear caused his parents to bury a coffin with a nameless child? But they didn't tell their son, or somehow, they meant to, but it never happened. I am sorry, Franny, I know you want to—"

"'The Musgrave Ritual,'" she said.

"I beg your pardon?"

"A Sherlock Holmes story. A ritual that leads to buried treasure is passed down over the years, but at some point, the meaning is lost and all they have is nonsensical words until Holmes figures it out."

"You are free to ask the Reverend Halliday if his parents gave him a ritual."

"I doubt it. But the Reverend Halliday was given something—he was given a name. Samuel. I remember now. There something odd about Samuel's birth in the Bible, wasn't there?"

Again, the archdeacon tweaked Frances by appealing to her maid. "Mallow, I'll wager you know the story of Samuel. Could you relate it for your mistress?"

"Oh, yes, sir. A very nice story it is. His mother was sad because she was barren, so she prayed and cried at the great temple in Jerusalem. A priest upbraided her, thinking she was drunk at the temple of all places. But she told him she was just upset because she was childless, and the priest felt bad because he saw she was a good and pious woman. She even said that if she had a son, she'd give him to the service of the temple when he was old enough, and the priest added his prayers to hers. And soon she found she was with child and did as she promised, and he became the great prophet Samuel."

"Nicely done, Mallow," said the archdeacon. "Accurate in all respects." Frances turned and gave her maid a quick wink and smile.

"As a reward that at least *one* of you here knows something of the Old Testament, I will bestow on you one more piece of knowledge," said the archdeacon. "I don't know if this helps, but the name Samuel comes from Hebrew, meaning, 'God has heard.'"

Inspiration hit Frances, and she practically jumped out of her chair. "But that's the epitaph on the gravestone! Didn't you see it? I thought it odd and wondered what meaning it could have. 'God Has Heard.'"

"Remember, Frances, I only saw the gravesite at night, and the light was focused on the pit, not the stone," Archdeacon Ffolkes said.

"But have you ever seen that phrase on a tombstone?" The archdeacon shook his head. "And yet there it was, a reference to Samuel. But Samuel—that is, Samuel Halliday—lives. But how? It doesn't . . . but there must be . . ." She lapsed into thought, as if Mallow and her cousin weren't even there.

The archdeacon chuckled again but not unkindly. "I can't help you, but I know you will figure it out, dear cousin. When you get on a horse, you ride it to the end." He paused and then laughed loudly. "I didn't think what I was saying—what a perfect reference. I'm thinking now of your attempt at steeplechase as a girl. It was horrifying, but I admired you for it. Mallow, did your mistress ever tell you about the time she dressed in her brother's clothes, hopped on his horse, and took him on a gallop? It took half the grooms in the county to catch her."

"A slight exaggeration," said Frances.

"I confess, sir, that that particular event was much discussed belowstairs."

"I'm sure it was," said the archdeacon. "Franny, you'll be glad to hear that the bloodline from Seaforth Star continues. That rich brown coat and fine spirit remains in his descendants. You can't hide a good bloodline. I know, with the exception of that stunt, that you have little interest in horses, but even you could easily tell all the horses who trace their ancestry back to Seaforth Star. They all look of a kind. When next you travel to Seaforth Manor, do make a visit to the stables."

Frances stood. "I will. And thanks for your expert advice today. I had hoped for more, but that's hardly your fault. I know now that the Hallidays did send a message, however subtle, to their son. I can use that to capture his interest, and together, we can . . . we can proceed." She had been going to say, "force something out of Emma Lockton." Emma, whose name also sent a message, from Shropshire. But there was no need to involve her cousin in all of that. "Come, Mallow. We have work to do. We're almost there." They made their good-byes, and the amused archdeacon saw them out. A few moments later, the two women were in a hansom back to their rooms.

"Was my ill-advised riding adventure really the subject of talk belowstairs, Mallow? I was just making a point, even as a little girl, that having to ride sidesaddle was unfair."

"It was discussed, my lady, but always in a respectful tone, and the general thought was that your performance was most impressive." *There was also a healthy dose of pity for your parents*, Mallow thought but did not say.

Frances laughed. "I'm pleased to hear it. Maybe the next time we travel down to the estate, I'll see if I recognize any of the horses. As my cousin said, you can't disguise a bloodline."

Bloodlines, Frances thought. Horses apparently looked like their parents. Well, why not? People often did. For example, everyone knew Frances was her mother's daughter. People looked alike. Hair color, a pleasing face. A handsome vicar. The beautiful Susan Lockton and her plain mother. The picture on Frances's uncle's candy box—"chocolate-box prettiness." The handsome horses on the Seaforth estate. Would Mary and Charles's child favor the mother or father? Helen, the beautiful Helen. The portrait of Louisa with the world's most kissable mouth . . .

Frances cried out and threw her hands up in surprise.

"My lady, are you unwell?"

"I'm fine. But oh, my dear Lord, oh, Mallow, your mistress is the stupidest woman in all Christendom. However, it's all right; it's all clear now, staring me in the face all this time. I was an utter fool, but now I have the last piece of the puzzle. Oh, dear, Mallow, it was brilliant, absolutely brilliant. A cool plan, probably made at the very last minute, but with such daring it held up for years."

"Do you know where Helen is, my lady?"

Frances gave her maid a mysterious smile. "Helen? Oh, Helen is well and truly dead, Mallow. But we were engaged to find Louisa Torrence. And we will have her. However, it's bringing her out that's going to be tricky. Not impossible, but tricky. A woman who disappeared. A lost soldier. A killer. We'll bring them all out, Mallow. I'll tell you all. And we'll plan our revelation."

"I am delighted to hear your ladyship has come to a successful conclusion. I will help in any way I can."

Frances put her hand on Mallow's. "I know. You've been invaluable so far, dear Watson."

"Thank you, my lady. And if I may be so bold, just now, you sounded very . . . commanding, my lady, like the prince at the end of the play last night."

"Yes, Mallow. What did he say? 'All are punish'd.' Yes, Mallow, I'm afraid all are punish'd." Then she smiled. "Or will be."

Chapter 29

Frances immediately started planning with Mallow. They didn't even break for lunch; Frances sent one of the hotel maids out for fish and chips. Their greasy fingers stained the papers as Frances made lists and charts, explaining it all to Mallow and tossing off ideas for forcing secrets out of those who still kept them.

"It's one thing to know, Mallow. It's another to prove. As you can see, there are multiple secrets here and a thirty-year connection between the disappearance of Helen and the murder of Mattins. They're related, but no one knows the whole story. Except us, of course. It's rather like pulling up weeds. If you just grab the stem and rip, the roots remain, and a few weeks later the plant comes up stronger than ever." Or so she had learned one summer as a child, when her mother had tried, and failed, to interest Frances in gardening.

"Anyway, there's so much illusion, Mallow. I've been thinking about what Mr. Shaw told us. Actors are full of illusions, but so are playwrights and directors. I'm going to create my own play. There's another piece by Shakespeare—*Hamlet*—and the main character uses his own words to solve a mystery: 'The play's the thing wherein I'll catch the conscience of the King.' So I'm going to be a playwright and director, and you're going to be a stage manager."

"I beg your pardon, my lady—a stage manager?"

"Yes. That's the job the late Mr. Mattins had. The stage manager is in charge of what goes on behind the stage. I guess you could say that if a director is like the master or mistress of a house, a stage manager is like a butler or housekeeper."

"Very good, my lady."

"Do you think you'll be able to get them to listen to you, Mallow?" asked Frances in a teasing tone.

"I have full confidence they will listen to me, my lady," said Mallow without cracking a smile. Frances had no doubt either.

After lunch, Frances made another list.

"I'll need you to visit Lockton's and have a private talk with Susan. We'll need her, of course."

Mallow listened to her ladyship's instructions and nodded. "We got on well, my lady. I'm sure she will be agreeable."

Frances then said that she'd be getting her bicycle and they would meet back later.

First, she was off to the St. James Theatre, where the doorman told her where she could find her friend and jujutsu partner, the musical actress Marie Studholme. Frances met her in her dressing room, examining various outfits.

"So, Frances, which color works for me? The pale rose? It contrasts nicely with my hair. But look who I'm asking. I'm sure that Mallow is the one who makes sure you're properly dressed every morning. If I didn't like you so much, I'd try to steal her from you."

Frances feigned shock. "She would never. Even a mistress who lives on her own and speaks publicly on women's suffrage is more respectable than an actress."

Marie laughed. "Mallow is absolutely right. But Frances, I should ask if you have recovered. All of London is talking about how you gave a sound thrashing to a thief. I confess to being wildly jealous that you got to put our jujutsu training to use before I did."

Frances sat down and groaned. "All of London? My sister-in-law heard, and I'm just waiting for my brother to find out. Ah, well, I've gotten rather good at soothing him. It's just more of the same."

"Oh, I'm sure you'll be able to handle it. Now tell me, how did that absolutely delicious fiancé of yours take it? It happened in his house, I understand."

"He behaved rather splendidly," said Frances.

"Good for him—and good for you! He sounds like a man worth keeping." There was a hint of sadness in her smile. Marie was one of the few people Frances knew who was divorced. Yes, Hal was worth keeping. But did he think the same of her, no matter what she did? *No—focus on the case now.* There would be time later to think about Hal. To think about marriage.

"Yes, there aren't many men who would put up with a suffragist consulting detective. But that brings me to why I'm here. I'm about to solve a case, but it's rather tricky. It's an old story, you see, and I thought I could catch my suspect by revealing his deeds in a play. Correction, my *suspects*. More than one, but they're not connected and are working at cross purposes. So I'm going to write a play—a narrated pantomime, really, to keep it simple. I made a list of actors I want to hire from your company—not the Green Players, since this involves them. If I can rehearse here in the off hours and then perform it at the Emerald, that would be ideal. I'll pay standard wages, if you can help me with the cast."

Marie's eyes sparkled, and that lovely mouth of hers curved into a knowing smile. "Is there a role for me here?"

"I'd love to have you, but I daresay you'd exceed my budget."

"But it sounds like so much fun! I'll do it for free. Tony Mattins was well-known and liked in every theatre in London. If this will help catch his killer, you can depend on me."

"Delightful. I want your beautiful face well-lit front and center and your golden voice reciting the story. Get me the actors, and I'll work on a script." She gave her friend's arm a squeeze, and then it was off to the Emerald for a talk with Mr. Rusk.

When she got there, she saw the new security wasn't a rumor. She carried her bicycle inside and was prepared to walk right by the porter, but he stopped her.

"Sorry, my lady. New rule. No one who isn't part of the company can walk beyond the lobby. Mr. Rusk's rule."

"But you know me. I'm hardly going to pinch anything."

"I'm sure, my lady. But Mr. Rusk was absolutely firm. No one outside of the company. But if you're wanting Mr. Rusk, I'll send a lad for him." The porter opened the auditorium door and said a few words to a boy who was no doubt working inside. A minute or two later, Rusk appeared in the lobby.

"Lady Frances," he said. He didn't look particularly pleased to see her. Frances wasn't surprised, after their discussion—and the overheard conversation—the other night. "Is there something I can do for you?" He paused and forced a smile. "More tickets?"

"I just wanted to thank you. And ask a favor. Actually, by doing me a favor, I can do one for you."

He looked nervous and quickly licked his lips. "Come to my office," he said. She followed him down the hall.

"Your porter said there are new policies in place for visitors."

"Oh, that? Just something from our new owners. They're afraid, rather needlessly in my opinion, about theft. So they have asked me to restrict access."

Even if Frances hadn't overheard the discussion he had with Prescott, she'd have known he was lying. His voice and his shifty eyes gave away everything.

Once they were in his office, Rusk gestured to Frances to take a seat.

"Thank you again for the opening-night tickets to your delightful production," she said. "And for allowing me to stay for the party. The king and Mrs. Keppel seemed to enjoy themselves."

"Yes, His Majesty was most complimentary." He cleared his throat. "You seemed very well-acquainted with them?" It was only half a question.

"Society is so small, Mr. Rusk, and the Seaforths have been at court for centuries. But I know you're busy, so I'll get to the business at hand. I would like to put a show on in your theatre. The audience will be private—we'll do it on a night you're not performing. You're 'dark' at least once a week, I believe. Your cast will be invited. In fact, I'm sure they will enjoy it. I will be insulted if they don't come. We can pick a date in about two weeks' time. Will that be satisfactory?"

Rusk stared at her for several long moments. "I don't know what to say, Lady Frances. I guess the first question is why?"

"Oh. Didn't I say? It's about the tragic death of Anthony Mattins. But even more, it's about Helen. It's about the Oath of Tyndareus. One night. One performance. And a chance to reveal some long-held secrets."

"My lady. I don't see how—"

"You don't have to see how," said Frances. She also could act, and she put every ounce of her patrician background into her voice, now cold and commanding. "You just have to remember your oath. You said it was silly, but it was real. This is about Helen. If you ever cared for her, you will agree to this. You will be there. Mr. Prescott will be there. Now I suggest you get out your calendar and work with me to pick a date."

Mr. Rusk just kept looking at her, and Frances stared right back. *Oh, please, don't challenge me again. Just do what you're told. If you really cared for Helen . . . if you really believed that a soldier with a bayonet was seeking vengeance . . .*

"Very well, my lady." And he consulted his leather-bound diary. They settled on an evening, and then Frances thanked him and retrieved her bicycle. Just one more visit today, one more effort at diplomacy.

She parked her bicycle inside the gate of Lady Torrence's house, and the butler quickly answered the door. "Her ladyship is in the drawing room, my lady," he said. He showed Frances into the room, where Lady Torrence looked up hopefully as Frances took a seat.

"You look . . . excited, Lady Frances. Have you come to report?" she asked. Frances saw she struggled to keep her voice steady. She must've been living on a knife's edge these past days, wondering if her daughter was dead or alive— or if her fate would remain a mystery.

"Yes, I have something to report." She took a breath. "I can tell you that I will produce Louisa for you. I can't do it now, but I am confident I can do it in the next couple of weeks."

Lady Torrence nodded. "I am . . . astounded. But I don't entirely understand what you're saying. Where is she, if you know she lives but can't produce her immediately?"

"I wish I could tell you more. I know a woman who can bring her forth, but it will take some convincing and a little money."

"Money? I'll give you everything I have!" Her voice cracked.

"Hardly that. I wrote out some numbers. It may vary slightly, but these are my estimates." She handed Lady Torrence a piece of paper.

"This is very little. I'd pay ten times this. I'll have a check sent to your residence tomorrow. Will that be satisfactory?"

"That is sufficient." She stood. "I have plans to make. I wish I could tell you more."

"So . . . I will see Louisa again?"

It has been a long time, thought Frances. *Would she like what she saw? But I never promised her peace of mind. Only the truth.*

"Yes, Lady Torrence. You will see Louisa again."

Mallow, meanwhile, was on an assignment of her own. She carefully timed her arrival at the shop for just as the store was closing. Mrs. Lockton and Susan were turning off the lights and covering the counters against dust. As they were leaving, Mallow came upon them.

"Good afternoon. I'm so glad to catch you before you left. Miss Lockton, I had some more thoughts about your desire to become a dressmaker. Her ladyship has given me leave to discuss it with you, as my guest at a tea shop, if you have time now." She turned to Susan's mother. "With your permission, of course, madam."

It seemed a little unusual, thought Mrs. Lockton, for Lady Frances to give money to a servant to take her daughter out. But it was kind, and she had no wish to offend Lady Frances, as eccentric as she was.

"That is very thoughtful. Please thank her ladyship on my behalf. Susan, I'll see you at home after your discussion."

Susan seemed pleased and curious. She and Mallow got themselves a table at a nearby tea shop and ordered tea and cakes.

"This is very nice of you, Miss Mallow," said Susan.

"It is my pleasure. And her ladyship's. She is very impressed with you," said Mallow in a tone that indicated that very few people impressed Lady Frances. "She will be speaking to her dressmaker at her earliest convenience. But meanwhile, she has a job for you. Both of us will be working together in the coming days. Her ladyship will be writing and directing a play."

Susan almost spilled her tea. It was unheard of, a woman—a titled lady!—involving herself in the theatre. Was Miss Mallow having a joke at her expense? But Mallow reassured her with a gentle hand on her arm. Her ladyship had said this might be a little difficult to arrange, but Mallow was determined not to let her down.

"It's a special project, Miss Lockton. Special and secret, to help a friend of her ladyship's who's also a lady. We need your help."

"As a costume seamstress?"

"No. As an actress."

Susan blinked. "But my mother doesn't even like me working as a seamstress in the theatre. Can you imagine if I worked as an actress? Miss Mallow, I couldn't possibly . . ."

"But it's not really a performance. It's a special project, just for a few people. It's very respectable, Miss Lockton. Lady Frances is the daughter of a marquess, and her brother is a marquess now and very important in the government. You can just tell your mother you are working on a special project for her ladyship, which is the truth."

Susan still looked doubtful as she drank some tea and picked up a little cake. "What will her ladyship pay?"

"Twice what you make as a seamstress. And it will be after your work in the store."

"But to be an actress," said Susan, shaking her head.

"Just this once. And it doesn't really count, because only people her ladyship invites will come."

Curiosity and desire for money won out.

"Very well," said Susan. "Tell her ladyship she can rely on me."

Mallow sighed with relief. The two young women proceeded to finish their tea and the plate of delicacies.

"So Miss Mallow, I daresay this is the most unusual thing her ladyship has ever done," Susan said.

But Mallow just shook her head.

"Miss Lockton, not even close."

CHAPTER 30

Frances and Mallow found themselves very busy over the next few days. First, there was the writing, as Frances dashed off page after page of script. Mallow was given the task of making lists of costumes and the various items the actors would use, which her ladyship said were called "props."

It got a little crowded in their rooms when Frances engaged a typist to print a final version of the script. As the typist was a woman, the hotel rules did not forbid Frances from having her—and her machine—in their rooms. But it was hardly traditional, and Frances had to reassure the manageress, Mrs. Beasley, that the typist would only be around for a few days. She decided not to tell her that she was already planning to purchase one of these machines herself and to ask the typist to train her in its use.

After a few days, Frances said that the actors were ready to start at the St. James Theatre, where her friend Marie had helped her collect them. They gathered their papers and hailed a hansom.

"This is very exciting, Mallow. We are not only solving a mystery but entering a whole new world."

"Yes, my lady. But I do want you to know I will never leave your service for full-time theatre work."

"I am glad to hear it. Although I do want to reassure you that what we are doing is perfectly respectable."

"I am sure, my lady." Mallow seemed to take some assurance from her words nonetheless. It wasn't like they were *actresses*.

The St. James was similar to the Emerald, and Frances and Mallow quickly found their way to the stage, where the cast had already gathered. The actors looked curious and amused, knowing little except that a rather odd titled lady wanted to direct a play and was paying good money. Susan Lockton and Marie Studholme were also present.

"Thank you all for your cooperation on this play that will run for only one performance but will be remembered for a long, long time," Frances said. "It will be pantomime, so it will be mostly about movement. The action will be narrated by Miss Studholme, so there will be few lines to memorize. I would like to introduce you to your stage manager, Miss June Mallow. Although she is new to the theatre world, she is exceptionally well-organized, and I am sure I can count on you to follow her directions. Now the name of my play is *Death at the Emerald*—"

"Excuse me, my lady," said one actor. "If I may give you some advice, I'm not sure that is the most engaging title. May I suggest another one?" He was young and good-looking, and Frances was sure he knew exactly how handsome he was and relied on that. Dealing with actors was going to be a little more of a challenge than she had anticipated. She saw her friend Marie just raise an eyebrow and wait to see how this would play out.

It was Mallow who spoke first. "Excuse me. You—the one who just asked her ladyship a question. What is your name?"

"Winslow Gardener, at your service, Miss Mallow," he said.

"Well, Mr. Gardener, in the future, if her ladyship wants your opinion, she will ask for it."

That wiped the smile off his face, and there were snickers among the rest of the cast.

"Is that what a stage manager does, my lady?" whispered Mallow.

"Absolutely, Mallow. I see you have a talent for this." Then to the company at large, Frances said, "If there are no more questions or comments, we will get started. Miss Mallow, please hand out the scripts, and we will begin."

It didn't take Frances long to realize that, just as Mallow was going to be an excellent stage manager, she herself was well-positioned to be a director. She started out giving directions, then began actually positioning the actors and actresses, turning them around the stage as if they were full-sized dolls. "Stand like this, only three-quarters to the audience . . . Now let's be a little more enthusiastic here; you're young and in love . . . Say, we're going to need some special lighting here. Mallow, didn't we engage a lighting designer?"

"Yes, my lady. He will be available for discussion later this week."

"Excellent. Now let's do a run-through once more . . ."

And so it went for the next few days. Frances had told the cast in a vague way that this was going to help in her investigations of who killed Anthony Mattins. Not that they entirely believed her. During a break, she definitely heard one actor say to another, "Our director is as mad as a March hare."

Well, let them think that, she thought with some amusement. The less seriously people took this play, the more likely it would work. Meanwhile, the actors did what they were told, and Mallow performed her role with serious determination, as if she were the housekeeper in a great country mansion organizing a formal ball.

Working with the lighting designer was a fascinating experience.

"I don't know the correct term, but I believe there is a way to send a shaft of light into a particular place?" Frances asked him.

"Bless you, my lady, there is. It's called a baby lens, and we have a hundred watt one here. A watt is—"

"Thank you, I am familiar with watts. Can you show me?" Frances and Mallow climbed to the top of the theatre, and the designer was pleased to show them the powerful beam.

"And can you use lighting to put someone in a half shadow?"

He chuckled. "With the right lighting, my lady, you can do anything."

"Very good. Would the Emerald have a similar lighting system?"

"I'm sure, my lady. All the big theatres have the latest electric lighting nowadays."

"Good. Thank you." They clambered down, and later, while they headed home, Frances said, "Mallow, we are well along here. It's time to make sure of our audience. Inspector Eastley, of course, and Constable Smith. I did promise them that they would be present for any arrests. And Mrs. Lockton, of course. Her presence is essential."

"I imagine she'll be upset to see her daughter on the stage, my lady."

"I think that by the end of the play, having a daughter on the stage will be the least of Mrs. Lockton's worries," said Frances.

Mallow nodded. "I see your point, my lady."

Once they had returned to Miss Plimsoll's, Frances dashed off a note for Inspector Eastley, inviting him to come with Smith and two constables who would need to remain hidden.

"Getting Mrs. Lockton will be a little harder, I'm afraid. She isn't going to want to come anywhere near the Emerald Theatre. We need to give her a motive."

The next day was Friday, and during their final rehearsal, Frances congratulated her cast for bringing it all together so neatly.

"I will see you all for our opening—and closing—night on Monday at the Emerald. Miss Mallow and I will be there early and have arranged for the costumes to be brought over." They'd be wearing clothes of the last generation, which more than one actor remembered from their youth.

"For now, Mallow, I'll leave you at Miss Plimsoll's and have a final talk with Mrs. Lockton. It'll be a little difficult. Our last conversation did not end well. I'll have to give her a very strong reason to attend."

"And what will that be, my lady?"

Frances smiled. "Nothing less than the triumphant return of Helen to the London stage."

The salesgirls were helping other customers when Frances arrived at Mrs. Lockton's store, and when one was free, Frances gave the girl her card and asked if she could possibly speak with Mrs. Lockton in her office. She headed to the back, and Frances wondered if Mrs. Lockton would dare refuse to even speak with her. *Oh, I bet she'd have the courage to refuse me, but she's too curious, too concerned about what I might know to not speak with me.*

She was right, and the girl showed her to the office.

"Please take a seat, Lady Frances," Mrs. Lockton said as they entered. "Thank you, Bessie. You can close the door on your way out."

When they were alone, Mrs. Lockton looked at her as if she was trying to figure out what Frances was thinking. She started on a neutral topic. "Thank you for offering my daughter employment. She was a little unclear about the nature of the work. Sewing for some charitable activity?"

"Yes. That's a good way of putting it," said Frances, smiling at her, "but it isn't Miss Lockton I'm here to speak with you about. Our last conversation ended on an awkward note. I am sorry about that. I understand you have deep feelings for the Halliday family, those who are living and those who are deceased, but I need to find Helen. I think you overestimate the dangers to her or to anyone else's reputation. I would like you to come to a performance at the Emerald Theatre on Monday evening. Much will be revealed."

She had already decided that Mrs. Lockton was brave, but there was no hiding her nerves now, made clear by the beads of moisture on her forehead.

"Are you planning to reveal what happened to Helen?" Mrs. Lockton asked.

"I will reveal the truth, and I know you will regret it if you don't come. What happens will happen whether you are there or not. But as the owner of a business, you know full well that you can better manage any problems in the moment rather than hours or days later. Again, it's Monday at two. If you want to bring a companion, that will be acceptable. Either way, I will expect you. Good day."

She stood and turned around but heard a chair pushed back as Mrs. Lockton stood quickly.

"Lady Frances. You have no idea . . . there are men involved—"

"I know there are men involved. But you and I are women. If we can't trust each other, what hope is there?" Frances didn't wait for a response and left the store. She knew Mrs. Lockton would attend. She wouldn't like it, but she would come.

Chapter 31

Monday came soon enough. Frances found herself fidgeting and going over every last detail of the show. If nothing else, she thought, this was giving her a greater appreciation of actors and all the work involved in creating even a short and simple play. She'd never look at a performance the same way again.

Mallow was looking forward to the event as well. She had taken a certain pride in organizing the show but had had her fill of actors for a while.

"Miss Forbes keeps entering later than you ordered, my lady," said Mallow on their way to the theatre. "I have had to remind her of this twice. I can only think of what any good housekeeper would do with a maid who had to be told twice to clean the grates. Not that I am complaining, my lady. It has been a most interesting experience. But I think I'd go mad if I had to live my life in their world."

"The reverse is also true. Most of them would go mad if they had to live in ours."

The actors were waiting for them, and Mallow quickly took charge of Susan. She was a nervous and awkward actress but had endeared herself to Mallow by taking her role seriously and following her ladyship's directions as best she could.

"This afternoon, for the performance, I'm to do your hair up proper," Mallow explained and brought the girl into a dressing room, where she quickly stripped off her plain dress. They had found a pale dress that set off her black hair nicely. Then Mallow sat her on a chair in the dressing room in front of a mirror. She opened the folder her ladyship had given her and looked at the photograph. It was an old-fashioned hairstyle. Mallow had seen a similar style in a portrait of one of her ladyship's aunts at Seaforth Manor. She had never done hair up like that herself but felt confident she could copy the photograph.

"No one has ever done my hair, except my mother when I was a little girl. We have a maid at home, of course, but mother always said she had real work to do besides pampering me."

"Ladies of quality always have maids to do their hair," said Mallow. *Even if they don't always cooperate.*

"Miss Mallow . . . can you tell me now what this is all about?"

"Don't move your head," said Mallow. "All I can say is that her ladyship feels it is very important for justice to be done."

"Isn't that what constables and barristers are for?"

"Her ladyship believes they need assistance every now and then."

"It's something to do with my mother, isn't it?" Susan said it in a tentative, small voice, as if she was afraid of the answer. "I know Lady Frances has been talking to her. She's seemed a little nervous."

"I'm sure I couldn't say." Mallow's nimble fingers quickly did up her hair, and when she was done, Susan stared at herself in the mirror.

"I look like a proper lady," she said with a giggle.

"Yes, you do, miss."

The girl smirked. "I wonder what the Reverend Halliday would think if he saw me like this."

Mallow sighed. "If I may make a suggestion, I would not hang my hopes on the vicar." And then, overriding Susan's protests, "Just be still for a moment. A little powder to take the shine off your face."

There was time for one more run-through before the audience came. It was what her ladyship said was a "dress rehearsal," which meant everyone was in their costumes. With a grim determination, Mallow made sure Miss Forbes made her entrance on time. When the show reached its successful conclusion, she ensured that the props were put back where they should be.

Frances meanwhile was up in the rafters again with the lighting man.

"If you think this is impressive, my lady, I've heard the Metropolitan Opera House in New York has some of the latest and most impressive electric lights of any theatre. I'd love to see it."

"I attended a performance there when I was living in America, but it never occurred to me to look at the lights. The next time I'm there I will." Her brother had mentioned an upcoming family trip to New York to visit to the diplomatic community in Washington. It would simplify everything if she and Hal were married by then. Could she be a married lady by then and still have Mallow dress her up for the opera, just so she could spend the evening observing the opera's lighting system?

A stagehand called from below, "Mr. Rusk wants to know if he and the audience can enter now, my lady."

"Have you checked with Miss Mallow?" she shouted down.

"Yes, and she said everything is ready backstage."

"Very good then. Let them in. I'm coming down." As part of the deal with Mr. Rusk, he and all the members of the Green Players had been banned from the theatre for the dress rehearsal. Frances and Mallow had made sure all the doors were firmly closed.

"You might want to keep an eye on the back doors," Rusk had advised before he left the theatre that afternoon. "We're still concerned about securing the building in the wake of Mr. Mattins's death."

"I'm not worried," Frances had said with a faint smile. Mr. Rusk had looked like he was going to argue the point but then had just shrugged and left.

They all came in now, the members of the Green Players. Rusk appeared concerned and behaved like he was expecting a disaster at any moment. Prescott had a look of amusement. Everyone else seemed curious. There weren't many who had known Helen, but everyone had heard of her, the legendary beauty who had married for a "normal" life overseas.

There were no tickets for that afternoon's performance. Everyone found their seats. Frances peered out from behind the stage. Where was Mrs. Lockton? But then she entered after the initial rush, wearing the same good dress she had put on when visiting Frances at Miss Plimsoll's. Frances had wondered if she would bring a friend for support—but no, she had brought the Reverend Samuel Halliday. Frances smiled—she had not expected that, but it was of no matter. In fact, it would make things easier in the end. Mrs. Lockton leaned on his arm, and he looked down at her with great kindness.

Just as well, thought Frances. Emma Lockton would need the comfort of a vicar before the afternoon was over. The comfort of this vicar in particular.

And finally, in came Inspector Eastley. Even from a distance, Frances could see his hard eyes sweeping over the other audience members. The huge Constable Smith, however, looked over the theatre itself. Had he ever been in a place like this? Or maybe his assessment was just professional, as he considered all the nooks and crannies a theatre contained, so many corners where miscreants could hide in the shadows. A few actors regarded the two men curiously, but no one spoke with them. They took two seats on the aisle, by themselves.

Very well. All was set. "Did you give the letters to the messengers?" Frances asked Mallow.

Including one to Lady Torrence, boldly promising that she would meet Louisa later that afternoon. *Will my own arrogance finally be my undoing?* wondered Frances. *Old nannies and governesses will be laughing at me all over London.*

"Yes, my lady. I sent them all with strict instructions to Lady Torrence, Lord and Lady Freemantle, and the Reverend Halliday."

"The Reverend Halliday is here anyway. He'll miss his letter, but he will just find out earlier."

"Very good, my lady."

At one minute past two, Frances nodded to Mallow, who told a stagehand to raise the curtain for *Death at the Emerald.*

A baby lens spotlight poured down on Marie, wearing a simple yet elegant dress. She stood behind a podium, and her voice, rich with of strength and music, filled the theatre as Frances grabbed Mallow's hand and gave a squeeze.

"Once upon a time, there was a beautiful actress named Helen, and six men loved her most deeply." Six men, from young to old, filed onto the stage. Frances heard a ripple in the audience as the Green Players recognized the signatories of the Oath of Tyndareus. There was Rusk, not quite as round, dressed a little better than the rest to show his ambitions toward management; Prescott, lean with his sardonic smile; the boyish Alexander Braceley, dressed like a dandy; and the rest of them.

And then a woman danced onto the stage—but she wore a mask, like an ancient Greek actor. The men surrounded her, entreating her to love them.

"But poor Helen was overwhelmed by their attentions, and feeling distraught at causing the object of their desire so much distress, they signed an oath—a fierce and terrible oath based on ancient words—swearing to uphold Helen's choice of spouse. And so she made her choice. But he wasn't one of the six."

A man in a sober business suit entered: Douglas MacKenzie, the Emerald Theatre accountant. He danced with Helen and swept her away into the darkness upstage.

"Thus Helen's brief career on the stage ended." The mask was tossed away into the light. "Those who signed the Oath of Tyndareus went on with their lives. They resumed their careers, and some found other worthy partners to marry. But one couldn't resume his life. He loved her so much, he was driven to a frenzy. If he couldn't have her, no man would. This man broke the oath and killed Helen's chosen husband." MacKenzie, stumbling now from a mortal wound, collapsed in the pool of light on the stage.

Frances was watching from backstage. At this point, the actors in the audience were looking stricken. Rusk and Prescott were looking stunned, and Emma Lockton had gone pale.

"But who did it? Which faithless suitor broke the oath, broke the laws of God and man, to kill Helen's husband? Which man—"

"Enough!" A cry came from offstage. Marie looked startled at the interruption, and everyone turned to see who had broken into the play. Into the dim light walked a man dressed in a soldier's uniform, the old uniform of those who had fought and died in the Sudan. A helmet shadowed his eyes, and he carried a rifle. He could've easily slipped in. After all, Frances had dismissed Rusk's warning about securing all the doors.

"Enough," he said again, lower this time but more menacing. "Lady Frances Ffolkes, I know you're backstage. I know you're behind this. And I want this mockery, this foolishness, stopped. You and I will have a reckoning later. For now, I'm here for the man who broke our oath, who destroyed Helen's chance for happiness. For all I disagreed with her choice, I was not faithless. I can tell myself that much. There was only one thing that kept me from dying in the Sudan, one thing that let me hold onto a spark of life: the thought that I had kept my oath. I made it back to London, prepared to start a new life, only to find out what none of you apparently knew—that Helen's husband had been killed, and she had fled in terror."

Frances couldn't fully see the shaded face, but there was no doubt all knew who he was. Alexander Braceley. He had survived the Sudan, and he had come home. Frances switched her attention back to the audience. Rusk and Mrs. Lockton continued to look dumbfounded, but Prescott looked absolutely terrified.

Braceley walked downstage, right to the edge of the stage. "Gil Rusk. My God, you filled out nicely. I always thought you were the smart one here, but you never knew what happened to Helen. Still, I don't blame you." Then his voice got harder. "I blame you, Quentin Prescott. You pretended to be me, didn't you, chasing poor Lady Frances around London?" Braceley laughed without humor. "Well, she got the best of you, she and that precious maid of hers. Still, she had it coming, considering all she did."

Frances and Mallow remained where they were, watching this new drama unfold.

"But that's all by the way, Quentin Prescott. That's nothing compared with what else you did, stabbing Douglas MacKenzie in the back like that. I ought to turn you over to the constables. But we swore an oath, a sacred oath. Do you know what happened in ancient Greece to those who broke their oaths? They faced the wrath of the Furies. And today, Mr. Prescott, I am one of their number."

From his shirt pocket, Braceley produced a cartridge and loaded it into his rifle with a sharp snap. He took aim at Prescott.

"No!" cried Prescott. "For God's sake, mercy!"

"Why should I have mercy?" demanded Braceley, sighting over his rifle.

"It was an accident. I just wanted to talk to him, and we had words. I swear, I didn't mean to kill him."

"Oh, really?" He didn't sound convinced. "And Tony Mattins? He was one of us. How could you?"

"I didn't kill Mattins!"

"Liar. If there is to be any hope of mercy, you will tell the truth."

"Again, it was just an accident. We had words. He was going to tell—" Prescott sounded desperate now. "He was going to break the oath, not me. He was going to tell Lady Frances everything, violate Helen's trust."

"And reveal your crime," said Braceley. "I bet he always suspected. You have two murders on your conscience. Two violations of your oath. And you will pay. You will pay now. Say your prayers."

"For God's sake, mercy!" screamed Prescott again.

Braceley pulled the trigger—but nothing happened. Nothing except the fall of the curtain, as ordered by Mallow, indicating the end of act one. Only Braceley was left visible, standing on the apron in front the curtain. He shouldered his rifle and took off his helmet. In the full light, he really didn't look much like Braceley, as Lady Frances had heard him described, but it had been good enough.

He wiped his forehead on his sleeve. "My God, these helmets are hot. How the soldiers managed is beyond me." He called out to the wings. "Lady Frances, did I do all right? I had to improvise, as you said I would. I hope I performed correctly."

Lady Frances, followed by Mallow, strode onto the stage. "You were splendid, Mr. Archibald. I almost believed you were Alexander Braceley himself. Very nicely played."

The actor, Mr. Archibald, specially recommended by Marie Studholme, bowed low. "Thank you, my lady," he said and walked off stage.

It took everyone a few long moments to figure out what had happened. Frances had fooled all of them, ending act one of her play with what seemed to be an interruption but was really just a trick of the eye. An illusion.

And Quentin Prescott, suddenly realizing he wasn't going to be shot in the Emerald Theatre, had come to the conclusion that he had given himself away. That Lady Frances had fooled him.

Enraged, he prepared to jump onto the stage. "You bitch, you hellcat—" But the only place Prescott was going was up, thanks to Constable Smith, who had moved surprisingly quickly for such a large man. He lifted Prescott by the collar and pushed him back down into his chair.

Inspector Eastley, hiding a smile behind his mustache, approached the seated man.

"My goodness, Mr. Prescott. I never would've thought such an experienced actor as you would be fooled like this. But then again, Lady Frances set a very impressive trap for you. She sent me a note explaining what was going to happen, and even so, I almost believed Mr. Braceley had come back."

Lady Frances smiled grimly down at Prescott as the rest of the audience was still trying to take it all in. Mallow glared with absolute disdain. Emma Lockton looked like she might faint. But no. She was strong. Frances knew that much.

"Thank you for the compliment, Inspector," Frances said. "Yes, Mr. Prescott killed Helen's husband, Douglas MacKenzie, in a jealous rage. I think that Mattins always suspected and was going to help me when I came asking about Helen, but then Prescott killed him to keep him quiet. It was a bayonet—an old prop, perhaps—that had the advantage of throwing blame on Braceley. I thought it was Braceley myself for a while, but that poor man died with the rest of his company in the Sudan. You had a cloak, Mr. Prescott, but it was a cheap costume, not heavy army quality. Illusion. Nothing but illusion. And by the way, you played Mercutio, not Romeo. Fortunately, Mallow and I found the program before you broke into his room looking for any mementos."

"How the hell . . . ?" said Prescott.

"Please, Mr. Prescott. Watch your language in front the ladies," said Inspector Eastley.

"Oh, let him speak, Inspector, for all the good it will do him now. You know, I thought that he was insisting he was Romeo just out of vanity. But no—he didn't want me to think he was Mercutio for another reason. Mercutio dies halfway through the play, giving Prescott enough time to run out and kill MacKenzie. If he had been Romeo, he'd have had an alibi. He was furious when another actor acknowledged him as a master with a blade when he should've been flattered, but he had killed two men with a blade."

"It's all talk," said Prescott sullenly.

"Oh, but there's more proof. Mallow and I left serious marks on him. There should be a bruise on his right shin from where I tripped him and another on his back between his shoulder blades."

"Is that true?" asked Inspector Eastley. "Lady Frances, I would love to hear that story later. But for now, Mr. Prescott, could you raise your pant leg and then give us a chance to peer down your shirt? If you want, I could have Constable Smith help you, but you'll find him much less gentle than your usual dresser."

Looking very unhappy but seeing no other choice, Prescott obliged with his leg. Inspector Eastley raised an eyebrow at the results.

"Lady Frances. Did you leave this bruise on him? My goodness." He shook his head and turned back to Prescott. "You are under arrest for the murders of Douglas MacKenzie and Anthony Mattins and for the attempted murder of Lady Frances Ffolkes. Constable Smith, please turn over Mr. Prescott to the two uniformed constables outside. Take care of the details, and see that Mr. Prescott speaks to no one until we return."

Mr. Prescott tried to grab onto some final dignity, walking as if he were making a grand exit instead of being arrested. The company was still speechless, but as he was marched down the aisle, the place exploded in whispers. Rusk, however, looked absolutely broken as he tried to take in that a man he had known for most of his life had killed another friend and his great love's husband. He buried his face in his hands.

And Emma Lockton? She was still upset, but there was something else there. Was it relief? Even triumph? Reverend Halliday, like everyone else, seemed a little stunned, and Frances could see him gently reassure his Aunt Em.

Well, we shall see, Mrs. Lockton, thought Frances. *This is just beginning.*

CHAPTER 32

The conversation was getting louder, and the audience was starting to get up. Frances clapped her hands sharply.

"Thank you all for coming, but we're not done. We still have act two." That got everyone's attention. Considering what had happened so far, they were inclined to stay for more. Emma Lockton looked surprised, and wariness crept into her features, but she showed no signs of leaving. Mr. Rusk glanced up. All was lost, he seemed to think. No point in leaving now.

It took a few moments for everyone to settle down. Mallow gave a signal to dim the houselights, and Marie, after a quick congratulatory smile to Frances, began speaking again.

"Despite the tragedy, that wasn't the end for Helen. She had lost her husband, but she was strong; she would lead her life."

Into the light stepped Susan Lockton, still playing Helen. But Helen was no longer an actress, and she had lost her mask. She was well-lit and could easily be seen, wearing the hair done up just as in the portrait of Louisa Torrence that hung in her old room.

Magnificent, thought Frances. They had really done it. Mallow had put up her hair with perfect fidelity, and the dress from another generation had completed the picture. Emma Lockton cried out from the audience, incoherent, and Gilbert Rusk choked out, "Dear God!" Susan stood as the entrancing Helen, with her midnight-black hair and a creamy complexion possessed only by women just out of girlhood.

"Fortunately, Helen had good friends," continued Marie. "Fleeing the theatre world forever, Helen took refuge with an older married couple, pious folk who lived in a town not far from London." The actors playing the Hallidays came onstage—a sober, middle-aged pair. "With hard work and trust in the Lord, they had prospered and chose to share their good fortune with others, reaching out to those in the theatre to provide assistance and bring them closer to God. They took in poor Helen, offering her support and safety. Who knew if the traitor who had taken her husband from her was also planning to kill her too?"

Onstage, the Hallidays embraced Helen and led her to a few sticks and a sheet that represented a comfortable bed.

"And as the days went by, it seemed that Helen had indeed found a refuge. Mrs. Halliday was with child, and Helen was a kind and helpful companion. They assumed she would help when the child arrived. But Helen suddenly took a fever . . ."

Frances continued to look at Mrs. Lockton. The more Marie spoke, the more nervous Emma Lockton got, even more than in act one. She was practically shaking as the actors moved onstage, and Marie's voice had cast a spell on the entranced audience. Frances could hardly breathe. Would it happen as she had planned? Would Emma Lockton do what Frances expected her to do?

". . . and as fate would have it, on a dark night, one woman was bringing life into the world, as another was planning to leave it. At least, that's the story as it came down to us. But that's not actually what happened. Helen herself—"

"No!" screamed Mrs. Lockton, and it came deep from within, as if she was being tortured. "For the love of God, no." She gave a strangled cry, and before the Reverend Halliday could react, she had launched herself onto the stage. Once there, she didn't seem to know what to do, however, as if she had hoped her presence would end everything. She looked around wildly.

The audience was momentarily surprised, but after the first shock, Frances felt a sense of disappointment from them: *All right, we admit the first surprise was well done, but to do this twice in the same short play? Really, Lady Frances, do you take us for fools?*

Frances took a deep breath and walked onto the stage. Looking over the skeptical audience, she said, "I assure you, this is not part of my play. Mrs. Lockton, please explain yourself."

Mrs. Lockton turned to Frances with such rage in her eyes, Frances wondered if she would be physically attacked. "Oh, don't be so modest, my lady. You know exactly what is happening here."

"I gave you a chance," said Frances coolly. "Now give me a reason to end this play now, or I will have constables remove you and finish it myself. Show me Helen."

Rusk now joined them onstage. Frances thought he might oblige them.

"Lady Frances," he said with forced patience, "we are in your debt to a great extent for uncovering a murderer in our midst. But he was a man we've known for years—for decades—and we have been through enough. If you have more to say, just say it. We have had ample drama for one day."

Frances arched an eyebrow and looked into his eyes. So much pain and confusion there, and she felt a pang at what she was doing. But it would come out all right in the end—she hoped. For a brief moment, she became aware again of her enormous arrogance, moving people around like this. More than once Sherlock Holmes had let a guilty man go free when he thought it was right to do so. *How flexible are my ethics?*

She forced her voice to be steady. "Mr. Rusk. Perhaps you could somehow take charge of Mrs. Lockton. After all, she is a member of your company."

"Is that a joke? I've never met this woman before today, I assure you."

"Oh, for heaven's sake, Mr. Rusk. The truth is staring you in the face. I deduced it, and I wasn't even here thirty years ago."

Frances now saw a change in Mrs. Lockton. She knew now it was over, but she wasn't going to cringe from the truth. She looked down at the Reverend Halliday, watching her, still in utter amazement. There was love in those eyes. Oh, yes, she loved the vicar, loved him so deeply.

Mrs. Lockton then sighed—and smiled—and turned to Rusk. "Dear Gil. I thought you of all of them would remember. It's been a long time, though. Still, I can recall the words I used when I first met you. You thought I had rehearsed them. I had, of course. 'I'm a good hard worker, Mr. Rusk; I'll remember my lines, follow all direction, and never give you a moment to regret engaging me.'"

Relief poured through Frances. She hadn't realized how tense she had been and felt almost dizzy. She looked at Mallow in the wings and winked at her. And Mallow unbended enough to wink back.

"No . . . it's not possible," said Rusk. "Helen? My God, it really is you." He turned to the audience. "Do you see? Helen has come back." And seemingly without any thought, he flung himself at her, embracing her. After a few moments, Helen embraced him back.

"I always knew it wasn't you," Frances heard her say quietly. "Not my dear Gil."

Frances was most amused that the first person in the audience to applaud was Inspector Eastley, looking up with his wry smile. And a few moments later, everyone else joined him. She rather thought it was a triumphant end to her first—and last—outing as a theatrical impresario.

But there would be time enough to reflect later. Members of the audience crowded the stage. Frances whispered to Rusk to take Mrs. Lockton to his office, and they left quickly. She turned to the vicar. "Reverend Halliday, Mallow will show you to Mr. Rusk's office. You must have a thousand questions, and we will answer them, but Mrs. Lockton needs you now. Inspector, my deepest thanks for trusting me."

"And my trust was not misplaced, I see. I have a feeling there are more secrets here, but can I assume they are not legal ones?"

"Just emotional," said Frances.

"The worst of all, my lady, but fortunately, not part of my remit. I will take myself off. There's a prisoner who needs questioning." He and Smith made their way out.

"Thank you for coming," said Frances to everyone else remaining. "I thought that, as members of the Green Players, I owed you a chance to witness the return of one of the most celebrated members in the long history of your company and the arrest of the man who killed her husband and your great friend and colleague, Mr. Mattins. Thank you all, and good evening."

With that, she left them to gossip among themselves and quickly followed Mr. Rusk, Mrs. Lockton, and Mallow to Rusk's office. Susan dashed over to her. "Lady Frances, I don't understand. Why was my mother here? Why was she so upset? Why were people calling her 'Helen?'"

"Oh, Miss Lockton. I'm glad you're here. I was just going to send Mallow for you. Come with me, and we'll answer all your questions." She took the girl's arm and led her to Rusk's office.

"My mother is going to kill me when she discovers I was an actress. I thought she wasn't supposed to find out I was doing this."

"I think your mother may be a lot more understanding than you think."

It was a little crowded in Rusk's office, but Mallow had asked a couple of stagehands to push his desk against the wall and bring in some extra chairs. They sat in a circle—Frances and Mallow; Mrs. Lockton, being comforted by a still confused Reverend Halliday; Gil Rusk, looking steadily at Mrs. Lockton as if he couldn't believe Helen had come back; and a fearful-looking Susan. Mrs. Lockton spared a quick look for her daughter, but it was a loving one, not angry.

Mrs. Lockton spoke first. "Very well, Lady Frances. I told you that it wasn't just my secret, but others'. But it's too late to stop this now. You'll take the blame for any consequences."

Frances just met her gaze. She rather admired Mrs. Lockton but had had enough of her completely one-sided point of view. "I'll accept my share, Mrs. Lockton, but you must take the blame for not telling the story for all these years," she said coolly. "But there's no point in looking back. Would you like me to tell it? Or should you?"

Mrs. Lockton smiled. "I was just an actress. You're the playwright, my lady."

"You were an *actress*?" asked Susan.

"Yes, your mother was the most beautiful actress in London, I've heard it told," said Frances. Susan lightened the mood by giggling at that, and Mrs. Lockton just shook her head. "But I will tell the story. As I showed in my play, a beautiful young woman—about your age, Miss Lockton—showed up at the Emerald Theatre and got herself a place in the Green Players. She had come from a wealthy, prominent family, but she wanted another life away from a strict father who could only see one path for his elder daughter."

Helen had chosen another path, thought Frances, entering a world where her father had humiliated her mother with a succession of mistresses. What a message to send—joining the same milieu where her father had misbehaved so shamelessly.

"She changed her name and called herself Helen. Once settled among the Green Players, six men wooed her. I think one truly loved her"—her eyes darted to Mr. Rusk—"and one saw her like a daughter. One lusted after her, seeing her as a challenge to his pride. At least one obsessed over her. But she married an accountant. You see, Helen never fit into the theatrical world, and once the initial excitement was over, she decided she wanted a balanced, modest life and an equal partnership with a man, where she could raise a family. They planned to move far away, where she would never be recognized—but one of her former suitors could not let her go and decided if he couldn't have her, no man would. And so, he killed her husband. You saw the results of that in act one."

Mrs. Lockton started to quietly cry, and the Reverend Halliday put his arm around her. "You don't have to stay for this, Aunt Em. I will take you home."

"No—let's finish," she said.

Frances continued. "And so Helen, not even sure who had killed her husband—and afraid she might be killed next—turned to the Hallidays, who had established a mission in the theatrical community. We were told Helen died of a fever, but there was something about her that was hidden, something I didn't realize myself until recently. Helen had been a married woman, if only briefly. And Helen found herself with child, just like other married women—and just like Mrs. Halliday. This is when it became very complicated. The two women delivered their children on the very same night. Reverend Halliday, you commented on the sad irony that your mother, sickly and getting on in years, delivered a healthy child, while Helen, young and healthy, died quickly from a fever. But that's not what happened."

Frances paused. She had everyone's attention, and Mrs. Lockton was clutching the Reverend Halliday as if she'd otherwise collapse. "In fact, Mrs. Halliday was the one who lost her child and her last chance to be a mother. Helen had no fever. She was young and healthy, and so was her son. But what could she do? Return to making a precarious living on the stage, where she might be killed? Crawl back to her parents and live in quiet humiliation for the rest of her life? She had no skills for any kind of work, no way to support a baby." She turned to Mrs. Lockton. "So in your pain and fear, you forged a brilliant plan with the Hallidays. It was put out you had died, and no one outside of that small household had even known you were with child anyway. In fact, you turned over your baby to the Hallidays to raise as their own, and the Halliday baby was put in your grave."

Mrs. Lockton buried her face in her hands and cried, just as Lady Torrence had when talking about her daughter's disappearance. The age and circumstances didn't matter, Frances saw. They were mothers who had lost children.

"With a fevered haste, everyone went to work that night. Mr. Halliday was a builder, but he had started life as a carpenter. He quickly built a coffin. A sexton worked in ignorance and was paid off, along with the midwife. The late Halliday baby was buried in an adult coffin to keep up the pretense, and the vicar was convinced to play along for everyone's good. Church records disappeared in an 'accident.' And for all that the Hallidays loved their adopted boy, they never forgot the child born to them, and so they gave him an impressive monument and visited the site regularly."

The Reverend Halliday frowned. Then, as if he was afraid of his own words, he said, "Lady Frances, are you saying that Mrs. Lockton is my mother?"

"Yes," said Frances softly, "that is exactly what I'm saying. Did you ever see the way she looked at you? It was clear to me how deeply she loved you when she spoke of you and when I saw the two of you together. I am deeply ashamed of myself for misinterpreting that love at first. She loves you as a mother loves a son."

"So, Reverend Halliday, I guess you're my brother?" asked Susan. "No wonder my mother didn't like me to—well, never mind." She blushed. If the scene hadn't been so full of emotion, it would've been funny.

"I didn't want this to ever come out," said Mrs. Lockton, looking at her son for understanding and forgiveness. "Please, if it had not been forced from me, I would've taken my secret to my grave."

"But why?" asked the vicar. "Where is the harm or embarrassment? What you did, what my parents—that is, the Hallidays—did, was out of love. There is no shame to you, me, or Susan." And crying louder than before, Mrs. Lockton threw her arms around her elder child. Frances nodded to Mallow, who produced a bottle of sherry and a glass. Frances filled it and pressed it onto Mrs. Lockton.

"Sip it. It's all out now. It's almost over." Mrs. Lockton did what she was told and gathered herself.

"How could you possibly have known?" she finally got out. "Everyone who knew is long gone."

"There were clues. And in some sense, Reverend Halliday, I think you suspected something was wrong somewhere."

"I knew there was a secret," he said cautiously.

"Just look at the clues. Your name to start with—Samuel. Thanks to Mallow here, I was reminded about the story of the pious woman whose prayer for a child was granted. 'God Has Heard,' was carved into Helen's stone—that's what Samuel means in Hebrew." The Reverend Halliday nodded, looking a little embarrassed that he hadn't figured it out himself.

"And then there's the visual proof. I should have seen that right away." She turned to Mrs. Lockton, who seemed more composed now that the worst was over. "Susan looks like you did at her age, the same creamy complexion and midnight-black hair, the same mouth. I should have seen it earlier. Prescott noticed—I even overheard him saying Susan reminded him of someone. Perhaps later he would've remembered. Mrs. Lockton, you didn't want Susan working here because you were aware she looked like you and didn't want anyone to look at her and see Helen. And you, Reverend Halliday. You also took after your mother. The same jet-black hair and pleasing features. It finally became clear. But where was I? Oh, yes, the brilliant plan. Mrs. Lockton, you still needed to find a place in the world, and you wanted to be near your son, even if you couldn't acknowledge him—and the Hallidays were pleased to help. So you went away, perhaps to trusted friends or relations of the Hallidays. And then you came back to them. You had a new name, made yourself a little dowdier. It was the new name and the story you gave yourself that confused me at first, but that was also a final clue. The Torrences had a history with Shropshire."

"Perhaps I should've picked another name, another place?" asked Mrs. Lockton. "I never thought I'd be subject to such an inquisition."

"Oh, but it made a lot of sense," continued Frances. "If you had said you came from a place you didn't know, you could've been caught in a lie if you met someone who had actually been there. You did know Shropshire from your childhood visits, so you could talk about it with confidence. And the name—Emma Bradley. Your childhood playmate, a friendship your father ended. A memorial to the Emma Bradley who died as a little girl."

Mrs. Lockton sighed and then smiled at Lady Frances. "I'm a little pleased it took a woman to find me out."

"I'm a little pleased it was a woman who fooled me so thoroughly. So I think that's all of it. And now to the conclusion. This started because I was engaged by a client to find her daughter. I've done that, so I made arrangements. Mrs. Lockton, I'd like to take you to meet your mother. Miss Lockton, Reverend Halliday, you have a grandmother. Also, Mrs. Lockton, I sent a note to your sister and her husband."

That got Mrs. Lockton's attention. "Sarah? You've seen her? How is she? I have missed her so much."

"She is well. Happily married with two sons who are doing well. Her husband is someone important in the City."

"I so wanted her to be happy. I read the social news regularly," said Mrs. Lockton. "I saw she had gotten married but no other details."

"If you read the Society pages, you know your father died some years ago. Your mother is alone and very old. The man who killed your first husband is behind bars and never will get out."

Surely, you're not going to be difficult now, thought Frances. *You will agree to see your mother after all I've done, won't you? Did Sherlock Holmes ever have to go through this?*

"For uncovering my first husband's murderer, I'm sure I owe you. Very well, Lady Frances. It's time to see my family again."

For the second time that afternoon, Frances relaxed. "I think this meeting is over then. I have arranged for transportation outside."

Everyone stood a little unsteadily. Rusk was still looking at Mrs. Lockton.

"Helen?" he asked.

"I think Helen was dead and buried a long time ago, Gil. For the last thirty years I've been Emma, and before that, I was christened Louisa." And then she gave him a full, warm smile that shed years from her. For a moment, Frances fancied she could see the beautiful young woman she had been. "However, if you would like, you can still call me 'Helen.'"

"Then I shall. I married but am a widower now. I have two grown children. I would like to talk with you again." Mrs. Lockton looked amused, then produced a card. "I run Lockton's on Bond Street. I need a week to recover from this excitement, but after that stop at the shop at closing someday, and I'll let you buy me a dinner. For now, I want to see my mother and sister."

Chapter 33

Rusk seemed pleased with Mrs. Lockton's response to his invitation. Mrs. Lockton, still leaning on the vicar's arm, swept out of the office, making sure Susan was following her.

"Mother, were you really a celebrated actress?" Susan asked as they headed down the hall. Frances and Mallow hung back. Susan seemed more excited than scandalized.

"Imagine that, Mallow. Finding out that one's dull and serious shopkeeper mother was once the toast of the London stage with dozens of men lining up to take her out to dinner." Frances thought of her own mother, standing up to her father to allow her to go to Vassar in America.

"Certainly a surprise, my lady."

"A good surprise or a bad one, Mallow?"

"I fancy Miss Lockton found her mother's past . . . admirable, my lady."

"I fancy you're right. But Mr. Rusk, you look like you have a question?"

"A hundred, my lady. But one for now, if you please. You knew one of us had killed Helen's husband and then Mattins. But you seemed to know it was Prescott, not me. I wondered why."

"Oh, that was easy. I realized eventually it was an actor stalking me, one who was comfortable in women's clothes. I thought of those early days, as you told me, when men played women's roles. Which Prescott did once. And you're not an actor, Mr. Rusk."

He laughed. "I had hoped my warm and pleasing personality would have spoken for me."

Frances laughed right back. "So much is made of the cleverness of women. Sherlock Holmes would joke about it, according to Watson, until he met his match in Irene Adler. But as a consulting detective, I have to deal with something more solid. Mr. Rusk, I owe you thanks as well as apologies for putting you through so much. I look forward to your next production. Mallow, we are off."

They left Mr. Rusk in his office to contemplate his past and future. In the lobby, Marie was waiting for them, eyes sparkling.

"Pure genius, my lady." She gave Frances a kiss. "Thank you for allowing me to be part of it."

"Thank you for gracing us with your beautiful voice. We have another jujutsu lesson in two days. I'll see you there."

As they headed outside, Mallow asked, "Do you think Mrs. Lockton and Mr. Rusk will start a romance, my lady?"

"If I were a bookmaker, I'd be inclined to give short odds, Mallow."

"My mother always said gambling was a fool's game, my lady."

"Especially when it comes to love."

In silence, Frances and Mallow joined Mrs. Lockton, the Reverend Halliday, and Susan in a hired coach for the trip to Lady Torrence's house. Once there, Mrs. Lockton headed directly up the front steps, her daughter close behind her. The vicar stayed back for a moment. "Lady Frances, Miss Mallow. God go with you always."

He quickly joined the two women on the steps. The butler admitted them, and they disappeared inside.

A few moments later, an elegant new motorcar pulled up. A well-dressed woman—Lady Freemantle—let herself out without even waiting for the driver to open the door for her and ran as fast as she could in her dress. A moment later, she too had entered the house.

Looking a little amused, Lord Freemantle waited for his chauffeur and followed at a more sedate place. But then he stopped and turned to see Lady Frances. He gave her a welcoming smile and approached. He tipped his hat and bowed.

"So it is true, Lady Frances? My wife received a note saying if she called on her mother at this time, she would see her sister. I take it Louisa is now present in the drawing room?"

"Yes, Lord Freemantle. And Lady Freemantle will also be meeting a new niece and nephew."

He arched an eyebrow. "I look forward to the whole story. Meanwhile, I've summoned both my sons, who are traveling to London as quickly as possible to meet their aunt for the first time. For now, Lady Frances, I just want to tell you how impressed I am."

She gave him a cheeky smile. "Not angry? You bought an entire theatre just to stop this investigation."

He shrugged. "I was afraid that Louisa would never be found and all that would be uncovered would be scandal. But in the end, seeing how happy this has made my wife, I would endure any amount of scandal."

"Why, Lord Freemantle, I never thought City gentlemen could be so warmhearted. I am surprised."

"Not as surprised as I am that a suffragist could be so coolly logical. Are you coming in, my lady?"

Frances looked wistfully at the house. "I do want to see the results of my investigations, but it's a deeply private reunion." Again, she wondered if Sherlock Holmes would've had such scruples.

"Oh, come, Lady Frances. You're the last one I'd expect to stand on ceremony. You have a right to be there, and I'd expect by now the first tears are over. My mother-in-law will want to thank you." He held out his arm. "Let me escort you in." That was all the encouragement Frances needed. She took Lord

Freemantle's arm, and over her shoulder she whispered, "You come too," to Mallow.

The butler let them in, and he seemed calm enough. But Frances's restless eye landed on the maid, Simpkins, the only servant still in the household who had known the young Louisa. Frances had thought her hard but saw the traces of tears on her face. Their eyes met, and Frances fancied she saw gratitude in them.

She saw more tearstained faces inside but smiles too. Louisa sat on the couch, flanked by her mother and sister, the Reverend Halliday seated opposite them looking half delighted and half bewildered.

Lady Freemantle saw her husband and said, "Come, dear, and greet your sister-in-law, niece, and nephew." He was more than up to the task, despite the complex series of events that had led to this reunion, and he kissed the ladies and warmly shook Halliday's hand. "It's a pleasure to have the family together again," he said.

Lady Torrence, meanwhile, looked up at Frances. "I am glad you are here, Lady Frances. My gratitude is more than I can ever express, and I know I speak for everyone in saying that."

"I agree there with my mother," said Louisa. "Despite my reservations, I am forever in your debt, to you and to Miss Mallow." Louisa turned to her mother, and Frances saw a trace of the rebellious girl she had once been. "Dear Mama, has Lady Frances, London's first female consulting detective, changed your mind about women's place in the world?"

"My dear, I still have to say, no woman in this family has worked, especially not in trade. And now that I see I have a daughter running a shop and a granddaughter aspiring to be a dressmaker . . . I envy you both, choosing a life not open to me. We shall have a lady's luncheon soon to discuss every detail of the business. I am consumed with curiosity." Mrs. Lockton and her daughter smiled. And now Lady Torrence turned to her grandson. "And I am not leaving you out, Samuel. I am honored to have a vicar in the family. I shall be in your church next Sunday. My hearing is not what it was, so I expect you to speak loudly."

"I shall see you there. I think for my sermon I'll be drawing some lessons from my namesake, the prophet Samuel." He looked up at Frances. "God has heard."

Maids came in with refreshments, and Frances caught Lady Torrence's eye once more before she and Mallow slipped away. The butler saw them out, and a few moments later they were back in their hired coach.

"Mallow, we have done something wonderful. But now our part is over. They will have to find a way to reestablish the family. We cannot help them with that; it is up to them. But they seem to be off to a grand start. We're going home."

"Very good, my lady." They sat in silence for a while, each woman lost in her own thoughts. After a few minutes, Mallow brought up a new subject. "I fixed the hem on your blue dress if you want to wear it to dinner tonight."

Frances squeezed her maid's hand. "Thank you, Mallow. I'm sure that will be fine."

She suddenly felt a little limp—so much time on the case, and now it was done! Frances was exhausted, and yet the whole day played in her mind again and again, the performance and its dramatic conclusion. Well, a return to normality might be just what she needed.

She had a pleasant surprise when they returned to the hotel, a note from Hal. "Mr. Wheaton is having me for dinner tonight, Mallow."

"Very good, my lady. The blue dress may not be elaborate enough. Perhaps the green, which shows off your hair so nicely. Speaking of which, for your hair, I thought we would—"

"Very well, I'll submit. But then you're off for the evening, and I'll have a little something else for you in this week's pay. Stage managing is not in your term of service, so you deserve something extra."

"Thank you, my lady. I assume our theatrical careers are over. But if your ladyship ever wants to produce a motion picture, I will of course support you in any way I can."

Frances always liked to think that it was hard to surprise her, so she later excused what happened by telling herself she was physically and emotionally drained after a long day. When she was admitted to the Wheaton house, she was stunned into speechlessness at seeing Hal saying good-bye to Winifred Elkhorn in the foyer.

"Frances! I'm pleased to see you again," said Mrs. Elkhorn. "I hear word that you have been up to some remarkable things. I must be leaving, but I look forward to hearing more about it when next we meet." She gave a sidelong glance at Hal, who was looking on with a benevolent smile. "Meanwhile, I'll let Mr. Wheaton tell you why I was here. Mr. Wheaton, thank you again. Frances, until our next meeting."

"Well?" said Frances when she and Hal were alone.

"Well, what, my dear?" said Hal with that same bland smile, hiding secrets. "Some sherry before dinner?"

"Hal, be serious." She followed him into the library, where he poured drinks. "Why was the president of the League for Women's Political Equality here?"

"Franny, she is your mentor, but that doesn't mean I can't talk with her too."

"Hal. This isn't funny." She knew she was being unreasonable. Hal was entitled to meet with whom he pleased. So was Mrs. Elkhorn. But her mentor and her fiancé meeting in secret without telling her? She couldn't bear not knowing. She couldn't bear Hal's secretive smirk—the reminder that, for all he was an amiable suitor, he was also one of the most distinguished solicitors in London, a shrewd thinker, and a keeper of secrets.

"Of course not. It's legal business, and legal business is never funny."

"So you've taken Mrs. Elkhorn on as a client?"

"I couldn't tell you. My client list is private. You know that. But you're partly right. Here's some very good sherry. Sit and sip it while I try to satisfy the curiosity of the insatiably curious Lady Frances."

"Very well. But I'm only being nice because I still feel bad for inadvertently leading a criminal into your house."

Hal laughed, poured drinks, and sat down opposite her. "Franny, I've been thinking about us, our engagement and eventual marriage, and your desire for a partnership where we are together and equal. To that end, I invited Mrs. Elkhorn here to volunteer my firm's services to the League, giving your organization free legal advice. I'll be working with your dear friend Thomasina Calvin, who I understand supervises research activities, and her constant companion, Gwen Kestrel."

After Frances got over her shock, her first emotion was anger. How dare Hal do this without talking to her? How dare he intrude on what was *hers*? But no, he was right. A marriage of true partners. She'd have to start thinking less of *his* and *hers* than of *theirs*. Mrs. Elkhorn knew that; that's why she looked amused when she departed. *She probably knew my first reaction would be anger,* thought Frances. *But after all, I did bring a criminal into his house—what will be* our *house. We are tied together more than I realized.*

She took a deep breath to control herself and had some sherry. "This is what you said you were secretly working on when we dined at Simpson's, wasn't it?"

"Yes. You were concerned that your staid husband would be sitting in his office growing increasingly frustrated that you were getting yourself into all kinds of trouble. Well, dear Franny, let's get into trouble together." He looked at her closely. She was still frowning, and he frowned too. "But did I guess wrong? Does this have to be something separate for you? Perhaps, then . . ." His voice trailed off as he apparently grew afraid of what her answer might be.

Frances shook her head. He was trying hard. This was a major step for a man in his position to tie himself to the suffrage movement. She had underestimated him. Again. Marriage would be a risk but not half the risk of running away from home and becoming an actress. How Mrs. Elkhorn would laugh at her if she shied away from this one.

She gave Hal a broad grin. "No, Hal. You are absolutely right. I'm just wondering who will bail us out of jail if we both get into trouble." And at that, Hal laughed and took her in his arms.

Well, Louisa Torrence managed to forge a life on her own terms, Frances thought as she kissed Hal. *And I shall too.*

CHAPTER 34

It wasn't until the small hours that Hal saw Frances into a hansom. Thoughts continued to race through her head, shifting from Hal to the family reunion at Lady Torrence's house and back to Hal.

The night porter let her in, and Frances found herself looking forward to the sameness of her routine. Mallow, despite instructions to go to bed, was no doubt gently napping in a chair in their sitting room with her knitting in her lap, waiting for her mistress to come home. She'd help Frances get out of her dress, they'd have a quick argument about brushing out Frances's hair, which Frances would lose, and then she'd read for a few minutes before going to sleep.

But the day had one more surprise for her.

"You have a visitor, my lady," said the porter. Hearing voices in the foyer, a man was already stepping out of the lounge. It was her brother, Charles, in military uniform. The last thing Frances wanted that night was an argument with her brother, but there was no avoiding it.

"Charles. Everything is well? Are you off to war again?"

"No. A regimental dinner. Franny—"

"Was Mary with you?"

"No. It was a dinner for officers, not the annual regimental ball. Franny—"

"Because she needs to be careful in her condition."

Charles grasped for words, which amused Frances. "Mary said she wasn't telling anyone yet, not even her mother. How did you—?"

"Silly Charles. Did you really think you could keep a secret like that from me? I'd love a niece I could take to suffrage meetings, but I know you'd like a son, and I know Mary would like to give you a son, so I will pray for a nephew. I suppose you'll name him James after Father, which would've delighted him."

"Thank you," he said. "We'll discuss that later. Anyway, where have you been so late? I asked that maid of yours, and despite all my questions, all I got was her usual, 'I'm sure I couldn't say, my lord.' She knows every little thing you're up to."

Frances thought of the evening just ended and suppressed a smirk. *Not everything.* To her brother, she said, "Charles, it's very bad form to question a lady's personal maid like that. Can you imagine father doing that to mother's maid?" She watched him try to control his temper.

"Franny. Stop changing the subject. Mother didn't get into fistfights with criminals in the homes of London solicitors. Yes, it was quite the topic of conversation this evening, whether the sister of the Marquess of Seaforth was looking for a position as a sergeant major."

"I'm sure that's an exaggeration," she said. "I just ran into some brief difficulties when acting for a client."

"A *client*?"

"Yes. I've recently become London's first female consulting detective." Charles lost all power of speech now. Frances rolled on. "You may have heard that I was attacked by a veteran of the Suffolk Rifles, all of whom perished in the Sudan, as I'm sure you know. You may have also heard that I was looking for an actress named Helen, who vanished thirty years ago. Maybe you even heard that I wrote and directed a play at the Emerald Theatre to uncover a terrible crime. Do take Mary to their production of *Romeo and Juliet*, and mention my name to the manager, Gilbert

Rusk. Also, Mallow and I met the king there by the way, and he was angling for another invitation. And we'll need to talk next week about you hosting a motion picture party. It sounds like great fun. Now it's very late, and we both should be off to bed."

But Charles wasn't going to be pushed away so quickly.

"Franny, I didn't understand half of what you said. Thank God. You've always made a case for living your own life, and I've accepted that as best I could. But when word of your exploits involving physical violence get back to me at my club and regiment, it is no longer just your life anymore."

She smiled sweetly and spoke softly to contrast his rising voice. "Dear Charles, what did you hear? That a soldier attacked me? But no, he died decades ago. It was just an illusion. That I found an actress named Helen? She was also an illusion. An empty grave in Maidstone? Also an illusion. There was never any danger—illusion again and again." She kissed him on the cheek three times. "For you, for Mary, and for your child. Know this, that the only reality is love. All else is illusion."

And with that, she swept upstairs, leaving her brother yet again in silence.

Oh, what an exit. I really am the most marvelous theatrical director.

Acknowledgments

Once again, many thanks to so many people who help keep Lady Frances rolling along. First, deep appreciation to my peerless agent, Cynthia Zigmund, who's always in my corner and serves as Lady Frances's godmother. As always, the fantastic crew at Crooked Lane Books—especially Matt Martz, Sarah Poppe, and Jenny Chen—are not only a pleasure to work with, but they help me improve with every book I write.

My sister, Abby Koreto, stage manager extraordinaire, helped me with the theatre scenes. Martial arts practitioner Bryan Kapustinski made valuable suggestions in choreographing Frances's fight scenes. For background in the early days of motion pictures, I relied on Filmsite.org, Northern State University's online "Brief Outline of the History of Stage Lighting," and Filmreference.com. Any errors or anachronisms are entirely my responsibility.

My family continues to give me the extraordinary support I need to keep writing. Without the continual help, encouragement, and advice from my wife, Liz, there would be no Lady Frances at all.

Historical Note

Lady Frances brushes up against some historical people and circumstances in this book, some of which may look anachronistic but are a matter of record.

I came across the Edwardian musical star Marie Studholme when first researching this book. A beautiful and by all accounts talented singer and actress, she was the toast of London in her day. She is known to have studied jujutsu with Yukio Tani, one of the first Japanese teachers of martial arts in the West. Suffragists also studied martial arts and used them to great effect against the male opponents who attacked them while protesting.

Shaw's *Major Barbara* premiered in 1905, so Frances would've been familiar with it. Shaw teases Frances about basing Barbara on her. In fact, it is believed Shaw did base some of the characters in this play on real-life individuals, including those he knew personally. The Emerald Theatre is fictional but based on similar venues. The St. James Theatre, where Frances meets with Marie Studholme, was one of London's leading theatres from 1835 until it was demolished in 1957. A favorite theatre of Queen Victoria, it saw the premier of *The Importance of Being Earnest*, and later Lawrence Olivier and Vivien Leigh would star together in performances of both Shaw and Shakespeare.

Frances and Mallow meet King Edward VII and Alice Keppel at the Emerald Theatre. Mrs. Keppel was the king's mistress in the last years of his life. Beautiful and charming, she managed her position with tact and discretion. Outliving the king by nearly forty years, she died just a couple of months after the birth of her great-granddaughter, Camilla, who is now Duchess of Cornwall and Prince Charles's second wife.

The film studio Frances and Mallow visit is based on real studios. It's often assumed that motion pictures began with Charlie Chaplin, but the film industry was well under way in Edwardian times, as pioneers worked to develop film, lighting, cameras, and projectors that could keep up with their increasing ambitions. The first commercial feature-length movie, *The Story of the Kelly Gang*, was released in 1906. Although the British film industry continued to grow and thrive, a few years later filmmakers began gravitating to locales with a more reliable source of sunlight, especially a little town in California called Hollywood.